FIRE BASKET

FIRE BASKET

JUNE SHANDLEY

ATHENA PRESS
LONDON

FIRE BASKET
Copyright © June Shandley 2010

All Rights Reserved

ISBN 978 1 84748 780 3

First published 2010 by
ATHENA PRESS
Queen's House, 2 Holly Road
Twickenham TW1 4EG
United Kingdom

Printed for Athena Press

Author's Note

The author   Edith

My book is based on my mother, Edith, her life and experiences throughout the Second World War. The start of war brought changes that no one could predict. The horror and realisation of what was happening brought fear and stress. However, being British, we showed strength and pulled together. My mother had to cope alone, like so many others. With the comradeship of neighbours and friends, she drew strength and courage, and managed to survive those dark days.

Prologue

The days I remember are so clear that the years roll away and I can begin to recall my life as it was then. But this was September 1939, the start of the war. I noticed the silent anticipation of the inevitable that lay ahead. It was sunny and bright outside and appeared normal – traffic and people trundling along – surely it couldn't be happening? It must be wrong. Suddenly my thoughts were interrupted by a shrill scream.

'Mum, William has pinched my sweets –' sob – 'and I was saving them for tomorrow!'

'No, I have not,' a voice from below screamed back. 'She gave them to me, so they're mine.'

Children, I thought, always fighting over something. I had better go and see what's going on.

I had finished making the beds and there was plenty to do downstairs. I reached the landing and there was Jane, sliding down the banister.

'Don't do that,' I yelled, 'you'll break your neck!'

She slid down with a bump at the end.

'I told you not to do it, but you never listen – none of you children do! William, I want you to go to the corner shop; the bread has all gone and we need bread for tea. Take Jane and Maggie with you; Larry can stay and fill the coal scuttle and clean the grate. It's his turn, and anyway he's going to Tony's party this afternoon. Take this sixpence and there's a ha'penny each for the three of you. Now off you go and behave. Hold hands going down the road, and don't pick the bread on the way back! Watch the door and don't bang it on the way out!'

Bang!

'Sorry, Mum.' And then there was silence.

This was absolute bliss: peace for a little while, I thought. I watched Larry with the coal scuttle. He was a good boy – he never argued, just got on with things. My thoughts started to drift. I was thirty-two years of age with four children and another on the way, a husband away. He had enlisted already, not much choice really, with very little money coming in. With the war on our doorsteps, there would be a shortage of food. Where did it all begin?

Yes, I remember, it was the Rhondda, the Rhondda Valley, South Wales. I was one of a family of thirteen children. Life was very hard. My mother worked so much to keep us all together; feeding hungry mouths, especially thirteen children, was a tremendous responsibility, and everyone worked down the mines, from my father to my uncles.

I remember the time when there was a miners' strike. Everyone came out except for a few, who they called scabs, and one of those few was my grandfather – and later my father, who went on strike. Everything was scarce and there was very little money to live on. Most of the children were running ragged and didn't have any shoes on their feet. Times were really hard.

We were a close-knit community. Everyone looked out for each other, but then we always did. Everyone attended chapel on Sunday no matter what, scrubbed faces and clean pinnies and full of pride.

There was no drinking on a Sunday and everything was closed, although I knew that my grandfather had a secret drink put aside – my grandmother had no idea. I knew because my grandfather confided in me and it was our secret. Anyway, my grandfather could not afford to go on strike and early one cold morning he set out to face the strike line. It was grim to see the faces of these men. They challenged him.

'Go back!' they yelled. 'You won't get through.' They were armed with sticks and batons. My grandfather carried on walking, determined to get through. He had mouths to feed; he had no choice. And then to everyone's astonishment there, a few yards behind, was my grandmother marching along holding her apron up full of scraps of coal she had picked up on the way. She was going to defend my grandfather no matter what. The men in the picket line shook their heads and dropped their sticks; one by one they walked away. That was one day and there were many others in those sparse years.

Part One
London

Chapter One

I was born in the year 1907 and christened Edith May Faulks. I left school at the age of twelve, mainly to look after my brothers and sisters, working whenever I could. There was so much to be done. My mother took in washing to help make a living. My father died when I was eleven, so we were the breadwinners and there was ironing and cooking to get through. Whenever I had a free moment, I would go with my friend Enid and we would climb to the top of a mountain and we would sing and chat, laugh and giggle and dream of when we would find our fame and fortune in London. I knew in my heart I would do one day… and I did.

At the age of sixteen I found a job in service, in Muswell Hill in London. I was so excited to be in the big city, with everyone bustling about, busy streets and traffic, shops that I had never dreamed of. My Aunty Gwen had travelled with me on the train to London to settle me in and to make sure that I was going to work for decent gentry people. I was allocated a room in the topmost part of the house, which I shared with the pantry maid, Rose. The room consisted of two small beds, a washbasin with a jug and a large closet to hang clothes. There was also a chest of drawers with an oil lamp on top.

Rose was instructed to show me around the house before I was taken to see the housekeeper, who informed me of my duties. These consisted of cleaning the main rooms on the ground floor, polishing the brass and silver and serving afternoon tea. Both Rose and I had to be on duty by 5.30 a.m. Rose had to stoke the fires and make sure the kitchen floor was scrubbed; everything had to be gleaming. My jobs were to clean the fireplaces in the main rooms and light the fires. I had one half-day off per week and once a month I had a Sunday (a complete day). My wages were two shillings and sixpence per week plus board and lodgings.

Every month I sent five shillings to my mother, who relied on the extra money coming in as she wasn't well and found it difficult to carry on taking in laundry. The doctor had told her that her heart was weak and she should try and take more rest or bear the consequences. I wrote to her every week telling her all about my job and the various happenings that occurred in the household. There was so much tittle-tattle flying around, there wasn't a dull moment I can truthfully say, and I thrived on it.

My mother longed for me to go home as she needed my help, but she also needed my contribution of half of my wages. It was so hard not to drop everything and just go home, but needs must and I knew that I was helping more by staying.

The work was long and hard and I was at everyone's beck and call, but I had made friends and Rose was my closest. We made light of everything, even when it became almost intolerable. We would cry together and then laugh it off and occasionally we would have an evening off together and end up roller skating. We had so much fun, flirting with boys, falling over on purpose in order to attract attention. It worked, as one day I was skating around and suddenly my legs gave way beneath me. Whoops – I landed face down. I felt people whizzing pass me and I gasped for breath. A searing pain shot through my left leg. I felt I couldn't move. Suddenly a pair of strong arms lifted me up.

'Hey, are you all right?' a voice called. 'Hold on to me.'

I looked up into the face of a very handsome young man; he had piercing blue eyes and the nicest smile I had ever seen. I was absolutely smitten.

'Don't try and stand,' he said, 'you have more than likely sprained your ankle.' I felt dizzy, the pain was unbearable and so I hung on to his arm. 'Come on,' he added, 'you need to have it looked at.'

He almost carried me to the first aid tent. In the meantime, Rose, who had been ahead of me, suddenly turned around to see what had happened.

'Edith,' she screamed, 'what have you done?' She raced across to where I was sat. 'You look awful,' she said. I felt awful. My ankle looked really swollen and I felt sick.

The first aid man put a cold compress on and said, 'Never mind – you will have to put your feet up for a few days. The best thing you can do is have a sweet cup of tea and then go home.'

'I'll go and get us all one,' said the young man. 'I'm Peter, by the way. I'm pleased to meet you, Edith? Your friend is—'

Before he could finish, Rose interrupted, saying, 'I'm Rose. So pleased to meet you, I'm sure.' She gave a little giggle.

'Likewise,' Peter said. 'Three teas with sugar coming up.' And off he went.

'Who is that?' asked Rose. 'He's really handsome.'

'Yes,' I said. 'And he's mine,' I added jokingly.

That day I shall never forget. It was the beginning of my friendship and romance with Peter that lasted until I was nearly twenty-three.

Chapter Two

My first few years spent in service were a chapter of my life that opened my outlook completely. The Welsh way of life was so introverted and guarded in comparison to how it was in London. I knew nothing of life, the hidden dangers that walked the streets, and the manipulative people. The housekeeper, Mrs Baker, gave us all a talking-to, strongly advising us all never to go out alone at night unless we were chaperoned, and of course she was right.

I spent as much time with Peter as I could on my half-day and the occasional evening. We had formed a very strong friendship since the day of the roller-skating incident. Peter was training to be a banker in London and came from a middle-class family. He had one sister (whom I met during our friendship), his father was a GP and his mother was a retired nurse. Peter spent every other weekend with his family, whom he thought very highly of. I knew in my heart that my friendship with Peter would not be approved of by his parents, although no comments were made. I didn't have to be told; we came from different backgrounds and that was enough. Our respect for each other was such that we never discussed our families or class distinction. It never really mattered that much to us as we enjoyed being together and made the best of those years.

My employers, who were titled people (Lord and Lady Havis), had discovered that I was clairvoyant. This had come about when I had read Rose's tea cup one day. I had sworn her to secrecy because I didn't want anyone else to know. It was considered a gift within my family that you just kept to yourself. My mother and my grandmother were both clairvoyant and very superstitious about others knowing – bad luck, along with other superstitions, was part and parcel of my Welsh heritage. Although Rose meant well, she just couldn't keep a secret and told the cook and the housekeeper, who in turn asked me to give them a reading.

Of course, I was annoyed with Rose for betraying a confidence; however, I was plied with tea and cream cakes from the cook and everyone gathered in the kitchen below stairs to hear their fortune. At first I would only consider one person present at a time, but as time went on it didn't matter, as everyone seemed to enjoy the whole idea of fortune-telling. It was entertaining, and I enjoyed being the focus of attention.

So it came about one day that Lady Havis decided to check the evening dinner menu with Cook and caught us all sat around the kitchen table laughing and giggling with cups upside down on the saucers.

'What's all this?' Lady Havis demanded. 'Is it someone's birthday?'

Our faces were a picture, especially Cook's.

She immediately jumped up, her face reddening, saying, 'Please excuse us, My Lady, we are only having a little bit of fun. Nothing too serious.'

Lady Havis immediately questioned the cups and saucers.

'Why are they upside down?'

There was a reaction of silence. Each one of us sat with our hands covering our cups looking at Cook's face, waiting for her reply.

'It's fortune-telling, My Lady,' Cook replied.

'Fortune-telling, Cook. What are you talking about?' said Lady Havis.

Cook by this time was beginning to twitch.

'Our Edith has a gift, my Lady,' she began to splutter. 'She is able to read the future by reading tea leaves. We have all benefited by Edith's readings.' Cook's voice started to tremble. 'We didn't mean any harm, my Lady.'

'And what do you think of all this, Mrs Baker?' asked Lady Havis, swinging around to confront the housekeeper, 'Have you had your future read too?'

'Yes, My Lady,' Mrs Baker replied. 'I have and I am truly impressed by what I have learned. Edith is truly gifted, and may I say that she was reluctant to participate in our afternoon party because of her position here.'

With authority in her voice she said, 'I take full responsibility for any indiscretions that you might think have taken place. I can assure you, My Lady, it is for amusement only during our rest period and no harm was intended.'

'Well, we will see,' said Lady Havis. 'Cook, I need to check the evening menu with you – the rest of you, go about your business.'

'Yes, My Lady,' we all said in chorus, and hurried out of the kitchens. Rose and I made our way to our room and locked the door.

'Oh, Edith,' Rose cried. 'What is going to happen now? We might get the sack.'

'Well, if we do, then that's that, but I think it will be just me. Don't worry, Rose, I'll make sure you keep your job. I'll explain everything to Lady Havis and she will understand.'

'But I don't want you to leave,' Rose cried. 'You are my best friend and we have such good fun together and I couldn't share with anyone else. Honestly, Edith, I couldn't.'

Rose wailed, 'No, please no.'

'Don't get into a panic, Rose,' I said. 'I'm sure Mrs Baker will take care of everything, so come on; we have to wash and starch our aprons. I have to serve afternoon tea and if I'm late I shall really be in hot water.'

The rest of that day went smoothly, although there was a little bit of tension between us all.

Nearly a week later, Mrs Baker summoned me to her office.

'Edith,' she said, 'Lady Havis has asked to see you in the drawing room prompt at 3 p.m., and before you ask, I know nothing. And make sure you are looking presentable.'

Mrs Baker's authoritative manner made me tremble.

'Yes, Mrs Baker,' I said. 'Thank you.'

'Off you go, girl,' said Mrs Baker. 'And don't be late.'

I remember feeling quite sick. What can it be? I thought. If I was going to be dismissed, Mrs Baker would have given me notice; that was part of her job. However, something had to be important for me to be summoned to her Ladyship. What it could be? My mind was in turmoil.

I continued with my duties and at 12.30 p.m. I went for my lunch. Below stairs there were two kitchens, a pantry room and the staff dining room. There were a further two rooms which were used for the yard man, a real jack of all trades, and Charlie, the valet, who polished all the shoes. Other cupboards were for storage.

I made my way to the dining room and sat down alongside two other maids and Charlie. There was homemade vegetable soup and newly made bread for our lunch. Normally, I would be feeling pangs of hunger, but my stomach felt heavy and I pushed my bowl aside.

'Hey, gal, what's your problem?' said Charlie. 'Ain't you hungry?'

'No, Charlie,' I said, 'I'm not. You can have mine.'

'No,' said Cook, 'I'm having none of that. Now, Edith what is wrong? It's not like you not to eat yer food. Come on, tell us.'

'It's nothing, really, Cook,' I said. 'I have to see Her Ladyship this afternoon. Mrs Baker told me this morning that she wanted to see me and I don't know what it's about.'

'Goodness me,' said Cook, 'that is serious. Come on, girl, it won't be that bad. She might want you to be her personal maid.'

'I wouldn't think so,' said Charlie, butting in. 'I know that for a fact. Anyway, her Ladyship ain't taking on anyone else. His Lordship only said yesterday that she had too many maids, in front of me, too! I pretended not to listen,' Charlie chortled. 'Anyway, Their Lordships have to tighten their belts now because they are going to buy a country home, somewhere in Dorset, and it's going to cost a whole heck of money.'

'Really, Charlie,' said Cook, 'd'ya have to use those kind of words? It sounds really common. And another thing, Charlie, you shouldn't gossip. Whatever 'appens, we will still have our jobs here. I know so, because Mrs Baker was summoned to the drawing room last week and was told of their plans. We will all hold the fort while they are away, and that means no one takes advantage. We will have our duties to do, and our hours will be the same, so don't get any wrong ideas, Charlie. I'll be keeping my beady eye on you!'

With that Cook turned around and said, 'Edith, eat up. You won't feel any better by starving yourself. I'm sure you haven't anything to worry about.'

And with that everyone continued with their meal. I managed

to eat the rest of the soup in silence and afterwards made my way upstairs and worked until 2.30 p.m. I normally had two hours' free time until I served afternoon teas at 4.30 p.m. However, I had my appointment with her Ladyship at 3 p.m., so I made my way up to my room to smarten up.

I put on a clean starched apron and cuffs, brushed my hair and powdered my nose. That will have to do, I said to myself, looking into the mirror and seeing my image. Not bad, boyo! Goodness is that the time! Looking at the clock, I had five minutes. Down the stairs I leapt, through the corridors and down another flight of stairs until I reached the drawing room. I stood outside and held my breath.

I tapped the door twice. A voice called, 'Enter.'

I pushed the doors open gently and let myself in. Her Ladyship was sat near the fire alongside a coffee table where tea had been served, and another chair had been placed on the other side.

'Edith,' Her Ladyship said, 'sit with me and have some tea, I need to talk to you. There is no need to be apprehensive; this is just a friendly chat. Please sit, Edith.'

And to my utter astonishment, I was poured a cup of tea by Her Ladyship.

'Do have a biscuit, Edith,' she said. I sipped my tea slowly while Her Ladyship carried on talking.

'Now, my dear,' she said quietly, 'I wish to put a proposition to you. Would you be prepared to give an afternoon in the week to entertain a few of my friends with your tea-leaf readings? It would give me such pleasure, and there would of course be a contribution for you, and of course you would be relieved of your afternoon duties on those days.

'Now, Edith, I want you consider this. You are under no pressure, my dear. Think about it and let me know your answer in the next few days. Mrs Baker thinks very highly of you and informs me that you work well, and are pleasant and friendly with other members of staff. We pride ourselves on having a happy and contented household and hope to maintain that for the future. Well, that's all for now, my dear, and on your way out would you inform Mrs Baker that I wish speak to her?'

'Thank you, My Lady,' I said and hurried out. As I gently

closed the doors, my heart was in my mouth, and I just couldn't believe it. Edith Faulks to entertain the gentry? It was unbelievable! I walked along the corridor and found my way to the back stairs. Mrs Baker's quarters were on the second floor. They consisted of a sitting room, a wash room, and a bedroom. They were really very cosy and nicely furnished, and I quite envied her. I tapped on the door.

'Come in,' Mrs Baker answered.

I pushed the door open and walked in. Mrs Baker was busy sewing; she had a treadle machine which she used regularly for repairing household linen and staff uniforms.

'Well, Edith,' she said, 'what is it?' She moved her feet away from the pedals and folded her arms, which I found intimidating.

'Her Ladyship wishes to see you, Mrs Baker,' I said breathlessly.

'Ah, I thought as much,' Mrs Baker said. 'I think I know what it is about, and by the look on your face you do as well. Off you go, I'll speak to you later.'

I left quickly and made my way to my room where Rose was waiting with bated breath. 'Well,' she said, 'what 'appened? Are ya in trouble? Have ya got the sack?'

'Calm down, Rose,' I said. 'No, I haven't; quite the opposite, in fact.' I began to tell her all that had been said.

'Well, I'm dumbstruck,' said Rose. 'You have fallen on your feet, right enough, mixing with the nobs. You'll be wearing a tiara soon,' she said, rolling over laughing. 'Wait until everyone else knows.' Rose was so excited.

'I don't think we should say anything just yet,' I said. 'Her Ladyship might not want it spread around, and we don't want to upset the applecart, so keep it secret, Rose.'

The next few months seemed to fly by. I enjoyed my afternoons with Her Ladyship and her friends, who were so enthralled by the novelty of it all, and I gained respect. Rose and I still went roller skating, and Peter came whenever he could. My friendship with Peter grew, although I never divulged to him about my afternoon readings; I felt that was something best kept to myself, and Rose knew that.

Chapter Three

I valued my friendship and time with Peter, we had grown close together. He loved my Welsh accent and I loved his dry sense of humour. We went to the pictures now and again, for walks through the parks, had picnics and boat rides; we enjoyed everything in the time we spent together. I remember going home to see my mother and family. I was given time off because my mother was unwell. Peter saw me off at the station.

'I shall miss you,' he said. 'Please write.'

I replied, 'Of course I will,' and I did.

My time spent with my mother and family went very quickly. I had been missed at home, and in the village everyone wanted to know how life was in London and the things that I did in my everyday life. They all wanted to go roller skating, have trips down the Thames and picnics in Hyde Park. Life was so different for them. I knew that I could never go back to how things used to be; my life had changed and I had, too, and there was no going back.

My mother was quite poorly and wasn't able to do very much; making a cup of tea was an effort for her, leaving her quite breathless. Her heart condition had deteriorated, leaving her very frail. She had been overjoyed to have me home and any worries I had of her I hid inside me. She had been so strong for all of us, for all of her life, and now it was our turn to be strong for her. We spent hours chatting and planning. We were going to paint and paper the parlour, the next time I was down. Irene, my sister, would make new curtains and covers for the chairs. Also, I would buy some cushions from a London shop and bring them with me when I came on my next visit. It was so exciting for my mother, it seemed to give her renewed strength, and I was sad to have to return to London. The days had flown by and I already missed my family on the long and tedious journey back.

The weeks and months passed by, the winter and then spring,

and I reached the age of eighteen. Cook had baked a cake and decorated it with candles. It was a jolly afternoon with everyone gathered around the kitchen table singing Happy Birthday, and although I felt excited, I also felt a tinge of sadness. I missed my family. My mother had sent me a card with a handmade lace handkerchief enclosed. I wished I could be with her.

My sister had written to me two weeks previously telling me how Mother was – her medication was keeping her going, but she was very weak. She looked forward to my letters every week and was counting the days to when I make my next visit. 'Please let it be soon,' my sister said, 'we all miss you.'

That day I arranged with Mrs Baker to have a fortnight off in June so that I could visit my mother and family. I posted a card that day to let them know; only then could I relax and enjoy the rest of my birthday. In the evening I went out with Peter, who gave me a bouquet of flowers and a silk scarf. I was overwhelmed by such a lovely ending to the day.

That summer Lord and Lady Havis travelled to their country home in Dorset to spend the summer months and would return in September. There was a skeleton staff left behind, including Rose and myself, Cook and Mrs Baker, and of course Charlie. Everything ran smoothly, things were more relaxed and we had more free time. We completely spring-cleaned from top to bottom, and the evenings were spent playing cards, sewing, telling stories and generally having a good time. I saw more of Peter during that time, and Mrs Baker said I could invite him for supper one evening – curiosity was one reason. Cook made a very special evening meal, which included a glass of wine. Peter was very impressed, and Mrs Baker and Cook were very attentive along with us all. We all chatted through the evening and it was late when Peter left.

The following day we all felt very tired and it took us a while to get motivated. Charlie complained of a migraine and was given the morning off. It was early afternoon when I was summoned to Mrs Baker's office. Her face looked sombre.

'There is a telegram for you, Edith,' she said.

My heart began to beat. A telegram for me; it must be serious. I quickly opened it. It was from Aunty Gwen, telling me to come home as soon as possible; my mother had taken a turn for the worse and was asking for me. Mrs Baker comforted me and made arrangements for me to travel home. Charlie escorted me to the station and saw me off. I hadn't time to let Peter know. However, Mrs Baker said she would contact him for me and let the other staff know.

The journey seemed never to end and when I did arrive there was no one there to meet me. I looked around and the platform was empty. I couldn't understand it. I had sent a message to say the time I would be arriving. This terrible feeling I had made me think I was too late. The evening was drawing in, and I knew I would have to start walking before it became dark. I had only walked a few yards when I heard the rumble of wheels. I turned the corner and there was old Mr Thomas from the village with his horse and cart.

'Sorry, luv,' he said as I climbed aboard. 'We haven't much time. Your mother is very, very weak. No one could leave her, so I came for you myself. Prepare yourself, Edith, luv.'

We arrived in minutes. Irene met me in floods of tears.

'Edith,' she cried. 'Mam is waiting. Quick, be quick.'

I hurried into the parlour and everyone moved away. I knelt down and held my mother's hand. She sighed and whispered, 'You are a good girl,' and then she closed her eyes like she had fallen asleep, but she had gone. A glimmer of light shone through the window; it was like my mother had waited for me. The tears flowed. The pain I felt was unbearable.

'Mam,' I cried, 'I'm so sorry. I wish I could have been here sooner.'

'Now, now,' said Aunty Gwen, 'your mam knows, and we wouldn't wish her to suffer any more, so let her rest.'

We all gathered in the pantry where tea was being brewed. The doctor had been waiting while we said our goodbyes. He then checked that everything was in order and left.

Those next few days were like a bad dream. Everyone seemed in shock. The funeral came and went; we all wore black and curtains were drawn. The neighbours baked and cooked for us, everyone pulled together and somehow we coped through those dark days. Aunty Gwen and my family begged me to stay longer but I knew I would have to return to London soon. However, Mrs Baker had telegraphed to say that I could stay longer; everything was running smoothly. Although I was sorely missed, they were coping and wished me well.

We all pulled together and in the next weeks the house was transformed from top to toe. There was an organised rota (which was left to me to do); each one had their chores and it kept us all from dwelling on the loss of our mam. We talked through our childhood memories, our ups and downs, the good and bad times, but most of all the future ahead. Our plans, our dreams; through this we laughed and cried, and our family bond was stronger than ever. We had each other.

Chapter Four

Then the day came when I had to return to London. My heart was heavy. I didn't want to leave my family. However, I knew that my life was there and I missed my friends and most of all Peter, who had written to me every other day, supporting me through those dark days. I couldn't wait to see him. He had come to mean so much to me. I knew I loved him very much, and although he hadn't declared his feelings for me, I instinctively knew he felt the same. On my journey back to London, these thoughts were with me.

Arriving at Waterloo, there was this air of expectancy, the hub bub and noise of the station, the smokey air and the chatter of people. My heart was beating fast. I was so excited that Peter would be there. To feel his arms around me and feel safe and happy, I couldn't wait. I stepped off the train, lifting my luggage on to the platform. I looked up, squinting through the sunlight. I then looked around and coming towards me was Peter. He was smiling. The happiness he showed made my heart beat even faster. He threw his arms around me.

'I've missed you so much,' he said as we held each other, not wanting to let go. He lifted my face towards him, kissed me, and said, 'I love you, Edith, you are everything to me.'

I was trembling and crying with happiness.

'I love you, too, Peter,' I said.

He wiped the tears from my eyes and said, 'That's all I wanted to hear. Come on, let's go and celebrate. This is what your mother would have wanted for you. I'll take care of you.'

With that he lifted the luggage with one hand and held my hand with the other, and we strolled down the platform, both feeling light-headed with happiness. The future for me seemed complete, and arriving back at Muswell Hill to my place of work, I was greeted with such warmth. Everyone was pleased to see us; my face was flushed with excitement and anticipation. Rose couldn't stop chattering, wanting to know all the news.

Mrs Baker and Cook were there and Mrs Baker gave her condolences and said how sorry they all were at the sad news of my mother. High tea had been prepared and we all sat down to home-cooked ham with freshly baked bread followed by apple pie and custard. We all chatted away. Mrs Baker told us that Lord and Lady Havis would not be returning for another three weeks; however, they were expecting everything to be tip-top on their return. Time flew by with everyone enjoying themselves and soon it was time for Peter to leave. We arranged to meet the next day. I felt a pang of sadness watching him make his way through the throng of people. He turned and waved and disappeared. I closed the door and went upstairs to my room where Rose was waiting,

'It's good to have you back, Edith,' she said. 'We have all missed you.'

'And I have missed you, too,' I said. 'I have so much to tell you.'

We chatted through the night until we fell asleep through sheer exhaustion. The following day, feeling very tired, I made my way to Mrs Baker's quarters to be informed of my duties for that day.

'I want you to spring clean the drawing room,' she said, 'and then after lunch, the music room. It hasn't been touched since Lord and Lady Havis left. The covers will need to come off and the brass polished around the fire hearth, so you have a busy day, Edith.' She eyed me up and down and added, 'An early night tonight for you, young lady: you are looking quite pale and tired. These weeks must have been hard for you. However you must take care. Now off you go.'

The day seemed so long. I couldn't wait to see Peter again. Every chore felt harder than before. I wanted to shout above the roof tops that Peter loved me; the feeling of elation was absolute bliss. The grandfather clock was chiming 4 p.m. when I left the house to meet Peter. I had dressed in my Sunday best, a dress with a lace collar and cuffs and lace-up boots, gloves and a hat trimmed with a silk flower, all in powder blue, Peter's favourite colour.

I skipped down the road, my heart beating fast, in and out of the throng of people; I felt no one could feel the joy I was experiencing. At last I reached the tea rooms where Peter and I had arranged to meet. There inside was Peter and sat alongside was a young woman, very pretty. They were both laughing together, completely oblivious to anyone else around them. My heart missed a beat, feeling a pang of jealousy.

Who could this person be? I asked myself, and at that moment Peter saw me. He jumped to his feet and like a gentleman he opened the door for me.

'Darling Edith,' he said, 'I would like you to meet my sister.' A feeling of relief swept over me.

'Fanny,' Peter said, 'this is Edith. Isn't she lovely?'

Fanny's eyes swept over me.

'Hallo, Edith,' she said, 'I'm so pleased to meet you. Peter has told me so much about you. In fact that's all he's talked about recently, and I can understand why.'

The warmth I felt from Fanny was genuine. I knew we would get along fine. We ordered tea, the introductions over. The time flew by; we never stopped chattering, and there was so much to talk about. However, Fanny was due back at the hospital for evening duty so we made our way to the corner where she caught the tram. Peter held my hand.

'I'm delighted that you and Fanny get on so well. This wasn't prearranged. Fanny contacted me last night, to arrange to meet to catch up on all the news, so I thought it would be a good opportunity for you both to meet. You didn't mind, did you, Edith?' he said.

'Of course not,' I said. 'Your sister is a lovely person and I'm looking forward to seeing her again. I couldn't be happier.'

'Good,' he said and held my hand tighter. We ambled along feeling a sense of contentment. What a lovely day it had been; the tiredness of the morning had gone from me and I didn't want the day to end. We finally arrived home and arranged to meet the following Monday. Peter was spending the weekend with his parents. I wondered if he would mention his intentions to them. However, it was early days and Peter would do things in his own time.

The weekend passed by quickly. Rose and I went roller skating on the Saturday afternoon and talked incessantly and made silly jokes. I felt so happy; the thought of what laid ahead gave me a warm glow. Mentally I was making plans for the future.

Rose saw the look on my face and said 'Now, now, Edith, you mustn't rush things. Think carefully. Peter will have to work for promotion and that's another couple of years at least. And you haven't met his family. It will all take time; everyone has to get used to the idea. You don't want obstacles put in your way, do you, Edith? His family is posh and, to be honest, we are servant girls and you know what people are like – ideas above our station and all that. It ain't going to be easy, so take it slowly and it will work out right.'

My stomach turned over. My goodness, Rose was right. She talked a lot of sense, which to be truthful I had never given her credit for.

'Rose,' I said, 'you are my best friend and you are so honest. Thank you for bringing me down to earth. I was getting carried away and never stopped to think. I love Peter so much, I would not do anything to ruin what we have got, and I couldn't imagine my life without him. I will be patient. Come on, Rose, I'll treat you to a cream tea. What would I do without you?'

And with that said we made our way to the tea rooms.

The following day we joined Mrs Baker and Cook and other staff members for a church service. Occasionally we were expected to do this (even though I was a Chapel girl). The Sunday lunch had been prepared early by Cook and Charlie, who always insisted that he stay behind to keep an eye on things. Arriving home from church, we were given sherry served up by Charlie (permission given by Mrs Baker) and then sat down to a roast-beef lunch and apple pie.

'Make the best of this,' said Cook. 'In two weeks Lord and Lady Havis will be returning from Dorset for the autumn and winter and we all will have to pull our socks up.'

Charlie muttered something about 'aving his socks up and chuckled at everybody. 'Charlie,' Cook said, 'mind your manners. Mrs Baker has allowed us all a fair and easy time and now we will have to knuckle down. Ain't that so, Mrs Baker?'

Mrs Baker nodded in approval and said, 'I want everything

polished and shining by the time Their Lordships arrive home, so starting from tomorrow I will have a rota made up with all your duties – for each of you there will be a list. Make sure your evening duties are completed today.' And with that she made her way back to her quarters, leaving us to clear away. The day ended quietly and we were all retired by 9 p.m.

The following day, Monday, we were up and about at 5.30 a.m. cleaning and polishing, preparing for the return of Lord and Lady Havis. We stopped for breakfast at 9 a.m. and continued through until lunch. I was starving, as I hadn't eaten much breakfast; my appetite had waned but I tucked into leek and potato soup with some of Cook's freshly baked bread.

'My, my,' Cook said, 'you were hungry, Edith. You will end up with indigestion eating at such a pace.'

'Sorry, Cook,' I said. 'I'm forgetting my manners.'

And with that I helped clear the table and gave Cook a hand with the vegetables for the evening meal. I was looking forward to the afternoon, when I would be meeting Peter. It had seemed ages since I had seen him and yet it was only a weekend. My heart was bursting with happiness. The day had started with beautiful sunshine, but by the time I left to meet Peter it had started to rain. However, that didn't dampen my enthusiasm. I opened my brolly and made my way to the tea rooms where we had arranged to meet.

Peter was waiting outside. His face lit up. 'Edith, I have missed you terribly,' he said, and putting his arms around me he planted a kiss upon my cheek.

'Come on,' he said, 'I'm gasping for a cup of tea and I have so much to tell you.' He led me into the tea room and we were shown to our normal corner table. After giving our order, Peter began to tell me all about his weekend.

'Edith, my darling, I have told my parents about us – I mean about you and our future plans – and they both would like to meet you.'

I felt my heart miss a beat. I couldn't believe it. I stuttered, 'Peter, you mean they really want to meet me?' I was breathless. 'You have told them everything?'

'Yes, everything, darling,' Peter said, 'and they are coming to

London in the next couple of weeks, so we will arrange to meet and I will introduce you to them. I know you will love them, Edith, and I know they will love you.'

My whole body was trembling. I didn't really expect this so soon. I so wanted to make a good impression.

'Edith, you are trembling,' Peter said. 'Please don't worry – everything will be fine.' And with that he held my hands tight and said 'I love you very much and I'm looking forward to spending my life with you.'

Peter's blue eyes gazed into my face. 'Always remember that,' he said. 'You do love me, don't you, Edith?' His face looked tense.

'I will never stop loving you, Peter,' I said. 'Whatever happens, I'll never stop, never.'

'That's all I wanted to hear,' Peter said. Suddenly we were lost in our own thoughts. It seemed almost magical, but then we were interrupted by the waitress asking us if everything was satisfactory and had we enjoyed our tea.

'Yes, lovely, thank you,' we said together, both smiling at the waitress. Peter paid the bill and we left the tea rooms. Making our way back, Peter suggested that we might travel to Hyde Park one day. It would perhaps be a good place to meet up with his parents. How would I feel about that?

'Yes, Peter, I think that would be a good idea,' I said, my voice trembling.

'Then that's settled. I will set everything in motion and will book a restaurant for lunch for all of us. It will be a day to celebrate for everyone.' Peter clasped my hand, 'Come on, Edith, we have to hurry you home, or Mrs Baker will be giving you your marching orders. And we can't have that, my darling, eh?'

Peter's face was a picture, his eyes twinkling, smiling mischievously.

I started to laugh and said, 'No, of course not. I will have to work on my day off and that would never do.'

We were both laughing together, the happiness we felt was equal, and at last we reached the house. I had five minutes before I was on duty. A brief kiss and a wave and Peter was gone.

I made my way into the house and rushed upstairs. I quickly changed and hurried downstairs just as the clock chimed 5 p.m.

Normally I would be on duty by 4.30 p.m. when their Lordships were at home, but this was to check the rooms and to see that everything was in order. The evening flew by and by 10 p.m. I was tucked up in bed, absolutely exhausted.

The following day, feeling very tired, I went about my duties in a trance-like state until lunch time. Cook eyed me up and down and said, 'You won't want Peter seeing you looking like this, my girl. It's an early night tonight for everyone. Too many late nights we've had, and it won't do. Their Lordships would be quite angry and annoyed to learn of this.'

'Yes,' I said, 'you are right, Cook, and I'm sorry. I promise to pull myself together before Mrs Baker sees me.'

'Right, Edith,' Cook said, 'now get some food inside you. That should bring you round and then have a nap before you go on duty.'

The rest of the day went by and we were all tucked up by 10 p.m. The following morning everyone seemed bright and cheerful and the time sped by. As I wasn't seeing Peter until the next day, Rose and I went roller skating. We knew that we had better make the best of things and our opportunities before their Lordships returned. The rotas could be changed and we would have different hours of duties and not have the chance to go out together so often.

The couple of hours we had roller skating seemed to go by quickly. We chattered and giggled most of the time, falling over because we weren't concentrating. I felt so happy; the prospect of seeing Peter the next day gave me a warm glow. My mind started to drift until Rose reminded me with a friendly push.

'Come on, Edith, we're going to be late. Mrs Baker and Cook will have us scrubbing floors for the next fortnight and bread and water to eat as well. Cor! I don't fancy missing them stews and soups, eh! I love my food too much. Edith, come on.'

Rose grabbed my arm and said, 'I'll race you back.'

Arriving back, both breathless from running, we were greeted by Charlie.

'Cor! What you two been up to? You looks like some old bloke's been chasing you. I'll sort 'im for ya!'

'No, Charlie,' we both cried, 'we had a race back because we didn't want to be late.'

'Well, you're not! It's only quarter past four,' Charlie said, 'so you have a few minutes spare, and guess wot? Their Lordships are coming back this weekend and we 'ave to pull our socks up mighty smartish! Don't let on that I 'ave told ya. Mrs Baker is gonna tell ya 'erself. Come on, let's 'ave a cuppa before we start; kettle's boiling and Cook's resting. She was snoring in the chair earlier on,' he chuckled, 'and I caught 'er. She didn't like it and sent me packing with a flea in my ear. Any 'ow, she is in 'er room now so let's 'ave that cuppa.'

The rest of the day and evening went by, ending with a game of cards with Cook in the kitchen. Rose and I chatted into the early hours until we fell asleep. We seemed to talk about everything and anything; what a pair we were.

The rest of the week flew by. Peter had made arrangements to meet his parents for lunch the following week. I had asked Mrs Baker if it was possible for me to have the day off that week, and with some reluctance she agreed, reminding me that Lord and Lady Havis would be home.

'I promise I'll make up for it,' I said to her.

'Of that you can be assured,' she replied.

The weekend came with the arrival of Lord and Lady Havis and entourage from Dorset. We all lined up in the main hall to greet them, each one of us looking smart in our starched uniforms. Mrs Baker was beaming from ear to ear and Cook looked flushed and slightly nervous.

'Welcome home, Lord and Lady Havis,' Mrs Baker said, with a slight curtsy. 'We have been looking forward to your return.'

Lord and Lady Havis smiled and greeted us all individually and then retired to the drawing room, awaiting afternoon tea. The kitchen was buzzing, Cook giving out orders to each of us. I was to serve afternoon tea to their Lordships, Rose was helping to prepare the vegetables for the evening meal and Charlie had to deal with the entire luggage. Everyone seemed to be dashing around.

Back to normal, I thought, everything on a tight rota. However, perhaps it was a good thing; we had been slacking quite a lot. With the tea trolley laden with tea and cakes, I knocked on the drawing room door.

'Enter,' a voice answered. I pushed open the double doors, steering the trolley through.

'Ah! Tea,' Lady Havis said. 'Thank you, Edith. Bring the trolley nearer to the fire. Do we have crumpets? Ah, yes we do. There is quite a chill in the air. Don't you think so, dear?' she added, turning to Lord Havis.

'Yes, my dear,' he said, 'you are quite right; the room hasn't been used for sometime. We must have a word with Mrs Baker about this.' And with a nod, he said, 'You can go now, Edith.' With a slight curtsy, I said thank you and made my way out, closing the doors quietly behind me. The rest of the day seemed like a whirlwind, constantly on the go, hardly any time to think, the bells in the parlour continually ringing, up and down stairs until dinner was served and we were able to relax and have our own supper and retire to bed. There was another busy day ahead.

The next week raced by and the day came when I was to meet Peter's parents. Although I appeared to be calm, I felt really nervous. This was going to be one of the most important days of my life and I wanted to make a good impression. Peter had assured me that everything would be all right.

'Be yourself,' he had said, 'everyone will love you. Don't worry; just remember I'm with you and that I love you.'

I knew he was right and decided to put on a brave face. I had everything to look forward to. Peter's parents had just arrived when we reached the restaurant; they were smiling as they came to greet us.

'Hello,' they said, 'we are so pleased to meet you, Edith.'

I felt an instant liking for them. Peter's mother had a round, friendly face with twinkly eyes, and his father looked like an older version of Peter, the same stance, the manner of a gentleman, and Peter's blue eyes. They both made me feel at ease and throughout our meal their conversation was unpretentious. We chatted and laughed and by the end of the meal I felt completely at ease. What a lovely day, such lovely people. It was so obvious how proud they were of Peter. I was in the clouds; this was the beginning of a new life. I felt so happy, especially when we all strolled together through the park. It was a perfect day.

We said our goodbyes at the station and an invitation was given by Peter's parents for us to join them for a weekend in the near future. We arrived back at Muswell Hill by early evening and I was reluctant to say goodbye to Peter. I just didn't want the day to end; we both wanted to be together and hated having to part. However we both knew that it would be a while yet and we had all of our lives to look forward to. We kissed and hugged and arranged to meet on my next half-day off.

Rose was waiting for me in the kitchen, along with Cook; the look of anticipation on their faces told me that I was in for a long evening.

'Well, how did you get on?' both said in unison.

'Make the tea, Rose,' Cook said. 'Edith needs a refreshing cuppa after 'er long day. Come on, Edith, sit yourself down; you look worn out. 'Ow was it, were they nice folk? How did ya like them?'

Rose interrupted, saying, 'Were they very toffee-nosed? How did they make you feel, like a servant girl or anyfing like that?'

'No, of course not,' I said. 'It was the most wonderful day. They made me feel like one of the family, and, guess what, we have been invited to their home for a long weekend, sometime in the near future mind.'

'Cor! Fancy that,' Rose chuckled. 'You will be going up in the world to be sure, eh? Cook, don't ya think, our Edith will be rubbing shoulders with posh folk?

'Now, Rose,' Cook said, 'just ya slow down and get ya breath back, it's early days yet. Ya can't rush these things. Peter's got 'is career to think of, promotion and all that. It all takes time, right, Edith? You've got your job 'ere in the meantime.'

Cook was looking very intently at me.

'Yes, Cook,' I said, 'you are absolutely right. Things will take their time and I want it to be right and work out for everyone so we will take one day at a time.'

'That's it, girl,' Cook squeaked. 'Ya keep that head screwed on and ya won't go far wrong.' And with that Cook uncovered a plate full of sandwiches, fresh ham and tomato.

'Come on, tuck in,' she said, 'I saved them for us so that we could have a good chinwag. Let's have a fresh pot of tea, Rose, luv; there's lots to talk about. Charlie is out so we shouldn't be interrupted.'

Two of the other maids came in to join us, wanting their cocoa and to listen in. Cook stoked up the fire and we all sat around the table eating sandwiches drinking and chatting. It was nearly 10 p.m. when Charlie returned.

'Cor! Wat's going on 'ere?' he said. 'Who's been 'aving earache?'

'Never you mind!' Cook squeaked. 'It's gals' talk. Now do you want some cocoa, Charlie?'

'Yes, a big one, Cook,' he said, 'and I'm starving.'

'How about a big please,' Cook said. 'Ya manners ain't up to much.'

'Sorry, sorry,' Charlie chortled, 'it's all this excitement; it makes me forget.'

'Well, that's most of the time, anyway,' Cook squeaked. 'I dunno what's going to happen to you, Charlie. You're a lost cause.'

And with that everyone started to giggle.

'That's it,' Charlie chortled. 'Poor old me: odd man out, put upon, at everyone's beck and call, but ya all love me really, don't ya?'

By this time everyone was screaming with laughter.

'Yes, of course we do, Charlie. We 'old our breath whenever we catch sight of ya. That's enough frivolity for now, we'll wake the whole household up,' Cook said. 'Come on, finish your drinks up – we have an early start in the morning.'

We cleared away and made our way to our rooms. Rose and I fell asleep almost straight away, and woke only when the alarm went off.

The weeks and months flew by quickly. There was so much to do, and with Lord and Lady Havis entertaining there were quite a few extra duties. I hardly saw Rose. With my duties being mostly upstairs, and our half-days different, we didn't go roller skating very often. We chatted in our room and that was a about it. Also, having extra duties, I had less time with Peter, once or twice a week maybe. However, we made the best of things and enjoyed our time together. Our weekend away hadn't come about and I was beginning to think that it had been forgotten until Peter mentioned that his father hadn't been well. He had contracted a throat virus which had turned into a nasty infection that had spread, leaving him very weak, Peter said.

'Mother has had her work cut out with father; it's an advantage to have been a nurse, although she is finding it all a bit much. The consultant was sure he had turned the corner and things were looking brighter. I'm going to spend some time with him and give Mother a break; I know you will understand, Edith. Fanny took time off to help, but they are short-staffed at the hospital so she has had to go back. I have got some leave due to me and I have arranged to travel down tomorrow, which sadly means I won't see you for a while. However, my darling, I will write as often as I can and the time will fly by. I shall miss you so much, but soon one day we will have all the time together that we want.'

'That's all right, Peter,' I said, trying hard not to show my sadness and disappointment, 'you must be with your family. I do understand because of my own mother and I know the stress it causes, and if there is anything I can do, please ask.'

'No, my darling you have enough to contend with here. All I want is for you to be here when I return.'

'Of course I will, Peter. There is no question of that, and I will count the days.'

'That's my Edith,' Peter said, 'and now it's time for a little surprise. I have booked our corner table at the tea rooms for 3 p.m. and we have just ten minutes to get there.'

Peter held my hand and we hurried along. The tea rooms were quite busy and as we entered the waitress greeted us with 'Good afternoon, madam and sir. Your table is ready.'

I thought this is a bit unusual; we didn't normally have this fuss. There was a pink tablecloth and napkins laid out with flowers in a beautiful vase, and as we sat down Peter ordered our tea. The waitress was smiling from ear to ear and curtseyed slightly and hurried away.

'I'm a little bewildered – what is going on?' I asked.

'You will soon find out my darling,' Peter said, as coming towards us was the manager of the tea rooms, carrying a tray with the most beautiful cake on it.

'Congratulations to both of you,' he said, smiling, 'we are so privileged to share this happy time with you both,' and with that he placed the cake in the centre of the table. 'And when you are ready to cut the cake, let us know,' he said, and disappeared into the kitchen.

I was at a loss. 'Peter,' I said, 'what is going on?'

'This,' Peter said producing a small box. 'Darling Edith, will you marry me?'

He took my hand and placed the box into it. I opened it, trembling with excitement. I saw the most beautiful diamond ring.

'Oh, Peter,' I cried, 'of course I will marry you! The ring is beautiful and I love you.'

Peter took the ring and slid it on to my finger.

'A perfect fit,' he said, 'for a perfect lady, who I love very much.' He kissed me gently on my hand and said, 'This is the happiest day of my life!'

I just couldn't believe this was happening; my heart was racing.

'Peter,' I said, 'I couldn't be happier, it's heaven.' With that, Peter waved his hand and a melodious sound of violins began to play, the manager came to cut the cake and a rapturous applause followed. It was absolutely wonderful. Everyone around us was smiling, and people from other tables came across to congratulate us. I never wanted that day to end; it will stay with me for ever.

The next few weeks seemed unreal. The household was buzzing with preparation for Lord and Lady Havis's guests, who were coming to stay for a very special function, and not being able to see Peter as well made it seem very strange. I missed him so much; my whole being ached for him. Peter wrote every week with all the news about his father, his progress and recovery. His mother was very tired and relied on Peter and Fanny for support. He couldn't return immediately, he had written in his letter, until he had found nursing help to ease the burden for his mother. However, the bank was awaiting his return and he had a responsibility to them as well.

'I'll let you know, my darling,' he had said in his letter, 'as soon as I know I'm coming back.'

Chapter Five

Those days and weeks seemed eternal, although we didn't have much time to dwell on anything. Rose and I only managed one half-day together, which we spent roller skating and we never stopped chatting most of the time. It was good therapy because we hadn't had much free time with all the extra work involved. This was made worse when Cook fell ill. The doctor had been summoned and she was ordered to rest for at least two weeks; she had high blood pressure, which had caused palpitations. Lady Havis made a rota up for us all to take turns in sharing the cooking and making up of the menus. Even Charlie had to lay breakfast trays and make tea.

'Not my job,' he had complained, 'it's women's work. I got other jobs more important. It ain't fair,' he kept muttering under his breath.

'It's not fair on any of us, Charlie,' Rose said, 'You're getting on my nerves moaning all the time. Cook isn't enjoying being sick, she can't help it. So just get on with it before I blow my top.'

'All right, all right,' Charlie said 'keep ya shirt on. You're not Mrs Baker so mind ya tongue.'

With that silence fell and both Charlie and Rose went about their business. Working relentlessly eight hours or more per day left us all completely drained and there was no time for petty arguments; just work, eating and sleeping.

The next two weeks sped by. Cook, now recovered, much to our delight, returned to the kitchen, giving out orders, with her finger checking for dust all around the shelves, muttering comments as she did.

'By gawd, it's a good thing I'm back; it's all but gone to the dogs! Come on, let's be having ya. There's work to be done.'

Our faces must have been a picture, totally dumbstruck. Cook had no idea the amount of work and effort that we had all put in while she was ill. Rose, I knew, would not stand by without commenting.

'Blimey, Cook, you got some nerve! We did double shifts in order to cover for you, and we were all worried sick about you, and that's the thanks we get!'

Rose's face was bright red and her expression was one of amazement; she realised she had spoken out of turn.

Cook spun round, her face twitching, her eyes wide open.

'Well, that's that, then,' she screamed. 'I'm supposed to be grateful, am I?' she slumped into the chair holding her head. 'Oh my gawd, I'm sorry,' she mumbled. 'I'm not thinking straight; it's been 'ard on you lot, I know. Sorry to all of ya. Put the kettle on, Rose, a cup of tea is in order.'

Rose immediately moved forward to fill the kettle. However, Charlie, who had been struck motionless by Rose's outburst, suddenly leapt forward and said, 'I'll do it, Cook. I've 'ad to do a lot of tea-making these last couple of weeks and I'm getting quite expert at it.' He smiled at Rose and winked. 'Ain't that so, Rose?' he said.

Rose looked bemused. Whatever is the matter with Charlie? she was thinking. Her face began to redden. Cook's eyes were darting from one to the other.

'Well, that's a turn up for the books,' she muttered. 'Gawd only knows miracles do 'appen, so get on with it, Charlie, or we will all die of thirst. Edith, fetch the biscuits; we'll all have a chat and catch up on things and whatnot, eh?'

We all sat down and each of us related to Cook the different things we had been doing. In the meantime Charlie couldn't keep his eyes off of Rose, and continually commented on how she had worked so tirelessly and without any thought for herself. Cook and the other maids seemed to be lost for words. It was apparent that Charlie was besotted with Rose, who was shrinking with embarrassment in her chair.

'Charlie,' she said, 'for gawd's sake! Don't go on so much, everyone did their bit.'

'Yes, I'm sure everyone did,' Cook said loudly, 'and now it's time to get back to work. Come on, you lot, let's be 'aving ya.'

So the rest of the day went by, with not a peep out of Charlie.

Poor Rose, trying hard not to make eye contact with him, continued with her chores. That evening we all retired to bed at 9.30 p.m., and once the door was closed Rose burst into tears.

'Edith,' she cried, 'I feel such a fool with Charlie going on like that. What was he thinking of? In front of Cook and everybody…'

'Come on, Rose,' I said, 'it's obvious why. Charlie admires you and he let his feelings for you run away. He probably feels a bit silly himself now; he hardly said a word throughout the rest of the day and I dare say he regrets making you feel embarrassed. Charlie is Charlie, Rose; he isn't a bad person, and having said that he is quite presentable when he's dressed up, and he wouldn't do anyone a bad turn. Be fair, Rose,' I said.

'Yes, I know,' Rose said, 'but I didn't think he liked me like that, Edith.'

'Well, he does,' I said, 'so you let him down gently if you're not interested. After all, you are a pretty girl and men are bound to notice you. Even Charlie! Sleep on it, Rose,' I added, 'you will feel different in the morning.'

Rose wiped the tears from her eyes and said, 'Do you really think I'm pretty, Edith? I never thought I was. I'm just Rose, the kitchen maid.'

'Yes,' I said, 'you are, and I'm a parlour maid, but that doesn't mean that we are not pretty or good people. This is how we earn a living and keep a roof over our heads. We were not born with a silver spoon and this is our life as it is. Time and change will come when it's ready, just think about it; we have to look forward to each day.'

'Yes,' Rose said, 'you are right, Edith, and you are very wise. I'm so glad you're my friend.' We carried on talking until our eye lids were so heavy we couldn't keep awake and drifted off to sleep.

The following day we were given instructions by Mrs Baker that everything that needed polishing had to be polished extra special, the reason being that Lord and Lady Havis were receiving a royal guest, a cousin of the king, and entourage, for a glittering banquet.

Only Mrs Baker and Cook had been told of the coming event; no wonder Cook had been so agitated. We were to be told on the day because of protocol. Our uniforms had to be starched and pressed, shoes polished and heeled, every member of staff had to remain on duty throughout the day regardless of rotas previously arranged.

The buzz in the kitchen was evident of how important this visit was. Special menus had been drawn up, and a delivery of fresh salmon encased in ice caused a stir in the kitchen. Cook was giving out orders to all and sundry. She surprised us all with her methodical instructions and by keeping her cool. Rose had been put in charge of arranging the salad bowls, which was quite an honour for Rose, who normally cleaned and washed up. Her face was full of concentration and there was an air of excitement everywhere.

Charlie avoided eye contact with Rose and never spoke out of turn; he went about his duties and was most polite to everyone. I noticed Rose giving him sideways glances when she thought no one was looking. Was she having second thoughts, thinking Charlie wasn't so bad after all? My mind was wandering. It's all in my imagination, I thought, so I dismissed it.

It seemed that I was running up and down stairs most of that day. Mrs Baker was giving out orders to everyone, and then out of the blue I was summoned to the drawing room by Lady Havis. Whatever could it be? I thought. I knocked on the door and entered.

'Ah, Edith,' Lady Havis said, 'I have decided to let you wait on table this evening, and there will be four of you so I shall expect impeccable service and manners throughout. I know I can rely on you, Edith; Mrs Baker will give you further instructions later today. That will be all, Edith.'

'Thank you, My Lady,' I said with a curtsy and left the room. Outside my heart was beating so fast, I clenched my hands with excitement.

I'm going to wait on royalty, I thought. Wait until I tell Rose and Cook! With that I made my way down the stairs. The time flew by, and although I felt nervous, I was looking forward to the evening.

The guests arrived and aperitifs were served in the drawing room. Conversations flowed throughout, and the house was alive and buzzing. The dining room was amazing. Candelabras had been placed on the table, along with beautiful flower arrangements, solid silver cutlery had been laid, beautiful linen napkins placed on gold-edged plates, and crystal glasses glittered. It was great splendour to behold, and the grandest experience I can remember in my life.

The banquet continued into the early hours of the morning, and most of us didn't retire to bed until two or three in the morning, apart from Charlie, who didn't get any sleep. He had to see everyone into their carriages, and that was well after 4 a.m. He never grumbled, though; he was quite star-struck! In fact, we all were.

The following day seemed quite hollow after all the celebrations. We were all too tired, and breakfast was eaten in comparative silence, each of us savouring our thoughts, apart from Cook.

'Thank gawd that's all done and dusted; too many of them banquets and we would be fit for nothing,' she said and looking at us with her face twitching, she added, 'What I say in my kitchen doesn't go any further than these walls. Their Lordships don't need tittle-tattle from anyone, ya hear me?'

We all nodded; no one would want to upset Cook. We all knew better from past experience that her tongue was sharp, but she had a heart of gold and we were well fed. Her cooking was excellent, and if any of us had any worries, she would always find time to listen; even Mrs Baker confided in her.

I remember on one occasion Charlie had come in late after his day off, his face downcast. Normally he was chirpy and full of himself, but this day was different. He went straight to his room, just grunting 'Goodnight' to us.

Cook called out to him, 'Don't ya want any cocoa, Charlie? What's up?'

'Nothing,' he mumbled back.

Cook waved her hand at us and said, 'It's time you lot got an early night –' with a nod and a wink – 'there is a busy day ahead tomorrow and you don't want to look all washed out, so off with you!'

The hint was loud and clear so we made our way to our

rooms, knowing Cook would sort things out. The next day Charlie was his normal self and it wasn't until some time later that we learned that Charlie's family had had a bereavement and he had become the sole breadwinner. It appeared that his mother and siblings relied on Charlie for financial help and whenever Charlie had his day off he would spend it with his family, helping around the house, doing jobs that his mother couldn't do.

Unfortunately there was a huge debt that had been left because of the bereavement and it had fallen on Charlie's shoulders to honour it. The bailiffs were threatening to come. Poor Charlie was beside himself with worry, and he was too proud to divulge any family business to anyone. However, he hadn't banked on Cook. She had taken Charlie to one side that night and whatever she said, Charlie had decided to confide in her. It was evident that Cook's advice had resolved things for Charlie, and he became his cheeky self again within a couple of weeks and no more was said. Mrs Baker had once said Cook was the salt of the earth, and she was.

The next couple of weeks sped by. The house had quietened down and Peter had returned from his parents' home and was back working at the bank. Our reunion was such a wonderful time; we had missed each other so much, there was such a lot to catch up on and every free moment I had I spent with him. We talked about our future together and the things we would do. It was all so exciting.

Peter's father had fully recovered from his illness and everything was back to normal. Rose and Charlie became good friends but wouldn't admit that they were courting to anyone, although Cook and I knew different. Cook wasn't so hard on Charlie and gave Rose more responsibility around the kitchen. Rose and I confided in each other still and shared our happiness. Looking back now, those weeks were so happy for all of us. We shared a household that wasn't harsh and cold like some houses where there was a strict regime, and even cruelty to the servants. Thank God we were so fortunate to have titled people who were genteel and compassionate towards all walks of life. Lord and Lady Havis knew how to be firm but kind and so theirs was a happy household. Everyone had a grumble now and again, and a few tiffs with each other, but, that was all.

Time flew by and I had reached my twentieth birthday. Peter had planned a celebration by booking a table for a dinner dance at a very upmarket hotel in London; this would include his parents and friends. I had saved and put aside enough money to afford a new dress for the occasion. Rose and I arranged a half-day together so we could shop and look around for something special. We found the most beautiful dress in pale blue edged with cream lace, with pearl buttons down the front and ruffled cuffs with a line of buttons matching. It was so pretty; Rose talked me into buying it.

'Edith,' she said, 'you'll look a picture. Gawd knows you deserve it! You will outshine everyone among all those toffs.'

I giggled at Rose. She was such a funny and good friend; what would I do without her? The dress was neatly packed in a satin box and tied with ribbon. I knew this was the most luxurious dress I had ever had and felt like it was a dream. The rest of the afternoon went by quickly. Even though Rose bought two outfits, we still had time for a cream tea.

Rose had confided in me that Charlie and she were courting (even though I knew already). Charlie she said wanted her to meet his mother and family, hence the new outfits. Rose said that she was amazed at her feelings for Charlie and how much he had changed: he was more responsible in his attitude towards everything, and he was so kind and gentle and couldn't do enough for her.

'Edith,' she said, 'I'm not boasting or anything, but Charlie is the most decent bloke a girl could have and that's why I love him.' The tears were welling in Rose's eyes. 'I've never been so happy, Edith. We're both are so lucky, aren't we?'

My eyes filled with tears.

'Rose, I'm so happy for you and you're making me cry. Both our dreams are coming true. We will always be best friends, I know, but let's promise never to lose touch, whatever happens.'

'Never,' Rose said, but little did we know what was ahead that would change our lives for ever. On returning we showed Cook our new clothes; she enjoyed sharing our excitement. 'Cor blimey,' she said, 'you pushed the boat out! I've never seen such posh outfits; still, you both deserve 'appiness. To be honest, you're like having my own kids and I know one day you'll be moving on and having your own families and whatnot. My life is 'ere,' she added. 'I'm 'appy enough, good job, and a roof over my 'ead, and I got you gals round me. What more could I ask for?' she winked at us and that said everything.

The following days sped by, my birthday came and included a lovely surprise from Peter, who had arranged for my sister Irene to join us. She had travelled to London the day before and was staying with a friend on the outskirts of town. I already knew of this friend from a letter that Irene had sent me telling me of her friend's good fortune on being left a legacy including a small terraced house. Irene had been so excited at the prospect of having the opportunity to be able to visit London, and of course being able to see me made the difference. We missed each other and of course I missed all the family as well.

It was a lovely day and evening and we had our pictures taken. I had one taken on my own, and looking back I thought I looked the bee's knees, but like everything, fashion changes with time. Irene had commented on how well and happy I looked, and I did. To me I had the perfect future ahead. Who would have thought that my life would have changed this much in a few years?

The next few weeks were quite hectic. Lord and Lady Havis entertained a number of different guests so we were all kept on our toes, running back and forward. One of the parlour maids became ill so I had extra duties, along with the others. It was difficult to see Peter very often because of time off: just one half-day off in ten days. Also Peter had been promoted to under manager on a trial basis. He had been quite excited.

'Edith,' he had said to me, 'if this promotion becomes permanent, I think we can start planning for the future, like looking for a home! What do you think, my darling?'

Chapter Six

Peter's face was a picture, his love and enthusiasm showing through. I just couldn't believe what I was hearing, and my heart was beating so fast I couldn't speak.

'Edith,' Peter said, 'are you all right?'

'Yes, yes,' I said, coming to my senses. 'It's such a wonderful plan, Peter. I'm so proud of you and it's so exciting.'

We spent our time together talking and making plans and arranged to meet whenever we could. The buzzing household continued; Lord and Lady Havis seemed to thrive on social evenings. Rose and I had very little time for chit-chat and what time we had we spent with our beaus, although we talked ourselves to sleep nearly every night.

Lord and Lady Havis went to Dorset to spend a couple of months at their summer home, and a skeleton staff was left behind, which included myself and Rose, Charlie, Cook and one other maid. Mrs Baker had travelled down with them this time to organise the running of the house and would return two weeks before Lord and Lady Havis returned to make sure that that their London home was prepared and ready for their homecoming.

We were left strict instructions of our daily duties, and rotas had been made up for those two months or more. Cook was left in charge and was responsible for keeping us in check. Lord and Lady Havis had arranged for workmen to come in to decorate the drawing room and library and other small rooms on the first floor; we were to clean and shampoo the carpets as each room was completed. Apart from Cook, we all had to work together, including Charlie. None of us seemed to mind, as it was a more relaxed atmosphere, with no bells ringing or running up and down stairs. Cook kept us on our toes by making sure we stuck to the rotas, our meals were always on time and she kept the workmen happy with tea and sandwiches. Apart from one or two mishaps, everything went along smoothly, until Rose slipped in the kitchen and dislocated her shoulder.

Poor Rose was in absolute agony. Cook was quite distraught.

'You silly gal! What were you thinking of? The floor was wet.' Cook's face was twitching (this happened every time she became agitated).

'Find Charlie, quick,' she said to me. I remember poor Charlie's face when I told him.

'Oh gawd! My poor love,' Charlie said, 'where is she?'

'In the kitchen with Cook,' I said. 'You have to fetch the doctor, Charlie, quickly.'

We raced down to the kitchens. Rose had been helped into Cook's armchair; her face was quite pale and she was grimacing with pain. Charlie wasted no time, and hurried off to fetch the doctor, who returned promptly with case in hand.

'My, my,' the doctor said 'and what have you been getting up to?' He patted Rose's hand gently. 'Let me see… Ah, yes, you have pulled your shoulder bone; it's only dislocated.'

He administered a sedative to Rose and asked Charlie to assist him by holding her around the waist.

'Look at me,' the doctor said, and before Rose knew anything had happened, it was all over.

'Ouch!' she cried.

'You need to rest now,' the doctor said, 'it will ache for a little while. I'll leave a sedative with you to take before you retire to bed, and you should be all right within a couple of days.' He turned to Cook and said, 'Fetch me if there are any problems.'

'Yes, I will,' Cook replied, 'and thank you, doctor.' Cook always managed to speak without abbreviating her words when certain people were around!

The doctor left and we made Rose comfortable in Cook's chair. Charlie made us all a cup of tea and it was quite apparent that Cook was relieved to know that everything was all right. Rose fell asleep with Charlie's arm around her. That was something you rarely saw; normally the rule was no fraternising at any time in the household, but this was different.

Within a week Rose was back to normal. The smell of paint lingered throughout the house and the workmen seemed to be in no hurry to finish. I think they enjoyed Cook's tea and sandwiches too much.

The next few weeks flew by and I was able to see Peter a lot more. Although he worked longer hours, we managed to meet in the evenings. Cook said that as long as the daily rotas were completed, she could see no reason why we couldn't have free time in the evenings, providing we were in by 10 p.m.

The evenings were warm and sultry; it being August, we were able to meander through the parks. There were bands playing and we were able to sit and listen in between making plans; there were pavement cafés where we could buy coffee and refreshments. For sixpence you could have as many cups of coffee as you liked; the waiters had a never-ending coffee pot! Those evenings together we both treasured. We had grown so close, and we both loathed parting at the end of the evening.

'Very soon,' Peter would say, 'we will be together in a home of our own.'

Those words were like magic. At that time I could not imagine my life without Peter. He was my rock, my future, and I knew that's how he felt about me. In my mind I didn't want to be a parlour maid for all of my life; I wanted a home and children and I wanted them with Peter. However, we would have to wait a little while. We decided that it would be nice to live on the outskirts of London, somewhere with a garden, but until Peter's promotion was confirmed we had to be patient.

Mrs Baker returned two weeks before Lord and Lady Havis had planned to return to London. We were pleased to see her, although Rose and Charlie said she wouldn't be as liberal as Cook: we certainly wouldn't be able to have our evenings off, just our allocated ones according to the rotas.

The evening Mrs Baker returned, Cook had prepared a special supper. She had missed having Mrs Baker around and to be honest she was Cook's only true friend. They both enjoyed evenings together, chatting and playing cards and occasionally they went to see a West End show; they both enjoyed their way of life. Their work was all they knew and cared about.

We were all interested to hear about her time away in Dorset, what the house was like, the countryside, the people and the villages. Mrs Baker had been quite impressed by everything. The way of life was different: much slower, no traffic, lots of fresh air and country walks.

'I would think it is something like Wales,' Mrs Baker said, looking at me and nodding.

'Well, yes,' I said, 'similar, but of course we have the mountains, which you wouldn't have in Dorset.'

'Yes, quite,' she replied, giving Cook a wink. 'I never thought of that.'

Was that a note of sarcasm?

Cook just smiled and said, 'It would be nice to have a holiday there, rather than work.'

'Yes,' Mrs Baker replied, 'it would do you good to have a break. A complete change is what you need, Agatha.' That was Cook's Christian name, which few of us knew.

Charlie's face said it all.

'You can take that look off your face, Charlie,' Cook said. 'You mind ya manners round me, and that goes for all of ya!'

'I never said a word, Cook! Would I ever?' he said, grinning from ear to ear.

The rest of the evening we spent chatting and playing cards. Charlie and Rose had finished their evening duties and at the suggestion of Mrs Baker they went for a walk.

'They make a good couple,' Cook remarked. 'I've had to eat my words, gawd knows! I never thought them two would make it, but what a change in Charlie, full of cheek and whatnot! Now he's a new bloke. Rose is a good gal, the best thing to 'ave 'appened to Charlie, and he worships the ground Rose walks on. They deserve to be 'appy, don't ya think?'

We all nodded in agreement. Cook never normally passed comment in front of staff, but this was her way of giving her approval, and Mrs Baker nodding her head sealed it. I ended up making cocoa for everyone and then we all headed off to bed.

The following day I had arranged to meet Peter at the teashop in the afternoon. I had two hours off and wasn't on duty until 4.30 p.m. and it was also Peter's half-day. We looked forward to our times together. We always had so much to talk about. However, this day was different. His face was happy but serious when I met him.

'Hello, my darling,' he said. Holding my hands, he murmured. 'I have some news for you.' His eyes were wide and piercing as he looked at me. He led me into the teashop and to our corner table, which luckily wasn't occupied. He ordered tea and then began to tell me.

'Edith, my darling, I have been offered a new post. It's with more prospects and opportunities, far more than I could dream of –' my heart was beating fast, I had a sudden dread – 'only, Edith, it means I will have to work in America. New York, to be precise. Only for a year, darling, but it would make such a difference.'

Peter's face looked anxious for I must have shown my feelings of complete shock.

'Are you all right?' he asked.

'Yes, yes, I'm sorry,' I said, 'it is such a surprise; it's the last thing I expected you to say.' My whole being was shaking. I could not imagine such a long time apart.

'Edith,' Peter said, 'I don't have to accept. You are more important than any promotion; you are my life and my future. I will have other opportunities come my way. I shouldn't be so thoughtless. It's happened so quickly, I never stopped to think how hard it would be for you and how much I would miss you.' He held my hands and I could feel him trembling as he said, 'I have a month to decide, but have decided I am staying here with you. I love you so much.' His expression was determined and the tone of his voice was sincere.

'Please, Peter,' I said, 'let's stop and think about all of this. We need to talk this through.' My voice was trembling with emotion. By this time, our tea was served. I started to pour but my hands were shaking so much Peter had to take the teapot off of me.

'Edith,' he said 'let me do this.' He poured the teas and we sat in silence until we had finished.

'You are right,' he said, 'we do need to talk this through, although my mind is made up. There is no way I'm going now. I feel that this has been too much for you today and talking can wait a little while longer.'

We made our way out of the teashop and decided to take a stroll through the park, Peter held my hand and we walked in silence for a little while, watching other people, listening to their chatter as they strolled by. It was almost 4 p.m. and I was on duty within the half-hour. I reminded Peter, who was reluctant to let me go.

'Time goes by so quickly,' he said. 'Is it possible for us to meet tomorrow, Edith?'

'Maybe in the evening,' I replied. 'I'll ask Mrs Baker. I'm sure she won't mind if I complete my evening duties first, but we must go now.'

We hurried through the park and made our way back. Peter hugged me and promised to meet me outside the following evening.

'We could go for a drink if you like,' he said, his face full of concern.

'Don't worry,' I said, 'just as long as we are together, I don't mind. Everything will be fine.' We kissed and I watched Peter as he made his way through the busy streets. He turned and waved and was gone. I quickly made my way in. I had five minutes to get changed. The evening sped by. I hadn't spoken to anyone about Peter's news. I just couldn't bear the thought of it; Rose asked if I was feeling well because I looked a little pale.

'Fine,' I replied, 'I'm due for an early night. No more late-night chats, Rose.' I tried to sound light-hearted, but Rose wasn't going to be put off easily.

'That's not like you, Edith. Something's up. God knows I can tell when you are hiding something from me. Have you had a row with Peter?'

'No, of course I haven't, Rose. It's women's problems; you know what I mean.'

'Sorry,' Rose said, 'I'll say no more. I'll make you a nice hot cup of cocoa and put the warming pan in your bed. OK, Edith?'

'You are so good and kind, Rose,' I said, 'what would I do without you?'

'For gawd's sake!' Rose mumbled, 'you'll have me in tears in a minute. Let's be 'aving ya.'

Although I thought I wouldn't sleep, the hot cocoa and warming pan did the trick. I slept soundly and woke with a clear mind and determination.

The morning flew by and Mrs Baker agreed to my request,

providing I finished my duties, for time off in the evening. Lunch was prepared by Rose. Cook had given her more responsibility. I think she was training Rose and teaching her cooking skills, for Cook knew that sometime she would have to retire and Rose and Charlie would make a good team within the household. It was common knowledge that Rose and Charlie had been offered living accommodation when they decided to marry. Lord and Lady Havis were delighted when they heard the news, which was surprising, for most households who engaged staff would not approve of fraternising. But this was different; they were going to be married and a couple that would be permanently living in and always available would be an asset to them.

Rose had excelled herself. Lunch was delicious: ham off the bone with freshly baked bread. Piping-hot tea was served by Charlie with a serving cloth draped across his wrist.

'Is everything satisfactory for madam?' he chortled, referring to Cook. She just gave him one of her looks. No need to say anything; that was enough.

'Whoops, sorry!' Charlie said and we all started to giggle. Cook just shook her head.

Later that afternoon, with two hours to contemplate, I decided what I was going to say to Peter and what I would have to do.

The evening came and I was anxious to finish my duties. I knew that Peter would be on time and it was important that I didn't keep him waiting. In my heart I knew that our lives were about to change and the pit of my stomach felt heavy. However, I had to show that everything was all right with me. I had dressed smartly in a two-piece, which was one of Peter's favourites.

'Hey,' he called out to me as I came around the side of the house, 'you look lovely. As you always do,' he said quickly. He kissed me gently on the cheek and held my hand.

'I have really been looking forward to this evening, we have so much to talk about and I have found a quaint pub for us to have a drink in.' He was smiling, his eyes twinkling. 'Come on, Edith,' he said, 'the night is young but we have only two hours before you have to be in.'

'Yes,' I said, 'so let's go.'

We held hands and made our way through the winding streets.

Everything about the pub was quaint. The tinkling of a piano made the atmosphere friendly and warm and people were beginning to drift in, ready to enjoy a pleasant drink and evening. We managed to secure a table by the window, the lamp on the table casting shadows around us, which gave out that cosy glow. It made us both feel relaxed as the barmaid came across to take our orders.

'Wot ya 'aving, my luvvies?' she said, picking up some empty glasses from the table. We both decided to have light ale, something I wasn't used to, but this evening was special. We both knew decisions were going to be made. I commented on how nice the pub was and the friendly atmosphere that surrounded us.

'Yes,' Peter said, 'I knew you would like it here.' And we continued to make conversation until I said, 'Peter, I have thought and considered all that has been said regarding your promotion. It would be foolish for you not take this opportunity, and I know it means a lot to you.'

Peter tried to stop me saying anything further.

'No, Peter,' I said, 'please listen. We have all our lives in front of us and a year away isn't that long. It will go by quickly, I'm sure. We can write to each other every week. Please, I want you to go; it is just as important for me as it is for you. I'm so proud of you, and you deserve this.' Peter held my hands and said, 'Edith you are unselfish, kind and loving and I am proud of you, too. However, I cannot leave you. Life wouldn't be the same, not being able to see you for so long.'

We continued to talk it over and by the end of the evening a decision had been made. Peter was going to America.

Time was of the essence and the next few weeks seemed unreal. I confided in Cook and Rose, who both looked stunned when I told them.

'Cor!' Cook said. 'It will all fly by and next fing he will be back in no time at all. Ain't that right?'

'Of course he will,' Rose said. 'You won't know yourself. Besides we are going to keep you busy!'

'I've got jobs lined up for ya already,' Cook chortled with a twinkle in her eye. I knew then that I had friends who would always be there for me and the time while Peter was away would be well spent. I wouldn't have any chance to feel sorry for myself.

The next weekend Peter took me to see his parents. I had been given the time off by Mrs Baker, who had made it clear that I would have to make the hours up later in the month.

It was the last weekend for Peter, who was sailing the following week from Southampton. Fanny, Peter's sister, joined us, too, which made it a family affair. A party had been arranged for the Saturday evening. It all went very well, everyone laughing and joking, not one tinge of sadness was allowed. We all raised our glasses to his success and future.

The following morning after breakfast, Peter and I went for a stroll by the duck pond that was nearby. This was going to be our last time on our own, in a sense, to gather our thoughts, to remember everything that we cherished.

'I'll write as often as I can,' Peter said, 'and Fanny will keep in touch with you and arrange to meet whenever she has the chance.'

'Yes, that would be nice,' I said, 'we could meet for coffee and a chat and catch up on all of the news.'

'That's my girl,' Peter said, with a gleam in his eye, 'I know I won't have to worry about you too much, my sweet girl!'

We carried on chatting and made our way back. After lunch we said our goodbyes and Peter's parents said I would always be welcome at any time and that we should meet sometime in London.

They had arranged with Peter to catch a connecting train so that they could see him board the Queen Mary and say farewell, which would be in a few days' time. Our journey home seemed too quick; we talked nonstop, both being over-cheerful.

'We must have a photograph taken together,' Peter said, 'I'll arrange it at the studio tomorrow and when they are developed you can send one on to me.'

'That would be lovely,' I said. Somehow it seemed to cheer me up. I felt a surge of relief flow over me. I would always have his face in front of me, something to treasure for ever.

'Wear your blue dress,' Peter said, 'it is my favourite, the one with the lace collar.'

'Yes,' I replied, 'I was just thinking of that. It's my favourite, too.'

Chapter Seven

We carried on chatting, oblivious to the fact we had reached home. We had such a lovely weekend together.

'Give me a hug,' Peter said. 'I don't want you to go in.' We held each other for a few minutes, kissed and said goodbye.

'Meet you on Tuesday,' Peter said and waved as he walked away.

Rose and Cook were in the kitchen, preparing the evening meal as I came through the door. 'Cor blimey! She's back already,' Cook called out to Rose and in one breath she said, 'Put the kettle on, Edith, and you can tell us all about ya weekend over a cuppa.'

Rose took my coat and bag and said, 'It's good to have you back, Edith, we missed you upstairs.' Even Charlie said so, too!

'I'll have to go away more often,' I said, 'if I am going to receive red-carpet treatment each time.'

'Get a way with ya,' Cook chortled 'I'll 'ave ya peeling potatoes if ya get too big for ya boots!'

'That's right, Cook,' I said, 'bring me down to earth. A cuppa for everyone,' I added, ignoring their grinning faces. What would I do without these lovely people, especially in the next few months? It was going to be hard, I was thinking, the next few days must be the best.

Tuesday came quickly. The morning duties I carried out mechanically. Lunch came and went; I finished my afternoon by preparing the tea trolley for Lord and Lady Havis's tea which was served at 4 p.m. I had two hours with Peter.

I was quite excited about having my photograph taken. I had laid my powder-blue dress out along with my gloves and purse early in the morning so that I could be on time. Peter was waiting outside, punctual as usual, looking very smart in a pinstriped suit.

'You look lovely,' Peter said to me. 'I am really proud of you, Edith, always looking elegant.'

'You will have my head swelling in a moment, boyo,' I said laughing. 'Anyway you are looking quite handsome yourself, if I may say so.'

'You may,' Peter said, winking wickedly. 'Come on, we have to be on time for the photographer, 3 p.m. on the dot. He only managed to fit us in because of a cancellation and it is important for us.'

Holding my hand, Peter hurried me along. We reached the studio at 2.55, both feeling relieved that we were not late. There were people there who were just leaving after having their portraits taken. The photographer was a portly man with a red robust face and moustache. He greeted us with a 'Good afternoon, madam and sir,' and led us into a room that was draped with curtains in fine cloth. A chaise longue and soft quilted chairs rested on a raised platform, which was covered in deep rich carpet, with arc lamps placed on either side.

He then proceeded to tell us about his technique in photography. Most are in sepia finish or hand-painted, he told us.

'I can do both if you wish,' he said, gesturing with his hands. 'Of course hand-painted is dearer but gives a beautiful colour, natural and enhancing,' he turned to Peter for his approval. Immediately Peter said, 'I think perhaps my fiancée can make that decision.' My face must have been a picture of surprise, because Peter started to laugh and said, 'What do think, Edith, one of each?'

'I really don't mind,' I stuttered, feeling slightly embarrassed.

'Well, that's fine,' Peter said, 'we could have two of us together and one on our own. Yes, I think that would be good, and we would have a memento each, Edith.'

'That would be lovely,' I replied. The photographer clapped his hands together and said, 'Good, please sit over here.'

We sat down on the chaise longue while the photographer arranged the lights. He said we could hold hands if we wished. He then disappeared under a cloth covering the camera and called out for us to hold very still but smile. It seemed like eternity and suddenly a great flash. We had four taken altogether, including one of us each on our own. It took nearly an hour and we were told to call back in two days when the sepia photographs would be ready. However the hand-painted ones would take longer. He requested a small deposit and said he looked forward to seeing us again shortly.

We were both gasping for a drink by that time and I had just under an hour before I was on duty. The coffee shop around the corner was quite full but we managed to squeeze in by the window and enjoyed a welcome pot of tea. In no time, I was back on duty, knowing that in a couple of days Peter would be sailing to New York. We spent our last evening together having a meal and a stroll. Strangely enough I felt calm and contented. The bond we had would keep us together no matter how far apart we were.

Our goodbye was a tender and lasting embrace; the look in Peter's eyes was full of love, which I shall never forget for the rest of my life. It seemed hazy and unreal, especially when I waved goodbye and watched Peter disappear in the distance knowing I wouldn't be seeing him for another year. Part of me wanted to run after him and beg him not to go, but I knew that it would be selfish and we would both have regrets. We had years ahead.

Time will fly by, I told myself as I went inside.

Chapter Eight

Rose was waiting for me, her face looking serious until I smiled and said, 'I hope you have put the kettle on. I shall need my cocoa tonight.'

'Cook's already done that,' Rose replied, 'and I've made some biscuits, still hot from the oven, and you won't be able to dunk them, eh, Cook?' she said, turning to wink at her.

Cook had been standing by the open cooking range at the far end of the kitchen, stirring the pot.

'That's right, Rose,' Cook replied, 'and I've made us a nice cuppa. It's a bit early for cocoa, Edith, and besides, we are playing cards and tea and biscuits go down well with a touch of brandy. Come on now, let's be 'aving ya before Charlie and the rest come and scoff everything.'

'That's my Charlie you're talking about,' Rose retorted, giving me a wink. 'He won't miss a game of cards and most of all my home cooking, don't you think, Cook?'

Cook's facial expression was a picture. 'And when did ya become a cordon bleu? Cook chortled. We were all laughing when Charlie appeared.

'Wot's going on 'ere?' he shouted. 'Enough of this frivolity.' He started to stutter. 'Cor! That's a – um – big word for me, ain't it, Rose?'

'Yes, it is,' she replied laughing, 'and it's all because of my biscuits that I've made. Come on, Charlie, sit yourself down before we all get bellyache!'

The rest of the evening was spent playing cards and drinking tea. The cheerful atmosphere made me feel heady and not once did anyone mention Peter. This was their way of showing support and acknowledgement of their friendship when I needed it most, and it saw me through the next months when I felt the emptiness of Peter's departure. Surprisingly enough I slept that first night.

A letter arrived nearly three weeks later from Peter saying how New York was fantastic and how much he missed me; he would like to show me New York one day. His apartment was big, he wrote, the buildings were quite intimidating and life never stopped night or day. It would be some time before he became accustomed to their system of banking and their way of life, but he was determined to work hard and reach his goal.

> I long to hear your voice, that lovely Welsh lilt which I miss so much. I hope you are not gadding about on your days off!

Knowing Peter this was his way of reassuring me. There were six pages altogether and a promise of a telephone call one day, which the bank would allow him. He would write again and give me the times and details. 'Please write soon,' he ended his letter.

I kept that first letter in my apron pocket and at every opportunity I had I would read it until it became crumpled. I sneaked upstairs to my quarters, ironed it smooth and then placed it in my drawer wrapped in pink ribbon, and all of the other letters that came were put together in the drawer. Through the weeks and months I read through each letter over and over again. It made me feel close to Peter and sometimes I would sleep with them under my pillow.

The phone call was arranged (with Mrs Baker's permission) from New York. It was 3 p.m. one Tuesday afternoon. The signal was poor and Peter's voice sounded hoarse and crackly, but it was wonderful to be able to talk to him. We had five minutes and it all went too quickly. Peter promised to ring again in a few weeks, all being well, and we both promised to write. I was walking on air for the rest of that day.

It took Rose to bring me down to earth with, 'Edith, I think I've got a boil on the back of my neck! It's agony! Will you put a poultice on it? Charlie and Cook are too squeamish to do it and I can't do it myself.'

'Calm down, Rose,' I said, 'of course I'll do it. We will need a bowl of boiling water and a piece of lint and antiseptic. Ask Charlie to make tea. You'll need a cup, a sweet one, after I have finished with you.'

'Oh gawd!' Rose cried. 'Is it going to be that bad? I can't stand pain!'

'Come on, Rose,' I said gently. 'It will hurt a little bit, but it needs to be done. I'll be as gentle as I can, I promise. If you like, Charlie can hold your hand.'

'No thanks, Edith,' Rose cried. 'Charlie is better staying with Cook and holding hers! I only hope that they don't ever have a boil!'

By this time Charlie, who had been listening, had placed a chair and towels in the scullery with a bowl of boiling water on the table. Cook scuttled in with the lint and antiseptic looking very sheepish.

'You're going to be all right, Edith,' she said, trying hard not to make eye contact with Rose. 'I've put the kettle on for a nice cuppa, when you've finished.'

And with that Cook scuttled back into the kitchen, where Charlie was laying out the cups and saucers nervously.

'Careful, Charlie,' Cook said, 'ya don't want to crack anything.'

Charlie muttered something which was out of ear's reach, the door closed and I proceeded to place the poultice on poor Rose's neck. It was quite inflamed and nasty and Rose cried out in pain and I could feel her body shudder.

'Oh my gawd! Oh my gawd!' she kept crying out. 'Please let it stop.'

'Sorry, Rose,' I said. 'It's all over – just the antiseptic.'

Rose laid her head on the table crying with relief. 'Thanks, Edith, thank gawd! Never again, please.'

'You are run down, Rose,' I said. 'You need to drink cabbage water more often. It's an old remedy, keeps away boils and spots. My mam used to swear by it.'

'I bet she did,' Rose cried, 'it would make anyone swear! I'm not drinking that, ugh!'

And before I could answer the door swung open and Charlie rushed in.

'Are you all right, Rose, luv? I'm sorry, it must 'ave been 'orrible.'

By this time Rose had calmed down. 'Come here, you big softie. I'm OK,' she said. 'It's done and dusted. Edith should be a nurse! To be honest I don't think I could do it either.'

'You would, if you had to,' I said. 'Let's have that cup of tea. I'm gasping for one and you certainly need a drink and a good rest.'

'It's all ready,' Charlie said, 'piping hot and on the table, and Cook has given her chair for you to sit in. Plenty of cushions and by the fire.'

'Gawd, what a fuss!' Rose muttered. 'I'm truly honoured I'm sure, but a wooden chair would do fine.'

'I heard that!' Cook called from the kitchen. 'I wouldn't look a gift 'orse in the mouth if I were you! Let's be 'aving ya before it all goes cold and the rest come in for their break.'

The rest of the day Rose was allowed to take it easy. She sat down to peel vegetables, and Cook allocated other chores to a new kitchen maid, who was too timid to refuse. I served afternoon tea and supper in the evening and by 10 p.m. I was feeling so tired I just fell into bed. For the first time, as far as I can remember, Rose was already asleep without having a natter first; it had been quite a stressful day in all.

My feeling of emptiness began to fade and in the weeks ahead I kept busy, taking on extra duties whenever needed. I had always kept a diary and jotted things down each day, but since Peter had gone I had made a conscious decision to fill two pages every day with all that was happening so that I would be able to keep letters to Peter interesting.

Each fortnight I would receive a letter, each one full of optimism and stories about how well he was doing. He had made friends with one or two of his colleagues, who in turn had taken him out to see the sights of New York, Broadway and an evening watching a James Cagney film. He had visited New Jersey and the Statue of Liberty, and went to the top of the Empire State building.

> One day I hope to show you all of this, but in the meantime keep writing to me as I need your letters to sustain me, they are so interesting and I visualise you all of the time.
> I hope you are keeping in touch with Fanny and my parents. They regularly write to me and they would like to visit me in New York, hopefully in a couple of months. They will sail from Southampton all being well.

The knowledge that his parents would be seeing Peter in a few weeks' time made me feel unsettled. I had been dealing with the void that I had been feeling without him, my whole being wanted to be with him and I knew it wasn't possible.

How could I last another six months or more without seeing him? It just wasn't fair. It should be me going to visit him, I told myself, and then I realised I was being selfish. Peter's parents hadn't enjoyed good health in recent months, and as he was their only son, who they absolutely worshiped, they were entitled, and I realised how hard it must be for them.

My letters had to continue in the same way and I would get in touch with Fanny so that we could meet. I would also send a card to his parents, wishing them well. With this in mind I threw myself into my work and continued to look forward to Peter's letters. A month later I heard from Fanny.

> Please can we meet? We have so much to catch up on and I have some free time on a Wednesday afternoon.

Arrangements were made for the following week and to my surprise Fanny had managed to include her mother and father, who greeted me with open arms.

'So lovely to see you again, Edith. You are looking well, my dear, and we know you must be missing Peter as much as we do; there is so much to talk about.'

The afternoon sped by. I felt relaxed and was able to talk naturally. I now could feel part of the family. Already, Fanny was like a sister to me, she had Peter's humour and twinkling eyes and made everyone feel at ease. We chatted about the trip to New York and it was obvious that the parents were very excited. This would be a dream holiday combined with seeing Peter, a once-in-a-lifetime adventure. I thought, maybe one day it will be me. I felt a pang of regret that I wasn't going, but it was only momentary and it passed.

I had knitted Peter a scarf, which I gave to his parents to give to him when they arrived. Fanny had bought a book for him; he enjoyed reading, especially thrillers.

'He will think it's his birthday all over again,' she laughed, and so the afternoon ended. We said our goodbyes with promises of letters and cards and meeting again in a couple of month's time, although I would see Fanny before then which she reminded me of. I had promised to teach her to roller skate.

The journey back was quiet and I felt pensive and contented, time would fly by if I kept busy. Another seven months and we would be together. That's what I told myself; there was so much to look forward to.

It was six o'clock when I walked into the kitchen. Cook was having a nap before serving dinner; everything had been prepared earlier. No one else was around and only the ticking of the clock broke the silence. I tiptoed out, not wanting to disturb Cook's slumbering, and made my way to my room, thinking Rose would be there. However, it was empty; it looked like she was with Charlie. It gave me the opportunity to read through Peter's letters once again, which I treasured. The silence was golden.

I was able to read without any interruptions; it was my own little world and I savoured every moment. Now was the time to write to Peter in peace and quiet. I related the events of the day in every detail. In all I wrote six pages and by the end I was exhausted and fell asleep. The next thing I was woken by Rose gently shaking me.

'Cor blimey, girl! You must be tired to miss supper. Cook was getting worried, wasn't sure whether you had come in yet. Anyway there is supper on the stove, keeping warm for you.'

'Thanks, Rose,' I said, yawning and stretching. 'I'm starving. I'll just brush my hair and come down. Will you wait for me? I have lots to talk about.'

'Can't wait,' she said. 'Charlie is on duty tonight; their Lordships have a bridge night so he is going to be kept busy and we can catch up on everything. Cook is eager to hear all the news and Mrs Baker is going to join us at 8.30 for a game of cards and it's nearly quarter to eight now, Edith! Come on, be quick.' Rose grabbed my arm. 'You look fine.'

With that, we hurried down to the kitchen where nibbles had been prepared for Charlie to serve later. Cook's face was one of astonishment.

'Where in devil's name 'ave you been?' she screamed. 'We've been worried sick, Edith, all sorts going through our minds.'

'Sorry. I'm sorry, I should have let someone know. You were asleep when I came through and I didn't like to disturb you,' I said sheepishly.

'Well, all's well that ends well,' Cook retorted. 'You better eat supper. It's on the stove. Get it down ya before Mrs Baker arrives; all this should've been cleared away ages ago.'

'Thank you, Cook,' I said, 'I'm starving.'

'I'm not surprised,' she mumbled as she arranged the cups and saucers. 'Rose, make the tea. I'm parched with all of this 'anging around.'

The rest of the evening went by quickly. I was able to tell the events of the day by the time Mrs Baker made an appearance and then it was an hour of playing cards with everyone; we were all in bed and asleep by 10.30.

The following morning was an early start. I was in the drawing room cleaning the hearths at 5.30 and 8.30 serving breakfast to their Lordships and overnight guests. This was going to be a busy day with all of the extra work and by 9.30 I was longing for a cup of tea. My stomach was rumbling with hunger so I tucked into boiled eggs and toast and two cups of tea. I expected Cook to comment, but she just patted me on the head and continued to give instructions to the new kitchen maid.

That afternoon I had two hours' free time which I badly needed. I had a letter to post to Peter and ironing to see to, and I also felt really tired. My day hadn't ended; at 4.30 p.m. I was serving afternoon teas and 8 p.m. dinner that evening, so I decided to have a short nap before anything else. Rose promised to wake me in time, and said she would join me for a walk.

'Don't worry about the ironing. I've bits to do and yours isn't much. It'll give you more time to dream,' she giggled.

'You are good, Rose, even though you drive me mad sometimes,' I murmured as I drifted off.

'Watch it!' I heard her cry.

The next thing I was awake with Rose tapping me on my shoulder.

'Come on, wakey, wakey! I've bought you a nice cup of tea,' she said, smiling. 'We need to get going or we will be late for evening duty.'

'Thanks,' I said. 'You are an angel. The tea is most welcome, and I'll be two ticks.'

We managed a short walk, posting my letter to Peter on the way; there was a café nearby alongside the local park.

'Fancy a cream cake, Rose?' I asked. 'My treat?'

'Well, go on then,' she said half-heartedly. 'I've got to watch my figure if I'm getting spliced next year. I don't want Charlie complaining.'

'That would never happen,' I replied quickly. 'He loves you too much and there is nothing of you anyway. Come on, before I change my mind.'

We found a little table outside the café facing the sun and ordered a cream tea which we tucked into leaving cream around our mouths.

'Cor! Edith, look at your face. You've got cream all round your mouth!'

'Yes, I know,' I laughed. 'You should see your face. That's the trouble when you eat creamy cakes; there is no way to avoid it.'

By this time two people sitting the other side began to giggle. They had the same problem and asked the waitress for some napkins, which we all shared to clean ourselves up. The time had sped by and we had fifteen minutes to get back and change, which we did by the skin of our teeth!

Later, Cook, who had prepared tea, couldn't understand why we were not hungry.

'You're not coming down with something? It 'ain't like ya both. Still I dare say supper won't be wasted, eh!'

'No, Cook,' we both replied quickly. 'It's lunch; you fed us too much.'

'I'll remember that,' she mumbled, giving us a knowing look. 'Off ya go! Be on time for supper or else!'

During the next couple of weeks I tried not to dwell on the coming events; however, the day came when Peter's parents were sailing to New York.

I had sent them a card wishing then bon voyage and my love. I imagined what it must be like to be on board a huge liner, all the excitement. What a marvellous journey to make and at the end of it there would be Peter waiting for them at the docks.

I just wished I could be there. However, wishing was one thing and it wasn't going to happen so I had to be patient. I would soon hear again and he would have received my letter by now. The best thing for me to do was to keep busy. Some of my afternoons were spent knitting and at least once a month I was asked to entertain Lady Havis's guests with my tea-leaf readings.

I didn't spend as much time with Rose as I used to because of Charlie and that was understandable. We occasionally went roller skating and sometimes for a walk, but that was all. Fanny and I went skating one day and it was hilarious. She just couldn't keep her balance, and spent most of the time on her backside!

'I'll never be any good at roller skating,' she laughed. 'I'll stick to nursing and riding a bike.'

'Don't give up so easily,' I said. 'It's your first time and everyone falls over a few times.'

However, Fanny never tried again – once was enough. We met for tea now and again in the following months and kept up with the news. We had become really good friends and I valued that.

Nearly two months had passed when I received a letter from Peter's parents. It was an apology.

> We are so sorry for not writing before now and we sincerely hope you are well. Our time spent in New York was wonderful, quite formidable at times, and Peter spent all of his free time with us. The apartment was large with modern appliances; an electric cold storage to keep the food fresh. Absolutely marvellous! We could easily become used to it.

The rest of the letter was filled with their different experiences of New York and a promise of meeting up soon. They had a gift to give to me from Peter.

'Perhaps we could arrange for Fanny to join us as well and catch up on the news?' they asked.

A few days later, a letter was delivered to me from Fanny.

> Would you be able to meet next Saturday afternoon? Mum and Dad are coming for the weekend, so it means we could all get together for tea and a natter. Let me know soon.

Fortunately for me, I had already arranged to have a half-day that Saturday to go roller skating with Rose. I knew she wouldn't mind under the circumstances.

'Don't worry about it,' Rose said. 'Lord knows this is important to you! I've got Charlie to nag, eh!'

So that was that. Saturday was arranged and we all met up at the tea rooms. Tea was ordered, and while we were waiting, presents were handed round. Peter had bought a beautiful pendant for me, heart-shaped, 'with love' engraved on the back.

'That is lovely!' Fanny exclaimed, 'shall I put it on for you?'

'That looks lovely, Edith,' they all said, smiling at me.

'I shall treasure it for ever and ever,' I said, blushing.

'There is one from us, too,' his mother said, handing it to me. I quickly untied it to find a silver-coloured box, embossed on the outside, which was quite exquisite.

'We thought you would find it useful, perhaps to keep your letters in,' she said, smiling. Peter's father was nodding in agreement with a twinkle in his eye.

'Thank you both very much,' I said. 'I shall treasure this also; it's like a birthday all over again.'

'Yes, you are right,' Fanny cried. 'I didn't expect this.' She had received a coloured comb for her hair from Peter and a pin-on nurse's watch from her parents, who sat looking proudly at her.

By this time the waitress had brought the teas along with a choice of cream cakes, which we duly tucked into. We continued chatting until it was time to leave. I felt a moment of sadness as I waved goodbye. However we had promised to keep in touch and of course I would see Fanny in a couple of weeks.

Once in, I went straight to my room and sat in front of the mirror to admire the pendant. It was beautiful, something I had never dreamed of. I'll wear it all of the time, I told myself. I put the box in my top drawer after I had placed the letters inside. I really felt privileged to have Peter's family in my life and I knew my mam would have been happy for me.

With renewed optimism I carried on working, taking on extra duties. I wanted to save as much as I could in the next few months. In no time Peter would be home and I wanted to have an ample bottom drawer. He had hinted at marrying the following spring in his last letter.

I hope to be home for next Christmas. I have heard from Head Office that there will be an opening for me in the New Year, but not in the centre of London. I don't know exactly where at the moment. They will inform me nearer the time, but wherever it is, we will make our home. That thought gives me great incentive and I shall work harder for it. Your letters inspire me, so keep writing, my darling Edith. I will telephone you within the next two weeks if possible.

Love you always.

PS Hope you liked the pendant.

The feeling of joy of knowing that I would be seeing him within a few months kept my spirits up. Rose and I confided in each other, secrets that we would not divulge to anyone else. We talked ourselves to sleep nearly every night.

Lord and Lady Havis were preparing for their summer holiday. Firstly they would visit Paris for a month and then travel back to Dorset and return to London in September, which meant there would be a skeleton staff left to run the house. Mrs Baker informed the staff that any time needed for visiting relatives or holidays should be requested while Lord and Lady Havis were away. Certain members would be required to travel to Dorset later to prepare the house, including Mrs Baker herself.

Chapter Nine

This time Rose and Charlie were included, much to their delight.

'Cor! We 'aven't ever been outside London, let alone going to Dorset,' Charlie cried, with Rose jumping up and down with excitement.

'Cook will be in charge of running the household,' Mrs Baker continued, 'with Edith upstairs keeping check and Freda, our kitchen maid. Daisy, downstairs parlour maid, should suffice. If, of course, there is any heavy lifting to be done, I have arranged for Albert from the Deanswall household next door to call in occasionally to check with Cook and for any emergency that might arise. In the meantime, I suggest you put forward any requests you might have in writing and return them to me as soon as possible.

My first reaction was to request time off to visit my family in Wales. I hadn't seen them for some time and I really missed them, especially with Peter being away. I arranged to have ten days off in June providing I worked extra duties if required. Mrs Baker would have preferred me to have the last two weeks in May before Rose and Charlie left for Dorset.

However, Cook intervened and said that it would be very quiet and she could manage with the remaining staff, bless her!

The next few weeks sped by I found so much to keep me busy. I was looking forward to seeing my family and catching up on the news. Rose said she would miss me, even though she was excited about going away and being with Charlie as well.

'Will you write to me, Edith,' she begged, 'and let me know everything? You know I'm no good at writing, but maybe a card, eh!'

'Don't worry, Rose,' I said, 'I'll make sure you hear all the gossip and any bits of news. I shall have plenty of time to catch up on everything and I shall miss you, too.'

Lord and Lady Havis left for Paris the following week with their entourage. Rotas had been made up for the following weeks for each of us, and so we would be kept busy. Mrs Baker seemed to relax more and joined us for supper in the evenings.

'I'm going to approach Lady Havis while we are in Dorset and see if we cannot arrange for you to try your culinary skills there,' she said. 'After all, Agatha, you deserve a break. We could do an exchange. Besides, you are far the best cook.'

'Don't start worrying about me,' Cook replied, 'I don't want to cause any trouble. If their Lordships are 'appy with the arrangements then that's that.'

'We will see,' Mrs Baker said quietly. 'I am not without influence,' she added, tapping her nose, but then, realising that we were in earshot, she changed the subject. 'Are we playing cards? Shall we have a debate instead?' she added, looking at us with a half-smile on her face,

'No, thanks, Mrs Baker, we'd prefer to play cards,' we replied quickly.

'Well, that's settled then,' she said. 'Agatha, you deal, and one of you girls make the tea.'

'Yes, Sergeant Major!' Rose muttered under her breath as she scurried into the pantry. Cups and saucers were laid out and we all settled down for the evening and were later in retiring because we didn't have to be up as early as normal while their Lordships were away.

Within a week I had received two letters, one from Peter and one from Irene, my sister. I felt quite excited; two in one week was unusual. Peter's letter related to his trip to New Jersey and a forthcoming month in Chicago working at one of their banks for general experience.

He was quite excited by the prospect.

Irene's was about my visit to the Rhondda and how they were all looking forward to seeing me and catching up on everything.

We are all coming to meet you off the train, including Enid. Unfortunately she is in the family way. She got mixed up with a bad lot and is not receiving any support. Everyone is gossiping and tittle-tattling. She almost gave up. Her mam is standing by her, thank God! And of course she has us. You were her best friend and we know that you will always be there for her, but I thought I had better warn you in advance. She is beginning to show, so don't look surprised when you see her.

After reading Irene's letter, to be honest, I felt quite shocked. Poor Enid! Her family was staunch Chapel people and would be feeling the shame. With some narrow-minded neighbours, it would mean total seclusion from them; the stigma would live with them for ever, and fire and brimstone would be preached. Having a baby before marriage was a great sin, and human nature was cruel, but we lived in times that were harsh and lacked compassion.

That afternoon I spent my time writing letters. In all, it took me three hours to write just two, one to Peter and the other to Irene, as there was so much to write about. I managed to post them later that day.

My thoughts were with poor Enid. How fortunate I was in comparison. I was betrothed and had work and a roof over my head. I had a future, but she had a long, hard road ahead and needed her friends to support her. I decided that when I had posted the letters, I would buy some wool and a knitting pattern and make a set of baby clothes. In my spare time, I could finish the set before my visit home, which was in a couple of weeks. I chose the colour lemon, soft baby wool, as it would suit a boy or girl.

In the evening, after supper, I confided in Rose and Cook about the news that I had received about my friend Enid and her terrible situation. Both were sympathetic and offered to knit some clothes. Cook said she would like to crotchet a jacket, and offered to teach me how to do it. I had always wanted to learn how to crotchet and this was the opportunity. From then on, once the rotas had been completed, we spent our time knitting. It was good fun and even Mrs Baker took an interest.

Charlie, poor man, seemed a little bemused by it all; this just wasn't his scene and he kept in the background playing cards with Freda and Daisy.

That weekend, Mrs Baker, Rose and Charlie left for Dorset. I felt a pang of sadness as we waved goodbye.

'The place will feel hollow,' Cook remarked, 'not so much chit-chat. Gawd knows I need peace and quiet! With you gone next week, Edith, I am sure the silence will scream at me.'

'Yes,' I said, 'but it will be only a couple of weeks and you will have less cooking to do. You can knit and read to your heart's content. Freda and Daisy will keep you company.'

'Get away with ya!' Cook chortled. 'Let's 'ave that kettle on, I'm gasping.'

The days flew by and I was all packed and ready to leave on the Monday. Fortunately for me, Albert from the Deanswall household next door had popped in to see Cook regarding any chores that might need doing and he offered to help me to the station with my luggage.

'Our lot's away,' he said with a wink and a nod. 'I 'ave the use of the facilities so, my luv, I am at your service.'

Cook's face said it all.

'I wouldn't look a gift 'orse in the face, Edith,' she said, smirking. 'Times are changing, that's for sure; a ride in a posh car can't be sniffed at, so off ya go!'

The journey to the station only took a few minutes, and Albert carried my luggage to the train and insisting on making sure I was safely aboard.

'I'll keep an eye on Agatha,' he shouted as the train pulled out. 'Enjoy yourself.'

He then disappeared from sight, the smoke of the train enveloping the platform. I settled down to reading a book; it was going to be a long journey and I didn't want to be bored. I felt quite excited and was looking forward to seeing everyone, catching up on news, sharing my future plans with my darling Peter; there was so much to talk about.

The sun came filtering through the window as I read. I was beginning to feel drowsy and fell asleep, and was later woken by the conductor announcing that afternoon tea was being served in the dining carriage. Realising I hadn't eaten since breakfast, I decided to treat myself to tea. I was starving and tucked into jam scones, which were served with a pot of tea. I shared the table with another young woman who chatted away. She was a nanny to a well-to-do family in London and was given leave to visit her mother and father whom she hadn't seen for sometime.

'My ambition is to be a nanny to our Royal Family,' she said. 'I have all the qualifications, you know,' she added, waving her spoon in the air. 'My parents have high expectations and are so proud of me.'

I smiled back. Come home, Rose. All is forgiven, I thought, pretending to take an interest.

'I'm sure they are,' I answered, stirring my tea. A word came to mind; like, pompous!

Thank goodness she wasn't sitting with me for the rest of the journey; it would have been a nightmare. Finishing my tea, I excused myself and made my way back to the carriage. Another two stops and I had to change trains to reach the Rhondda.

It was quite a welcome I received when I reached home. They were all standing on the platform waving when they caught sight of me. I noticed the changes in them. They were more like adults now, with Irene playing mum. Enid stood behind them, almost trying to hide herself from me. I felt quite emotional at meeting them all and it was hugs all round. Tears were streaming down Enid's cheeks as she moved towards me.

'Come here,' I said. 'What's all this about, you silly girl? You're my friend and I have missed you, but I'm here now and there is a lot of catching up to do.'

The luggage was taken from me and as we made our way out of the station everyone was talking at the same time. Myra and Millie, my younger sisters, were tugging at my arms, asking if I had brought them anything from London.

'It's a surprise,' I said, whispering to them. 'Wait until we reach home and you will see.'

'We can't wait, Edith!' they yelled in excitement, while Irene wagged her finger, reminding them that they were young ladies, not children.

'For goodness sake, girls, give Edith a chance,' she said. 'Let's all have a cup of tea before we catch the bus. I know I could do with one. What say you, Edith?'

'Yes, that would be lovely,' I said quickly. 'It's my treat.'

The station café was heaving with people and we pushed our way through. Irene nudged Millie.

'Save the table in the corner,' she whispered, 'or we will all have to stand.'

It seemed ages before we were served. Laden with trays we

jostled our way to the table. Enid was chatting away and looked a lot brighter. We all managed to sit down, even though it was a little cramped.

'We have just a half-hour before the bus leaves,' Irene said. 'Sup up; there isn't another one until tomorrow.'

Looking at me she added, 'Of course, you wouldn't know! We have a bus now and don't have to rely on old Mr Thomas and his horse and cart, bless him! Of course, we need him on a Sunday – buses are not allowed to run on the Sabbath – but it is still a blessing and we appreciate that, don't we, girls?'

'Yes,' they all answered, 'it makes a difference. We can go into town now and again.'

We carried on chatting until the driver called out that the bus would be leaving shortly. We gathered the luggage together and made our way out of the station and climbed on board. It was standing room only for part of the way, but we found a seat for Enid who was looking a little pale; probably feeling a little claustrophobic, with everyone huddled together making it overpowering.

It wasn't very long before we reached home and there waiting at the bus stop was Ivor, our brother, who had come to visit. He had been working in Doncaster and had come home on leave, which coincided with my visit. This was such a nice surprise; I had no idea. Irene and the girls kept it secret at Ivor's request. He wanted to see my face, he said; we hadn't seen each other for nearly two years, since Mam had died.

'Come here,' he called out. 'Well, well, you are looking rosy-cheeked and bonnie considering you live in London.' He gave me a hug.

'It's lovely to see you too, Ivor,' I said, my voice trembling with emotion, 'you never change.' Ivor's skin had always been pallid through working down the mines. 'You been working hard, I take it?'

'Yes, Edith! What else? You know me: no time for pleasures, eh?'

By this time everyone was chatting excitedly. Ivor had taken hold of the luggage as we made our way to the house. The houses in our road were built into the side of the mountain, in tiers.

They were all terraced with winding steps to the front doors and a communal path that led across the top, making it easier for neighbours to pop in for a cuppa! Not many locked their doors. There was no need; it was a trusting and safe community to live in. Everyone was poor and helped each other. Apart from being narrow-minded, they were lovely people.

The table had been set for supper and the smell of stew and dumplings, which were cooking on the stove, wafted around the parlour.

'Ivor has been cooking,' Irene said. 'Lord knows he is a god-send! Baking cakes, making teisen laps – it's been heaven. We could do with you here more often, boyo!' Irene chuckled winking at Ivor, who was grinning from ear to ear.

'I would if I could, but it's not possible,' he answered. 'That's where the work is, in Doncaster. My dearest wish is to be able to come back home for good, and keep an eye on you girls, too! Maybe when things get better and there is more work. In the meantime let's tuck in. You all must be hungry; I know I am.'

We didn't need asking twice and there was silence apart from the clink of the cutlery as we all relished the food, when suddenly the door burst open!

'Sorry, Rene and Ivor,' a young man said. 'I forgot the time!'

I looked in amazement at this tousle-haired boy who stood in the doorway. This couldn't be my baby brother, Bryn! He had grown so much since I had last seen him.

'Come here, you,' I said. 'Boy, you have changed.'

'I'm nearly fifteen now, Edith,' he cried, putting his arms around me, 'and I'm working. I'm a delivery boy for the bakery, and sometimes help make the bread as well.' He sounded breathless with excitement, 'I can't wait to tell you everything, but I'm hungry so I'll eat first.'

'Yours is keeping warm in the oven,' Irene said, waving her arm. 'Wash your hands first and come and sit down, Bryn love.'

It was obvious that Irene adored him; he was the baby of the family and when Mam died he was completely beside himself. No one could comfort him, apart from Irene and me. He said that I looked like Mam the most out of all the girls. Unfortunately I was working in London and was only able to stay for a few weeks, so Irene had become a surrogate mother to all. It had been hard for her, taking on all the responsibility. Our other sisters, Blodwin, Phoebe and Ada, had flown the nest, two in Scotland and Ada in America. Two of our brothers died of diphtheria when I was twelve; the other two, Thomas and Michael, went to make their fortunes in Australia and had lost touch with us, which was sad because they were not aware of Mam dying and there had been no forwarding address. It was hard not to dwell on it sometimes. It left a void in our lives. However, we had to carry on and make the best of things and concentrate on those around us.

The next two weeks, my life was busy with making visits. Aunty Gwen invited us around for her birthday party, which included the neighbours. Her house was heaving with people, but that was Aunty Gwen; she loved it, the more the better.

I spent some time with Enid. She was delighted with the baby clothes that had been knitted. We talked about almost everything, from the early days up to the present day, but her fears of being isolated and the future of her unborn baby was foremost in her mind.

'I know my mam will always be there for me,' she said, 'and Da is gradually coming round to accepting my situation, but the rest around here are giving me the cold shoulder; the Jones family at the end of our road are the worst,' calling me names. Mam found out and went to see them and put them right on a few things. She was blue in the face with rage. Apparently Mrs Jones was forced to get married, if you get my meaning, and of course my mam reminded her! What a shock, eh? I think I can cope. Mam is going to look after the baby when she or he is born. I will need to find a job; Da has made that quite clear. I know this sounds harsh, Edith, but it's all for the best.'

Enid's voice began to tremble. 'Already I love the baby I'm carrying. I will do for the rest of my life and I'll try to be a good mother. It's the shame I have brought upon everyone which is hard to bear.' Enid began to sob. I put my arms around her.

'Let it all out, have a good cry,' I murmured. 'You have a family and loyal friends, always remember that. You have to be strong, Enid, for your baby and ma and da. Come on, wash your face, comb your hair, then we'll go for a walk and blow the cobwebs away. You'll feel better then.'

A feeling of despair swept over me. Poor Enid, I thought, life is hard, and hers will be a long road; while I'm here I must support her.

With all the goings-on and being back in my own environ-ment, I had pushed Peter to the back of my mind. I began to wonder what he was doing, how different it must be to live in New York. One day I would like to go there, I thought, maybe with Peter; that's what he planned. In the meantime I can dream.

The evenings were spent in the parlour with the family. We talked about my wedding plans, the girls being bridesmaids, what we'd wear, who would be coming – it was all quite exciting.

I wanted to ask Enid to be a maid of honour, but under the circumstances it would be like rubbing salt in the wound so decided to wait until it was the appropriate time, and in any case, nothing would happen until the following year, and maybe not until the autumn. Before that, Irene and I thought it would be a good idea to all meet up, for an introduction; they didn't want to be strangers. It wouldn't be fair on Peter, poor man. It would be overwhelming to meet all my brood!

The dreaded day came, as Bryn called it, for me to return to London. It had all gone so quickly. Part of me wanted to stay. However, my life had changed and there was no going back. There were tears and hugs with the goodbyes. It was hard to board the train without feeling emotion. Bryn had come to the station this time; before he just couldn't do it. Now he was a lot stronger and had come to terms with the loss of our mam. Irene had promised to bring him to London one day with the girls, with the promise of writing.

I watched through the window as the train left the station. They were all waving, the smoke of the train enveloping them, and they disappeared from sight. For the first time I felt the pangs of emptiness at leaving my family; no matter what there would always be a tie. My roots would be with me for ever.

My journey home was uneventful. I read a book, ate my sandwiches and slept. I reached London in the late afternoon, thinking that I would have to catch a bus to Muswell Hill. I was more than surprised to see Cook and Albert waiting for me at the station!

'Thought we would have a trip out,' Albert chortled, winking at Cook.

She quickly added, 'Couldn't let ya struggle with them cases! We knew the time of the train and Albert kindly offered to meet ya! And I 'aving time to spare, came for the trip.'

Looking at Cook's face, I detected a slight blush; was something going on here? There she was, wearing her Sunday best, and this was Saturday! Maybe I shouldn't read too much into it, but something had changed since I had been away. We arrived back at the house, which seemed eerily quiet without Rose and Charlie. Nobody was around apart from Daisy, our parlour maid, who had laid tea. There were fresh-baked scones and jam, napkins alongside the plates, the best china!

Yes, I thought, there is definitely something going on; mum's the word! Tact would be needed where Cook was concerned. In her own time she would let us know. None of our business! We knew better than to pry.

Cook asked, 'Ready for a cuppa, Albert? Have some fresh-baked scones and homemade jam to go with it.'

'Yes, please, Agatha,' Albert answered quickly. 'Don't mind if I do.'

'Sit yaself down then; you girls, too,' she said, looking straight at me to see my expression.

Not blinking an eyelid, I said, 'Thanks, Cook, I'm gasping.'

I sat next to Daisy, who had a strange grin on her face. I nudged her gently. She was just sixteen and found romance in older people amusing. This wasn't going to be easy, pretending not to notice, but in Cook's case you had to!

Albert proved very interesting to talk to. He had a way with words that caught everyone's interest. And he was very respectful of Cook, too. With his jovial personality, he was likeable to all. At the end of tea, he helped to clear the table without hesitation.

'I'm well trained,' he laughed. 'I have had to be in my line of work; just have to get on with things. Must say, though, today has been a treat, eh, Agatha?' He gave a knowing smile to her.

'Yes,' Cook replied, trying not to smile too much, 'made quite a pleasant change. I enjoyed the drive.'

Her voice and speech had altered; she wasn't abbreviating her words (her posh voice, Rose would say), which meant that she wanted to impress those around her. Albert didn't seem to mind one way or another; what you saw was what you got! That was his motto. He was down to earth and a rock to lean on. It was obvious that he had taken a liking to Cook and vice versa. Maybe this would be the turning point in her life.

Bless her, I thought, she deserved some happiness, but it would have to be slow and steady. Cook was a very shrewd woman and would take one day at a time until she thought it was right. Albert knew this and was quite prepared to go along with whatever pace she took.

'Well, I must get back,' he said. 'I'm keeping an eye on things this evening. I'll pop round in the morning to see if you need any help if that's OK with you, Agatha?'

'Very kind of you, Albert,' Cook murmured. 'We do appreciate all of the things you've done, don't we, girls?' she added, turning around and nodding her head at us to agree.

'Yes, thank you, Albert,' we both answered.

'My pleasure. I've enjoyed it. See you in the morning,' he said and left.

The following day was spent cleaning carpets, one of the jobs on the rota which Mrs Baker had devised. Cook was making sure that everything was carried out to the letter. In my mind there was a definite sparkle about her when she was giving out orders, even when making our morning tea! Which was out of character; it normally was left to the pantry maid. Maybe her orderly life had changed because of Albert! Nevertheless, for whatever reasons, this rosy-faced and plump woman had changed, and was more relaxed and tolerant.

Albert joined us for our morning break which was at 10 a.m. He brought with him some freshly baked biscuits that he had been given by Mrs Braithwaite, the Deanswalls' cook.

'Thought you might like these to have with your cuppa,' Albert chuckled. 'They smell pretty good!'

Looking at us with a sly grin he went on to say, 'Not often do

I get any treats like this. I must be doing something right, what do you say, girls?'

Cook and the rest of us nodded in agreement. Albert's eyes were twinkling with delight. Daisy remarked that he looked chuffed. She was sat next to Freda, who nudged her and giggled. Cook looked amused and said, 'Thanks, Albert, very thoughtful of ya! Sit yaself down and I'll pour the tea. Daisy, pass the biscuits round and mind your manners!'

Cook was half-smiling and coughed gently as she poured the teas. We had a half-hour chatting before we returned to our duties. Albert had to leave to pick up a parcel from the station, and we heard him whisper to Cook, 'Shall I call in this evening after supper? Game of cards would be nice, Agatha. Including the girls, of course,' he quickly added, looking at Cook's face changing. (It wouldn't have been proper without us, in Cook's eyes.)

'If it is what you would like,' he continued, stepping back a little.

'You would be very welcome, Albert,' Cook replied gently. 'Shall we say 8 p.m?'

'Fine, perfect!' Albert said. 'Won't be late,' he added and made his exit.

The weeks went by and Albert became a familiar figure around the kitchen. He called in every morning to check if anything needed doing, which was just an excuse really to have a natter with Cook. However, he had grown on us; he was always cheerful and obliging, nothing was too much bother and made each one of us feel important. Cook reminded him that when Lord and Lady Havis returned, including the Deanswalls from next door, his visits would be less frequent.

'It would almost certainly be disapproved of by both house-holds. Make hay while the sun shines,' Albert would say. 'We'll cross that bridge when we come to it.' And he was right; there was no harm done. It was a respite that we all enjoyed.

Mrs Baker, Rose and Charlie were returning ahead of Lord and Lady Havis. I had received a card from Rose, which read, 'See you soon, luv, Rose!'

She wasn't able to write very well because of her poor reading ability.

'I get by,' she would say, 'don't need to know everything, do you? Common sense is more important, my mum used to say.' And in Rose's case, yes it was. She was happy with her life and Charlie had made it complete. What more could one ask for?

It suddenly came to mind that I hadn't received Peter's letter. Normally it would arrive every two or three weeks depending on any shipping hold-ups. He must have received mine. Cook had been dealing with the post while Mrs Baker was away and she commented on the fact that I hadn't heard.

'Them banks make you work 'ard,' she said, 'and I dare say that the poor lad hasn't 'ad a lot of time! You're bound to 'ear soon. Who knows, he might be on his way 'ome!'

'Wishful thinking, Cook,' I murmured. 'Peter would have sent a telegram. It's probably the post that has been held up. He might even telephone. I'll just have to be patient.'

It seemed in no time at all that Mrs Baker, Rose and Charlie had left for Dorset, and here they were back again. Rose was full of stories to be told, and the whole house was alive with chatter; we couldn't get a word in edgeways. Constant cups of tea, along with souvenirs brought back from Dorset.

Mrs Baker was a little quiet when she discovered that Albert had struck up a friendship with Cook. I thought perhaps she felt that she would be losing Cook as a friend and needed reassuring. She made no comment as such but it was obvious.

Albert, meanwhile, kept a low profile. He called in one morning and had coffee with Cook and stayed just twenty minutes. Rose and Charlie were highly amused.

'Good luck to them,' they both said when we were alone. 'Gawd knows nothing surprises us these days! But who would 'ave thought, Cook and Albert! Wonder what their Lordships will 'ave to say if they find out?'

'None of anyone's business,' Charlie cried. 'What they do in their own time is private! And anyway, I 'eard them arranging to meet later. It's their free time; don't matter what anyone else says!'

'Yes, Charlie,' I answered, 'and the least said the better. Cook wouldn't approve of us gossiping and we have to remember that Mrs Baker isn't too happy about it and if she heard us nattering on it would make it worse for all of us.'

'Mum's the word!' they all said together, and surprisingly enough no more comments were made.

Two weeks went by. Lord and Lady Havis returned to the household, bringing with them guests from Dorset. Everyone was running back and forward for the first couple of days until the old routine had been re-established. The very early morning starts proved to be very tiring. We had become lax while their Lordships were away and it was back to the grindstone, leaving us all exhausted by the end of the day. Most evenings I was in bed by 9.30 p.m. Rose followed later because of time spent with Charlie.

Chapter Ten

'I shall be glad when we get spliced!' she cried. 'It ain't half awkward sometimes 'aving to sneak around! Edith, are you listening?'

I was pretending to be asleep, but Rose still nattered on until I gave in.

'I'm listening,' I said, yawning. 'It won't be for ever, so in the meantime let's get some sleep.'

'Sorry,' Rose muttered, 'blimey! We've worked, bells forever ringing, we haven't spoken two words apart from this evening. When we were in Dorset it was a lot quieter, even though there were gentry staying; they didn't have as many parties, spent time outside, picnics and suchlike. They spent the evenings playing cards; sometimes they went horse riding – they have stables and whatnot! We had to feed the stable lads, the head groom and the gardeners. Quite liked it, though. They were a friendly lot. We had a party in their quarters one night when their Lordships went to a summer ball. They didn't come back until the morning, so we got away with it!' Rose nattered on until she was exhausted and we fell asleep.

By the end of the week all the guests had left and life seemed more normal, certainly quieter. The bells had ceased to ring in the kitchen and Cook welcomed the tranquillity. We saw less of Albert; his lord and master had returned and he was kept busy with household duties. Although, having said that, the little time he had off, he managed to spend with Cook, who managed to combine her free time with Albert. Mrs Baker had resigned herself to the fact that Cook was enjoying the company of a male friend. Despite Cook reassuring her that their friendship would remain the same, a touch of jealousy was evident because Mrs Baker had never imagined that Cook of all people would have a beau at her feet! However, there was very little she could do but accept the situation. Both Cook and Albert were the height of respectability in their behaviour and certainly not neglectful of their duties, and I for one was very happy for them.

Rose and Charlie were given the following Sunday off together to visit his family. They were arranging their wedding, which was to take place the following spring. They rarely had an opportunity to visit, so Mrs Baker had given permission for them to have time off. The household was free of guests and Lord and Lady Havis decided to enjoy time on their own. I had two hours' free time that Sunday afternoon and decided to have a stroll through the park just to have some fresh air and to blow the cobwebs away.

The day was warm and sunny, which brought people out. Children were feeding the ducks laughing and playing. It was lovely to watch. I found a bench to sit on and watched everyone strolling by. This is wonderful, I thought. The sun felt warm upon my face and my thoughts began to drift. I focused on Peter. It wasn't like him to be late; his letters were always on time. Maybe there was some kind of hold-up with the shipping or the sorting offices. I was beginning to feel worried. A kind of sixth sense if you could call it that, made me feel uneasy. I shouldn't be feeling like this, I told myself. It was a beautiful day, the sun was shining and everyone around seemed happy and I should be on top of the world, singing. But I had this niggling feeling of apprehension. I knew sometimes I felt insecure with Peter being so far away, but this was different. My heart began to flutter and my mouth felt dry and I suddenly jerked. A voice out of the blue brought me to my senses.

'Are you all right, my dear?' Sitting beside me was an elderly lady. 'I hope you don't mind me asking,' she murmured, 'but you looked a little pale and worried. Are you sure you are all right?'

'Oh yes,' I answered quickly. 'I was far away. Thank you for asking.'

'Oh that's good,' she said. 'I am a good listener, you know,'

For the next half-hour she chatted away. Her name was Victoria and she lived and shared a house with her younger sister, who ruled the roost.

'I love her dearly,' she went on, 'but sometimes I have to get away from it all. She is always nagging me to do this and do that.

She means well, but there are times when enough is enough, so I bring myself here where there are friendly faces all around, and of course I love to feed the ducks.'

It was obvious that she was very lonely. She had never married and her sister was her only family. It made me realise how very fortunate I was to have friends and family and a future husband. It took this elderly lady to put me in focus again. We made arrangements to meet one afternoon to have tea. Her face was all smiles as she said goodbye.

Arriving back at the house, I was greeted by Daisy, who seemed a little anxious.

'I was just coming to look for you, Edith. There's a lady to see you. Her name is Fanny and she has been waiting for some time. We made her comfortable in the parlour, but Cook was getting really worried and asked me to come and find you.'

'Thanks, Daisy,' I murmured. 'I'm here now.' This is a surprise, I thought, Fanny normally lets me know well in advance if she is paying a visit. I had to ask for permission to receive visitors and she was aware of that, so it had to be important. I hurried through to the parlour, where Cook was making small talk to Fanny, keeping her attention. They both looked up as I entered the room.

'Gawd! Where have ya been?' Cook cried. 'Thought you were going for a short walk and back again. Young Fanny's been waiting ages!'

'Sorry, Cook,' I said. 'I'd have come back earlier if I had known.'

'Never mind, you're here now,' she said. 'I'll make some more tea.'

She rose from her chair and left the room calling out for Daisy as she closed the door. Looking at Fanny and her expression, I knew something was wrong.

'What is it, Fanny?' I asked. My heart raced with anticipation.

'Edith,' she murmured gently, 'I'm afraid it's not good news.' She held my hand tightly. 'We have received information from New York that Peter never returned from Chicago, which should have been three weeks ago. It seems that he didn't board the train that was bound for New York. There would have been different connections to be made, but Peter's luggage was found on the platform at Chicago!'

Fanny started to tremble. 'He has just vanished, Edith! No one seems to know anything; the police are completely baffled. Mother and Father are in a terrible state; they wanted to tell you but couldn't and asked me to contact you. I couldn't just telephone. It's all so cruel!' she cried, putting her arms around me. 'This is terrible news for me to give you.'

My whole body felt numb with shock.

'No, Fanny,' I screamed, 'it can't be true! Peter wouldn't just disappear; there must be some logical reason.' My head started to spin and my legs were trembling. I held on to Fanny as fear and dread swept over me. This couldn't be happening; it was all a bad dream. Peter was my whole life. We were going to be together for ever, and nothing could have prepared me for this news.

Fanny was sobbing into my shoulder as she tried to comfort me. By this time, Cook had returned with the tea and almost dropped the tray when she saw our distress.

'Gawd! What is it?' she cried. 'I knew it! Is it bad news?' She placed the tray on the table, trembling as she did so. 'Oh, Edith,' she cried, 'please tell me.'

Cook knelt down besides us. Wiping my face with her apron, she asked, 'Is it Peter?'

Fanny began to explain, holding on to me as she did. 'Yes, I'm afraid it is,' she murmured and briefly gave Cook the details of what had happened. The voices seem to fade in and out as I took in the stark truth and suddenly I felt myself being lifted up and almost carried to the sofa in the far corner, a blanket wrapped around me.

'You are shivering!' Fanny cried. 'This should keep you warm.'

'A hot cuppa with a touch of whisky is what you need,' Cook said. ' 'Ang on a moment and I'll fetch some.'

By this time, Daisy and Freda had appeared looking quite concerned.

'Don't stand there gawping!' Cook shouted. 'There's chores to be done. Freda, you will 'ave to serve the teas to their Lordships. Edith's in no fit state to do anything. Off with you now!'

Poor girls, they didn't know what was going on. They would be kept in the dark for a while. In the meantime, Fanny had composed herself and was helping Cook with the tea. I sipped the cup of tea with a tot of whisky which was placed in my hand.

'Drink this – it will do you good,' Cook whispered to me. 'You've had a shock and you need to rest a while.' She turned to Fanny, who was standing next to me, and said, 'This can't be easy for you, luv, seeing it's your brother and all. You look pale; sit down before ya fall down!'

There was no arguing with Cook and Fanny knew that.

'Thank you,' she murmured, and sat down next to me. Cook offered her a tot of whisky, but she declined. 'No, thank you, but you are very kind. I cannot stay; I have to get back. I am on duty this evening and have to cover for someone who is off sick.'

'Rest a while and get ya colour back before leaving,' Cook answered. 'No one will thank ya for it. This is a terrible time for everyone.' She patted Fanny's hand and left the room. The momentary silence was welcome. I had recovered enough to realise that I had to keep calm and collected. Reasoning with what had happened would give us a better perspective of the whole situation. We sat there for a while and talked things through and arranged to meet the next day. Not long after Fanny left, Rose and Charlie returned, rosy-faced and full of chatter until Cook broke the news to them.

Rose cried, 'Oh no!' Where is she?'

Cook replied, 'In the parlour, and feeling fragile. She shouldn't be alone at a time like this, better off with us in the kitchen keeping busy.' And of course, Cook was right; I didn't want to be alone feeling the emptiness and the hollow thoughts. Nothing made sense at this time. Everyone fussed round me for a while, as I helped prepare the evening meal, and Mrs Baker, who Cook had sent for, arranged for Freda to serve dinner to Lord and Lady Havis.

'I will explain everything,' she said. 'You have had a nasty shock and need to rest.' Her voice was full of compassion and I realised how fortunate I was to be working in a household with people that were my friends and cared.

After dinner, Mrs Baker and Cook allowed me to sit with them.

'Best to talk about it, Edith, better out than in,' Cook murmured. 'Most of the time it takes the pressure off.' She carried on for while until Mrs Baker interrupted her.

'Agatha! Let Edith explain in her own time.'

'There isn't much more that I can say,' I replied. 'Fanny told me all that she knew; it is just waiting for more information. Not knowing is the worse part and I have to keep it together or I shall go mad.'

'That's not going to happen. We are here if you need someone,' Mrs Baker said. 'We are all your friends here and if you need to talk you only have to ask.'

'Thank you,' I said. 'Thank you, both.'

Rose and Charlie appeared with hot cocoa for everyone.

'Good night's sleep is what we need,' Charlie murmured, with a half-smile. Cheerful Charlie, bless him.

The following morning, with the events of the previous day still fresh in my mind, I tried to cope with the early duties, feeling dazed and unreal, not wanting to believe all this was happening. I automatically went through the motions and was unaware that I was running late. Rose appeared in the drawing room, slightly out of breath.

'Oh, Edith, there you are! Cook is getting worried. You haven't been late for your breakfast ever! Gawd! I know what you're going through, but this isn't the answer.' She put her arm around me and said, 'Peter is out there, somewhere. It's a big world. I know Peter – he will be back!' Those words would echo in my mind for ever.

Somehow, not hearing any news gave me a renewed strength, and in the weeks ahead I went through the motions of everyday life, trying to feel normal. I had contacted Irene, who wrote every week. Everyone was thinking of me and to keep my pecker up, she wrote in one letter. I wasn't to give up hope. The police in Chicago and New York were completely baffled and were in touch with London police headquarters regularly. Any information received was passed on to Peter's parents who, in turn, wrote to me, letting me know every scrap of news. They tried hard to sound cheerful and optimistic; however, I knew from Fanny how it was taking its toll on their health. She met up with me at least twice a week and we would talk, not always with despair but hope. We kept each other strong and vowed we would never lose touch, whatever the outcome.

Six months passed by and there was no further news. The police search continued but they gave out very little hope of finding Peter, at least alive. The realisation of never seeing him again brought me to the depths of despair; trying to imagine a life ahead and a future seemed unlikely. I became quite depressed, more so when news came that Peter's father had passed away. His health had deteriorated and he seemed to lose his willpower. Peter had been the apple of his eye.

Fanny left London to live with her mother and found work at a local hospital. She kept in touch by telephone and letter, but it wasn't the same. I missed her so much; she was my only contact with Peter, some of their mannerisms were the same and it brought a closeness that kept him clearly in my mind.

Cook and Rose were remarkable. Between them they help me keep my sanity. Not once did they tell me to pull my socks up, which in the normal run of things they would have done. Instead, Cook made sure that I was eating properly and Rose made sure that I had a stroll each day, mostly to the park. We met Victoria several times; she would squeeze my hands each time and reassure me that everything would be all right. She was a lovely lady, and even though she was old, her optimism was immense.

'There is a bright future ahead, my dear. You are young; make every day worthwhile.' Victoria was very wise and became a dear friend in those last months.

Chapter Eleven

Lady Havis summoned me one day to the drawing room. Not knowing what to expect I spruced myself up. It had occurred to me that perhaps that they had certain reservations about my health and well-being. I had taken several days off through the last months. Freda and Daisy did extra duties to cover for me but it didn't go unnoticed by their Lordships. Mrs Baker, although a disciplinarian, had showed compassion throughout and turned a blind eye on several occasions. However, needs must prevail and in all fairness, enough was enough! So expecting the worst and looking fairly presentable, I entered the drawing room expecting to see their Lordships grim-faced, but to my surprise it was only Lady Havis present. Smiling at me, she said, 'Come and sit down, Edith,' beckoning with her hand to a chair placed by the fireside. I gently curtsied and sat down.

'Well, Edith,' she continued, 'these last months haven't been very pleasant for you and we all sympathise and understand. We admire your courage and stamina. However, you need a change of environment, so, my dear, we suggest that you come with Mrs Baker in the spring when we leave for Dorset. You will, of course, have certain duties to perform, which Mrs Baker will attend to. The country air will put the roses back in your cheeks, Edith, and perhaps give you a different perspective on everything.'

To say I was surprised would be an understatement. I couldn't believe my ears.

'Thank you, My Lady,' I murmured. 'I appreciate it very much.'

I rose from the chair, and with a quick curtsy I left the room. I felt a surge of relief sweep over me. I wasn't going to be dismissed after all and maybe going to Dorset would be the best thing in the long run. Fanny would be able to contact me with any news. My head started to buzz and for the first time in months I was beginning to plan ahead. I raced along the corridor and down the stairs to the kitchens to find Cook and Rose. Cook was rolling out pastry for a steak and kidney pie, His Lordship's favourite. Rose was in the scullery with Daisy, peeling vegetables. Charlie had just come through the door and stopped in his tracks when he saw my face.

'Gawd, Edith! What's up?'

My face must have told a story. Cook spun around when she heard Charlie speak, and looking at me she said, 'Something wrong?'

'No, Cook,' I answered quickly, 'nothing's wrong at all. In fact, I thought that I was going to be dismissed; instead I have been asked by Lady Havis to accompany Mrs Baker to Dorset for the summer months. I think it's a good thing, don't you, Cook?'

'Well, well, that can't be bad,' Cook answered wiping her hands with her apron. 'You need a break from here, that's for sure. You'll be sorely missed, but it's an opportunity not to be sniffed at. Charlie, put the kettle on,' she said, all in one breath, 'a cuppa is called for. I'll get this pie in the oven before we sit down. Rose, Daisy!' Cook called out. 'Finish them vegetables and come lay the cups and saucers. Edith, you fetch the biscuits.'

With Cook giving out orders, everything suddenly felt normal. Rose gave me a hug and jokingly murmured, 'I'll have the room to myself for a few months. Peace and quiet, eh!'

Charlie gave her a knowing look, which Cook noticed, and cried, 'Don't get any ideas –' winking at me with a wicked smile – 'you will be too busy to be spending much time in your room. I'll have you spring cleaning everywhere in the house, and I have a list as long as ya arm for Charlie. Extra work means extra pennies, eh?'

'Just joking, Cook,' Rose replied quickly glancing at Charlie, who by this time had moved away to the other end of the kitchen to make the tea. He had learned not to argue or comment where Cook was concerned; you couldn't win and he had a lot of respect for her. And it was through Cook that they had been offered quarters after their marriage in the following autumn. Cook had persuaded Mrs Baker to have a word with their Lordships regarding their status. They were to be given two rooms on the third floor: a bedroom and a sitting room and the use of the wash room at the end of the corridor, which Rose and Charlie were grateful for. This would give them a good start until such time they were able to have a home of their own.

The pie was finished and placed in the oven and everyone sat at the table while Charlie and Rose poured the teas. I had placed plates of biscuits at either end of the table so everyone could help themselves. Feeling more light-hearted I joined in the chatter that filled the room. Freda had just arrived, bringing with her the new maid. She was from Poland and spoke very little English and had been engaged as a scullery maid. Rose had been promoted to assistant cook, mainly making salads and trifles, which she was highly delighted with, so the vacancy for a scullery maid had arisen. Her name was Anna (at least, that's how it was inter-preted); she looked very thin and undernourished and seemed quite nervous. However, Freda, who was kind and compassionate, was given the task of looking after her and showing her the ropes, and also teaching her some English. Once all were seated, tea was served and biscuits passed around. Everyone was chattering away and never noticed or heard Albert entering the kitchen.

'Well!' he said very loudly. 'This is what you get up to! I've been knocking on the door and no one seems to have heard me so I let myself in.'

'Don't you always?' Cook answered sharply, but with a smile on her face. 'We're having our afternoon break; you are welcome to join us. Their Lordships are not due home until later so take a chair and sit down.' She asked Daisy to fetch another cup and saucer.

Cook then proceeded to tell Albert about the events of the day and my forthcoming trip to Dorset. Albert thought it was a good idea; he had visited some years before, and found Swanage in Dorset a beautiful place.

'Lovely there,' he said. 'Sea and countryside, good healthy air, which gives you an appetite. Been meaning to visit again, but never got around to it, maybe next year, eh?' He looked at Cook with a half-smile; it was only momentary but Cook blushed slightly. The next half-hour was spent chatting and I felt more positive about the forthcoming months. That evening I wrote to

Fanny, telling her of my working visit to Dorset in the coming weeks. I would send her my address, I wrote, and asked her to keep in touch and let me know any news.

The following day seem to fly by and it was almost 3 p.m. Rose and I managed to sneak out for our afternoon amble through the park, posting my letter to Fanny on the way. It was a fine, warm afternoon and we sat near the lake, chatting and watching people feed the ducks. Suddenly we remembered that we had promised to meet Victoria at the café and we were late. We hurried along and found her feeding biscuits to the birds.

She looked up and said, 'Oh! There you are. Wasn't sure you were coming today but I'm pleased you have,' she smiled cheerfully. 'We can order tea now!'

Both of us had come to treasure Victoria's friendship and Rose had promised me that she would continue to meet her whenever she had the time while I was away. I explained to Victoria about my plans and promised to send her a card while I was away.

She said, 'I shall miss you, Edith, but it will be good for you, my dear.' She patted me on the hand. 'Change is as good as rest and you need it.'

We talked for a while longer before we made our way back. Cook greeted us with, 'You had a telephone call, Edith. It was Fanny. She says she will call back at 8.30 p.m. Mrs Baker agreed the time because dinner will have been served well before 8.30, so take note and remember the time.'

'Thanks, Cook,' I said trying not to smile too much at the seriousness of Cook's manner. 'I will not forget,' I whispered.

Cook waved her hand and said, 'Off with ya! You'll be late on duty… Rose, get a move on: I need the salads for the starters.'

We both hurried off to get changed before more was said. Dinner was served at 7.30 and by 8.30 everything was cleared away. I had a hurried supper, anxious not to miss Fanny's call. Maybe there was some news concerning Peter. However, in any event I would be able to tell her my news, regardless of the letter. I made my way to the main hall just in time to hear the telephone ring.

Mrs Baker appeared, waving her hand. 'Take the call in the library. Please don't be too long – it's late,' she said in a whisper.

'Yes, Mrs Baker, and thank you,' I said quietly. The telephone had been placed on the table near the window with a view of the courtyard, it was so tranquil. I gently picked the telephone up and whispered, 'Hello.' Fanny's voice sounded clear and positive.

'Hello, Edith,' she said. 'I hope you are well. Everything is fine here, my dear.' She continued to natter for a few minutes and then her voice began to falter. 'I don't know how to tell you, Edith, but the police here have informed us that they have heard from the New York Police Department regarding Peter and they have now listed him as a missing person and have closed the search until new evidence is brought forward. They have tried every avenue, but only deadlock. All Peter's personal belongings will be sent back to England and then returned to us.'

'I'm so sorry, Edith,' she said. 'I know this isn't what you want to hear and I wish I could be there with you and would have come up, but mother, although well, is becoming frail and I really don't wish to leave her for too long.'

Fanny continued to explain everything and her voice seem to fade. I felt numb and empty, unable to speak. How could this happen? Don't give up, I screamed inside. Peter is indestructible; he is out there somewhere!

Suddenly I was jolted back to reality by Fanny. 'Edith, are you still there?' She sounded distraught.

'Yes, I'm so sorry, Fanny,' I cried. 'I just can't believe it, but I know it's true and thank you for telling me.'

We continued to talk for a few more minutes and promised to write. I didn't have the heart to tell her of my forthcoming trip to Dorset, but just said that there was a letter already on the way. I placed the telephone receiver back on the hook. I stood for a few moments, gazing down into the courtyard, a feeling of emptiness sweeping over me. I could not accept that this was the end of all hope for Peter. Panic and nausea gripped me. I started to tremble and felt I was unable to move. I couldn't breathe. Suddenly the voice of Mrs Baker calling, 'Edith!' brought me to my senses.

'What on earth has happened, girl? You look terrible!' she said. 'Come on, back to the kitchen. A cup of sweet tea is called for and you can tell me what has happened.'

Cook and Freda were sat chatting at the far end of the kitchen as we entered. Little Anna was sitting at the table, her face intent, trying hard to listen and understand the conversation. Cook looked up and immediately knew that something was wrong.

'Kettle's on,' she said. 'Freda, a fresh pot of tea, please, and then explain to Anna her duties for tomorrow. You can do that in the scullery! Edith, sit down before ya fall down!'

She didn't stop for breath and continued issuing orders until Mrs Baker coughed and said 'Agatha!' and gave Cook a meaningful look.

'I think Edith needs to talk,' Mrs Baker whispered. 'She has had a bit of a shock so let's all sit down and give her chance to speak.' After a few moments, and holding back the tears, I blurted everything out. Silence followed. Cook and Mrs Baker, unable to say anything, just looked at each other until the bell rang from the drawing room, which was a summons for Mrs Baker, who hurried out, patting my shoulder as she left.

'I'll be back as soon as I can, Agatha,' she whispered and then there was silence again. Cook rose from her chair and went to a small cupboard at the end of the kitchen which she called her 'medicinal stores'.

'A drop of brandy is what ya need, my girl,' Cook said. 'Hold your cup up and no arguments! It will put the colour back into your cheeks.'

At that moment, the kitchen door opened and Rose and Charlie appeared, their eyes immediately focusing on Cook. Rubbing his hands together, looking straight at the bottle of brandy in Cook's hand, Charlie cried, 'That for us? Ooh!'

'Watch your manners! This is medicinal. Edith has had a bit of a shock,' Cook cried, 'so make yaselves useful: see to the supper!'

Both Rose and Charlie looked amazed.

'What on earth is going on?' Rose yelled. 'We're not clairvoyant! How are we supposed to know?'

'Calm down,' Cook replied. 'I'm sorry I yelled at ya both, but ya don't think up 'ere,' she said, pointing to her head, 'so please bear with me.'

Rose and Charlie nodded in agreement and set about preparing the supper while Cook related all that had happened. Shortly after, Mrs Baker returned and joined us for supper, which meant that everyone had to watch their manners. By 10 p.m. nearly everyone had retired to bed. Rose made a jug of cocoa, at Cook's suggestion, to take to our quarters.

'This will send us to sleep with a bit of luck,' Rose whispered to me, 'but you know what I'm like.'

'Thank goodness I do,' I replied, yawning. 'What would I do without you? In fact, all of you have been kind and understanding. I couldn't have managed on my own.'

'Don't be daft,' Rose cried. 'You'll get through this. It isn't going to be easy, but you will. Come on, let's have that cocoa before it gets cold.' Surprisingly enough, we fell asleep after a few sips, even though Rose tried hard to keep talking.

We were woken the next morning by Freda, who had been knocking on the door.

'You've overslept,' she cried. 'It's quarter to six. You had better hurry before Mrs Baker and Cook find out.' She bent down and picked up a tray holding two cups of tea. 'Here,' she said, 'drink this quickly. I'll see you later; I've got to get back to Anna.' And she hurried away.

'Cor,' Rose shrieked. 'What was in that cocoa? Gawd knows we better make a move, quick! Edith, are you listening? Wakey wakey!'

'Sorry, Rose,' I said leaping out of bed and grabbing my clothes. I splashed my face in cold water, which did the trick. I was soon awake. Rose handed me a cup of tea.

'Get that down you,' she said. 'It's a good job Mrs Baker and Cook don't get up early. We'd better hurry.'

Within ten minutes we were attending to our chores and by breakfast we had caught up. With all the panic and rush, I hadn't had time to dwell on the events of the night before. Although I didn't have much of an appetite, I managed to eat a little. Cook had her beady eye on me, making sure that I did.

No more was mentioned regarding Peter and I realised it was for the best. This was my home and my friends were here. I had my family in Wales and of course I would always have Fanny to write to and remember Peter with. Deep down I would never give up hope, but I knew I had to go forward and try to put everything behind me, and that's exactly what I did.

Part Two
Dorset

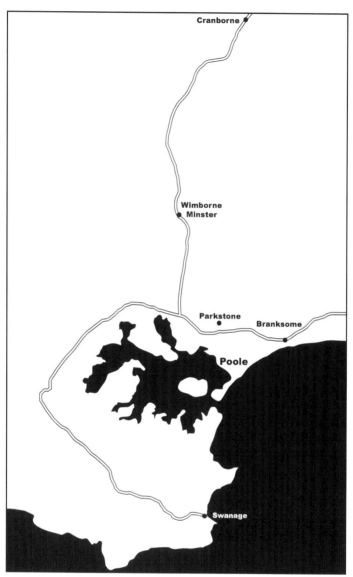

Dorset in the depression

Chapter Twelve

The day came when we set off for Dorset. The hustle and bustle of everything was quite exciting. Mrs Baker had given her last-minute instructions to Cook for the remainder of the staff, the rotas, and so on. Lord and Lady Havis had left two days previously to attend a wedding party and would travel to Dorset later. We were waved off by Cook, Rose and Charlie.

'Don't forget to write,' Rose called out, her face lighting up when I waved back. Fortunately for us, Albert was able to take us to the station. The Deanswall household were away for the summer months, which gave Albert a free hand, there was just a few staff left. Albert was in charge. I could tell by Cook's face that she was looking forward to seeing more of him. I felt a pang of sadness. I would really miss them all. However, I was looking forward to my time in Dorset and seeing the countryside.

Once on the train, we settled down. Mrs Baker had brought her knitting and a book to read for the journey. I was too excited to read and chatted for a while until Mrs Baker decided to read. The carriage was half full and I gazed around looking at the different faces. What were their lives like? I thought. Where were they going and where did they come from? My mind started to drift and I fell asleep. The next thing I was woken by Mrs Baker, who said the buffet car was open and serving teas and we should take the opportunity for refreshments, as it would be some time before we were able to sit down again to eat.

We made our way to the buffet car and ordered sandwiches and scones, which were served with piping-hot tea. We sat in silence, listening to other passengers chatter while enjoying our food. I realised that we hadn't eaten since breakfast and how hungry I felt, so I really tucked in, to Mrs Bakers surprise. She raised her eyebrow and said, 'You seem to have a healthy appetite, Edith. Let's hope it remains so. You are far too thin, my girl, and need building up so I shall see that you are served adequate meals while you are in my care. The Dorset air will make a difference.'

No more was said and we returned to our carriage. In no time at all we reached our destination, Verwood Station, Dorset. We were met by Giles, who was Lord and Lady Havis's chauffer-come-gardener at their country home. He was a rosy-faced man with a portly stance.

He tipped his cap and greeted us with a smile and said, 'Hello, there. Nice to meet you again, Mrs Baker,' and turning to me he said, 'You must be Edith. Pleased to meet you, my dear. Let me take them bags from you both.' His Dorset accent was strong and appealing and I warmed to him straight away.

'It's a balmy evening, so I've let the windows down in the car,' he whispered, placing our bags in the boot. 'Nothing I like better than a drive in the country. Them cities like London are fine, but you can't beat the open land. Born and bred 'ere, don't know any different. Don't want to, either.'

We set off with a gentle breeze cooling the air; he carried on chatting and pointing out places of interest until we reached Cranborne. I was enthralled by it all.

'We are nearly there, my dears. Chatscott Hall is a half-mile up the road. Lovely place,' Giles said, 'see for miles on a good day.'

Mrs Baker turned and half-smiled at me. It was obvious that she had a regard for him. She found him refreshing and highly amusing, a cheerful person at all times and a wise one, which I learned in the time that I was there. My first view of Chatscott Hall was through the huge iron gates that led to the big house. Giles stopped to open the gates and I was amazed at the vastness beyond. There were woods on either side of the drive and as we drove along it opened out to views of a meadow and a stream running along side. Opposite, standing majestically was Chatscott Hall. It was breathtaking. Surrounding the house were landscaped gardens and I remember the huge fountain as we drove around to the servants' entrance.

We were greeted by Florence Hewitt, the resident cook. Flo was her nickname. She was a tall, thin woman, contrary to belief that all cooks were of large build. She stood with her arms folded, and alongside her was one of the kitchen maids.

'Lord be!' Mrs Hewitt called out. 'We thought you would never get 'ere. Them suppers will be all dried up!'

'Sorry, Flo,' Giles cried, 'we took the long way round, the scenic route. Your favourite,' he said, winking at her. Mrs Hewitt's face reddened and she replied curtly, 'Get away with you, Giles! Let's be 'aving you!'

She turned to us and said, 'Lovely to see you again, Mrs Baker. And this must be Edith. Welcome, my dears. I expect you are more than ready for your suppers. Everything is warming in the oven so let's not waste any more time. Giles will help with the bags; leave them by the back stairs.' She gave Giles a meaningful look.

We were led into a huge kitchen. The oven range took up one side, pots and pans hung from above and a solid wood kitchen table dominated the centre. The aroma of food wafted through. Another door led into the dining area which had been set for the evening meal. Once seated, Mrs Hewitt offered Mrs Baker an aperitif.

'Would you care for a sherry, my dear? I keep it for special occasions and this is one,' she said, smiling.

'How can I refuse?' Mrs Baker answered her face lighting up. 'I would love one.' It was obvious that Mrs Baker was held in high esteem; she ran the household through the summer months while at Chatscott Hall and her word was master.

We all sat down to supper, which consisted of vegetable soup to start with, roast lamb, potatoes and fresh bread, and home-made lemonade was handed round to the rest of us. Everything was delicious. My appetite had returned. I hadn't felt this hungry for some time. I sat next to Catherine, who was a house parlour maid, next to her was Walter, a young lad of fifteen, fresh-faced and cheeky. He cleaned boots and so on, but mostly was a Jack of all trades. Then there was Betty, the kitchen maid, who was sat next to Charlotte, a rather aloof person. She was a personal assistant to Mrs Baker, to be more precise a general dogsbody; she helped out when Lord and Lady Havis had extra guests and that would mean cleaning and polishing, which she considered beneath her!

Last but least was Giles who sat at the end of the table with his pint of brown ale. Raising his tankard, he cried, 'Cheers, every-one! Down the hatch!'

It brought smiles to all of our faces, apart from Mrs Baker and Mrs Hewitt, who raised an eyebrow at him in disapproval. It was apparent that young Walter was impressionable and didn't need any encouragement. His face was a picture!

Once supper was over, I was shown to my sleeping quarters, and to my surprise I had been allocated a room of my own, small but compact, high in the rafters. All of the staff quarters were in the west wing. The next room to me was Betty's and Catherine's, who shared a bedroom. Mrs Baker's quarters were at the end of the corridor, fortunately far enough away from us!

After I had unpacked my bags, I was taken on a tour of the house to familiarise myself. Charlotte had been given the task of showing me. Her manner was rather austere. She pointed out the rooms that I would be in charge of.

'We keep a clean and tidy house,' she said. 'The standards are very high here.' Her voice was pitched with a hint of authority, which brought a smile to my face. Poor girl, I thought. I wasn't at all impressed. It crossed my mind how Rose and Charlie would have reacted! For Charlotte had only arrived two weeks previously to help prepare the house for the arrival of Lord and Lady Havis and hadn't had any experience working in domestic service and certainly not with gentry. She had previously worked in her aunt's corner shop. Unfortunately the business was sold and she was left without work, and although her parents supported her for a little while, money became tight and there was no alternative but to find her a suitable job. Hence the 'personal assistant' and she was living up to that!

The evening ended with everyone gathering in the kitchen for hot drinks. Last-minute instructions were given out by Mrs Baker for the following day. Lord and Lady Havis would be arriving in the evening so everything had to be completed by late afternoon.

'I suggest we have an early night,' Mrs Baker said. 'We have a tight schedule to complete and I want you all bright and bushy-tailed; an early start for all of us!'

Mrs Hewitt nodded in agreement. Giles, of course, wasn't included. He lived in the gatehouse and took his instructions from Lord Havis. Looking back now, I didn't realise that this was going to be a turning point in my life. Coming to Chatscott Hall would change my future and Giles would be a dear friend and father figure in the weeks ahead. My head had hardly touched the pillow that night before I was asleep.

The sound of footsteps awoke me the next morning just as the sun was rising. Voices from outside drifted through my window. I suddenly realised where I was and jumped out of bed. What time was it? I was late!

Feeling confused, I checked the clock on the mantle piece, it had just turned 5.30 a.m. Thank goodness I didn't have be on duty until 6.30 a.m., just for this one day. I looked out of the window which overlooked the stables and saw Giles and young Walter talking to two young men. It seemed to me that they were the stable lads from the village. Charlotte had mentioned that Lord and Lady Havis enjoyed horse riding; they had inherited four horses and stables when they purchased Chatscott Hall and occasionally joined in the hunts.

I couldn't hear all of what was being said as it was a distance away, but I gathered that instructions were being given by Giles regarding the tasks of the day. Realising I was still in my night attire, I quickly moved from the window and drew the curtain. I had almost washed and dressed when I heard a tap on the door.

'Hello, Edith,' a voice called out gently. 'Can I come in?' The door opened and Betty appeared. 'We thought you might like a cup of tea. It's your first day and it can feel strange,' she whispered. Behind her was Catherine, carrying the tea, her face smiling.

She said, 'Morning! Hope you slept well.' Her eyes flitted around the room.

'Yes, thank you,' I said, 'this is very kind of you both.' I felt at ease and knew I had already made friends.

'We are working together today,' Catherine said quickly. 'Mrs Baker thought it would be easier until you find your way around. Breakfast is at 8.30, so when you are ready I'll be next door.' Turning to Betty she said, 'You had better hurry: you know what old Flo is like if you are late!' She was referring to Mrs Hewitt, who was a stickler for time.

'I know!' Betty cried and hurried off.

My first day at Chatscott Hall went very quickly. It was quite a novelty to work in such a grand house. The rooms were amazing, each one opulent. The drawing room opened out on to the gardens, which had a croquet lawn, the French doors were open and the country air filled the room. Working alongside Catherine was a joy. She was thorough and quick, full of humour and highly intelligent. She knew all of the history of Chatscott Hall, Cranborne, and so on.

'I love to read,' she said. 'I'm a bit of a bookworm. Betty hates it! It stops me from talking and she can be a bit of a chatterbox, but we get on well and she has a heart of gold. You will enjoy your time here. There are lots of things to do and see. We're not a bad bunch!'

That I found out in the weeks ahead.

Lord and Lady Havis arrived just after 6 p.m. The whole house was buzzing they had brought two guests with them, Sir John William and Lady Elizabeth Jane. Mrs Baker informed us that we should expect to work late with just a break for supper. Although it was an informal visit, the dinner and evening entertaining could last into the small hours, which would mean that Mrs Baker and Giles would be on call. Charlotte and I were told that we would be serving at the table.

'Speak only when you are spoken to,' Mrs Baker said. 'Remember your manners, and your dress must be impeccable. I know I can rely on you both, so don't let me down.'

Charlotte, surprisingly, appeared to be nervous. 'Have you served titled people before?' After reassuring her, the coolness towards me the previous evening seemed to have disappeared and she was only too pleased to have me working alongside her. In retrospect, this was all new to her and she lacked the ability to make friends, which made her isolated. However, by the end of the evening she was laughing and chatting, especially at supper.

Mrs Hewitt kept giving odd glances towards her and I could tell that this was out of character when she, Mrs Hewitt, referred to me as a 'ray of sunshine', which brought smiles to everyone's faces, Charlotte just looked confused! By midnight we were back in our quarters. I was more than ready for bed. It had been quite an eventful day and one I had enjoyed.

The days seem to fly by and I soon settled in. The work was hard and at times back-aching. I never had time to brood and thoughts of Peter were becoming distant; a new environment and the country air seemed to be doing the trick. Catherine and Betty became my firm friends – at times we were a giggling trio! And of course we were reprimanded on several occasions. Charlotte, although friendly, kept her distance.

'She's old before her time,' Catherine would say. 'Doesn't have any fun, on her half-day she visits her parents and that's it! Too stuck up for us!'

It wasn't exactly true, because I had accompanied her on country walks and found her to be quite introverted, until she felt she knew and trusted you, and then she would open up and chat away. I told her about Wales and London, which she found enthralling.

'Do you think that Lord and Lady Havis will ask me to work in London one day?' Charlotte said eagerly. 'I have never been out of Dorset apart from when I went into hospital in Salisbury to have my tonsils out. All my family live in and around Cranborne and never had any desire to travel.'

'Well,' I whispered, 'if I get the chance when I return to London, I'll put a good word in for you. However, Mrs Baker is the one to speak to, and it is Lord and Lady Havis's decision in the end.'

She seemed to accept my word and said she would miss me when I returned to London for she found it difficult to make friends easily, especially being an only child. I told her that she should mix more and join in with everyone.

'When you work within a household such as Chatscott Hall, you become one of a team, working and living under the same roof, and it is important to bond.'

Charlotte nodded as if in agreement, and to be fair she really did try. However, she was still regarded by some as Miss Snooty!

During my time at Chatscott Hall, I learned to appreciate the countryside surrounding me. At times it took my breath away. The beauty and the vastness was awesome, and any opportunity I had I would walk to the village or through the country lanes. Although I loved Wales and was proud to have come from the

Rhondda Valley, it lacked the freedom from mines and slag heaps, smoking chimneys and low-lying clouds. Although harsh, it was part of an industry that supplied coal to other parts of Britain!

On one of my walks, I discovered a footbridge that led over a river to a bank that stretched for some distance. There were several anglers dotted along. The atmosphere was peaceful and relaxing. I ambled along, gazing at the men fishing, who seemed oblivious to their surroundings, deep in thought, hoping for a catch. It was their heaven! I smiled to myself and thought the tranquillity here, compared to the hustle and bustle of London, was amazing. No smoke, no grime, just pure fresh air.

I had walked some distance when a voice called out, 'You be a long way from home.' I recognised the Dorset accent straight away and looked around. It was Giles from Chatscott Hall. He was perched upon the bank, with fishing rod and tackle, grinning from ear to ear. He said, 'Well, I'll be darned! You be the last person I would expect to see in this neck of the woods! It's young Edith, isn't it? You've come some way, my girl. It's a good two miles from the Hall and more. Don't be wandering too far. Best sit yourself and have a lemonade. Freshly made by Flo, bless her heart. She is a little darling! Looks after me all right, eh?'

'Thanks, Giles,' I murmured, and sat down. 'I have another two hours before I have to be on duty and this is just what the doctor ordered. It's a beautiful spot. I had no idea you were keen on fishing.'

Giles's face lit up. Tapping his nose, he said 'It's my favourite pastime. Not many people know, my dear. I come here 'cause it's peaceful and it clears them cobwebs away. Them town folk don't know what they miss, but you, Miss Edith, you are a different kettle of fish, there's no doubt! You see and appreciate this lovely Dorset! You be a Welsh girl, so tell me all about your country. I've never been no further than Salisbury. Oh! I tell a lie: I've been to Beaulieu in Hampshire. I drove their Lordships to Palace House; big posh do! Never got back until the early hours. Anyway that's enough about me; now tell me all about your life.'

Well, I thought, where should I start? It all seemed so far away. These few weeks in Dorset had made a difference; my life in London had been put on hold. I had grown to love the countryside and the people; it had helped me to forget most of the sadness I had brought with me. I would never forget Peter, or love another so much. However, I knew that I had to go forward; life was for living. Somehow I was able to talk to Giles with ease, not faltering or feeling nervous. His manner was fatherly and kind. Sitting there seemed so natural with the sun dancing on the water. All was well with the world, so it appeared. That day was the first of many that I shared with Giles. Not having a father and being able to talk to someone like him, a fatherly figure so to speak, gave me renewed strength and he became my rock.

Most weekends Chatscott Hall received visitors. At one time there had been twenty, all needing attention, and extra staff from the village had to be called in. Mrs Baker, poor woman, was beside herself trying to organise everything. Charlotte was given extra duties, which included helping out in the kitchen in the evening. Betty found it quite amusing, for she had to show her what to do, and that was beneath Charlotte! However, everything seemed to go according to plan and the splendour of the occasions made up for all the hard work, and to be fair we were allowed staff gatherings. Mrs Hewitt's famous punch and pasties went down very well with everyone. Young Walter played the fiddle, country ditties, and he was very good. With Giles playing the mouth organ, it was definitely music to our ears! Those times I shall never forget.

Chapter Thirteen

Then came the day when Lord and Lady Havis instructed Giles to fetch an antique clock from a shop in Swanage, which they had purchased on one of their visits.

'We won't be needing the car today,' they told Giles, 'so when you have finished your morning duties and when you have had your lunch, you may go.'

'Thank you, your Lordships,' Giles replied and tipped his cap. Later at lunch, he was chatting away. 'Pity you be working,' he whispered to Mrs Hewitt, 'a nice drive through the countryside and a cream tea in Swanage would do you the world of good, eh?'

'There's no chance of that,' Mrs Hewitt replied quickly. 'Their Lordships are playing croquet this afternoon and they are expecting visitors to join them. I've cakes to bake, no time for gallivanting around. Young Walter and Betty, they be working as well, so be off with you, Giles, and don't be wasting my time!' Mrs Hewitt's bark was worse than her bite for she smiled and winked at us all.

Catherine, who had been listening with great interest, cried out, 'It's my half-day and I would love a trip to Swanage.' Turning to me she said, 'Edith, it's both our half-days: would you like to have a trip out?'

My first reaction was to say, 'Yes, please,' but the expression on Mrs Hewitt's face stopped me in my tracks.

'I don't think Their Lordships would approve,' she said. 'Remember your place, Catherine. Anyway, if you are that keen you can catch a train from Verwood. Cars, indeed,' she muttered. 'I don't know where you young people get these high ideas from! Come on, let's get moving. This is going to be a busy afternoon.'

Catherine's face was one of disappointment.

'Never mind,' I said gently, 'we can have a walk instead. Fancy a walk into the village?'

'Thanks, Edith,' she answered. 'I would love to. Come on, let's get ready, then.'

The sun was shining and there was not a cloud in the sky as we set out. We meandered along a path that ran through the meadow, which led to the road that would take us to the village. We were busy chatting away when we heard the toot of a horn. It was Giles trundling along in the car.

'I been looking for you two! You be hard to find,' he called out. 'Do you still want to see Swanage? Come on, climb in, and not a word to no one. What's the harm, anyway? Flo worries too much! Quick, before I change my mind.'

We didn't need asking twice. It was so thrilling. We laughed and joked all the way until we reached Swanage. The views were spectacular. The sea was glinting in the sun, people bathing and picnicking on the shore. It was unusual for me; I could only remember a couple of times being taken to the seaside. There was a paddle steamer alongside the pier, which appeared to have just arrived full of day trippers. The sounds of their voices echoed across the water, a hint of excitement in the air. My pulse seemed to race; the smell of the sea and the colour of the downs was exhilarating.

Catherine was tugging at my arm. 'This is wonderful!' she cried. 'What shall we do first?'

Before I could answer, Giles said, 'Why don't you walk up to the downs? Best views to see and you can walk into the village from there; nice shops to look at. I've got to fetch their Lordships' clock and then look in at the tackle shop, so I'll meet you girls back here at 4 p.m. Can't afford to be too late, so off you go!'

'Thanks, Giles,' we said. 'See you later,' we added as we waved goodbye.

The first thing we did was to buy an ice-cream cornet with a cherry on the top, much to Catherine's delight.

'This is the life,' she cried. 'I love all that summer brings; everyone is happier when the weather is warm and of course I can read to my heart's content. Just sitting in the sun with my favourite book is heaven!'

Listening to Catherine was a joy; she was so positive and nothing seemed to bother her. She was always good company to be with, which I needed at that time. On reaching the downs we looked about us. There were hotels nestled around and the one that stood out was the Grand Hotel looking magnificent and appealing.

'Looks quite posh,' Catherine remarked. 'People must have money to spend a holiday here. It's got everything.'

'Yes,' I replied, 'you are right. Let's have a wander before we walk to the village. I love all the views. It's quite stunning. I could live here!'

'Nothing is impossible,' Catherine said. 'That is, if you set your heart on it. Anyway, you are lucky to work in London, all the bright lights. Maybe I might work there one day, who knows!'

We carried on walking until we found a bench that wasn't occupied, from which we could see across the bay. It was lovely just to sit and talk, but the sun on our faces made us slightly drowsy, so we decided to stretch out on the grass and sunbathe. It seemed only a few minutes when we heard voices and the sound of heavy feet coming towards us.

'Oh dear!' Catherine muttered. 'I think we are going to lose our bench.' She looked up and then nudged me. 'Don't look now,' she whispered, 'but there are two handsome beaus walking our way!' She started to giggle and nudged me again.

'Catherine, behave!' I said laughing, and sat up, squinting at the sun. I looked to see who she was talking about. Looming in front of us were two young men, one taller than the other, both lightly tanned, slim in build and quite attractive. They were both smiling, and were aware that we had noticed them.

'Good afternoon, ladies,' the shorter of the two said, bowing slightly. 'Hope we haven't disturbed you, but we were heading for the bench, not realising that you two lovely young girls were here, of course!' The words fell from his mouth like they were rehearsed. 'I'm Daniel and my friend is Leslie. May we join you?'

Catherine's face was one of astonishment, and before we could answer they sat down beside us. Daniel continued to chat away, making it clear that he was interested in Catherine. It was quite amusing, even though I felt quite shy, and Leslie hadn't managed to get a word in edgeways. A much quieter person, I thought. Looking at him I could see that he was slightly embarrassed. He had a quirky smile with determined features, grey blue eyes and mid-brown hair. He seemed hesitant at first, not knowing what to say, glancing to one side, and then plucking up courage to ask me my name.

'Edith,' I replied, trying to sound confident, and continued to make conversation. I explained that we had only come for the afternoon and it was my first visit to Swanage and how much we were enjoying our time. Leslie's face was quite intent. He told me that he worked at a hotel in Bournemouth and was employed as a hotel porter.

'It's only a temporary measure,' he said, 'until I can find other work. I fancy driving, maybe a chauffeur or driving a charabanc. I prefer to be outside more. It's long hours at the moment and very few breaks in between.'

He seemed more relaxed now and continued to chat away. In no time at all we had to leave; there was just an hour left before we had to return to Chatscott Hall. Catherine seemed hesitant. It was obvious that she had taken a shine to Daniel. However, I reminded her that if she wanted to browse the book shop, we didn't have a lot of time. Saying goodbye was slightly awkward, for we were not sure whether we would meet again.

'It's been a pleasure meeting you both,' Daniel said, not taking his eyes off Catherine. 'It's a shame you have to go, perhaps we will meet again.' Catherine nodded and smiled at me.

'Oh yes,' I replied quickly, glancing at Leslie, who stood in silence with that quirky smile. 'Maybe we will make another trip to Swanage.'

'Yes, please,' Catherine blurted out. 'We have the same half-day next week. We could come on the train!'

I found myself blushing at Catherine's enthusiasm. 'Well, we'll see what happens,' I said quietly, 'but we really do have to go.' We shook hands and said our goodbyes and made our way to the village. Catherine glanced around to catch a glimpse of them.

'They haven't moved,' she cried, waving her arms. 'I think they wanted to come with us, Edith.' Her face was full of disappointment.

'Yes, maybe,' I said, 'but we don't know anything about them and if fate deems it, we will see them again! Come on, Catherine, let's have a cup of tea. I'm gasping.'

Fortunately for us, the tea shop was next to the book shop,

which gave us twenty minutes for each and then it was a dash back to meet Giles at the car.

Catherine seemed subdued on the journey back and buried her head in the book that she had bought. Giles chatted away and asked how we had enjoyed ourselves.

'It was absolutely lovely,' I cried. 'We must go again when we get the chance, eh, Catherine?'

Her face lit up and she grinned at me with that knowing look, which meant we had a secret. Giles, whose outward appearance gave the impression of being oblivious to situations, laughed out loud and said, 'What 'ave you two girls been up to? Daresay it must be young lads involved. I know these things.' He tapped his nose. 'Two young ladies, single and fancy free, I remember those days. Nothing I don't know and 'avn't done! But mum's the word, eh? Flo would never feed me again, especially me giving you girls a ride after what she said. No, best thing all round is to say nothing and we will live to see another day!'

Giles continued to chuckle to himself, as Catherine and I couldn't stop giggling. Giles was humour personified!

We were dropped off at the end of the drive when we reached Chatscott Hall and made our way back slowly, giving Giles time to deliver the clock to Their Lordships, and of course Mrs Hewitt would be less suspicious of our arrival.

As we were nearing the house, Catherine, who had been dragging her feet, suddenly swung round and cried, 'Daniel gave me a telephone number; he pushed this piece of paper into my hand when we were saying goodbye. What do you think I should do? I didn't know what it said until I read it in the car, and I do really like him, Edith.'

Catherine's face was flushed with excitement. She grabbed my arm and said, 'He has given me a time when he will be able to speak to me: after 8 p.m. on Tuesday or Thursday.'

'Well, you had better ring him, then,' I whispered. 'You will have to ask Mrs Baker's permission, though. She doesn't mind if you let her know in advance. There's a telephone in the library which staff are allowed to use in an emergency. Mrs Baker allowed me to use it the first week I arrived. I had a special reason. You don't have to say anything other than that you wish to make a call. I was always able to in London, so I cannot see a problem.'

Catherine squeezed my hand tightly and cried, 'This is our secret, Edith. Promise not to tell anyone! But of course I will have to tell Betty. She is my friend and would be really hurt if I didn't tell her, but no one else just in case!'

'Don't worry,' I whispered, 'your secret's safe with me. Come on, I'm starving and we have given Giles long enough to cover his tracks. Mrs Hewitt will have no idea!'

By this time, we had reached the staff entrance and were greeted by Betty.

'You two have been ages,' she said, 'did you go to Swanage?' Her face was full of anticipation.

'Yes, we did,' Catherine answered excitedly, 'and after supper we will tell you, but not in front of old Flo! Please, Betty, not a hint.'

'You know me, Catherine. Mum's the word,' Betty whispered. 'Hurry up, though; you know she is a stickler for time.'

We hurried in and were greeted by young Walter, grinning from ear to ear. 'Thought you got lost. Nearly had a search party out looking for you!' he said jokily. Mrs Hewitt's face was bland.

'Walter, behave!' she muttered. 'And you two girls,' she added, looking straight at us, 'remember I do not tolerate lateness at mealtimes. Please lay the table. We have had a very busy afternoon, not a minute to ourselves, and Their Lordships have guests arriving tonight, which means another late night! So come along; we have Mrs Baker joining us this evening, so lay an extra place.'

Silence reigned for about five minutes while we quietly set the table. However, once Giles walked in that was the end.

'Cor! It be just like a funeral parlour,' he said, 'not a sound. 'Ave you been on your high horse again, Flo? 'Tain't natural, expecting young people to be quiet. Rules are one thing, but we all work hard enough and this time of evening is for 'aving a break and a laugh. You be a hard woman, Flo, at times.' Giles winked at Mrs Hewitt, whose face was a picture.

'I be doing my job, let me tell you, and mind your own business,' she muttered. It was obvious to everyone that she was trying hard to keep a straight face; her mouth was twitching. 'Sit yourself down and behave, Giles,' she started to laugh and turned around to see our reaction. We burst into a fit of giggling, unaware that Mrs Baker had entered the kitchen 'I could hear all of this frivolity halfway down the hall,' she cried, 'I take it, Giles, that you are behind all this?'

Looking directly at him, she seemed amused, even though she sounded serious. 'We must keep some kind of decorum and show an example to our young staff, don't you think?'

'Pardon me, Mrs Baker,' Giles said, 'I will remember your words.' He winked and nodded, which made us giggle more. Knowing she was on a losing battle, Mrs Baker just tutted and took her place at the table.

Once supper was over, those who were not on duty were able to return to their quarters. Catherine appeared highly excited; she was anxious to confide in Betty all that had happened. However, Betty was working with Mrs Hewitt throughout the evening, with Charlotte on call to serve, so there would be no opportunity to have a tête à tête until much later. I had made a jug of cocoa and nudged Catherine and whispered that we could take it to our quarters and have a natter, away from prying ears! A smile passed over her face and she took the tray from my hands and hurried out of the kitchen. I don't think we stopped talking for at least two hours, plotting and planning.

To be honest, it gave me a boost, giving me renewed hope. My thoughts were of Peter… Perhaps… No, I mustn't. I had come to terms with the knowledge that he was no more. I had to move on. Being here in Dorset, and working with new people had given me renewed confidence, and with those thoughts floating through my mind, I returned to my room and fell asleep.

It was the sound of rain beating against the window that woke me in the early hours. It was very humid and sticky. The window had been left open and the sash belt was knocking against the window pane. It was just like a dripping tap, irritating. I rolled out of bed, not wanting to open my eyes. Better close the window altogether, I thought. Rain had leaked in and had dripped on to the floor so I used my flannel to mop up.

Standing by the wash bowl, wringing the flannel, out I gazed blurry-eyed through the window. Suddenly I saw a movement down below. I shook my head. Am I dreaming? I thought, and looked again. Yes, there was definitely someone or something moving. Regaining my senses I looked more closely. It appeared to be a man's form; his movements were slow and deliberate. He was heading for the stables. Maybe one of the horses was sick?

No, I thought, he hasn't a light to see with. What should I do? Horse thief, perhaps? You're being silly, Edith, I told myself. There was a simple explanation. However, I knew I just couldn't go back to bed. I quickly wrapped my bedgown around me, and checking carefully through the window again, I could see the figure enter the stables. Waiting a few minutes just to be sure that my eyes weren't playing tricks through the torrent of rain, a glimmer of light filtered through a crack in the stables. Dim, but definitely a light. He must have found a lantern.

Oh dear! I should do something; no turning back now. I quietly opened the door. I hesitated outside Catherine and Betty's room. No, I thought, it's best to inform Mrs Baker. That would be the sensible thing to do. Feeling quite nervous, I made my way along the corridor until I reached Mrs Baker's quarters. Gently tapping on the door, I called out in almost a whisper, 'Mrs Baker, Mrs Baker.'

Sounds of a door opening and shuffling of feet reached my ears and the beat of my heart grew faster. She isn't going to be too happy about this, I thought. The door suddenly opened. Mrs Baker's formidable form appeared draped in her night attire with a night bonnet, with a white chin strap (which was used to alleviate double chins).

'It's you, Edith!' she said. 'For heaven's sake, what is going on?'

'Sorry to disturb you,' I whispered, 'but I think someone has broken into the stables.' I explained briefly what I had seen.

'More than likely a tramp,' Mrs Baker muttered, 'however we cannot ignore it. You had better wake young Walter: tell him to fetch Giles from the lodge. I will get dressed just in case. Don't disturb anyone else, Edith. This could be a long night. Dear, dear,' she muttered and closed the door.

Waking Walter was difficult. The poor lad had worked late and was in a deep sleep. He opened the door, rubbing his eyes and having a job to focus. He looked at me if though he had seen a ghost.

'Cor! Am I seeing things? What's up?' he said sleepily. A few seconds later he appeared looking dishevelled. 'I'm on my way. Me and Giles will sort it out. Don't you worry, Edith.' He disappeared down the corridor.

I hurried back to my room and dressed quickly. There was no point in going back to bed and I wanted to see it all through. I was wide awake and feeling excited and nervous. I stood by the window, looking out. The rain had stopped and there was a clearer view. I turned to look at the clock on the mantle; it was almost 3.30 a.m. Any minute now, I thought. Peering back down into the courtyard and looking across to the stables, I could see the light was still there. Where was Giles? Almost instantly he appeared in the eerie half-light with Walter and someone else. They were treading lightly and from where I was stood it looked like they were carrying sticks or bats. Suddenly there was a tap on my door. It was Mrs Baker.

'I thought you might be watching,' she whispered, 'bit of a shock really. I have telephoned the police and they are on their way. Hopefully Giles will just lock him in.'

Peering across at the stables, she could see the three figures approaching the stable doors.

'Young Walter shouldn't be there. Whatever are they thinking of?' Mrs Baker became agitated. 'Where are the police?'

It seemed that they had been heard. The light showing through the crack of the stable door diminished.

'Oh! He knows they are there,' I cried. 'I hope he hasn't got a gun.' Turning to Mrs Baker, whose face looked grim, I said, 'They shouldn't go in. It's best to leave it to the police.'

'Yes, Edith,' Mrs Baker whispered. 'Don't worry – Giles will have his wits about him. He won't do anything foolish,' she sighed heavily. 'Thank goodness the police have arrived.' We could see the lights of the car flashing; it lit the whole of the courtyard. Within minutes it was all over. The police led the man, with his head bowed, out of the stables. There hadn't been any struggle. He looked a pathetic figure, tired and wet. He was bundled into the police car. Giles had a word with the officer, and then the car drove off.

'Well, that's that!' Mrs Baker said with a sigh of relief. 'We shall have to inform Their Lordships first thing. Come along, Edith, we had better go and find out what it's all about. No doubt everyone will be in the kitchen. I think a cup of tea is in order.'

The kitchen was buzzing when we entered. Walter was making tea. Giles and a stable lad, who lived in the gatehouse next door, were chatting away to Mrs Hewitt, who had been woken by all the activity, still dressed in her night attire. Apologising to Mrs Baker for her appearance, she then started to relate all that Giles had told her.

Giles interrupted her almost immediately by saying, 'Flo! Let me explain.'

Turning to face Mrs Baker, he said, 'It turned out to be an escaped convict – managed to get this far from Dorchester prison – went missing two days ago. Just needed a place to shelter. Harmless, really. The officer told me he was a first offender; stole food and clothes for his family – got caught of course, poor sod! Wet and hungry. He came away quietly; too exhausted, no fight left in him. It's the sign of the times – no work and people take desperate measures.'

'That might well be,' Mrs Baker retorted. 'But he could have been a murderer, and even so, breaking in to the stables was a crime.'

'Maybe,' Giles replied, 'but where is your compassion?'

All eyes were on Mrs Baker, whose face was bright red with embarrassment. Before any more could be said, Walter cried, 'Anyone ready for a cuppa?'

'That would be nice,' I replied quickly. 'My mouth is really dry and it's been a long night for everyone.'

The tension seemed to ease as we sat around the table drinking tea. I think we were all slightly traumatised, and the events of the night overdramatised. The time was about 5.30 a.m. Betty and Catherine entered the kitchen, looking completely amazed at the gathering.

'Are we late?' Betty exclaimed. 'What's going on?'

'You had better sit down,' Mrs Baker said. 'There is tea in the pot. Giles will explain everything to you. I must inform their Lordships as soon as possible. Of course, the police will be returning to take down statements. This is going to be a long day,' she muttered and left the kitchen. Within seconds the whole place was buzzing and for the rest of the day it was difficult to concentrate.

Lord and Lady Havis requested all of the staff to gather in the big hall after dinner, mainly to give a pep talk on the events of the day and the previous night. Lord Havis pointed out the need to be vigilant and thanked those who participated in catching the villain. He turned to me and said, 'I understand from Mrs Baker that you spotted the rascal first and foremost – most fortunate that you were up at that time and so alert. Well done, Edith!'

Everyone nodded in agreement, leaving me blushing with embarrassment. Lady Havis said a few words of encouragement and then we were dismissed. A few of us returned to the kitchens for our drinks of cocoa and Ovaltine.

Catherine nudged me and whispered, 'Should I ask Mrs Baker now about the telephone call?'

'You can,' I replied. 'But see what mood she is in first; don't forget, it's been a long day. Wait until she sits down and if she is chatty then it will be fine.'

Catherine nodded in agreement and waited for the right moment, which fortunately came when Mrs Baker asked her if she would mind working late the following weekend. Catherine seized her opportunity and asked if it would be possible to make a telephone call the following Tuesday.

'It will have to be after 8 p.m.,' Mrs Baker said, 'and remember to make it short; we are fortunate that Their Lordships allow us to do so free of charge.'

'Yes, of course,' Catherine replied. 'I do appreciate it. Thank you.'

Betty and Charlotte seemed to be intrigued by the clandestine atmosphere that seemed to surround Catherine.

'Family business,' Catherine muttered. Giles looked across, gave one of his knowing smiles and clapped his hands together and cried, 'Who's for a game of cards?'

Apart from Mrs Baker, who stated that she was far too tired from the day's events, everyone else decided to join in. By 10 p.m. everyone was feeling the effects of the day. I think we all slept soundly that night.

Chapter Fourteen

The next few days became difficult. The weather changed and we were into a heatwave. I remember the temperature rose to eighty-five degrees. Everyone and everything slowed down; early mornings were the only respite until the sun rose. Mrs Hewitt found the heat unbearable and became irritable. Most of us kept our distance when in the kitchen, leaving Flo to her own devices.

Their Lordships arranged to have their meals, apart from dinner in the evening, served outside under the oak tree which shaded the south wing. It was much cooler there and the views were breathtaking. Giles and Walter carried the wrought-iron tables and placed them under the tree, cushioned seats and parasols, too. Betty was given the task of serving and making sure napkins were placed correctly. It made life a little easier because there would be no running up and down stairs, using the drawing room as access. Mrs Baker had a rota made up and had rearranged duties for each of us. While the heatwave lasted, we were allowed to have our evening meals outside on the other side of the house. Mrs Baker provided picnic rugs. Mrs Hewitt had made iced lemonade and freshly baked bread, which we had with cheddar cheese and pickle. Those evenings I shall always remember, full of laughter and stories.

Tuesday came around and there was no containing Catherine's excitement. Betty and I knew we wouldn't have any peace and couldn't wait for the evening to come. On the stroke of eight, Catherine was waiting outside the drawing room. Five minutes later, Mrs Baker appeared. She checked to see that the room was unoccupied and nodded to Catherine that she could make her call.

'Five minutes,' she said, wagging her finger at Catherine.

'Yes, of course,' Catherine replied sheepishly. 'I promise.'

Mrs Baker walked away, mumbling, 'Make sure you close the doors after you!'

Meanwhile Betty and I waited in the kitchen, making ourselves busy by kneading bread for the following day. It seemed an age before Catherine returned. Her face was flushed and she was smiling, like the cat that had the cream.

'Well?' Betty cried. 'Tell us all about it!'

I nudged Betty and whispered, 'Not in here!'

By this time, Mrs Hewitt had taken notice. 'What in heaven are you girls up to now? All this whispering and goings-on; you be concentrating on kneading that bread and not so much chat!' Her bark was worse than her bite, so we nodded, smiling back at her in agreement.

'While you're here, Catherine,' Mrs Hewitt said, 'make yourself useful and make some drinks – mine's a cup of tea!'

Later we managed to escape outside where no one could hear us. The anticipation was too much for Betty. 'Did you speak to him? Are you going to meet him?' she cried.

'Calm down,' Catherine whispered, 'we don't want everyone to know. It's a secret for now.'

Betty's face was one of dismay. 'Sorry,' she said, 'I do get carried away.'

'Never mind, don't worry,' Catherine said. 'I would be the same. Anyway I have arranged to meet Daniel on my half-day.' Catherine's voice was trembling with excitement. 'We are meeting at Swanage, which will be Thursday. A walk first and then afternoon tea. I shall catch the 2 p.m. train from Verwood. Daniel is going to meet me the other end.'

She carried on chatting until she remembered to say, 'Oh, by the way, Edith, he also said to let you know that Leslie sends his regards and how much he enjoyed the afternoon. I think he likes you a lot,' Catherine whispered.

I felt myself blush and looked at Catherine and Betty, who were trying hard not to smile.

'For goodness' sake,' I cried, 'we only met for one afternoon. Besides I am not really interested. I shall be returning to London in September, so there is no point in talking about it.'

'If you say so,' Catherine murmured, 'but there is no harm in being friends. There are a few more weeks yet. Why not enjoy yourself?'

'Maybe you are right,' I said, 'but I think I'll wait and see what happens.'

My thoughts raced back to Peter. How could I contemplate another man in my life? Would I ever move on?

Suddenly I felt Betty's arm around my shoulder. 'Come on, Edith,' she whispered, 'it's beginning to grow dark. It must be quite late. Mrs Baker will be having a fit!'

We all burst into laughter; we had visions of her in her night-cap waiting at the end of the corridor, saying, 'What time do you call this?' Not a good time to be in her bad books.

After a restless night with only a few hours' sleep, I awoke to the sounds of horse's hoofs clapping around in the courtyard below. The sun had risen. I peered through the window to see what was going on. It had just turned 5 a.m. I thought, It's a little early for the stable lads to be saddling the horses. Their Lordships never rose earlier than 7 a.m. and they certainly wouldn't be riding at this hour, and then I heard Giles's voice. He came into view and crossed the courtyard.

'Morning, lads,' he said cheerfully. 'Them horses saddled and ready? Their Lordships request you take them round to the front of the house; it be an early morning ride before it becomes too hot. I know for sure it's going to be a scorcher! It's been forecast for another two weeks with thunderstorms in between. Don't get much sleep – too hot and sticky for everyone. Anyway, when you're done there's a cuppa waiting for you in the kitchen,' he whispered a few words and took his leave and disappeared around to the front of the house.

Having washed and dressed, I made my way to the kitchen. I was gasping for a drink and I wasn't on duty until 5.30 a.m. Mrs Hewitt was baking bread. The aroma wafted across. The smell of freshly baked bread gave me an appetite; there was nothing to compare it to, just like Cook's in London. The two stable lads were sat at the table and greeted me with a wave. 'Morning, sweetheart!' they both said together.

'Behave!' Mrs Hewitt said and turned to smile at me. 'Cup of tea, Edith? It's going to be another hot day: cold meat and salad for lunch. I can't be doing too much in this heat. Besides, their Lordships requested a picnic lunch.'

I sat and sipped my tea and listened to Mrs Hewitt's chatter. The two stable lads were nodding and grinning. Fortunately she was oblivious to anyone else. By this time, Charlotte, Catherine and Betty had emerged, nudging each other. It was obvious that the stable lads were having a joke.

'You girls had better make it quick if you want any tea. It's almost 5.30,' Mrs Hewitt said. 'We have a busy day ahead. I want this kitchen cleared in five minutes.' She gave the stable lads a knowing look. They quickly took the hint and left.

The morning passed slowly, and every task seemed to take longer. Lethargy had set in because of the humidity, we were perspiring constantly and feeling dehydrated, which slowed us all down, and I welcomed the afternoon break. I washed myself down in cold water and patted lavender water on to my wrists and brow. For some reason it was supposed to cool you down, something I had learned from my mother. It worked, anyway!

I had two hours before serving afternoon teas, so I decided to write a few letters. There were some huge trees around the back of the house, which edged on to the meadow, giving a lovely shaded cool spot to sit under. I gathered my things together and slipped out of the back entrance, hoping no one would see me. I needed to be on my own, to be with my own thoughts. To be honest, I had promised to write and send cards to everyone – Cook and Rose, my sisters, my little brother. They would all be wondering why they haven't heard. I wrote a long letter to my family, and picture cards to Fanny, Cook and Rose.

The time had sped by and fortunately for me the church clock in the village, which I could hear in the distance, chimed every fifteen minutes, so I was able to check the time. I had another ten minutes and I had to change into my uniform, so it was a quick dash. Their Lordships were expecting guests for a picnic tea, which made it more important that I was on time. Betty had already prepared the picnic tables, including pretty lace doilies under each cup. Lady Havis was most particular in the niceties; everything had to be just so. I served iced tea and home-made lemonade with freshly made fruit scones and little fancy cakes.

Unlike some titled people, Lady Havis always said thank you

and never made you feel uncomfortable and always asked how you were. That's how I shall always remember her.

That evening there was the most violent thunderstorm. We all gathered in the kitchen after dinner had been served. Nobody wanted to venture out, especially with the forked lightning and the lashing rain.

Poor Charlotte became very nervous.

'I really do not like thunderstorms,' she said, her voice trembling. Mrs Baker, who had joined us, suggested an evening of card games.

'Come along, Charlotte,' she said. 'It won't last for ever. You need something to take your mind off of it; be a good girl and fetch the cards from the cupboard. Catherine and Edith, you prepare the drinks, and when I say drinks I mean lemonade or tea, especially for you young people.' She turned to young Walter who had been rubbing his hands with glee. 'And you can forget any ideas of cider and ale, young man. We want you fit and well tomorrow,' she said. Mrs Baker had a soft spot for Walter. She knew he didn't have any family and needed some adult guidance; between her and Mrs Hewitt they kept a kindly eye on him. Giles entered the kitchen, completely soaked and bedraggled.

'It's not fit for a dog, a terrible night,' he cried. 'The lads are staying in the stables until the storm is over; the horses are in a nervous state to be sure. Their Lordships were quite worried until I suggested the lads kept an eye.'

'Yes, a good idea,' Mrs Hewitt commented, her eyes looking directly at the floor where Giles was stood – a huge puddle of rain water had formed. 'For goodness' sake, Giles, put your wet clothes in the scullery before we all drown in the flood!'

Turning to Walter, she cried, 'Go and fetch the mop.'

'Calm down!' Giles said. 'It's only a bit of water. Don't make such a fuss, Flo. I need a towel.'

Catherine, who found it all amusing, had grabbed a towel from the cupboard. 'Here you are, Giles,' she said, trying hard not to giggle. 'Give me your wet clothes. I'll hang them in the scullery for you.'

By this time, it was hard to keep a straight face; with all the tension of the storm we needed a little humour to break the atmosphere. Walter took one look at Catherine and that was that. We all burst out laughing, including Mrs Baker.

'Well, I'm glad you all think it's funny,' Mrs Hewitt said, 'but what's done is done, so let's settle down.'

'Good idea,' Giles replied. 'Any tea in the pot?'

The rest of the evening was spent playing cards and performing charades. It kept everyone amused until the storm began to abate.

By the following morning, the sun was shining and there was not a cloud in the sky. It was Thursday and both Catherine and I had a half-day. I had planned to walk into the village and post my cards and perhaps have some refreshment in the little tea shop and then meander back in my own time.

Catherine, of course, was meeting Daniel at Swanage. She had hardly slept a wink, what with the storm and humidity, and of course being excited of her forthcoming rendezvous didn't help.

'I really do not know what to wear, Edith,' she said. 'Betty thinks I should wear the lavender dress with the daisy pattern. I'm not sure. What do you think?'

'Wear what you feel good in,' I whispered. 'It won't make any difference. You are slim and pretty, he will be just glad to see you.'

Catherine's face beamed. 'You always say the right thing! Thanks, Edith.'

After lunch, Betty and I helped Catherine to choose her dress. She had three and chose the lavender one. She powdered her face and brushed her hair.

'Well,' she cried, 'will I do?' She looked a picture, quite stunning.

'You'll pass,' we both said. 'You should have your photo taken in that outfit, but never mind. As long as you enjoy yourself, you will remember anyway.'

We waved her goodbye and watched her disappear across the meadow. There was a path that led to the road where she would catch the bus to the station.

Betty sighed. 'I wonder if I will ever meet anyone and be as excited as Catherine.' Her voice faltered as she spoke. 'I have never had a beau, and I'm eighteen next birthday. I don't want to be a kitchen maid all my life. A home of my own and children is my dream, but there isn't much hope of that when I'm stuck here!'

Her demeanour was one of despair.

'Hey,' I cried, 'this isn't like you. Come on, you have everything to look forward to. You have a happy-go-lucky personality, which is very important. 'Your Mr Right will come along one day and you'll be swept off your feet!'

Betty began to smile and then she started to giggle. 'You really think so, Edith?' Her words came tumbling out. 'There is a boy who works in the village, in the butcher's shop. Mrs Hewitt sometimes when she needs fresh sausages asks me to run errands; that's when Giles is too busy. I borrow her bike, doesn't take long. His name is Arthur and he's ever so polite, but I don't think he notices me. Not in that way, anyhow. That's what I mean, Edith; it's never going to happen.'

'Well, that's where you are wrong,' I whispered. 'We will have to do something about it. We will arrange a half-day together and we will catch the train to Swanage. There'll be plenty of young men for you to see. Even go for a walk up on the downs and then have tea out. We can even have a picnic on the beach. The choice is yours, Betty,' I said smiling.

'That would be lovely,' Betty cried. 'I can't wait!' She chatted excitedly all the way back to the house. Looking at her face was a joy; she was bubbly and full of hope – how I used to be when I was eighteen, I thought. However, I had beautiful memories of Peter, which I would always treasure.

The walk to the village was so relaxing, even though it was extremely hot; the trees along the side of the road gave a shaded path and sheltered you from the heat. The area was mostly wooded, with very few houses to be seen. There was a bus into the village every hour but I preferred to walk; it was just under two miles each way. However, I sometimes caught the bus back if I felt tired. I reached the village just after 3 p.m. and went straight to the post office-cum-grocery shop. I needed some stamps to post my letters and some writing paper. The post mistress eyed me up and down.

Cranborne Post Office

'What can I do for you?' she asked without blinking. She had pointed features with tiny glasses perched on the end of her nose.

'Six stamps and a writing pad, if you please,' I said quietly.

'Thank you,' she said quite brusquely. 'That will be eight pence and three farthings.' Not once did she smile or show any warmth of character. I quickly left, thinking, What a sad person. If Rose had been with me she would have said 'miserable sod!', which made me realise how much I missed everyone in London; they were like a family to me. However, I knew I was enjoying my time here and would find it very hard to leave.

I posted the letters. The tea shop was just around the corner. I was looking forward to my tea and cake, the highlight of my day. There were just a few people inside, the aroma of fresh coffee wafted across mingling with the smell of baked scones. I settled in the corner.

'What will it be, my dear?' A rosy-faced lady approached me from behind the counter and asked, 'Tea, coffee, or ice lemonade? A nice cream scone? Everything freshly made.' Her eyes were twinkling as she smiled.

'Tea and a scone will do nicely,' I replied.

'Right away, my dear,' she said, placing a napkin and tea plate in front of me. My eyes wandered and I noticed the gingham clothes on each table. Everything was clean and sparkling, which made it very appealing. I must come here again, I thought. On leaving the tea shop, I meandered around. There was a haberdashery shop, a hardware store and, of course, the butcher's. Yes, I thought, I must take a peek. I wonder if I will be able to see Arthur, the young man who Betty liked so much. I scanned the window and sure enough he was there, scrubbing down the meat table. I could see why Betty was so besotted. Dark-haired and very handsome, he looked up and saw me staring and smiled. I smiled back and quickly walked on. I turned the corner and saw the local bus pull in. Just in time, I thought. Now it's here I might as well take advantage and save my legs, I really felt too hot to walk.

I climbed on board and sat next to the open window at the back. In about five minutes, the bus was half full. Once the driver had collected the fares we set off. My mind started to drift thinking of ways that could bring Betty and Arthur together.

Perhaps he had a girlfriend already, but even so Betty should at least try and find out, strike up a conversation – no, perhaps not. Maybe if someone else was with her she might not be so nervous. Oh dear, I thought, I'm getting carried away! Should mind my own business really. If Betty asks me for my help, than that is different, I'll wait and see what she has to say first.

By this time, the bus had reached Chatscott Hall. I thanked the driver as I got off and made my way to the path that led to the house.

It must be nearly 5 p.m., I said to myself. Plenty of time before supper, I'll do some crocheting; haven't done much recently. I was making some table mats; they were originally intended for my bottom drawer. I hadn't had much incentive in the last six months, so I must really try again. My room was very cool compared to the south side of the house; it was so hot I welcomed the thought of a cold wash and just relaxing. On reaching the house, I made my way to the servants' entrance to find Betty and Walter outside sitting on milking stools sipping lemonade. They were shaded by the porch overhang. Both of them greeted me with, 'Cheers, and where have you been?'

'The village,' I replied. 'Had a walk and then tea and back again.'

'All right for some,' Walter said, smiling, 'still it's my half-day tomorrow and I'm going fishing with Giles. How about that?'

'Sounds smashing. You'll enjoy it, I'm sure,' I said. 'Giles knows all there is about fishing.'

Walter's face beamed; he was so full of enthusiasm. Because he had no family, Giles had become like a father figure to him, like he was to me, someone to look up to. It was fortunate for Walter that he was working for such a nice household; he would be vulnerable in many others. There were many stories of maltreatment of young defenceless people with no families; it made me shiver to think about it. We were all fortunate!

Once in my room, I settled down to crochet. It felt a lot cooler and I was able to concentrate and I lost track of time until a tap on the door disturbed my thoughts.

'It's only me,' a voice called out, and in walked Catherine, looking flushed and breathless. 'Betty said I would find you here,' she said excitedly. She could hardly catch her breath. 'I ran across the meadow,' she gasped. 'Whew! I am so hot; I need a drink, please, Edith.'

'For goodness' sake,' I cried, 'come and sit down before you fall down.' I poured a glass of water and handed it to her. 'Here, drink this and sip it slowly, you will make yourself ill. It's far too hot to be rushing around.'

'Sorry,' Catherine whispered and flopped onto the bed, 'I've had such a wonderful time, there is so much to tell you.' She sipped the water gently until she was composed.

'That's better,' she said and reached for her bag. 'I have a letter for you. It's from Leslie. Daniel gave it to me to give to you.' Catherine's face was full of anticipation as she handed it to me. 'Go on, Edith, open it,' she cried excitedly.

It was a small sealed envelope with 'To Edith' written on the front. This was so unexpected that my hands trembled as I opened the letter. The handwriting was large and precise. I scanned the letter quickly before I read it out to Catherine. 'Well,' she said, 'what does it say?'

'It's an invitation out on my next half-day,' I said. 'If I let him know which day he will make arrangements. That's, of course, if I accept. He truly hopes so because he would love to meet me again! I can't believe it,' I cried, 'I never thought for one moment that he would be interested. Besides, I don't know him; I will have to think about it.'

'What is there to think about?' Catherine said. 'You liked him. You will never get to know anyone if you don't try! Come on, it will be good for you, especially after all that you have been through. There's no harm in it. He is really nice, quiet and polite. Daniel speaks highly of him.' She carried on talking relating to her time spent with Daniel that afternoon.

It was obvious that Catherine was smitten: her face glowed, her charismatic manner won everyone over every time.

'OK, maybe you are right,' I murmured. 'I will make sure of my half-day first. Perhaps we could all meet up together if it's possible. We both have the same half-day and it would make it easier for me, Catherine. Do you agree?'

'Daniel suggested that,' Catherine replied quickly. 'That's what I was hoping you would say.' She leapt up and gave me a hug. 'We'll have a lovely time, you wait and see.'

Catherine's enthusiasm seemed to rub off on to me and I began to feel excited.

'Yes,' I said, 'I think we will… but remember it's between us. I really don't want Mrs Baker to know. It's all very early days and she has been very kind to me throughout.'

'Mum's the word,' Catherine said. 'I understand, and it's nearly supper time and I am feeling hungry. We'd better not be late. Old Flo only needs an excuse and she will have us doing kitchen duties!'

We both burst out laughing – the image of Mrs Hewitt wagging her finger gave us a fit of giggles.

Because of the humidity, those of us who wished to eat outside were allowed to do so. We all seemed to find the picnic suppers exciting, only Mrs Baker and Flo didn't join the gathering. Young Walter couldn't be more pleased.

'We can talk about anything we like,' he said, laughing. 'Say one rude word, and it's "Watch your manners, young Walter! Remember where you are." Cor! Sometimes they are like two old biddies!'

Walter had us in fits of laughter throughout the evening until it was time for us to go in. We were beginning to feel tired and we all had an early start the next day. Having said that, it made little difference to Catherine and Betty, who sneaked into my room later to have a natter. Betty, of course, wanted to know all the news in detail, and so it was past midnight before any of us went to bed. The following morning I crawled out of bed looking hollow-eyed and wishing I could sleep for a week. Yes, an early night tonight, I said to myself. I need to look my best by next week if I was meeting Leslie.

My mouth was dry and I longed for a cup of tea. I had fifteen minutes before I started my chores, so it was a quick dash to the kitchen. Fortunately, Giles had arrived earlier and had made a huge pot of tea.

'Good morning, Edith, you be wanting a cuppa I dare say. You look if though you need one. Too many late nights aren't good.' He handed me the tea. 'Get that down you.'

'Thanks,' I said gratefully. 'And of course you are always right, Giles. What would we do without you?'

'Be off with you,' he said smiling. 'You'd best get going. Flo is on her way down, and she's not her best first thing in the morning.'

'I heard that, Giles!' Mrs Hewitt's voice boomed through the kitchen. 'Don't make me out to be a tyrant: I'm very tolerant with everyone,' she said, turning to look at me.

'Yes, of course, Mrs Hewitt,' I said quietly. 'Thank you for the tea.' I hurried out of the kitchen. Poor Giles, I thought!

The next few days were hot and sticky, with one or two thunderstorms in between. Lord and Lady Havis entertained a few guests, so we were kept busy. I managed a few walks in between, one with Betty. We were going to Swanage one half-day; however, Betty changed her mind after our walk to the village. She spotted Arthur cleaning the shop windows and realised that this would be her opportunity while she was with me. Courage seemed to take over and in no time at all they were chatting away. They were clearly suited, for the following week he invited her to a dance and no one could be more contented and happy than Betty.

Charlotte joined me on two occasions and was quite friendly and seemed to relax more. She regarded me as her friend and was able to confide in me. Her ambitions were high, but she lacked the confidence, even though she had a snooty air about her and gave the impression of being superior, underneath she was the opposite.

'You need to take every opportunity that comes your way,' I told her. 'You are very clever and astute; there is no need to be in domestic service for ever. One day it will happen.' I could see by Charlotte's face that she needed a boost now and again.

Thursday soon came around and arrangements had been made to meet Leslie and Daniel. Fortunately, Catherine and I were able to have the same half-day, even though Mrs Baker had wanted to change the rota. Catherine had pleaded with her that we had been invited to a poetry afternoon and we didn't want to miss it.

'Well, what can I say?' Mrs Baker said. 'You truly astound me! Poetry, indeed! What would Their Lordships think?' A note of sarcasm seemed to ring in her voice; no doubt she didn't believe a word of it – there wasn't much she didn't see through. 'How can I refuse?' she whispered. 'Culture is very important! So enjoy your afternoon.'

To be honest, I felt a little guilty. Mrs Baker could be brusque, but she had a kind heart and I had a lot to thank her for. However, it was only a white lie and I would have been mortified if she'd known the truth. Betty was sworn to secrecy and we promised to tell her everything on our return. We caught the 2 p.m. train from Verwood, dressed in our Sunday best, both feeling excited. Little did I know that my meeting with Leslie would change my life completely.

Chapter Fifteen

As the train drew into Swanage station, we scanned the platform to see if they were already there. We had arrived earlier than expected – in fact, ten minutes earlier – so we made our way to the tea room. A cup of tea would do the trick; it always had a calming affect and I certainly needed that.

Catherine could not stop chattering until she looked up to see Daniel squashing his nose against the window and waving his hand. He was quite amusing, making us laugh. Directly behind him was Leslie, who couldn't contain his amusement at Daniel's antics. It was then I realised how handsome he looked. I knew this day would be one I would treasure for a long time.

The afternoon sped by. At first shyness got the better of me and Leslie sensed it and put me at my ease. We walked up to the downs and then down to the beach, mingling with the crowds of sunbathers. The smell of the sea air and the warm sun was intoxicating; we paddled in the sea, splashing one another. Talk about children; we were worse! Any inhibitions we had were soon gone. A short walk from the beach we found a quaint tea shop. It was busy but we managed to find a table by the window. By this time we were feeling hungry so we ordered tea and sandwiches followed by scones. In those few hours we felt we had known each other for a long time.

Leslie was easy to talk to and not overfamiliar. We talked about our jobs, where we lived. It was all light-hearted and for the first time in ages I didn't feel the pang of loneliness of missing Peter. I was enjoying myself and knew I was attracted to Leslie. Like everything, all good things come to an end and it was time for us to return to Chatscott Hall, as the train left at 6.15 p.m. We had twenty minutes so we walked slowly back to the station. Daniel and Catherine lagged behind, discreetly giving Leslie and I the chance to arrange another meeting. There was no doubt that we both felt the same attraction and wanted to see each other again, so we arranged for the following Thursday, all being well.

'Must make the best of it,' Leslie said, 'you will be going back to London soon and what will we do?' His face had that quirky smile as he turned to look at me. He held my hand for a moment and squeezed it reassuringly. I felt myself blush. At that moment we reached the station and the train was just pulling in. I didn't want it to end; we stood there for a few moments. Leslie gently kissed me on the cheek and helped me on to the train.

'You take care now,' he whispered, 'and don't work too hard. Look forward to seeing you soon.' He moved aside, allowing Catherine to climb aboard. Daniel lifted her up just like she was a feather, smiling into her face; there was no doubt that he was smitten. Catherine was a lovely girl in looks and personality so it was no wonder he was drawn to her. The whistle blew and the train chugged slowly out of the station. We hung out of the window waving goodbye. Leslie and Daniel stood on the platform until we were out of sight. Neither of us spoke for a few minutes; we were relishing the precious time we had spent with them.

It didn't take long before Catherine burst out, 'Edith! I can't believe it! Everything is wonderful; it's been a perfect day.'

There was no stopping us as we laughed and giggled and confided in each other what Daniel and Leslie had said, as all girls do. The time sped by and in no time at all we had reached Verwood; the last bus had gone so we had to walk.

'I hope old Flo saves us some supper,' Catherine said, 'I'm beginning to feel peckish.'

'I'm sure she will,' I answered, 'but you know she is a stickler for time so we had better put our best foot forward.'

That evening after supper, Catherine, Betty and I managed to sneak away from the others, who were playing cards, on the pretence that we were going for a short walk. The evening was quite sultry so we made our way around to the back of the house where no one could see or hear us. There was an old garden seat that nestled below the eaves of the west wing; the wall had clinging wisteria which gave it a tranquil atmosphere. Betty said it gave her a sense of secrecy.

'Yes,' Catherine murmured, 'and remember whatever we tell you must be kept secret between ourselves.'

'Yes, of course,' Betty retorted, sounding quite offended. 'You know me better than that!'

'Sorry,' Catherine replied, 'but it would be more than our jobs are worth if Mrs Baker and old Flo were to find out. We are not allowed to fraternise with anyone while we are living at Chatscott Hall; that is one of the rules. Lord and Lady Havis made that quite clear to Mrs Baker for any staff who are taken on. Flo keeps poor old Giles at arm's length and makes out she isn't interested, but I know for a fact that she had drives in the country with him. Mrs Baker turns a blind eye. After all, it is a bit unfair, don't you think?'

'Yes,' I answered quickly, 'it's very unfair. In London that rule doesn't apply to us, and it shouldn't here. I can't believe their Lordships would be so strict. Did Mrs Baker tell you that herself?'

'No, come to think of it, she didn't,' Catherine retorted. 'It was Flo. I remember now there was a new maid last summer who was doing Charlotte's job. She had a beau who lived in the village. He was a constant visitor and upset old Flo. She made the girl's life unbearable until she left. One night at supper she gave us a lecture about fraternising and how Mrs Baker had told her about their Lordships' rules. We all believed her at the time, but I think she made the rule up herself because she was jealous and bitter. Her husband had left her after six months of marriage and she never got over it – that's what I was told by the woman in the village store. I felt sorry for her at the time, but the penny's dropped and I can see Mrs Baker never once made any reference to any rule about having beaus.'

Catherine's voice sounded angry. 'How could she?'

'Well,' I whispered, 'you know now, but it's still best to keep quiet about everything. We don't want our lives being made a misery even though we know it's not true. I for one would feel uncomfortable, and it's early days, especially for me. No one knows how things will turn out, and in any case I shall be returning to London shortly and that's a world away from here.'

I felt a pang of sadness which showed in my voice. 'However, I don't see why we shouldn't lead our own lives in our own time.'

Catherine and Betty nodded in agreement and both promised to keep mum about everything. Betty was bursting to know the events of the day. Recalling everything was quite exciting and we got carried away, not realising how late it was until Giles appeared.

'My my!' he cried. 'What have we here? Mothers' meeting! Do you girls not realise what time it is? Mrs Baker was sniffing around, wanting to know where you was. I thought I'd find you here. Best be back to your quarters; early start for you all. Don't give them any excuse to have a go.' He tapped his nose and nodded as if he knew what was going on between us.

'Thanks, Giles,' I whispered, 'you are a good friend. We appreciate it.'

'Be off with you!' he said. 'Don't want to see you young girls in any trouble. I'll say goodnight, then.' And off he went. Fortunately we managed to sneak in without anyone seeing us.

Waking the following morning to the sounds of laughter brought me to my senses. Whatever time it is, I must be late, I thought. Leaping out of bed, I drew the curtain to see what was going on outside. In the courtyard below were young Walter and Giles. It appeared that they were chasing a piglet. I must be dreaming, I thought. Walter was in fits at his attempts to catch the animal. Giles was running one way and almost slipped up! My mind couldn't focus; this was like a silent film, but of course it wasn't silent! I gazed at the clock on the mantle; it had just turned 5 a.m. so that was lucky. Most mornings, Betty or Catherine would give me a wake-up call. They had a bell-ringing clock which obediently went off at 5 a.m. each morning. Betty moaned that it was worse than the church bells!

No sooner had I got dressed than there was a knock on the door. 'Rise and shine!' It was Catherine, who called out, 'Did you manage to sleep?'

She pushed the door open. For that time of the morning she looked bright and bushy-tailed, putting me to shame.

'Not as much as you,' I murmured. 'I feel like I haven't slept. A cup of tea is what I need.'

'Betty has already gone to make one before old Flo shows her face,' Catherine said sarcastically. She was stood by the window, watching Giles and Walter. 'Looks like we'll be having bacon for breakfast!' she laughed. 'Poor little thing!'

'How could you be so cruel?' I said, trying not to laugh and yawn at the same time. 'I certainly don't have any appetite at this time of the morning. Come on, we had better make a move.'

The morning, although busy, seemed to drag for me, my thoughts were confused. I had been so excited about the day before. I had enjoyed my time with Leslie and was looking forward to seeing him again, but I had a sense of guilt, as though I was betraying Peter's memory. It was early days and I was still grieving, and to be honest I didn't really believe that I wouldn't see him again. I was concerned about Fanny and what she would think. I knew that Rose and Charlie would be happy for me, but Cook and Mrs Baker, I felt, would take a narrow view. I had been so devastated and felt my life would never be the same again ever. Everyone had supported me at the time and I will be always be grateful for that, but I needed to move on. In any case, I would be returning to London soon and any contact with Leslie would be by letter only. Maybe it would fizzle out. In the meantime, I would enjoy the time I have and not put too much emphasis on a fun time.

Later that day I had an afternoon break and decided to go for a walk and made my way to the path that led to the river. It was much cooler there. One or two men were fishing along the bank making it very tranquil. Further on I spotted Giles. That's a coincidence, I thought. I felt I needed to talk to someone and Giles was the best person to open up to. He always had time to listen and you never felt it was an imposition. He turned around as I approached him.

'Well, what a surprise,' he said jovially. 'Sit yourself down. Nice to have a bit of company.' That was his way of asking if I wanted to talk. Of course I did, and he listened without interruption until I stopped.

'Edith, my girl,' he said, 'you are young and have all your life in front of you. What has happened is in the past and you mustn't feel guilty about it. Enjoy your life and take what it has to offer. Don't be too hasty in matters of the heart; if it is meant to be, it will happen.' He squeezed my hand reassuringly. 'You had better make a move if you are on duty, my girl. Don't want you being late, eh?'

'Thanks, Giles,' I whispered. 'You are a good, kind and wise man.'

'Be off with you! It isn't any trouble,' he murmured. 'Life's too short my dear.'

I waved goodbye and made my way back, feeling like a weight had been lifted.

My life changed completely in the weeks that followed. Any time I had off, I spent with Leslie. We sent each other letters and arranged the occasional telephone call. Mrs Baker never questioned me at any time, although I'm sure she suspected something was going on. However, she was a very astute person and knew that we would be returning to London shortly and any romance would soon be forgotten or fizzle out. After all, London was a distance away and life there was very different. I was beginning to dread the thought of returning. I would miss everyone and I had no memories here, not sad ones, anyway.

However, in retrospect, it would put things into perspective. I would know my true feelings, being apart. It would be some kind of test. Both of us needed to be sure and it was still early days. Once I was back in London among the household of Muswell Hill, maybe I would feel differently, but who was I kidding? Time would tell and I felt happy to continue with things as they were.

Mrs Hewitt had arranged a special supper for Mrs Baker, which included all of us, on the eve of her departure, and mine. We were returning on the first Monday of September, a week before their Lordships would return. I had planned to see Leslie on my half-day, three days before our departure. I knew this might be our last rendezvous for sometime and wanted to make it very special. Catherine and Betty didn't want me to leave and made me promise to write every week once I was back in London.

'One day we will come to see you and you can show us London,' they both said enthusiastically.

'I shall look forward to that time,' I said, smiling at them both. 'Let's see what happens.'

Thursday soon came and I felt excited and sad. I told myself that this wasn't the end but the beginning of a new era in my life. I remembered Giles and the advice that he had given me. We all had choices to make and I felt I would make the right one when the time came.

My afternoon with Leslie was wonderful. We walked and talked, even went for a trip round the bay at Swanage, ending with tea and scones at the tea room near the beach. Both of us wanted to make it last, for it would be some time before we saw each other again. We both agreed to write and send a snapshot of each other for a keepsake. The walk back to the station made everything seem final. Standing on the platform I felt lost for words until Leslie said, 'Don't look so sad, I'll make sure there's a letter waiting for you on your return. Besides I'm coming to London sooner than you think.'

He looked at me with that quirky smile and all my doubts vanished. He folded his arms around me and kissed me gently.

'You had better get on the train before I change my mind,' he whispered. 'I might not let you leave!'

He held my arm and helped me on to the train. 'You take care,' he said, and stood back. The train began to pull out. The whistle had gone. I stood by the window waving until he was out of sight. The hollow feeling I felt soon disappeared. I knew instinctively that we would be together no matter what.

Monday soon came round. I had packed, with the help of Catherine and Betty, the night before. We had all gathered for breakfast, including Giles, who was driving us to the station. Mrs Hewitt insisted that we should eat a cooked breakfast.

'You be going a long day without proper food,' she cried. 'It ain't good for you.' She turned to Mrs Baker and said, 'I've packed some sandwiches, fresh ham and tomato. Much better for you both than the rubbish they serve in the dining car. And you, young lady,' she said, turning to me, 'you look far better now than when you arrived here. You have roses in your cheeks and you're a little plumper. It be this Dorset air!'

Everyone burst out laughing. There was no doubt with her Dorset accent and her claim that she spoke proper English came over as very funny. To be truthful, under that hard exterior she could be kind and compassionate, regardless of her resentment towards the male of the species, apart from Giles. I would miss her. I would miss them all.

Giles had brought the car around to the staff entrance, with Their Lordships' permission.

'Let's have them bags,' he cried, 'the train leaves at 10.30 and it is always on time. I know Wilfred the driver; he be a stickler for punctuality, so we better make a move. Now!'

There were hugs all round and even one from young Walter. 'Come back soon,' he said, his voice faltering. 'Dorset is better than London. We are one big family here, so don't forget us.'

'Of course not, Walter,' I said, trying hard not to cry. 'You are like my younger brother and I will write to you.'

His face lit up, he grinned, and turned to look at everyone. Mrs Baker, who had stood by looking bemused, whispered to Walter, 'I'll make sure, don't you worry,' and patted him on the head.

We climbed into the car. Mrs Baker who normally didn't show any emotion sniffed at her hanky and waved to everyone. Charlotte who had stood in the background suddenly shot forward and grasped my hand.

'Take care, Edith,' she said, her voice faltering. 'Don't forget, will you?' She slid a piece of paper into my hand and whispered, 'Read it later.' Before I could answer the car pulled away and we had turned the corner into the drive. I looked back at Chatscott Hall, knowing this would be my lasting memory of this majestic place and the people in it.

We arrived back in London late afternoon. Albert was waiting for us at the station, his happy demeanour shining through.

'Nice to have you back,' he said jovially. 'Agatha has been looking forward to your return. You're been sorely missed by all. Let's have your bags; the car is a five-minute walk away.' Smiling at us he added, 'It's busy round the station today; an extra train has been put on. A rally in Hyde Park; something to do with the unions so I was told. We are well out of it.'

Albert picked the bags up and guided us through the throng. The afternoon sun was beating down. It appeared to be even hotter in London than Dorset. We were glad of the comfort of the car. It was cool and, when we were moving, gave out a gentle breeze. Most of the way we chatted and I could tell by Mrs Baker's expression and the way that she spoke that she wasn't sure how Cook's and Albert's relationship had progressed. For some reason, it made her feel insecure. I suppose Cook was her friend of many years, they had both been employed in the household for at least fifteen years and had relied on each other for friendship and maybe she was afraid of losing her confidante. Her husband had gone missing during the First World War. Such was her loss, she vowed never to marry again. This I had learned from Charlie, who overheard their conversation one evening. Her life in service had been her future and she was contented with that. She enjoyed the responsibility of being in charge and never deviated from it. I would think the thought of losing her closest friend was too much of a challenge.

Arriving at the house, we were greeted by Rose and Charlie, who had slipped out of the house by the back door. It was amazing to see the change in them both in just a few months. Rose was definitely plumper and Charlie had somehow lost his paunch. They looked so happy. While Charlie and Albert sorted the luggage out and Rose attended to Mrs Baker, I made my way to the kitchens, to find Cook had prepared a high tea. The aroma of freshly baked scones wafted across. I could see a cooked ham alongside a salad dish, which included baby potatoes. This is the life of Riley, I thought. It's not what you know, it's who you know! This was for Mrs Baker's benefit, while their Lordships were away. There was no need for any doubts: Cook would always be her best friend what ever the outcome.

'Well I must say, you look a sight better now than ya did when you left 'ere!' Cook's voice boomed out as she appeared from the scullery laden with plates. 'Don't just stand there, girl, give me a hand!'

This was her way of saying welcome back! By this time, Rose had returned. She gave me a hug and said, 'Cor blimey, Edith we 'ain't half missed you! Ain't that true, Cook?'

'If you say so,' Cook murmured looking at me with a twinkle in her eye. 'I've had to keep a tight rein on things; Rose had her work cut out with the extra duties. Anna was very poorly at one stage. Doctor said she was run down due to being under-nourished when she left Poland. Anyway she is back on her feet now. Freda and Daisy, give them their due, got stuck in. It's all been done from top to bottom; no problems for Mrs Baker to worry about.'

Eyeing me up and down Cook, said 'You've got ten minutes if ya want to freshen up,' and turning to Rose she added, 'I take it Charlie has taken Mrs Baker's bags to her quarters. I daresay she is tired after the journey.' Looking at me again, she mumbled, 'You still here?'

'I'm off, Cook,' I said quickly and hurried out of the kitchen.

The feeling of being back home swept over me. I looked around me, taking in all the familiar things. Not much had changed. Rose's bed strewn with her clothes, like always; the smell of lavender water which she kept by her bedside; the chest of drawers; the wash bowl and jug with the crack down the side of it; my bed neatly made with clean sheets. That would have been Rose's idea, bless her. I looked again and noticed the photograph of Peter on the little table by my bed, a posy of flowers had been placed alongside. This was Rose, lovely Rosie, so thoughtful. The tears welled up in my eyes. The thought of having to say that I had met someone else felt like a betrayal; the love I had for Peter would always be with me. However, I had met Leslie and what I felt for him was different. None of it was planned, it just happened, and whatever the future had in store I would go along with. In any case, it was still early days, and who knew what the future would bring?

Later that evening, after supper, I confided in Rose, who had been looking forward to hearing all the news. At first I hesitated and told her how much I had enjoyed my time there and the friends I had made and what we had got up to and so on.

'Sounds like you had a working holiday,' Rose cried. 'Cor blimey! What will Cook say? She was really worried about you. Kept asking if I had heard anything, and then the cards arrived. Albert read them out for me. He's a good reader!'

Her voice suddenly fell to a whisper and she bent forward and murmured, 'I know you, Edith. You're not telling me something, I can tell by your face.'

Her mouth was twitching as she looked at me. I began to smile; there was no fooling her. And so it all came out. Not once did she interrupt, and at the end she held my hand and said,

'Good on you, gal! I'm happy for you, and Charlie will be, too, but it's best kept a secret for now. Cook and Mrs Baker… whew! Not a good idea, eh? They have old-fashioned views, so what they don't know, they can't talk about, and in a few months' time it won't matter anyway.' She was smiling into my face and said, 'Ain't I right?'

'Yes, you are,' I murmured, 'and you are a true friend, indeed.'

Chapter Sixteen

The next few months proved she was right. Leslie came to London on two visits and telephoned when he was able to, and of course I had to inform Mrs Baker if I was expecting a call and be there when the telephone rang. Fortunately, Their Lordships never used the telephone in the library, certainly not in the evening. Mrs Baker never questioned me, but her manner was abrupt each time, and I felt she was aware of something going on. There was one occasion when I entered the kitchen to find Mrs Baker and Cook in deep conversation and unaware of my presence.

'It's just a year since it 'appened,' Cook muttered. 'Can't believe she would behave like that, in any case—' Suddenly she stopped, realising that I was stood there. 'Cor blimey, Edith!' She began to stutter. 'You nearly gave us a heart attack, creeping in like that.'

Before she could say any more, Mrs Baker nudged her arm and said, 'Agatha! For goodness' sake,' and gave Cook one of her meaningful looks. Then turning to me she said, 'While you're here, Edith, you might as well make some tea. I think we are all ready for one – I am,' she said, smiling at me.

There was a short pause before Cook spoke. She sounded quite sheepish, muttering, 'There's some freshly baked biscuits in the larder, I'll fetch them.'

At that moment Rose and Anna appeared from out of the scullery. I could tell by Rose's face that she had heard some of the conversation. She had an I-told-you-so look!

Once tea was made, we all sat round the table discussing the evening ahead. Their Lordships were having a dinner party, so there was a lot of preparation to be done. The previous conversation was soon forgotten and the uncomfortable feeling I felt soon disappeared.

Christmas soon came and the household was buzzing with excitement. Their Lordships had invited guests for Christmas and the New Year, which would mean a lot of preparation for us all. I had received a letter from Irene. The family missed me and wondered if I would be able to come home for Christmas, that's if I was allowed the time. Ivor was travelling down to stay to have a family get-together and was hoping to see me as well.

My heart sank. I desperately wanted to be with them, but we had been firmly told by Mrs Baker that Their Lordships had stressed that everyone should be on duty over the yuletide celebrations so there was very little that could be done; our jobs were important. Any spare time that I had, I spent writing letters and Christmas postcards. I had kept in touch with Catherine and Betty, who in turn wrote to me with all the news. Part of the house had been closed off until next spring and those who had families were allowed to spend Christmas at home. Mrs Hewitt, Giles and Betty, and also young Walter, were spending it at Chatscott Hall. It made me feel that I wanted to be in two places at once!

During Christmas, Rose and Charlie announced that they would be tying the knot on St Valentine's Day, although they had planned to be married in the previous autumn. It was cancelled due to circumstances which had made it difficult for them. However, having talked it over with Mrs Baker and Cook, it was decided that 14 February would be ideal. They would be married in the register office nearby and a wedding tea would be provided by their Lordships as part of a wedding gift for their service and loyalty.

Charlie's family had moved to Leeds and unfortunately it seemed unlikely that they would be able to come, due to the distance and lack of funds. However, Mrs Baker decided that Charlie deserved a bonus for all his good efforts, which would go towards paying for his mother's fare and a new outfit. Charlie was over the moon. It would mean everything to him to have his mother present, the icing on the cake.

Rose, who had no family, was only too happy to have his mother witness their vows. She had already made her dress with the help of Mrs Baker and Freda, who were clever with the needle. Unlike most brides-to-be, Rose didn't mind everyone seeing it (apart from Charlie). She was so proud and the dress was beautiful, daintily stitched with rosebuds around the neckline and cuffs. The colour was cream with a white underskirt; Rose had saved enough to buy white stockings and shoes to match. Mrs Baker had also given her a pair of white lace gloves. Daisy and Anna had secretly made a blue garter for her.

'It's an English tradition,' Daisy explained to Anna, who had been mystified at first. She had never heard of it in Poland.

Throughout the festive days, we were working into the small hours. Although it was very tiring, we enjoyed the time of celebration; there was so much excitement, the whole household was buzzing and the knowledge of Rose's and Charlie's wedding in the coming weeks lifted everyone's spirits.

Rose had asked me to be her bridesmaid. I gladly accepted. We agreed that I should wear my powder-blue dress with the lace collar, which had been Peter's favourite. At first I had doubts about wearing the dress, as it was a reminder.

However, Rose made me see sense. 'You have to go forward,' she said. 'Peter will always be part of your life, but he has gone and you've met someone else who you care about. Don't waste your life thinking it's wrong, for Gawd's sake, Edith. You can't grieve for ever. You've done all you can!' Her voice lowered to a whisper. 'Be happy, like me and Charlie.'

The New Year came in with a bang, so to speak. Firecrackers were lit on the stroke of midnight and the New Year celebrations carried on until the early hours; we were all pretty exhausted the following day. Charlie had only managed to have few hours' sleep. He had been replenishing the drinks cabinet, so it was back and forth to the wine cellar.

Cook made sure that he had a hearty breakfast. 'You look fit to drop, Charlie,' she cried, 'all hollow-eyed. Early night tonight, lad! And that goes for all of ya,' she said, eyeing us up. 'After today, it's back to normality. Once the guests have left, there will be a lot of clearing up to be done. Mrs Baker is making a rota up for the rest of the week, so you will all have your work cut out.'

Poor Charlie, who was sat listening, just nodded in agreement. He was past caring! The rest of us knew it would be futile to comment; we were our masters' slaves! Most of New Year's Day went by quietly, everyone with their own thoughts, just going through the motions. Only at teatime did life begin to seep in. Steaming hot tea and biscuits seemed to do the trick.

Albert managed to pop in to say hello. 'It's been manic for the last two days,' he cried. 'I haven't had time to breathe. The last guest went a half-hour ago, so I've sneaked out. I could smell the biscuits; no one bakes them like you,' he said, winking at Cook. Not a word passed her lips; her look said everything. Albert knew when to stop, especially where Cook was concerned. He quickly sat down next to little Anna, who was trying very hard not to giggle. She found the idea of an older couple having an attraction to each other hilarious. Anyone over fifty was far too old. Rose had explained to her about Cook and Albert, that it was a friendship between them and it was to be kept very private; Cook would be very angry if she heard any tittle tattle. So Anna was sworn to secrecy. She knew it would be more than her job was worth. In any case, Anna was intimidated by Cook and always tried not to upset her.

After tea we were all given a two-hour rest period, which Mrs Baker had suggested under the circumstances.

'I want you all looking bright and perky. We have a busy evening, but not a late one,' she said, sounding relieved.

Fortunately for all of us, we were able to go to our quarters at 10.30 p.m., which everyone welcomed. My eyelids felt so heavy, and when my head touched the pillow, I fell asleep.

We must have been really tired, for the next thing I remember was Rose shaking me.

'The clock didn't go off!' she cried. 'It's nearly six! Gawd knows what trouble we'll be in. You'd better hurry up. No time for a cuppa.' She was franticly trying to put her skirt on and brush her hair at the same time.

I scrambled out of bed and focused my eyes. 'Sorry, Rose, you go on down. I'll get dressed and collect my dust box and start cleaning the fire places. Mrs Baker won't be up yet, and if Cook starts to yell, you tell her it was my fault. I didn't wind the clock up, or anything you like to think of. I don't mind.'

'Don't be daft,' Rose said, her voice sounding calmer. 'I'll just turn a deaf ear like I always do! I had better go.'

Just as she was about to open the door, I noticed she had put her skirt on inside out.

'Rose,' I called, 'your skirt!'

'Yeah, I know,' she cried, 'this side is clean!' Then she was gone.

Strangely enough, nobody had noticed our late appearance, so both of us decided to keep quiet. Cook continued to give out orders over breakfast, so nothing had changed. The next few days were uneventful as the household had quietened down. Their Lordships were back into their daily routine, which brought a peace and order below stairs; no continuous bell-ringing, which always brought on Cook's migraines, so all was well.

We spent our evenings playing cards and knitting. Most of January we had heavy falls of snow and it was bitterly cold, so we were glad of our warm kitchen. Their Lordships requested warming pans and fires in the bedrooms while the cold snap lasted. Rose and I heated flat irons for our beds, and wrapped them in cloth and placed them at the bottom of the beds where our feet would be.

'If your feet are warm,' Cook told us, 'it will keep your whole body warm,' which we found to be true.

In the weeks that followed, Leslie's letters increased in frequency; sometimes it was three a week. I was limited to one telephone call every seven days, and that was for five minutes only. The trouble was that we found it increasingly difficult not to be able to see each other. The winter made travelling less frequent, and this particular winter was very harsh. Railway lines had been blocked by snowfalls, and fierce blizzards had brought telephone lines down, which brought everything to a standstill.

Their Lordships never travelled very far in those cold weeks. They had a few bridge afternoons, which kept them entertained, and one or two visits to the theatre in the evenings, but apart from that they stayed in and had us running up and down stairs all through the day. We never dared grumble.

'That's what you're paid for!' Cook would say. 'We are paid servants and have to respect that; remember you have a roof over ya heads!' No point in arguing with that statement; she was right.

By the end of February the weather improved and things got

easier. Leslie wrote, saying he would be travelling to London at the beginning of February. His employers were sending him on an errand, and would it be possible to meet up sometime that day, in the afternoon, providing I could arrange the time off. It had been months since we last seen each other, and this was an opportunity that I wasn't going to let slip. I waited until lunch was over. I knew that Mrs Baker would be in her quarters and this was her best time of day; she was less tetchy. It seemed like she was expecting me, for when I reached her door, it was ajar. I gently tapped.

Mrs Baker called out, 'Come in, Edith.'

I was astonished to say the least. She was sat in her armchair with her glasses perched on her nose, holding the roster board. Eyeing me over her specs, she murmured, 'I assume you that you are here to rearrange your half-day… am I right?' To say I was lost for words was an understatement.

'Don't look so surprised, Edith,' she said. 'I have been aware of the changes in you for some time; with the amount of correspondence you have been receiving, I could not fail to notice. I do not wish to pry, but I have a duty while you are under my care to make sure you are not being led astray. You have been through a long period of stress and have been very vulnerable, and as you know their Lordships care about all of you. We are a hard-working and happy household and look out for each other, not like some I could mention.' Mrs Baker beckoned me to sit.

'Thank you,' I said quietly, 'I appreciate your concern and I apologise. I would like to explain.' The words seemed to flow out quite easily. I felt a sense of relief when I had finished. Looking at Mrs Baker, her face seemed almost expressionless.

'Well,' she murmured, 'you have it all worked out. You are in your twenties now, a grown woman. What can I say? You are very positive and sensible. However, you are still vulnerable and the fact is you both live a distance away from one another. What sort of courtship will you be having? Maybe it's a good thing that you have a period of separation. In any case, Edith, you have my blessing and our conversation will go no further. I can see no reason why you shouldn't have the half-day,' she added, removing her glasses and folding her arms, giving me a wry smile.

'Remember, you have your whole life in front of you, so don't rush into anything,' she whispered.

'Thank you, Mrs Baker,' I said, 'I do appreciate your advice and understanding. I will not let you down, I promise.'

'Off with you,' Mrs Baker said, rising from her chair, 'I have a pile of sewing to get through and you have tea duty this afternoon. Close the door behind you.'

I stood outside the door for a few minutes. I was so relieved. I need not feel guilty any more, I had nothing to hide.

Apart from Rose and Mrs Baker, no one knew of my rendezvous that day. I hadn't seen Leslie for some months and wanted to know how I would feel on seeing him again. Maybe we might feel differently about each other. However, I was so excited I wasn't able to eat my lunch.

Cook looked at me but never passed any comment. Charlie kept winking at me, and Rose kept nudging him to behave. The bemused looks on the other girls' faces didn't help, so I soon lost my appetite. Making my excuses, I returned to my quarters to get ready. It was still very cold, so I wore my only winter coat over a navy-blue wool dress, with a thick woolly hat and mitts that I had made, and wrapped a knitted scarf around my neck. Feeling very snug, I left to catch the bus at the end of the road, which left at 1.45. I had arranged to meet Leslie at 2.30. Providing there were no hold-ups, I should reach our meeting place well in time. Fortunately the roads had been cleared, but traffic was slow. I noticed the huge piles of snow that had been shovelled to the sides of the roads; it had been chaotic for all those who had to travel. Thank goodness, I thought, I had a live-in job.

My thoughts started to drift. I remembered when I told Fanny about Leslie. It was just before Christmas. We had met for tea to catch up on everything. We exchanged gifts and talked about my time in Dorset and her new nursing post, which wasn't far from Peter's home.

'It's ideal,' she explained, 'I work one week of nights and one week of days. I organise Mother so that she isn't left alone; she is quite frail now and needs constant attention, but of course she never complains and nags me to go out more. She was delighted to know that we were meeting today, and sends her love to you.' Fanny's voice faltered slightly. 'Of course she misses everyone, but life must go on.'

Looking at Fanny's face, I nearly lost the courage to tell her. However, Leslie was just a boyfriend, and there was no harm in that. Firstly, we talked about Dorset and the friends I had made, and Leslie being one of them. Fanny's face lit up.

'I am so pleased for you, Edith,' she said. 'We have all had a difficult and sad time, and you especially. You need to move forward; Peter would be happy for you.'

'Thank you, Fanny,' I whispered, 'that means a lot to me.'

She smiled and squeezed my hand and said, 'Let's have another cream cake, eh?'

That was the last time I saw Fanny. In the months that followed, Fanny sold the house and took her mother to Portugal to live. The climate was warmer, which gave her mother a new lease of life. Although she promised to keep in touch, I only received one card and heard no more.

Leslie was waiting by the bus stop when I arrived. Although he was wearing a thick overcoat, he looked frozen. I noticed the bunch of flowers that he was holding. My heart missed a beat. Seeing his face, I knew my feelings hadn't changed. I realised how much I had missed him. Leslie's face lit up when he saw me. I hurried towards him with a feeling of elation. The warmth of his arms around me assured me of his feelings. I had no doubts.

The few hours we had were spent talking. We found a Lyons tea room not far from the bus station. It was throbbing with people who had come in out of the cold. The smell of toasted teacakes and coffee wafted through. By sheer luck there was a table empty by the window, the waitress was clearing away the dishes and wiping it clean. We made ourselves comfortable and ordered toasted cakes and tea. Both of us were feeling hunger pangs from the cold.

The flowers that Leslie had given me were lovely, red and white chrysanthemums wrapped in white paper and ribbon; it was such a romantic gesture. At first, I was at a loss for words, but once we got talking, there was no stopping us. We got through numerous pots of tea, both of us telling each other all the events of the past months. There was so much catching up to do. Although we had only met the previous summer, it felt like we had known each other for a very long time. We made each other laugh and the happiness I felt, I couldn't describe.

Suddenly Leslie became serious. Holding my hand, he murmured, 'Edith, it's obvious to me that we feel strongly about each other, and living so far apart doesn't give us any chance to be together, so I want you to think seriously about my suggestion. I have been offered a job at the Grand Hotel in Swanage, as a trainee manager. It's a step up for me, the wages are better, and I have my own room.' His voice faltered slightly. Looking at me, he said, 'There are a couple of vacancies for waitresses, which will be available after Easter, and I know I can recommend you. That's if you want to do this.'

Squeezing my hand gently, he said quietly, 'Think about it seriously before you make any decisions. I don't want to push you into an awkward situation, or make you feel obliged, so don't say anything until you've had time to consider.'

For the second time that day I was speechless. A few moments of silence passed until I found my voice.

'Well, Leslie,' I whispered, 'you don't do things by halves. I certainly will think about it.'

His face had that quirky smile as he said, 'You do that!'

The bus left at 5.45. Leslie waved me off and left to catch the train from Waterloo. It had started to snow again and I huddled up to the window. I wrapped my scarf around my chin to keep warm. The bus was full apart from a couple of seats. Once the ticket collector had been around, I settled down, my mind racing.

I just couldn't believe all that had been said. I certainly hadn't expected Leslie's proposal; this would need a lot of thought. I loved my job, in as much I was part of a family. I had learned discipline, which in the beginning was very hard. The long hours and missing my family in Wales took some time to get used to, but my life had changed; it was a far cry from the stark hardships of home. I had independence, which gave me strength of character, and of course last but not least, there was Peter, who had become part of my life. All my memories were here. I would leave them all behind if I moved to Dorset. Could I really do that?

There was no doubt in my mind. I loved Leslie, even though it was different from Peter. Different personalities... different kind of love.

My mind started to drift and I suddenly felt tired. I closed my eyes. The next thing, the conductor was shaking my arm, 'Time to get off, miss,' he said, 'this is the station.'

Looking startled, I apologised, and scrambled off. I had missed my stop so I had a long walk ahead. The snow was still falling and the cold air took my breath away. The street lamps looked hazy through the winter fall. I hunched my back, pulled my hat over my ears, my scarf round my chin and set off. I arrived at the house just after 7.30, looking bedraggled and cold. As I entered the kitchen I could feel the warmth of the ovens that radiated around.

'Cor blimey!' Cook's voice boomed out. 'Where in heaven's name 'ave you been? You look frozen, gal!'

Rose and Anna appeared from the scullery to see what all the commotion was about. Their faces showed disbelief.

'Better get them wet things off. Fetch a towel, will ya, Rose,' Cook bellowed, making poor Anna jump. By this time I was beginning to shiver. I hung my wet clothes in the scullery and Rose wrapped the towel round me.

'You'd better sit near the oven to warm up,' she whispered, 'and I'll get you a hot drink. Cor blimey, gal, where did you get to?'

After I had explained what had happened, Rose called me a dozy devil and Cook suggested that a hot bath would be in order.

'Friday's bath night,' she said, 'but it won't matter if we make it tonight.' Three of us shared the water. 'You two don't mind,' she said turning to Rose and Anna, 'it's boiling all the water up. Best get it out of the way.'

They both nodded in agreement.

There was a tin bath in the scullery which we used, and it took some filling. It was curtained off to give us privacy. Charlie kept well away! So after supper we heated pans of water. I was first in – clean flannel and Lifebuoy soap. We were allowed five minutes each; the water only kept warm for a short while even though we topped it up, so we took it in turns each week.

By 10 p.m. we were in our quarters. I had heated a flat iron to warm the bed. The room was icy cold, even though we had burned a few logs in the fireplace earlier. Rose had insisted that I tell her all that had been said that day. I decided not to mention Leslie's proposal until I had made my mind up; it wouldn't be fair. Sleep on it, I told myself. By morning I would know.

Waking up after a deep sleep and feeling wide awake, I climbed out of bed, wrapping my dressing gown around me. I crept to the window. It was still very early, just turned 4.45. Rose had the covers over her head and was snoring gently. I wouldn't wake her yet – it was freezing. The window was covered in icicles and I could hardly see out. Looking at the fireplace, I could see a few embers shimmering. I noticed a log inside the basket. Rose had saved it, bless her. Within a few minutes I had managed to light a fire; blowing and puffing seemed to work. I rubbed my hands to warm them. Looking at the flickering flames, I recalled the events of the day before. In my heart I knew I had made a decision, one that would change my life for ever.

Chapter Seventeen

Valentine's Day arrived, and it was Rose and Charlie's wedding. Cook had been up since the crack of dawn, preparing food and nibbles. Everyone sensed the atmosphere, which was quite exciting. Rose had hardly slept for excitement.

'I'm full of butterflies, Edith,' she cried. 'In six hours' time I'll be married! Me and Charlie will be man and wife! It's really scary. Gawd knows how it's going to be, living together in the same room. I mean, you know, sharing the same bed! I don't know much about anything.' Her face was wet from tears.

'Look, Rose,' I whispered, 'it's wedding jitters. I've got butterflies, too, and it's not me that's getting married! You love Charlie, don't you? Trust me, Rose, everything will be fine. Charlie will cherish you. Both of you have so much to look forward to: your own quarters, making plans together, being Mr and Mrs Barlow. You are going to be so happy. Come on, Rose,' I said, 'wash your face and I'll help you get ready, but first I'll fetch you a cup of tea to calm your nerves. I know I need one!'

The register office was decorated with flowers when we arrived, and the sun filtered through the window. Rose looked a picture in her beautiful dress. She was a slip of a girl alongside Charlie, who looked smart in his new suit and buttonhole. There was just Charlie's mother, Mrs Baker, Cook and, of course, me to witness the service. Albert waited outside with a camera to take some photographs. He had borrowed a camera and tripod from a friend of his, much to everyone's delight.

Charlie's mother could not contain her emotions and wept throughout the service. She was so proud and looked pretty in her new dress, something she hadn't had for a very long time. Life had been very hard for her and the children. Charlie had been her rock for most of the time, but now he had his own path to follow. He adored his mother and would always be there for her regardless.

Lord and Lady Havis made an appearance at the wedding tea, congratulating Rose and Charlie and presenting them with a china teapot. Both Charlie and Rose were lost for words; this was the icing on the cake, and it could not have been a happier day, finishing with a champagne toast, courtesy of Mrs Baker. Cheers, everyone!

My quarters felt empty without Rose and in the weeks that followed I hardly had a chance to have a real natter with her. Rose and Charlie were inseparable. Any spare time they had, they spent in their quarters, painting and decorating. Their Lordships had given permission and supplied the wallpaper and paint. Mrs Baker made some covers for their chairs, so it was all very exciting for them both. There was some envy shown by the other maids, and I must admit I felt it, too. However, they both deserved a chance in life, and I could only wish them the best. Besides, they would have to work hard for it, always be on call whenever required, but to Rose and Charlie this was their home, and would be for some time.

Feeling somewhat on my own, I started to give more thought to my own future. Leslie kept in touch by letter and never once asked for my decision. We managed to speak on the telephone once or twice. It was very brief, just a few loving exchanges and how we missed each other. The ball was in my court and I knew that I had to take that step one way or another. Easter came, and the visitors, too. The household was buzzing once again and there was no time for brooding. The weather became warmer and the snow and ice disappeared; spring was around the corner. The daffodils began to bloom and the whole of Easter was blessed with sunshine, giving everyone incentive.

Shortly after Easter I handed in my notice. Mrs Baker wasn't surprised and said that she had been expecting it. Their Lordships were saddened, but wished me well. Rose and Charlie tried to talk me out of it, but knew it was futile. Cook was quite remote at first and never passed any comment until the day of leaving. She had packed me a lunch and Albert offered to take me to the station; the Deanswalls were away, which was fortunate for me. I didn't fancy the bus journey with my luggage. There were hugs all round and a few tears. Just as I climbed into the car, Cook stepped forward. She whispered, 'Don't ya forget, if things don't work out, I'll make sure there is a job here for ya – you're a good girl, Edith.'

All the emotion I was holding in suddenly gave way. The feeling of losing my friends swept over me. This had been my life for the last few years. Rose and Cook had always been there for me, not forgetting Mrs Baker, who had always been understanding and lenient. They were like my family and I would miss them very much. The car moved off and I waved until they were out of sight. The tears flowed. Albert handed me a hanky.

'You will feel better once you have got it out of your system,' he said. 'It's a big wrench, but you've got a lot to look forward to: a new life, the countryside with clean air, making new friends, a nice chap with a good job – what more can you ask for? So dry your tears, we are nearly at the station.'

Albert made sure my luggage was in place and I had a seat next to the window.

'When you arrive and are safely settled in,' he murmured, 'telephone Mrs Baker and let her know you are OK. Now you take care, young Edith. You never know, perhaps we might pay a visit to Swanage!'

Thanking Albert for his kindness, I kissed him on the cheek. By this time the whistle had gone and the train slowly moved out. I watched Albert walk away, turning to wave as he did so. That was the last time I saw him.

Leslie was waiting at the station when I arrived at Swanage, his face full of anticipation until he saw me step off the train, and hurried forward to help me with my luggage. The excitement I felt at seeing him again was overwhelming. Any doubts I had soon vanished. He put his arms around me and hugged me as if he would never let me go.

'I've been counting the days,' he whispered, 'and now you are here, this is just the beginning. I know you will be happy.' He smiled into my face and said, 'Fancy a cup of tea? I would think you must be ready for one.'

The tea room was quite busy so we shared a table with an elderly couple who smiled at us sweetly (love's sweet dream). Leslie explained to me that I would be sharing a room with another girl who worked at the Grand Hotel. 'She is a chamber-maid, a very quiet girl, but she gets on with her work I'm sure you will both get on together.'

He explained that I would be starting work the next morning and the head waiter would show me the ropes. He was a hard taskmaster but very fair: as long as you did your job properly, looked smart, and most of all were punctual, there would be no problems. My face must have given my thoughts away. It didn't instil much confidence. I had visions of a rather stony-faced man with a starched collar, clapping his hands together. Chop, chop!

Leslie burst out laughing. Holding my hand, he said, 'It's all right, Edith, don't look so worried. It's not like the workhouse! This is a first-class hotel with very high standards. You'll be fine. You have served gentry; that is your recommendation. Everyone one will love you!'

To my surprise, I settled in quite quickly. My first day saw me serving breakfast. I started at 6.30 a.m. The tables were laid the night before. Everything was immaculate, white starched napkins with polished cutlery. The hotel, which was quite opulent, catered for the wealthy. There were four waitresses and two waiters. I worked alongside Mary from Ireland. She was a cheerful person, and put me at my ease. She told me about Dennis, the head waiter.

'He's OK, but lacks a sense of humour. His bark is worse than his bite, bit of a loner,' she said laughingly. 'You'll get used to his funny ways to be sure!'

My quarters were below stairs; most of the staff that lived in were accommodated in the basement. I shared with Alice the chambermaid, a slight and inoffensive girl. Unlike Rose, she was neat and tidy, which was just as well, for the room was small and sparse but clean. My bed was by the window. We shared a wardrobe and a chest of drawers and a small washbasin in the corner. There was very little light coming through the window because of the basement wall, so the room was always dark. Fortunately there was a staff room on the ground floor with a few comfy chairs; most of the staff used it in their rest time. There was a staff dining room adjacent to the kitchens where we had our meals, the food was adequate, but not like Cook's!

Within a few weeks it was like I had been there for a long time. Although I missed everyone, I soon adapted and adjusted to the routine. Leslie made sure we spent time together, even though we had to be discreet. Most days we went for a walk, if only for an hour. It made all the difference. We went to the picture house once a week. Swanage had its own cinema, which was always full, and through the summer months there were two sittings.

Catherine and Daniel met up with us one Thursday. It was so nice to see them again. Catherine was over the moon and we had so much to catch up on. Leslie and Daniel left us to it and went for a drink. It was obvious to them both they wouldn't get a word in edgeways!

'I'm leaving Chatscott Hall,' Catherine said. 'Daniel has asked me to live with him. He has two rooms that he rents in Westbourne, not far from Bournemouth.' Her voice lowered to a whisper. 'Of course everyone is shocked, apart from Betty. Mrs Hewitt looked down her nose a bit. I think she is jealous really.' Catherine pulled a face.

'Charlotte doesn't talk to me. Giles and Walter – well, they don't have an opinion. It's my life and it makes no difference to them. Walter doesn't want me to leave. Which reminds me, he has kept all of your letters, and now you are working in Swanage he wants to know if you will visit Chatscott Hall before Their Lordships arrive. You would be more than welcome. Betty would be thrilled – her and Arthur are serious sweethearts. Of course, old Flo makes sure he doesn't come to the house and keeps Betty on her toes. If it wasn't for Giles having a go at Flo, poor Betty wouldn't last very long. I shouldn't say it, but Flo is a bitch! I honestly don't know why Giles bothers with her. There must be something!'

A week before Their Lordships arrived at Chatscott Hall, I managed to pay a visit. Betty met me at Verwood station, full of excitement.

She said, 'Catherine is on duty, but it's my half-day, so I caught the early bus. I've got lots to tell you! So much has happened. Come on, the bus goes in five minutes.'

She grabbed my hand and we hurried around the corner to

where the bus was waiting. It was already half full when we climbed aboard and to our surprise we spotted Charlotte sitting at the back. Betty stopped in her tracks. 'Oh! Seems we've got company. Just my luck!'

We had to acknowledge her, so we made our way to the back. Charlotte was more than pleased to see us. She had been to visit her aunt, who hadn't been well, and needed cheering up.

'I'm really pleased to see you again, Edith. You must tell me all about your new job.' Looking at Betty's face, I knew she was dying to tell me her news. However, it would have to wait until later. In no time at all, we reached Chatscott Hall. We cut across the meadow and I noticed newborn calves on the far side. It was that time of year: everything fresh, new growth, it felt good to be back. We reached the servants' entrance to find young Walter patiently waiting.

'Cor! You took your time. Thought you'd never get here.' He was smiling cheekily. 'Long time since we saw you,' he said. 'You look OK!'

I kissed him on the cheek. The poor lad blushed. 'Cor! I didn't expect that,' he said and hurried inside.

The rest of the day sped by. It was nice to see everyone again. Giles gave me a fatherly talk. Mrs Hewitt was very hospitable and showed interest in what I had to say. Her manner towards Betty had mellowed, she knew better than to show animosity in front of Giles. Betty managed to get me to one side. She was anxious to tell me about Arthur.

'We are saving up to get married!' she whispered. 'Arthur asked me if I would like to marry him. Can you believe it? It was like magic! I can't wait! I'm so happy. We will live with his parents for a while until we can afford to rent somewhere, and then we will start a family. It's so exciting. Edith, you must come to the wedding, it will be next year in the spring. Catherine will be my bridesmaid and Giles will give me away.'

Her voice suddenly changed as Charlotte approached us, and nothing more was said. I spent a little time with Walter. He was like a younger brother and I promised not to lose touch – and I didn't.

Giles took me to the station later that day, I felt sad as I waved goodbye. Part of me knew that I would not return to Chatscott Hall again. On reaching Swanage, the weather had changed and it had started to rain. Fortunately I had my brolly with me, and I arrived back at the hotel moderately dry. Leslie was on duty so I didn't see him until later that evening at supper. We talked about our day and ended the evening with a short walk on the downs.

Swanage became a haven for holidaymakers. The hotel was fully booked throughout the summer. We were all kept very busy and had very little time to ourselves. By September it began to slow down. Leslie suggested a weekend away.

'Perhaps the beginning of October,' he said. 'It will give us some time together. If you agree, I'll make arrangements. I can rearrange the rota, if head of management permits. It will be our first time together as a couple and I want you to be happy about this.'

His face looked anxious just for a moment. I sighed with relief. It was inevitable that we would get together at sometime although we worked close together, we had very little privacy and our strict upbringing dictated how we behaved. There was a certainty about our relationship that gave me confidence and I was sure of my love for Leslie. He never gave me any reason to doubt, and I knew I wanted to spend the rest of my life with him.

We decided on Weymouth. Leslie booked us into a bed and breakfast that overlooked the harbour. This would be my first holiday as such, never having one that I could remember. It was so exciting. Leslie said I was like a child who had been given some money to spend, but secretly he was just as excited.

Our weekend away was perfect. The weather, though cool, was bright and sunny. We had one day at Bournemouth. The paddle steamers were still running until the end of October, so we took the opportunity to have a trip across the water. It was absolutely wonderful. We talked a lot about our families.

Leslie was made an orphan at the age of eight and had been placed with an aunt. He had been separated from his sisters and the trauma of all that had happened made him unsettled and he ran away. Eventually he was taken to Dr Barnardo's home for children. In his early teens he went to sea. Although he had travelled the world, so to speak, he had found it stark and hard.

The brutal discipline that he endured made him vow he wouldn't go to sea again. Once on dry land, he managed to find a job as a labourer. It was short-term and eventually he found himself in Bournemouth and managed to find work as a porter in a hotel.

Within a short while he met Daniel, who was working at the Bath Hotel, which was close to the sea. They became firm friends and often went cycling together; they had purchased two second-hand bikes, which were quite rusty, and in their spare time they did them up, painting them and replacing the tyres, improving the brakes, and so on. It was shortly after that they discovered they could cycle to Sandbanks in Dorset and catch a ferry across to Studland, which lead them to Swanage. This they did several times and came back through Corfe Castle, which was a longer route, but very scenic. Once or twice they caught the paddle steamer from Bournemouth pier, and it was on one of those occasions that they had met Catherine and me for the first time, a day I shall never forget. It must have been fate!

Chapter Eighteen

All good things come to an end, so they say, and sadly ours did. Arriving back at the hotel, we knew it was back to the grindstone. A charabanc of visitors had arrived that morning and were booked in for a fortnight. Through the autumn and winter, hoteliers boosted business by allowing concessions for groups of people. With hotels it was seasonal and some staff were stood off for the winter months but fortunately Leslie and I were permanent. January to March was spring cleaning, so it was all hands to the pumps.

The evenings spent in the staff room were quite jolly, and we often had sing-songs. Mary from Ireland, who had a beautiful voice, would sing Irish ditties and melodies. The one I loved most was 'Danny Boy'. It had been a favourite of Mam's; she sometimes sang it while doing the laundry when I was a child. Her voice would echo through the house. She had been a Welsh soprano and had sung in the church choir as a young woman. If things had been different, she might have gone further with her singing. Being married at seventeen and having four children before she was twenty-five put paid to that. It was her choice, one that she never had regrets about.

Ten months had passed since I arrived in Swanage. It felt like I had always been there. My time in London seemed to fade, and although I kept in touch with Rose and Charlie, it all felt long ago. I was so happy being close to Leslie, and although the work was hard and long, and sometimes unrewarding, it was compensated by the plans that Leslie and myself had made for our future. We would talk about having our own home with a garden, somewhere in the south. It all sounded like a dream. We agreed to work tirelessly for a couple of years and save as much money as possible. It was made easier for us because we were live-in staff and our meals were included. Our wages were below average, but we made up for it in gratuities that the guests left. For the first time in my life I had a savings book. Every spare penny went into it, and I guarded it with my life!

Throughout the spring and summer the hotel was fully booked; most of the guests returned each year. One or two were residents and enjoyed the hospitality. The reputation of the Grand Hotel was high and respected, and the ambience it gave out drew a high clientele. Everything throughout was impeccable, including the staff, especially in appearance and manner. We all had our jobs and we knew our place. I had grown to respect Dennis as a head waiter; although strict and disciplined, he treated us all fairly. If you made an error, he would take you to one side and reprimand you, away from other staff. Fortunately for me it was very rare.

Betty's wedding took place during June. The invitation was for both of us, but it was the height of the season and Leslie was unable to go. I arranged time off in advance. I was made to understand by Dennis that I would have to work one week without time off to make up for it. Otherwise it would set a precedent, and the management would take a dim view of it all. I assured him that it would only be this once. My powder-blue dress came out of mothballs once again. I had my hair bobbed with crinkle waves, and I remembered thinking how fashionable I looked.

The wedding took place in a little church outside Cranborne. Catherine had met me at the station and we caught the bus that stopped just outside. There was a gathering of people inside the church grounds, none of whom I recognised until young Walter, who had been made an usher, appeared. It was quite a transformation. He was wearing a pinstripe suit and tie, including a buttonhole, his hair was greased and brushed back. His face broke into a smile when he caught sight of us.

'Cor!' he muttered. 'Am I glad to see you two. I don't know many people here. Old Flo is coming later. Their Lordships are keeping her busy: croquet afternoon with posh visitors. They weren't too pleased, having all the staff out. Snooty Charlotte, she is helping old Flo – Mrs Baker gave out the orders. Charlotte, by the way, is going back with Mrs Baker in September. She wants to work in London. There's an opening for a house parlour maid.

Good riddance, I say! Better get back… got to show people to their seats!'

Catherine and I were lost for words.

That was the last time I visited Cranborne. The wedding was idyllic. Betty and Arthur looked extremely happy, and everything went well. The reception, which was held in the church hall, ended the day with a toast to the happy couple.

During July and August, the weather became uncomfortably hot. Swanage was heaving with holiday makers, and the beaches were crowded with children with buckets and spades, youngsters with paddle boats bobbing up and down on the sea. As early as 6 a.m. you could hear people frolicking in the water; it was the only way to keep cool. The hotel was buzzing from early morning until late evening, and there was very little time for leisure.

Leslie and I managed a few walks in the evenings, providing he wasn't on duty. We both treasured the time we had together. We had become so close, at times it became unbearable. We were living in an age where it was inappropriate to fraternise while living under the same roof, but pretending we were just friends sometimes caused tension. However, we were determined to keep a low profile for the sake of our jobs.

September came and cooler weather with it. The wave of holidaymakers diminished, which gave us some respite. We managed to go to the picture house a couple of times, and on a day trip to Bournemouth to meet Catherine and Daniel, who incidentally had found a little cottage to rent on the outskirts of Christchurch. I found myself envying them, and even though I was pleased for them, I felt a pang of jealousy. Despite my feelings, I knew I wouldn't change my life as it was. I had Leslie, and that was all that mattered.

Towards the end of September I started to feel tired and lacked an appetite. It wasn't like me to feel so low. By October I made an appointment to see the local doctor, who gave me a brief examination. He removed his glasses and patting my hand he said, 'My dear young lady, you're not ill. There is no easy way of telling you, I'm afraid you are expecting a baby!'

To say I was shocked was an understatement. I sat frozen in my chair. It couldn't be true. My mind started to race. What would Leslie say? What would people think? This couldn't be happening. I didn't want a baby! The shame, all our dreams…

I suddenly felt faint, and the doctor handed me a glass of water. 'You need to make another appointment with me,' he said. 'My nurse will arrange a time. In the meantime you must rest as much as possible.'

He held the door open for me and signalled to the nurse to come forward. 'Please make another appointment for next month,' he said quietly, and closed the door.

The nurse smiled, and made out an appointment card. I noticed her look of compassion as she handed it to me. How could she tell? Of course, she had seen it all before. My heart sank. I suddenly felt vulnerable and started to shake inside. Oh my god, this can't be happening, what am I going to do? I thought. I stood outside the surgery, an air of silence all around me. I felt completely alone. My mind started to race. I needed to think clearly, I couldn't go back yet. My mouth felt dry and I had only eaten dry toast that morning. The tea shop wasn't far away; a nice cup of tea was a welcoming thought, and I could think things through. This was my half-day so there was no rush.

By the time I returned to the hotel, I had reached a decision. To try to keep it a secret would be impossible. The stigma of being in the family way would be too hard to bear. Firstly, I needed to talk to Leslie. It was his concern for me that had led me to the doctors.

'You are probably run down,' he had said, 'a good tonic will put you right.'

Nothing will prepare him for this, I thought. We had both taken good care. However, it had happened. If the worst came to the worst, I would go back home; my family would stand by me.

Later that evening, Leslie and I managed to have some time alone (we always met up in his room when discretion allowed it). Earlier, Leslie had asked me how I had got on; I said I needed to talk to him.

'I'm off duty at 8 p.m.,' he whispered. 'Don't look so worried, you'll be fine. See you later.'

Sitting there in his room that evening I felt far from fine, but somehow I managed to tell him. The initial silence was deafening.

Looking into Leslie's face, I could see he was shocked. He leant forward for his cigarettes, looking away from me. He lit up and moved across the room. His silence made me tremble. Tears welled up. I couldn't contain them any more and I started to cry quietly. Within seconds I felt Leslie's arms around me. 'It's all right, Edith,' he whispered, 'we'll sort it all out. I love you and I'll take care of you.'

His words were comforting; that was all I needed to know. A feeling of relief swept over me. He held me in his arms while we talked. By the end of the evening we had decided what we would do. For the first few months we would stay where we were, the autumn gave some respite. Christmas would be the only busy time, and after that, the months leading up to Easter were quiet. In the meantime, Leslie would look for work in Bournemouth. We realised that it wouldn't be appropriate to stay too long. We'd made the decision not to tell anyone; it would have meant instant dismissal for both of us.

During the next few weeks I managed to keep working normally, but the feeling of nausea in the mornings was hard to disguise. Irish Mary seemed to sense that something was wrong.

'Are you losing weight, sweet girl? A bird couldn't live on what you eat. You are much too thin.' Her voice was full of compassion. 'You're not fretting over anything? To be sure, you can trust me if you need to talk. Not a word will pass my lips, not a soul will know.'

She was wise beyond her years and I dearly wanted to confide in her, but I couldn't take the risk. It was still early days and until we had some idea of what was ahead, it was best kept quiet.

My visits to the doctors were kept to a minimum. He had prescribed iron pills for a short period. My blood was thin and the doctor was concerned about my weight loss.

'You need more fibre in your diet, young lady. There are two of you to consider now, you must eat well and no late nights.'

His kind manner towards me was comforting. He never took any moral high ground and never questioned me, which made it easier for me to visit him. My next visit was due after Christmas, but, like everything, circumstances change. Leslie had found work in Bournemouth, it was the end of November and his new employers wanted him to start straight away. However, the understanding was he would have to work a fortnight's notice.

To say it came as a surprise to everyone was an understatement. The management were not too pleased, especially when they discovered the two of us were leaving. The atmosphere was tense and corner whispers everywhere. Apart from Irish Mary and Dennis, I was ignored by most of the staff. Fortunately, Alice, who I shared with, was more amenable and although she never said much, she went to the trouble of bringing me a cup tea whenever she could early in the morning.

She said, 'My sister found that a sweet cup of tea first thing helped her through the day.' Her perceptiveness amazed me; she was quiet but shrewd, and didn't judge me.

Although it was difficult in that fortnight, we managed to leave unscathed. Leslie had contacted Daniel for help regarding lodgings in the Bournemouth area. As luck would have it, there were two rooms for rent in Lower Parkstone, which were a few miles out of Bournemouth. Quite a nice area, Daniel had said. I went round to have a look: it was very clean and not bad-sized rooms, and it was also on the bus route. We were more than thankful for Daniel's help, and of course Catherine's loyal friendship throughout that time was a blessing.

We soon settled in. Although it felt strange at first, living together seemed so natural after a while. Leslie started his job almost straight away. He had been engaged as a night porter in a hotel called the Hermitage, which was quite close to Bournemouth Square. Consequently I had the days to myself while Leslie was sleeping. In the beginning I found enough to do, cleaning out cupboards and arranging things differently. Making it into our home was exciting. We had the use of a kitchen, which was shared by another couple, and the bathroom. Fortunately we managed not to clash and it worked out well.

During the first few weeks I managed to find my way around. I walked into Ashley Cross, which was lower Parkstone; there was a park nearby, a railway station and several shops, all in walking distance.

One day just before Christmas I noticed a card in the newsagents' window. It was advertising for a general help in a guest house for three days a week. Although Leslie had stressed that I needn't work, I felt the need to. I had so much time on my hands. I had always worked and this would be ideal. The extra money would come in handy, especially when the baby was born. Fortunately no one would suspect that I was expecting. I hardly showed a bump to speak of, the morning nausea had ceased and I felt a lot better, but of course I would have to ask Leslie.

With Leslie's approval I applied for the job. The newsagents gave me the card and directions to the guest house which was a short bus ride away. The proprietors were a pleasant couple and took to me straight away, probably because they had Welsh relatives. They made it clear that they had other people to see and would let me know in due course. In retrospect, I felt a little guilty knowing that if I was lucky to be offered the job I would only be there for a short while, but I needed to keep busy, if only until Easter. The days were long and the nights were lonely. I didn't know anyone. It was difficult with Leslie sleeping through the day – he was out to the world – so the work would be an outlet. As luck would have it, within two days of my interview I received a note asking me to call back. I was offered the job on a temporary basis, which suited me. Feeling quite excited at the prospect, I hurried back. I couldn't wait to tell Leslie.

Christmas came and went and I settled in quite quickly. Although it wasn't that busy, I had plenty of work to do. I served breakfast, made beds and cleaned. There was just me and a lady called Vera, who did some of the cooking. She was quite a chatty, cheerful person who you couldn't help liking. On days when the proprietors were out, she would give me freshly made scones to take home. It was a rare treat, a far cry from London.

Shortly before Easter, Leslie asked me to marry him. By this time I was nearly seven months into my pregnancy, which was obvious. The landlady at first raised her eyebrows when she discovered our situation. We thought she would ask us to leave. However, times were hard and she needed the rent. Fortunately she had a soft spot for Leslie and, never having children of her own, the idea of a baby in the house appealed to her.

It was Leslie's night off and he suggested a walk to the park. It was spring and the lighter evenings made it very pleasant. We found a bench and sat down. I could feel the baby move. Leslie was completely in awe, especially when he felt the baby kick.

'That is quite incredible,' he whispered. 'We have a little person that will be sharing our lives very soon.' Turning his face towards me, he said, 'Better get married, hadn't we, Edith? I love you, and we have the baby to think of. We will soon be a family, and being married would make it right. What do you say, Edith?'

My face must have said it all! The happiness I felt at that moment I would always remember.

We decided on a quiet ceremony with just Catherine and Daniel as guests, Daniel being best man. As much as I wanted all of my family and friends to be there, it wasn't possible. I wrote a couple of letters, one to Irene and the family, also Rose and Charlie, letting them know of our plans. Months before I had plucked up the courage to let them know about the baby. It had come as a shock to them, but they rallied round. Irene suggested that I went back home.

'We'll look after you,' she had told me. 'Mam would have wanted us to. If it doesn't work out between you and Leslie, you will always have us, this will always be your home.' I must admit I cried with relief.

Shortly after Easter we married in the Baptist church at West-bourne. It was a simple ceremony without a reception. We had decided a light tea at home would be enough. Catherine and Daniel had bought a fruit cake and decorated it with lucky horseshoes. They had wanted to contribute in some small way. Catherine, who had a few tears through the ceremony, confessed to me that she would dearly love to be married, but Daniel felt there was no need make a commitment.

'We are perfectly happy: why change things?' he had said to her. However, Catherine felt differently. The stigma of living together was very strong in those days; they both loved each other very much, so why not get married. Daniel disagreed, and refused to broach the subject again.

The next weeks sped by as I prepared for the baby. We had been given a cot from one of Catherine's new friends, which was gratefully accepted. Nappies and bottles I bought with my wages, which I had earned working at the guest house. The doctor that I registered with put me in touch with a midwife called Winnie, who visited me every ten days to check that all was well. Her clinical appearance went with her personality: a plain-looking woman with a shiny complexion, a little intimidating in her manner, but very thorough. I knew that I would be in good hands when the time came. She had told me that firstborns normally took about ten hours in labour.

'Learn to breathe properly and it will make things easier,' she said. To say I was a little afraid was an understatement. Winnie sensed that I had reservations. Looking straight into my face, she said, 'There is nothing to be afraid of. I've brought hundreds of babies into the world. It's painful, but once baby is born, you won't even remember what all the fuss was all about.'

Ten days later her words came true. I had woken up just before five that morning in May. I realised that my waters had broken, and the labour pains were every ten minutes. I felt a moment of panic. Leslie was on night duty, and wasn't due home until 6.30. I needed to call the midwife. The telephone was in the hall below, and I knew that I wouldn't be able to make it down the stairs. Fortunately there was a brass bell on the landing table. The landlady had placed it there in case I ever needed help – she hoped not that time of the morning. You could hear a pin drop, but needs must, and I rang the bell with great determination. The sounds were deafening, but it brought everybody out. The landlady in her curlers and dressing gown, looking hollow-eyed, took one look at me, and was on the telephone within seconds. The young couple living next door peeked out, and then quietly closed the door. I must have looked a sight.

Winnie arrived promptly. She stripped the bed and remade it with clean dry sheets. I vaguely remember her telling me to breathe properly. The contractions were much closer and I wanted to scream out loud, but each time Winnie would whisper, 'Calm down, calm down.' The silly old bitch! I thought. How would she know what it was really like? She didn't have any children. This is the worse pain anyone could experience, how much longer?

Leslie had arrived home to be greeted by the landlady, who, bless her, had helped the midwife with hot water and towels.

'I don't think you will be allowed to see Edith,' she told Leslie. 'The midwife is pretty strict about fathers being present.'

Knowing Leslie, I guessed he wouldn't take no for an answer and barged straight in. Fortunately Winnie was used to dealing with anxious fathers, so calmly and firmly she told him that he would be of greater use in the kitchen, boiling water and making tea. I can recall seeing his face through a blur. I wanted to swear at him, I was in so much pain, but in retrospect giving birth makes you say and do things which you don't really mean, and I can honestly say that once William was born, all eight pounds of him, shortly before 1 p.m., it had seemed like eternity.

I felt happiness and joy beyond belief. He was a beautiful baby, and Leslie was over the moon. I can remember feeling completely exhausted and slept until teatime. The midwife called in later that evening to see how we were all doing. She gave instructions to Leslie and said she would call in the next day. The next few days were almost unreal. Leslie had taken time off, just a few nights in order to give me some rest, and between him and the landlady everything went like clockwork. I was waited on hand and foot. Winnie ordered bed rest for a fortnight. 'We don't want you having baby blues,' she said firmly. 'The first few weeks are critical.' I remember thinking years later how right she was.

She examined William and weighed him. 'We have a very healthy baby here,' she said. 'I've left you instructions. Any problems, you can contact me, otherwise I'll see you in a month. I'll see myself out.' As Leslie opened the door for her, she was gone.

Being left to our own devices brought with it a few problems. However, we were determined to cope, and we did. Leslie went back to work and I began to adapt to the daily routine. We had bought a pram from the second-hand shop, which I scrubbed clean. Each day I would take William for a walk, most times to the park, which gave Leslie a chance to have some rest.

I made friends with a young mum called Maud, who had twin baby boys. 'They are quite a handful,' she told me, 'it's hard to cope sometimes. If it wasn't for my mother, I don't know what I would do, especially when they are both crying at the same time. Billy, my husband, hasn't any patience. "It's women's work," he says, and lets me get on with it, and goes to the pub!'

My heart went out to her. I couldn't contemplate having two babies to cope with. Little did I know!

Chapter Nineteen

Months went by and I was enjoying motherhood. The landlady was smitten with William and gladly babysat whenever Leslie and I wanted to have an evening at the picture house. Catherine and Daniel were frequent visitors and enjoyed walking with us. Strangely enough Daniel, who became William's godfather, adored William, yet didn't really want any children of his own. This was a bone of contention with Catherine, who couldn't understand his attitude.

'I cannot imagine a future without children. It isn't natural,' she cried. 'What am I to do, Edith?'

For me to advise her was impossible. How could I? All I could offer was my friendship and the knowledge that I would always be there for her. Sadly, a year later, Catherine left Daniel and returned to Cranborne.

William was eighteen months old when I discovered that I was expecting again. It came as a shock. Leslie wasn't happy at all. Although he loved William, he hadn't planned on having any more children, at least not until he had become established. I understood this because we both wanted a home of our own. Living in two rooms was almost unbearable, and we only just managed to cope. Leslie had already changed his job, as working nights became too difficult with a baby. Taking on a job as a day porter meant less wages and we only just managed. Through those next months I noticed Leslie changing. He seemed tired and distant. He worked long hours, so I put it down to that, but gradually any spare time that he had, he spent at the pub, mostly with Daniel. I tried talking to him, but he just made excuses. I felt completely excluded.

Shortly before the baby was due, I had a visit from the doctor and midwife together. Winnie said, 'Don't be alarmed, but I thought it best for the doctor to examine you. It looks like you are expecting a large baby, and we need to make sure that all is well.

Nothing to worry about I'm sure,' she said, looking directly at the doctor, who in turn nodded his head and smiled at me.

'Won't take long,' he murmured, and proceeded to listen to the baby's heartbeat. After a few minutes of prodding, he took Winnie to one side. Alarm bells started to ring in my head and I felt my heart race. I couldn't hear what they were saying, but by the look on Winnie's face, I knew it wasn't good news. I sat bolt up, not daring to move. Turning to me, the doctor said gently, 'There is no need to be alarmed. It appears that you are expecting twins! I detected two sets of heartbeats!'

To say I was shocked was an understatement.

'Two!' I cried and burst into tears.

'Now, now,' the doctor said, 'everything will be fine. Winnie will take care of you. Just try to stay calm. I'll come and check on you in a few days. In the meantime, rest as much as possible.'

He gave Winnie instructions and left. For a few moments there was complete silence until Winnie said, 'I'll put the kettle on and make some tea. Sounds like William has woken up, too.'

While she was in the kitchen I fetched William, who had begun to cry. I cuddled him.

'It's all right, I'm here,' I whispered. I still felt a little wobbly and tearful, but knew I had to come to terms with it. How would Leslie take the news? Things were bad enough without this bombshell. How would we manage?

By this time Winnie appeared with a tray of tea and a drink for William. Taking one look at me she said sharply, 'For goodness' sake sit down before you fall down! You really need to rest. I know it isn't easy having William to look after as well, but you do have a husband to help you. Maybe… Perhaps you would like me to have word with him? Are you finding things difficult?'

My silence said it all. Winnie was a very astute person and nothing got past her. She had sensed something was wrong for a little while but never asked any questions until now.

'You are going to have three children. It's not going to be any tea party, and both parents share the responsibility when it comes to families. Your blood pressure is low and you need to slow down. I'll call back later and speak to Leslie. In the meantime try and eat something,' she gave William a pat on the head and left.

Leslie arrived home just after 8. I had made a shepherd's pie for supper, which was one of his favourites. He looked tired and needed a shave, so I decided not to break the news until later. William was ready for bed. He looked forward to being tucked in by his father. It was quite rare these days; some evenings Leslie didn't arrive home until after 9 p.m., and William was in bed asleep, so this evening was an exception. It raised my hopes when I saw how he adored our son. Perhaps I was over reacting. We would be fine, times were hard. However I still felt uneasy.

Once supper was over I checked to see if the kitchen was being used. I decided to wash up while Leslie relaxed with a cigarette. A few minutes passed and Winnie arrived. She popped her head around the kitchen door and whispered, 'Is Leslie home?'

I nodded and said, 'I haven't told him yet. He looks so tired and he has only just had his supper.'

Winnie raised her eyebrow and said, 'He has to be told. No time like the present. Come along.' Her voice was gentle but firm. The look on Leslie's face when he was told was of utter shock.

'Are you sure?' he started to stammer. 'This wasn't planned, it's… well… I had no idea.'

'Yes,' Winnie replied, 'no one did until today. There is no doubt, the doctor confirmed it, so there is preparation to be made. Turning to me, she said, 'Maybe you would like to have a rest while we make some tea, if that's all right with you, Leslie?'

'Of course,' he replied, trying hard to smile. He got up and went straight to the kitchen with Winnie right behind. Whatever was said in there certainly did the trick, for Leslie's attitude changed for the better. After that he came home on time, bathed and put William to bed, even cooked the supper a couple of times, insisting that I rested. I must admit that I welcomed all of the attention and help, and on the day the twins were born, Leslie was there helping the midwife.

It was a difficult birth. Two girls, the second born three hours after the first. It was exhausting, but soon forgotten. Leslie's face was covered with beads of perspiration and as he held the twins in his arms he smiled proudly at me. The joy I felt was uplifting. Later that evening Leslie fetched William, who had been cared for by our landlady throughout. His little face looked a picture. We had explained to him that he was going to have a brother or sister, but two! Well, that was too much for him to understand. He clung to me at first and then after a while he slowly came round.

We named the twins Jane and Maggie. Jane, being the bigger of the two, left poor Maggie behind. Her weight plummeted at first and caused concern, but within a few weeks she perked up. It was chaotic trying to look after three children with little space. The landlady was helpful and understanding, but she made it clear that we would have to find somewhere else. She had other tenants to consider, and to be honest it was a nightmare sharing the kitchen and bathroom and not fair on any of us.

Leslie had become desperate and spent his time off searching for a larger place to rent. Fortunately for us, Daniel knew a property agent called Fred Miller, who conducted his business in a shop at Upper Parkstone. Daniel had a word with him, and as luck would have it there was a house for rent in Cheltenham Road, which was Upper Parkstone. We were overjoyed. It had two bedrooms, a kitchen and a washroom, a large front room, an outside toilet, a coal house at the back, and also a small garden. It was a dream come true.

The house was unfurnished, so at first it was quite difficult. We had very little furniture, just two fireside chairs, a table, a bed, the cots and some odd and ends, but somehow we managed and we settled in. My family paid us visits. It was so nice to see them.

Leslie was more contented and managed to find a job as a coach driver. It was better pay and he enjoyed being out and about. Although times were hard because of the slump and money was scarce, overall we were happy and the children were healthy. I baked my own cakes and pies, and knitted all the children's jumpers and cardigans. Leslie even grew some sweet peas and sunflowers and also had a vegetable plot for carrots and beans.

Once a month we went to the pictures at the Regal on Ashley Road. Leslie had made friends with two elderly spinsters, the Haynes, who ran a second-hand shop not far from where we lived. They had supplied us with several bits of furniture and had taken us under their wing; well, at least Leslie. They treated him like a son, so whenever we needed a babysitter, one of them would always oblige, providing my friend and neighbour wasn't able to. I sometimes felt uneasy about leaving the children with them, but it was only for a couple of hours. Leslie thought I was being overcautious and slightly paranoid. However, I was always relieved to be back at home.

Just before William's fourth birthday I found I was expecting again. I felt dismayed. Things had become easier with the twins walking, and William was quite grown-up. He played with the twins and kept an eye on them while I got on with washing and baking. However, there was very little I could do. Leslie seemed indifferent when I broke the news, had his dinner, then went off to the Retreat, our local pub, on Ashley Road.

When he returned, he said he had been talking to Daniel, who suggested he worked a couple of night shifts at a local factory. Although it didn't pay well, the extra money would ease the financial burden.

'My wages are already stretched,' Leslie said. 'Something has to be done. Daniel is going to find out for me.'

He lit up a cigarette and muttered something under his breath. I felt a surging anger well up inside me.

'What did you say? Did I hear right?'

'Yes, you did,' Leslie shouted. 'I said you should take more care! Daniel says there are ways and means of preventing pregnancies, and it's up to the woman!'

To say I was lost for words was an understatement. The silence was deafening until I found my voice.

'It takes two to tango!' I screamed. 'I'm sick of Daniel giving out advice. Our lives are private; it's got nothing to do with Daniel. He might be your friend, but he certainly isn't mine! Look what happened to Catherine; he almost ruined her life!'

By this time my whole body was shaking. I felt quite sick. I sat down and buried my head in my hands. I began to sob uncontrollably. I heard Leslie mutter, 'I'm going out, I can't stand this!' The door slammed and then there was silence. I sat for few minutes. I looked up and saw William standing by the door. His face was red and tears rolled down his cheeks.

'Mummy,' he cried, 'I don't like shouting. I want a cuddle.'

He held his arms out to me. Holding him tightly, I reassured him that everything was fine, that Daddy and me weren't cross with him, and we both loved him very much. I vowed then whatever it took I would protect the children from any further upsets.

The atmosphere for the next few days was quite tense. Leslie played with the children, but hardly spoke to me unless he had to. I tried to be congenial, but I felt empty inside. This wasn't the man I had married; the quiet, shy Leslie had changed. I felt quite bitter towards Daniel. He seemed to have a manipulative hold over him. Who would have thought, knowing Daniel a few years back, especially with Catherine, that he could change so much. In retrospect, I suspected that he was jealous of Leslie, having a family, always there for him, something which Daniel really craved but was too selfish to make the sacrifices needed.

A few days later, Leslie arrived home early, looking quite sheepish. He handed me a bunch of flowers, the first ever, and said, 'I'm sorry, Edith, for treating you so badly. I should have talked things over with you. I've been under a lot of pressure recently, but I promise in future I'll make more of an effort. I've got some extra work. I start tonight, just two nights a week. It won't be for ever, but the slump is worldwide, and everybody is in the same boat.'

He put his arms around me and whispered, 'We will just have to take one day at a time, and count the pennies.'

Three months passed and everything was back to normal. Leslie, although tired from working long hours seemed more contented. He spent less time at the pub and saw less of Daniel, who had been promoted to manager. He worked evenings, which I secretly felt pleased about. Leslie had invited him home a couple of times. He had tea with us; he enjoyed playing with the children. Not once did I show any ill feeling. He was Leslie's best friend, and I couldn't begrudge that. His behaviour was always polite and courteous and he insisted on helping with the washing-up, but, each time I was glad when he left.

My instincts had always been good. Being clairvoyant, my perception was high, and I could weigh up a situation. One afternoon, I was alone in the house. Joyce, my neighbour and friend, had offered to have the children for a couple of hours while I caught up on the laundry. I washed and starched shirts for various people to bring in extra pennies, which I tried to save. I had just finished hanging them out to dry when I heard a knock on the door. To my surprise it was Daniel.

'Hello,' he said, 'just thought I'd call in for a chat. My, you look well!' He was smiling into my face.

I said quickly, 'Um! Leslie is working; he won't be home until 6.'

'I know, Edith,' he murmured, 'I've come to see you. We need to set things straight. I really need to apologise to you. I know things in the last few months have been difficult. Perhaps I stuck my nose in where it wasn't wanted, but honestly I was only trying to be a friend. You know how much I admire you. Leslie is a very lucky man.' He started to eye me up and down. 'Your bump is beginning to show. What are you, six months now? Not many women look appealing to the eye when they are pregnant, but you, well… let's say you appeal to me.'

By this time I was beginning to feel afraid, but I knew not to panic. I was alone. I had to think of something quick.

'Would you like a cup of tea, Daniel?' I tried to speak without trembling. 'I was just about to put the kettle on. Joyce will be back shortly with the children. We always have tea and cakes. Perhaps you would like to join us?'

Daniel's face darkened. He muttered, 'You are so naive! Don't play the innocent with me.'

He lunged at me just as I moved towards the door. I reached for the rolling pin that was soaking in the sink and lashed out blindly. I heard Daniel swear, 'You stupid bitch!'

I wanted to scream, but could hardly breathe. I almost fell through the doorway. If it hadn't been for Joyce returning at that precise moment, I don't know what would have happened.

'My God!' she cried. 'What is going on?'

Looking straight at Daniel, she snapped, 'You disgusting, evil man. I heard you. Get out! Before I call the police.'

Daniel stumbled through the door, losing his shoe as he did so. Joyce picked it up and threw it at him. 'Go on, get out, you animal!'

Fortunately the children never witnessed anything. They had

stopped to play with a stray kitten that had wandered into the front garden. That was a relief! Joyce stayed with me as I could not stop shaking. Ted, Joyce's husband, had fetched the doctor. I had started to have stomach cramps, which was due to shock. Leslie arrived home just as the doctor was leaving. He took Leslie to one side and explained what had happened. 'She needs to rest; I've given her a mild sedative. The baby appears to be fine, however, keep an eye on her, it's been quite an ordeal. I suggest you call the police, this man should be locked up. Your wife could have lost the baby.'

Leslie was beside himself, full of anger and disbelief. 'My God, Edith! How could he? I promise you it will never happen again. Wait until I get my hands on him. I'll kill him!'

Putting his arms around me, he said, 'I had no idea. Daniel was a friend, someone I trusted. You were right all along. Don't be scared, I'm here now.'

Later Leslie called the police. They came round and took a statement from me. Leslie gave details of Daniel's address and place of work.

'We will be in touch,' the constable said. 'In the meantime, if this man tries to contact you, let us know. I'll bid you goodnight, then.'

Two days later the police informed us that Daniel had been arrested and charged. He had admitted the assault, and was released on bail pending a date for a court hearing.

'Strangely enough,' the constable told us, 'when Daniel was arrested, he sported a black eye and a bloody nose.' Addressing Leslie, he murmured, 'Seems he fell over, sir. Nasty that!'

It was obvious to me that there had been a confrontation between Leslie and Daniel. He had kept that quiet. After a few days, we decided to withdraw the allegation. Apparently, a couple of days later Daniel had got very drunk and walked into the sea at Bournemouth. If it hadn't been for another reveller who spotted him, he would have drowned. After hospital treatment he was sent home to discover he had lost his job. News travels fast. Consequently we decided that he had been punished enough and with the baby coming we didn't need any more stress. The last we heard, Daniel had gone to work in London. We never saw him again.

Chapter Twenty

Three months later, Larry was born. It was a sunny October morning. Leslie had gone to work early. I had only been up an hour when I went into labour. Thankfully, Joyce was there and took the children next door when the midwife arrived. Within ten minutes of her arrival, the baby came into the world.

'This young man isn't going to hang around,' the midwife quipped. 'You won't have any trouble with this one. It might be an old wives' tale, but it's true!'

Looking at Larry, who was placed in my arms, I had no doubts. He had beautiful brown eyes that stared into my face as if he could see me clearly. He was a beautiful boy. The midwife was right: Larry was never any trouble. The children were allowed to come in to see their new baby brother shortly after the midwife left. They were so excited. The twins wanted to hold him, but William wasn't too sure. However I had Jane one side of me and Maggie the other, and their little faces marvelled at Larry's tiny fingers.

William, bless him, said, 'When he grows up he can play with me, and I'll make sure he doesn't fall over.' Looking at William with his round, rosy face, I felt so proud. He was a wonderful little boy.

There was no way of contacting Leslie. He left very early because he was driving to Windsor with a coach full of day trippers and wouldn't be returning until late evening. I was still asleep when he left; there was no inkling of what lay ahead. The baby hadn't been due for another ten days. He was in for a surprise, especially another boy! Joyce and Ted were a godsend. They took charge, between them they organised everything. Ted, who did shift work for the local baker, took the children to the swings at Alexandra Park. He had the use of the baker's van. It was such a treat for them. I could hear their screams of delight as they clamoured into the seat. Joyce laughed as she waved them off from the window.

She turned to me and murmured, 'I don't know who the biggest kid is. I think Ted is! He loves children and would have loved a big family, but when I had our David sixteen years ago, that was it. I couldn't have any more. Doctor said I damaged my womb giving birth. Mind you, our David brought us joy and we are very proud of him. He is training to be an accountant in London. Lives in digs, so we don't see much of him. Coming home next weekend though!'

There was no doubt of the excitement in her voice. I realised what a lovely person she was: selfless and kind, the best neighbour and friend anyone could wish for.

When Leslie arrived home, he couldn't believe his eyes. Joyce had just finished washing up and the twins were tucked up in bed. William had been too excited to sleep. He couldn't wait to tell his daddy that he had a new baby brother. He was sat on Joyce's lap clasping his Rupert Bear book. He had pretended to read it to Joyce, but really it was all from memory. We had read it to him so many times, he knew it word for word!

'What's all this?' Leslie's voice sounded worried. Before Joyce could answer, William shouted 'Daddy, Daddy, I got a new baby brother to play with!'

Leslie couldn't believe his ears. Swooping William up into his arms, he dashed upstairs. Larry, who was in his cot, had just stirred. I had woken up from a very welcome sleep.

'My God! Edith, you don't do things by halves! It's another boy!' Leslie's voice was full of emotion. He placed William on the side of the bed, and bent over the cot. Larry opened his eyes and didn't murmur… Leslie gently picked him up.

'You didn't wait for me little chap,' he whispered, 'you didn't hang around. I can see I'm going to have my hands full.' He sat down on the bed next to William. I'll always remember that moment, his adoration for his two sons.

Life was pretty hectic for the next few weeks. The midwife popped in a couple of times to check that everything was all right. The washing seemed never-ending, a line full of nappies every day. The line became so weighed down that the clothes prop snapped. We managed to get another one from the ironmongers, plus a bigger mangle. That was a godsend. I had to have two flat irons to cope with all the ironing; while one was on the stove heating, I was pressing with the other. There was no rest and as a consequence I lost weight, I plummeted right down to seven and a half stone. Leslie worried I wasn't eating enough. He made sure by coming home each evening and cooking a meal.

'You need two square meals a day,' he said. 'You're not eating enough through the day; you'll make yourself ill if you're not careful.'

Looking back on those days Leslie was a good husband and father. We were poor but happy.

By Christmas, we were more organised. The two Miss Hayneses found us a paraffin stove, which we used in the scullery to dry the washing. Otherwise, it was the clothes horse around the fireplace, which took away the warmth of the room. For Christmas we lit a fire in the front room. Joyce and I made some paper chains to hang, which was quite good fun. William loved it, he was able to join in, the twins wanted to help, so I gave them the coloured paper to play with. The atmosphere of Christmas was cheering, especially when Leslie brought home the Christmas tree, as well as a fresh chicken and sausages.

I had managed to buy some Fry's chocolate bars, oranges and sweets to fill the children's stockings. I had found time to make two rag dolls for the twins and Leslie had made a wooden train for William. Last but not forgetting Larry, we bought a rattle in the shape of a frog. We almost regretted it. He loved it, and in the following months he nearly drove us mad with the constant rattle. If ever we took it away, he would scream the place down; the soft toys he had just didn't interest him. Even when he was teething, he chewed on the frog, so we just put up with it.

The New Year came, and with it the snow and ice. It was very difficult to keep warm. When we run out of coal we would buy firewood and a bag of coke. The only thing was, it used to smoke badly. Sometimes the house would smell like a bonfire, but at least we kept warm. Leslie worked extra hours whenever he could. Food and rent was our first priority. Luxuries were a thing of the past. We were going through a worldwide slump, which was debilitating for all. We just kept going hoping things would change. Somehow we survived.

The spring arrived, bringing with it the warmth of the sun.

William started infant school at Heatherlands, a tall Victorian building. I remember his first day. It wasn't too far to walk, so I used the twin pram. Somehow I managed to fit Larry, Jane and Maggie inside, with William walking beside us. He was really looking forward to starting, dear little chap. He had a school satchel with a pencil box that Leslie had made for him. He was so excited, he ended up with hiccups! We stayed in the classroom for the first half-hour so that William could settle in. The teacher said it made all the difference. Some children found it difficult at first, but William was different. He immediately joined in with the other children and when we left he just waved!

Within three years, we moved to another house, which wasn't far from where we were living. It had three bedrooms and it was situated in Churchill Road. It was further from the school. However, it was bigger and had a downstairs bathroom and toilet, an absolute luxury for us, after being used to an outdoor lavatory. There was a large airing cupboard in the kitchen-cum-parlour, with a back boiler, which would heat all the water providing we kept the fire going. Just outside the back door there was a coal house built into the covered porch, which was ideal when the weather was bad. The garden at the back was narrow but long. It backed on to a bungalow at the end. Although it was fenced off, the children somehow managed to make friends with the two little boys that lived there. We called them the Curtis Boys! Mr and Mrs Curtis got to know us through the children, and we became good friends.

There was one drawback, our next-door neighbours. We lived in a middle-terraced house, which was one of four. The neighbours were elderly and had never had any children, so it was a bit of a shock for them, especially when they realised that we shared the back entrance. Children running back and forward did not appeal to them one little bit. The old boy was quite pleasant and didn't make so much fuss; in fact, he went as far as to buy a bag of sweets occasionally for the children to share. In one respect, it was a welcome relief for him.

Some days when the children were outside playing, I could hear her nagging. She would raise her voice at him and it seemed he could never do anything right. If the children played hop-scotch outside, she would send him out to wash the chalk off the pavement, poor man. The children nicknamed her Biddy. Our other neighbours in the middle house, Mr and Mrs Rogers, were fine, although a little bit toffee-nosed. They had two girls, Rita and Eileen. They never had muddy faces, always spick and span. Not really natural, I thought; too methodical in every respect. However, children find a way. They used to sneak up to the end of the garden behind the fruit trees, and they soon made friends. I could hear the screams of laughter until Mrs Rogers came out and called them in, but in the end she gave up trying. We always passed the time of day. In any case, I couldn't talk.

There was an Irish family living a few doors away, the O'Learys. They were a band of thieves. If something went missing, you didn't have to look far. Always scrapping, the children ran round ragged, never washed, and the house was filthy. Strangely enough they never picked up any illnesses. Most of the neighbours kept away from them. I warned the children to stay away mainly, because of the bad language and the fact they had head lice. I just couldn't deal with that. I had far too much to contend with.

My life in the next couple of years was filled with washing, cleaning and cooking with no let-up; I was up at the crack of dawn preparing breakfast and seeing to the children's school clothes. Having ironed them the previous evening, I then had to set them out, otherwise there would be ructions, especially with Jane and Maggie. With matching outfits, they never seemed to agree. 'Those are my socks,' and so on, never-ending bickering, until I came up with the idea of sewing their names inside their clothes. Why I never thought of it before, I really don't know all the woollies I had knitted myself. Jane and Maggie weren't identical twins. Jane was the stronger of the two and invariably got her own way. Maggie always gave way in the end.

Leslie worked long hours. He would have his evening meal, wash and shave and then go for a drink at the Retreat pub, so he spent very little time at home. The children had to be in bed before he returned as he liked peace and quiet after a busy day. Sometimes, after a few beers he would come home hungry and I would have to fry some chips. The smell would waft upstairs and the children, who were not asleep, would call out 'can we have some' or 'we want a drink of water', so in order to keep the peace I would take a few chips up on a plate for them to share and after that there was quiet.

Unfortunately Leslie had lost interest in the children. In the beginning he found time to play with them, but as time went by he made excuses not to and was always reprimanding them. So I found myself keeping them out of his way. Times were difficult and scratching around for everything sometimes caused tension. We had little or no money, certainly none to spare, and most of our clothes were second hand. On one occasion I had to pawn my wedding ring when things became desperate. Leslie never even noticed. Fortunately I retrieved it later.

William managed to get a paper round and every Friday he would hand over the few pennies he had earned, never asking for any of it for himself, bless him. He woke up every morning at five, completed his paper round and then come home, before having his breakfast and leaving for school.

While the children were at school I had a morning job scrubbing floors as it brought extra money in. My hands became chapped and hard skin started to form. The trouble was my hands were in water more than they were out. Eventually I had to give it up on doctor's orders. Not only that, I was expecting again, which didn't help matters. There was no way we could afford to have any more children. I dreaded telling Leslie, so I decided to keep it quiet until I found the courage to tell him. However, the decision was taken from me. I miscarried after ten weeks; Leslie never knew.

Part Three
The Start of War

Southern Daily Echo, *reproduced with permission.*

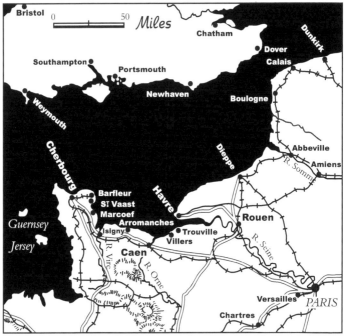

The invasion coast, showing the chief centres of activity between Cherbourg and Havre.
Latest German radio reports suggest new allied landings further north between Bologne and Calais.

Southern Daily Echo, *reproduced with permission.*

SOUTHERN
Daily Echo

REGISTERED AT THE GENERAL POST
OFFICE AS A NEWSPAPER

TELEPHONE: SOUTHAMPTON

Three Half-Pence

Vol. LVI.—No. 17235   SOUTHAMPTON, TUESDAY, JUNE 6, 1944   [NEWSPAPER DELIVERY]
[CHARGE EXTRA]

Allies Land in Northern France
EARLY MORNING SURPRISE FOR GERMANS
"Free Men Marching Together to Victory" *–Eisenhower*
KING TO BROADCAST TO-NIGHT

"COMMUNIQUE NUMBER ONE" set the world agog to-day. It was issued from Supreme Headquarters, Allied Expeditionary Force (S.H.A.E.F. for short) at 9.33 a.m., and said:

"Under the command of General Eisenhower, Allied naval forces, supported by strong air force, began landing Allied armies this morning on the Northern Coast of France."

IN this brief manner the United Nations, their enemies, and the peoples of neutral nations were told that "D Day" had arrived, and that the first stage in the liberation of Europe had begun.

Behind the bald announcement is the story of eventful hours crammed with radio flashes, the roar of countless bombers streaming towards the continent, jubilation and speculation in cities and villages.

For three hours before General Eisenhower released the momentous news German radio stations had been reporting "the invasion" with long accounts of battleships and destroyers off the mouth of the Seine, air-borne landings in Normandy, and air attacks on the vital coast between Cherbourg and Le Havre.

TIME OF LANDINGS
The Landings, it is understood in London, were made in Normandy between 6 a.m. and 8.15 a.m., minesweepers clearing a way. Naval bombardments, in which U.S. ships took part, were carried out, and airborne landings made, first reports being described as "good."

Before the assaulting troops embarked each man was handed a copy of a stirring order of the day issued by General Eisenhower and quoted on this page.

"MONTY" IN CHARGE
W. E. West, Press Association correspondent at S.H.A.E.F., says that General Montgomery is in charge of the Army group carrying out the assault, with British, Canadian and U.S. forces under his command.

Allied bombers roaring over at dawn gave British people the first hint that big events were under way. Almost simultaneously the B.B.C.'s French transmissions

began to warn French people to get away from costal areas, to avoid roads, railways and bridges.

HIS MAJESTY TO BROADCAST
The King is to broadcast to his people at 9 p.m. to-night.

General de Galle, who has arrived in London, and has had talks on military matters with General Eisenhower and Mr. Churchill, is also scheduled to give a radio talk to metropolitan France.

"GOING WELL"
Gault McGowan, representing the combined British Press, reporting from an English air field after watching the assault start from the air, said to-day: The situation seems to be going well. The Luftwaffe has not yet put in an appearance in strength, and the masses of manoeuvre on both sides are moving into position.

Before returning I flew for miles inland but saw no German armoured divisions on the move. The air umbrella exceeded Dieppe. No outfit seemed without its cover. There was so many of us in the air that we had to get up there by co-ordinated degrees to avoid crossing each others' lines.

BACK AGAIN IN STRENGTH
Little more than four years after the remnants of a British Army, battle-stained and weary, were snatched from destruction at Dunkirk, they returned to Europe ten times more numerous, armed with the weapons they then lacked and with the knowledge of a glorious record in North Africa and Italy to sustain them, was how W. E. West described the assault.

Plans had been made to the last detail for one of the greatest events in history. The men had been trained to the last ounce, skilled in the use of the most modern weapons and hardened like fine steel.

The three services are geared to the closest co-operation, as are the allied armies. Their air assault may be expected to rise to new heights. Every allied aircraft is operating in accordance with a single plan, under the single control of the Allied Air Commander-in-Chief, Sir Trafford Leigh-Mallory.

COMBINED ASSAULTS
To-day sees the first example in North West Europe of integrated or "triphibious" strategy, in which the Navy and the Air first help the army to gain lodgements in enemy held territory and the Army in turn, captures the ports and airfields essential for the efficient operation of its partners.

For months the air assault has been directed to crippling the enemy's aircraft industry and to minimising the expansion of his fighter force.

It is estimated that now the German High Command has at its disposal in the west some 1,750 fighters, about equally divided between single and twin enginned.

Three-quarters of these fighters were probably in Germany before the present operations began. There is no physical difficulty in transferring them to France or the Low Countries, and within a few days a very powerful force could be in operation there. But this would denude the home front of fighter protection, and no doubt the long-range bombing will be continued. Thus will the maximum damage and disorganisation be inflicted on the enemy and his fighter forces and anti-aircraft defences be stretched to the utmost.

ENEMY IN A DILEMMA
The enemy is, therefore, in a dilemma, but there is little doubt that he will feel compelled to move some squadrons from Germany, and fighting of some severity must be reckoned with before the Luftwaffe can be written off.

The enemy has a force of some 500 bombers in the west, and it must be assumed that he has been conserving these for just this occasion. They include a considerable number of aircraft especially designed for attacks on shipping, including torpedo bombers and He. 177 glider bomb-carriers.

The Salt of the Earth

They came from the North lands,
They came from the South lands,
They came from the mountains,
They came from the fens,
They drilled hard with rifle,
They drilled with their bayonets,
They practised with mortars,
They practised with Stens.

Now they're fighting our battles,
And in spirit we're with them.
They're fighting our battles,
And proving their worth.
They won't *all* get medals
They won't *all* get mention,
But they're *all* British soldiers,
The salt of the earth.

SALUTE THE SOLDIER

Let us Salute the Soldier by going without just a little more, by giving up just a little more, and by saving even more, not only during "Salute" Weeks, but all the time.

Issued by the National Savings Committee

Southern Daily Echo, *reproduced with permission.*

Chapter Twenty-one

There I was, September 1939, recalling all my yesterdays. How many tomorrows would there be? The reality was that we were at war and no one knew what lay ahead. The First World War was horrific. Although I was very young at the time, I remembered the stories, the terrible news of our boys, thousands dying in the trenches, with no protection from the elements. We were unprepared for such a war, so much loss, so much grief.

Would this war be any different? We had sophisticated warships and aircraft, and more advanced equipment than the last war, but would there be fewer casualties? I shuddered at the thought. Like many families, I would be coping on my own. I would have to be strong for the sake of the children. I felt afraid; the thought of bombs being dropped was inconceivable. Poland was already in the grip of the German Nazis. Being an island was no protection for us, which Mr Chamberlain pointed out. Poor man, he tried his best; many of our nation thought he was too weak to govern. His meetings with Hitler and his henchmen were wasted: one journalist writing for the *Daily Sketch* wrote, 'Hitler was an extremist who had visions of ruling the world no matter what the cost, a mad dictator who would go to any lengths.'

Suddenly my thoughts were interrupted by the children returning, the front door banged!

'Mum, we're back!'

Williams's voice echoed through the house.

'We haven't picked the bread. It's still warm; it's making us feel hungry though! Can we have some now?'

The smell of the bread wafted through the house and brought me to my senses.

'Just a minute,' I called out, 'I'll put the kettle on and we can have beans on toast.'

The next few weeks flew by. Everybody had been issued with identity cards and gas masks. The children had been given Mickey

Mouse ones, red and blue. To be honest, the children never realised the reality of war and thought wearing the gas masks was like an adventure. Fortunately we never needed to wear them. Shelters had been built outside the school and the children were drilled on what to do when the air raids began. Once the sirens went off, they had to walk in single file with their gas masks on their shoulders. They were told not to talk until they reached the shelters and were safe inside. William was full of it; he had been made leader of his class and thought it was great until one day a bomb was dropped quite close. The German plane had been heading for Southampton docks, had misjudged his target and the bomb had exploded a few miles down the road. The blast was felt for miles around. Many windows were shattered, including the school's. The children were terrified huddled together in the shelters, and that was only the beginning of many more.

Shortage of food was rife. Queues for bread became a nightmare, and in January 1940, food rationing came into force. We were all issued with buff-coloured ration books: four ounces of butter or lard, twelve ounces of sugar, four ounces of bacon and two eggs per person, per week. I had been issued with a grey ration book because I was pregnant, which gave me extra rations, but they didn't go very far. Vegetables, like potatoes and cabbages we grew in the garden; fortunately we had been warned in the early summer of 1939 to be prepared. Leslie had planted carrots in early spring and we had an abundance, which we stored in the shed, and when I was down to my last shilling I sold bunches of them to the neighbours to make a few coppers. Being desperate, we had to take desperate measures.

At times we all had to find ways round shortages. Some of us swapped food coupons for clothes coupons and vice versa, and borrowing became commonplace, especially cups of sugar! Home-made bread and cakes without the right ingredients tasted bland and not very appetising, but when you are hungry you'll eat anything. Sunday dinner sometimes was a tin of corned beef sliced and covered in gravy with a few potatoes and carrots.

For tea we had bread and jam or bread and butter; we couldn't afford to have jam and butter together. It was considered extravagant. There wasn't enough to go around anyway. Meat was rationed in March 1940 so occasionally we managed to have a piece of beef. It would be roasted on Sunday and any leftovers would be put through the mincer and I would make a cottage pie. The fat from the beef became dripping, which I stored in the larder. Through the cold months we had dripping on bread with a sprinkle of salt. It was delicious; it certainly kept the cold out and the children thrived on it. By the middle of 1940, everything was rationed, including tea. I rarely gave any of my tea ration away; a cup of tea was life-saving!

In April 1940 I was told by the midwife to expect an early birth. By my calculations, this was wrong; it shouldn't have been until May or June. However, after being examined by the doctor as well, who insisted it would be the middle of April, I accepted their diagnosis. Fortunately for me, my younger sisters, Millie and Myra, had moved from the Rhondda to Dorset two years before. Millie had been in service and had met her partner while working in Sandbanks and now lived in Ashley Cross. Myra had met her husband Albert while he was stationed at Blandford. They were living in a bungalow at Oakdale, so help wasn't far away.

I had written to Myra, who was living alone because Albert had been shipped to France. She contacted me, giving me a telephone number to call in case of an emergency. The corner shop had offered to take any messages for her. She had made friends with the couple who ran it and they were only too pleased to help. It was wartime and everyone pulled together: rich or poor, your chances were the same.

The air raids were becoming more frequent, especially the ones at night. We had no shelters and the houses shook with the ferocity of the blasts. It was so terrifying, I decided to hide the children and myself in the cupboard under the stairs, which housed the gas and electricity meters! I had been told that the houses that had been hit, invariably the stairs would be left standing. The cupboard also served as a larder. There was a wide shelf with a tiny window above and each time a bomb was dropped, it lit up like candle, even though I had taped over it.

It was difficult not to show fear, but when you have children you have to be strong for them. Poor mites, they would cry quietly. William tried not to: although he was very young, he was the eldest and he tried to take care of me. He worried about the baby I was carrying and was always making me cups of tea. The only thing was that he got a little above himself with the twins and Larry, and as a result there would be a few scraps!

One night, towards the end of May, the sirens went off. It was about midnight. I was laid on the bed fully clothed (there wasn't much point undressing with so many night raids). The eerie sounds of the sirens made me shiver. Not again, I thought. I felt so tired, utterly exhausted; my body ached from the weight of the baby, who had shown no signs of coming into the world. Just as well, I thought, how would I cope?

I pulled myself up and with great effort I roused the children, who were sleeping soundly. Surprisingly they had become almost immune to the sound of the sirens; their nights were constantly interrupted, which made them tired and niggly throughout. William was the first out of bed, grabbing blankets to take downstairs, Larry was stood on the landing, rubbing his eyes. He looked painfully thin, but he was wiry. Jane and Maggie were holding hands, just like they were taught at school, bless them!

Tucked safely under the stairs with blankets and a torch, we huddled together, waiting in anticipation. Our bodies trembled at the thought of more bombs. The first few minutes were eerily silent. Nothing seemed to happen, so I decided to check outside. William was reluctant for me to go.

'Don't go, mum,' he cried, 'a bomb could drop!'

'Just stay where you are,' I whispered, 'nothing will happen to me. I'm going to have a peep.'

I unlocked the front door and stepped outside. There wasn't a light to be seen; blackouts everywhere. Suddenly the sky lit up, as search lights outlined the barrage balloons. The drone of engines reached my ears and as I looked up I could see planes darting in and out of the search lights. The sound of the ack-ack guns echoed through the night sky as they began to fire.

'Oh my God!' I cried. 'I had better get in.'

I was just about to close the door when Mrs Rogers from next door came hurrying up the path with Rita and Eileen. They were dressed in their night clothes, almost hysterical with fear. Mr Rogers was in the Home Guard and wasn't with them.

'Can we shelter with you?' Mrs Rogers cried. 'Tom is on duty and we can't bear to be on our own.'

'Of course you can,' I whispered, not daring to speak too loud – for some reason I thought I would be heard above all the firing and the hellish noise. Somehow we all managed to squeeze inside the cupboard. We wrapped blankets around us not because we were cold but mainly to stop the trembling. It seemed for ever before the all-clear was given. A sigh of relief came from all of us.

The following day I learned that the dogfight I had witnessed was between two of our Spitfires and a German Messerschmitt. Unfortunately for the German pilot, the Messerschmitt was blown out of the sky. It was becoming a way of life, horrifying to contemplate, but one we had come to accept it and deal with. However, with the lack of sleep I started to feel unwell. I had let the children sleep late because they were exhausted. Mrs Rogers had popped in earlier with a half-packet of tea and some bread, thanking me for giving the children and her shelter.

'It was so kind of you,' she said. 'I just couldn't cope on my own. I don't know how you do it, Edith, night after night. If there is anything I can do for you, please don't hesitate to ask. Just send one of the children round.'

Thankfully that offer came in the nick of time. By midday my waters had broken and I went into labour. I had been listening to the radio; Mr Churchill had made a broadcast to the nation Mr Chamberlain had resigned on 10 May 1940. Mr Churchill had been made Prime Minister. He was stalwart in every respect and was held in high regard.

His voice boomed out, 'We will win this war. Each one of us will play his part.' Yes, I thought, and may God give you wisdom to see us through.

It was early afternoon when the midwife arrived; poor Mrs Rogers had panicked when I sent William round earlier.

'Mum is having the baby and we need to fetch the nurse,' he cried. 'Can you please stay with her? I have to go now, otherwise the baby will come without the nurse!'

'Oh dear,' Mrs Rogers cried. 'Yes, of course, you hurry off now; I'll come in straight away.'

She watched William tear down the road on his bike. 'Oh my

goodness,' she muttered. 'I'll need some towels. Tom!' she called out. 'I'm needed next door. Edith is having her baby, keep an eye on the girls.'

By the time the nurse arrived, Mrs Rogers had sorted everything out, boiling water ready and towels spread across the bed. Tom had offered to look after the children and give them tea. By this time I was past caring.

The midwife examined me. 'It's going to be at least another hour,' she said. 'Try and relax! I'll make some tea. I know I could do with one. You are my third baby today. It must be the shock of that air raid last night!'

She patted my hand to reassure me and then disappeared to the kitchen. Within minutes I felt the pain worsen. I knew the baby was coming. I could hear the chatter and the clinks of the cups from the kitchen. I screamed out for the nurse and by the time she reached me the baby was already born.

'My God!' the nurse cried. 'I got that one wrong! Well, my dear, you have a baby girl, a bonnie one at that. We must weigh her after we have tidied you up.'

Wrapping the baby in a towel, she handed her to me. She was a chubby baby with a mop of dark hair. She screamed non-stop for about ten minutes. We certainly knew she had arrived!

Later that day, Myra, who had been offered a lift in her neighbour's van, arrived. My sister was a pretty woman, even if I say so. Out of all my sisters she was blessed with beauty: dark sultry eyes, dark wavy hair, and beautiful, unblemished skin. She had a quiet personality and was unpretentious in every way. I looked at her slender form as she stood by the bedroom door. Her face lit up when she saw me with the baby, whom we had named Megan. Having no children of her own made it more poignant; her maternal instinct was strong and I knew she yearned for a baby of her own. However, she was only twenty-three so there was plenty of time, so I thought. This was my fifth child. I should be so complacent. No more! I had made my mind up. I wouldn't be able to cope; there was hardly enough money or food to go round. Besides, Leslie had made it clear that five was more than enough. However, best-laid plans and all that…

A camp bed had been placed in the front room; Myra had

insisted on this. 'Don't move the children for me. I'll be fine. I'm next door to the kitchen and I can prepare the breakfast without disturbing everyone early in the morning.'

She was in her element organising. The children loved her and were so excited about the new baby, and having their aunty staying with them was the icing on the cake. That evening, neighbours and friends popped in (including Mrs Curtis from the bungalow) bringing with them little gifts: a pair of knitted bootees, a hand-knitted bonnet and jacket, baby nighties and terry nappies that had been stored away in Mrs Rogers' linen cupboard for some years.

'Sentiment won't win the war,' she said laughingly. 'I certainly won't be needing them now!'

Mrs Chapman two doors away had made a jam sponge, a luxury for sure, even though it was made with dried eggs. It was equally shared out among us all with a nice cup of tea. Everyone had brought their own tea, milk and sugar. Rationing made you realise how scarce everything was and with my brood they didn't have the heart to do otherwise. Fortunately for us all, we had nearly twenty-four hours without any air raids.

With Myra's help, we got through the next couple of weeks. We had more air raids; one took place while the children were at school. They were in the shelters for over an hour. The German bombers were headed for Poole and had dropped their bombs before their aimed target because of the anti-aircraft guns below. Two German planes were shot down over the water near Poole, but the devastation they left behind was inconceivable. Many homes and shops were demolished, killing most of the occupants. Spirals of black smoke could be seen from a great distance, it was total chaos. Trying to cope with the nightly air raids became more stressful. Megan was restless and seemed to sleep only through the day. The nurse suggested that I bottle-feed her.

'The problem is,' she said, 'the baby senses your tension and it isn't good for her, so I recommend dried milk just for babies. You mix it with water, it's quite simple. Just make sure you have the bottle at the right temperature – test it on your wrist first. I'll call back later in the week to see how she is.'

Of course, like everything you can only try. However, Megan

reacted to it and was sick each time I fed her. In the end I became desperate and tried diluted condensed milk, which we used for our tea when there was no fresh milk. Whatever was in it, Megan seemed to like it and became more content.

The time came for Myra to leave. She had been told that young women without children had to either work in a factory or become postwomen because of the shortage of staff. Myra decided to work for the post office, which was close to home. She was lucky; some weren't given a choice. My heart felt heavy as we waved her off. I would really miss her, and of course the children would too. When Megan was constantly crying, Myra was there to help, and her quiet relaxed way worked wonders. How would I cope? My patience was wearing thin; I just needed one good night's sleep. On top of that, the children were always hungry and there wasn't enough to give them seconds. Most times I would make porridge with water and a sprinkle of sugar, sometimes a spoonful of condensed milk with it, but it was never enough. I longed for a banana or a juicy orange! Occasionally we managed to buy a couple of oranges; they were kept in cold storage and rationed out. Bananas we never saw, as the war prevented them being shipped over.

Fortunately, there was an abundance of apples. We had several orchards nearby and with our own fruit trees we managed to keep a store. However, it didn't stop the children from scrumping. I never approved and made it quite clear, wagging my finger at the children I told them in no uncertain terms that the orchards belonged to other people and it was stealing, regardless of whether everyone did it! To be honest, even in wartime some of the apples were left to rot, so people helped themselves. However, most of the children around found it exciting to scrump. One day Larry came home, doubled up with stomach ache. All the colour had drained from his face and he was screaming out. I sent William to fetch the doctor thinking that it was appendicitis.

'No such thing. Too many crab apples!' That was the doctor's verdict. 'A slap on the bottom if you eat any more, young man. A dose of syrup of figs should do the trick.' He winked at me knowingly. I sighed with relief and thanked him and apologised for wasting his time. From that time on, Larry never touched a crab apple again!

Chapter Twenty-two

Through the next few months, the air raids became more constant, through the day as well as night. The children's schooling was continually disrupted, they missed several days. At times it was too dangerous to venture out, all around us there was evidence of a bloody war. Many homes had been destroyed, whole families had been killed, people that we knew had died: it was like hell on earth.

I remember one early evening in August; I was bathing Megan in the kitchen. I had placed the enamel bath on the table. Megan was gurgling away, the gramophone was in the far corner playing my favourite record, Jane, Maggie and Larry were playing ludo and William had gone round to see his friend, Tony, who lived around the corner. Suddenly, without warning, there was the most horrendous blast that seem to come from nowhere. The kitchen window shattered and the back door blew open, throwing everything around.

I remember grabbing Megan and screaming at the children to run for the cupboard. It all happened so quickly, with no siren to warn us. I was shaking so much I almost fell over. Megan was screaming in my arms. The poor mite was dripping. I had managed to grab a towel and once under the stairs I realised that William was out. Instant panic took over.

'God! I cried. 'William is outside.'

I had visions of him lying under some rubble helpless. What could I do? Overhead we could hear the sounds of gun fire and dull booms from afar. The air was polluted with thick acrid dust which had come from outside and had filled the house. Being in a confined space, we could hardly breathe. The children were coughing and spluttering and crying at the same time.

'Mum, we are frightened!'

There was very little I could do but ferry the children outside. We needed air; our chances would be the same. It wouldn't make any difference; we would suffocate if we stayed. We huddled together in the porch. The air had cleared slightly and we were able to breathe. Megan was screaming and coughing. I had wrapped her in the towel and covered her face to protect her from breathing in the dust, but she was having none of it. She had a will of her own and that I found out in later years. The raid seemed never-ending and the noise was deafening. I could see spirals of black smoke above; the anti-aircraft guns were blazing away, with darts of red light shooting into the sky. The madness of it all was hard to contemplate. When would it ever end?

When it was all over, we crept back into the house. The quietness was eerie. Looking around me I could see the damage that had been done. The lid of the gramophone had been blown off, the mangle that had been stood by the sink had overturned with the force of the blast, and papers and clothes were strewn everywhere. The wireless, fortunately, had fallen onto the armchair and wasn't broken. Everything was covered in dust.

What a mess, I thought, but we are alive and I must find William. I told the girls to look after Megan while I went to search for him. Just at that moment he appeared in the doorway looking like a lost orphan.

'Mum!' he cried. 'Are you all all right?'

The joy we all felt was indescribable. We were all safe: there must be a guardian angel. Apart from burning eyes caused by the smoke, we had survived. The clearing up was a nightmare. Thick dust was everywhere, broken ornaments and shattered windows, only the blackout tape held the glass together. We had the help of Mrs Curtis from the bungalow, who had come to check if we were all safe and sound. Fortunately for her, the damage to the bungalow was minimal.

When we had finished, we all stood there surveying the aftermath. Everything was filthy, including us. I had lit the fire and pulled the damper out. We needed hot water for baths. Mrs Curtis offered a bath for the twins. She said, 'We have enough hot water to share and we can let you have some bundles of wood to keep your fire going. Thank goodness it's still summer, otherwise we would be scratching around!' That evening and night I shall never forget.

The following day was spent scrubbing and cleaning. Mr Curtis popped down to see the damage to the windows. The kitchen window needed replacing, as there was a gaping hole. The other windows throughout had cracks but weren't too damaged; we would be able to manage. However, the window in the kitchen couldn't be left and as luck would have it Mr Curtis had an odd pane of glass in his shed.

'Think it might fit. If not, I'll board it up,' he said cheerfully, 'nothing is impossible, we'll beat the sods, don't you worry!'

And off he went to fetch his tools. We found out that day that a bomb had been dropped three miles away. It appeared that the German bomber had been heading for Southampton and was hit by anti-aircraft guns. It almost dive-bombed but managed to recover and drop its evil cargo over our area, leaving devastation everywhere. A row of houses was demolished and most of the people living there were killed. I tried not to contemplate what it must have been like for all those poor people. What we had experienced was bad enough. The only consolation we felt was the knowledge that the German bomber crashed into the sea a few miles from Poole with no survivors.

Early September, Mr Churchill made a broadcast to the nation. He never cut corners; he told us how it was. Our casualties in all the armed forces were high, and Hitler's manic plans to rule the world brought about daily bombing raids. The Luftwaffe aimed for the English ports and aircraft factories. The Royal Airforce took to the skies. There were many battles between British and German planes over the Channel and south coast. The losses were high for our boys, but German losses were much higher.

Because of this, Hitler tried a new tactic to conquer Britain. He believed by targeting civilians he could force us to surrender and a few days later on 7 September 1940, the Blitz of London began: a daily bombing campaign of major cities, London being the main target. Casualties were high. On the first day, over 400 were killed and many injured. Within weeks the raids took place mostly at night to increase everyone's fears. People would be weaker through lack of sleep.

We had Lord Haw Haw spouting propaganda every evening

on the wireless: 'Germany calling, Germany calling.' He was a nasty traitor, supposedly one of us. He spoke perfect English. He was always trying to demoralise us, we all thought he was an idiot and he became a figure of fun.

There were many people who slept in underground stations for protection, and there were public shelters in most towns. However, the majority of people built Anderson shelters in their back gardens. You dug a hole quite deep and then placed the shelter in it. Most were made of corrugated iron, which was fairly strong, but some were made out of anything that would hold! You covered them with soil and prayed to God it would protect you!

The Blitz continued for nearly nine months, night after night, day after day, a constant battering. London had no respite. It was an act of God that anyone survived.

Christmas of 1940 was bleak to say the least. There was very little in the shops to buy, shelves were emptied within minutes of their being filled, and everyone queued for whatever there was available. As luck would have it, I managed to buy a small piece of beef. It was a couple of days before Christmas and I was passing the butcher's shop just before closing time. I noticed a tray of scrag ends of mutton in the window. There were only a couple of people queuing so I hurried in, hoping there would be enough for me.

The butcher must have noticed my look of anticipation for he scooped three handfuls individually on to sheets of paper, after serving the two customers in front of me. He turned and said jokingly, 'You only made it just in time: there's enough here to make a stew. Add a few onions and an Oxo, it will make an appetising meal. With all those mouths to feed, it can't be easy for you.'

With five children trailing behind, he couldn't fail to notice. He had a jovial personality that always made you feel at ease. He whispered, 'Have you got your joint for Christmas?' Looking round, making sure no one else was listening, he added, 'I have a spare piece of beef just right for Christmas. It'd be lovely with roast potatoes.'

'Yes, please,' I answered quickly, 'although I'm not sure whether I have enough coupons.'

My face must have been a picture for he laughed out loud. 'Never you mind. It's Christmas! I won't tell anyone if you don't.'

He hastily wrapped it in a piece of muslin and then folded some newspaper around it. 'Keep it in the coolest part of the larder. Should be fine, especially with this cold spell. There you go, that will be 2/9d, my dear.' His eyes were twinkling as he spoke.

'Thank you very much,' I said as I handed the money over. 'This will make a lovely Christmas dinner.'

'My pleasure, my dear. You take care with those young ones and enjoy the festive time. Let's hope the Germans call a truce and leave us in peace!'

There were very few presents for the children and Christmas day had arrived. Any money I had was spent on food. However, with a few nuts and sweets, crackers and comics, the children never noticed. We were invited to Mrs Curtis's for Boxing Day. A Christmas cake was the highlight, home-made and decorated with holly.

'All my own work,' Mrs Curtis said. 'Saved my coupons and bought some sultanas, flour and dried eggs, added some spice and a touch of brandy, so it should taste good!'

Two tables had been placed together to seat everyone. There were spam sandwiches and bread and butter laid neatly on her best china plates, a jam sponge and glasses of lemonade for everyone. The children's faces lit up. A real party, they thought. The excitement showed in their expressions. It brought tears to my eyes. We had spent two Christmases without Leslie. It was hard on them, I thought, but then again it was for everyone. No one knew who would come home. You just prayed. The afternoon passed quickly as we played games of pass the parcel and musical chairs. All of the children were in stitches, especially when Mr Curtis pretended to fall over every time he joined in. It was hilarious.

Sadly, though, just before 5 p.m. we heard the sirens go off. It was one mad dash to the shelter. Unlike us, they had built an Anderson shelter in their garden. It was very cramped with all of us huddled together, but we felt a lot safer. Waiting for the drones of the planes seemed like an eternity. Nothing happened and then the all-clear sounded. We never found out the reason why it was a false alarm; we were just relieved that it hadn't come to anything.

January and February of 1941 proved to be one of the hardest winters I can recall. We had everything from blizzards to black ice, icicles stuck firmly to the inside of the windows pipes froze. Fortunately, none burst. With very little coal or coke, we chopped up old chairs to keep the fire going. The children collected tree branches, which we dried out. We could only have baths once a week; most days it was washdowns by the fire, as it was so cold in the bathroom. The taps had frozen, which meant we had to boil pans of water to fill the bath. Consequently we all shared the same water! In between we coped with air raids and shortage of food. Beef-dripping sandwiches kept the cold at bay. The stark reality of war stared us in the face. Would there ever be a light at the end of the tunnel?

Each time I reminded myself of how London was suffering, many homes in the south and west of England had taken in hundreds of evacuees from all parts of London. They were put aboard trains with their luggage and gas masks, unsure of where they were going. The decision to take in evacuees was made for you. If you had the room you, were allocated one or two evacuees. Most were children, poor mites. They were at a loss, away from their parents and families. Some were orphans from losing their parents in the Blitz. It was so hard to contemplate that we were the lucky ones. Looking at my brood with their air of innocence and their complete trust in me no matter what the outcome gave me the inner strength to cope. The war united people, regardless of status or creed; we all shared the same goal. By helping each other, we would help win the war, and this was proved to me over and over again.

One example was when the children were out collecting wood, they had to pass the O'Learys' house. Although the family were volatile and always in trouble with the law, they still had to cope. Whether they had to steal to survive it, didn't matter to them; what was yours was theirs! Everyone kept an eye on their livestock, especially the chickens! However, this day changed my opinion of them, for shortly after the children trudged in with very little wood to show for their efforts, there was a knock on the door.

'William, will you see who it is?' I called out. 'I'm changing Megan.'

'Yes, mum,' he answered quickly. I could hear muffled voices and then William called me. 'You better come, Mum.' Lifting Megan up into my arms, I made my way to the front door. There stood the youngest of the O'Leary family, young Danny, clutching bundles of wood.

He stuttered, 'I was told by me mum, um, to ask you if you wanted some wood for your fire: we have plenty to spare.' With that he dropped the wood at my feet. He mumbled, 'Thanks, missus!' turned and fled down the path.

To say I was surprised was an understatement. Who would have thought that this act of kindness could come from a family who had shown no respect for the law, or their neighbours? I was speechless. Nevertheless, this showed that there was good in all of us. Later I sent William with a note saying thank you. After that, periodically we would find the odd bundle of wood or logs inside the gate. There was no need to ask who had left them there!

In the next few months, Morrison shelters were supplied to families who didn't have an Anderson shelter. Morrison shelters were for indoors. They consisted of a solid metal top and wire mesh sides, with not a lot of room inside. Once I had put the children in there, was only enough room for my top half, which was laughable really. Not a good safeguard.

'Mum!' The children would shout. 'The bombs will get your legs!' Out of the mouths of babes. I had put my trust in God.

London was still reeling from the bombardment of the Blitz. There was no let-up, and by April it was a mass of debris. Firemen and volunteers had their work cut out, but the stiff upper lip of the British showed through. We in Dorset had our fair share, but nothing to compare to London. However, wherever you were living, you had to cope and you were just as much afraid.

By May 1941 the Luftwaffe eased off, as Hitler turned to other tactics. Hitler's deputy, Rudolph Hess, flew to Scotland and bailed out. Parachuting into a field, he surrendered to a farmhand who was armed with a pitchfork. Hess spoke in English, and tried to explain his appearance! He was taken in by the local Home

Guard, who were completely baffled. One of the Guards mumbled, 'The wee man has lost his senses!'

The military and political experts could find no motive other than that he had gone mad. He was Hitler's right-hand man – was this one of Hitler's tactics? In my opinion the man was desperate. He was more afraid of Hitler than we were. He had very little power and was undermined by the top Nazis around Hitler. Whether he was mad or had a devious plan, no one ever found out; he was imprisoned and hopes of seeing Hitler again for him was never!

On Megan's first birthday, we celebrated by having a small birthday party. It was a Saturday and my sisters Myra and Millie, with her children, managed to visit us. We hadn't seen a lot of one another because of the air raids and lack of transport. The children were excited to see their aunts and cousins and so what we lacked in food we made up in laughter. It was a beautiful warm May day and we had put a trestle table out in the garden covered with an old bed sheet. Myra had brought a tin of peaches that she had saved. I had made jelly and some jam tarts, and there was bread and butter and lemon curd as a treat. Millie had bribed her local baker for some fruit buns with the understanding he would have a free pint of stout when he visited the pub that Millie worked in part-time.

'You don't ask, you don't get!' she quipped. That was Millie, always first in the queue! The afternoon went smoothly. Sitting watching the children play and laugh seemed almost surreal. Here we were, laughing and drinking tea, the sun shining, not a cloud in the sky: who would believe there was a war raging? Days like this were very rare and you made the best of it. In the early evening, Myra and Millie, with her brood, left to catch the bus. Once it was dark, the buses stopped running, so they couldn't risk being late. It was sad to see them leave as it was rare these days to have visitors. However, it had been a lovely, peaceful day, with fingers crossed for a peaceful night!

By 9 p.m. the children were all tucked up in bed, apart from William, who had gone round to Tony's. Megan was out for the count; the fuss and excitement of the day had worn her out, poor mite. She didn't understand what it was all about. Jane and

Maggie had taken it in turns to feed Megan, who wanted to feed herself, which amused Myra and Millie. Larry had been to play marbles with the Curtis boys after tea was over. He was sensitive to Millie's teasing and couldn't get away quick enough! I waited for William to come home and by 10.30 we were all asleep.

The summer of 1941 was hot and sultry, and with continuous air raids it became quite unpleasant. All of us huddling in the shelter was stifling. We couldn't have any windows open because of the raids and once or twice one of the children was sick. It was so claustrophobic that at times we had to abandon the shelter and hope for the best by sitting under the tables. What a nightmare!

Chapter Twenty-three

It was the last Friday in June and I was preparing the tea. The girls were outside playing hopscotch, William had gone to the shop to buy more bread. Around 5 p.m. there would be a new batch come in so we would try and be first in the queue. Larry had taken Megan to the Curtis family, who spoiled her, while I got on with things. I had the radio on, I loved to sing along to the music. Suddenly Jane came tearing in.

'Mum, Mum! It's Daddy, he's come home.'

I almost dropped the plate I was holding. 'My God! It can't be.' My voice trembled as I spoke. I looked up and there he was stood in the doorway with Maggie holding on to his tunic jumping up and down.

'Caught you on the hop!' Leslie said, laughing. My face must have been a picture. I burst into tears. I just couldn't believe it. I didn't think I would ever see him again. He placed his bags on the floor and swept me in to his arms. 'I've prayed for this day,' he whispered, 'coming home to you and the children kept me alive. This bloody war!' There were tears in his eyes as he spoke. 'God! It's good to be home, even though it's only for a little while. I've got to go back, Edith. This is only a short leave so we will have to make the best of it. Where is the baby? Megan!' he suddenly remembered.

'She's hardly a baby any more,' I said laughing. 'Megan is nearly walking. My letters, did you get them? I know it must have been difficult, but I hoped and prayed that they reached you.'

'Yes,' Leslie said, 'they were weeks old, but they were intact. I've still got them.' He looked around the room as if it was the first time he had seen it. As he eyed the food on the table, I could see he was hungry. 'Well, that looks a good spread,' he said cheerfully. 'I'm dying for a cup of tea; that's another thing I missed.'

Still feeling dazed, I murmured to Jane and Maggie to fetch

Larry and Megan. They dashed out the door, screaming with delight. It was like all their Christmases in one. Leslie flopped into the chair. It was obvious that he was physically and mentally tired. He had lost weight and his face looked gaunt. He was barely thirty but looked older. I wanted to ask whether he had been injured or not but felt it was best left for the time being. Just at that moment, William came dashing in. His face was one of complete surprise.

'Dad! How did you get home?'

Leslie rose from his chair. He couldn't believe the change in William, who had grown so much.

'Has your mother been feeding you on spinach?' he said, giving William a hug. 'I hope you have been taking care of everyone. You're the man of the house while I'm away.'

Leslie's face was beaming with pride. Thinking back, I recalled how he had lost interest in the children, but war puts things into perspective and it was best forgotten. The smell of bread wafted through the room.

William suddenly remembered. 'Oh! The bread, Mum, they let me have one small and one large loaf, just come out of the oven!'

'That's good,' I said smiling at him, 'you're a good boy. Go and wash your hands and help me with the tea while your dad has a rest.'

The sound of children's voices could be heard from outside. The door burst open and in came Larry holding Megan. He was speechless; his eyes like saucers! Megan looked baffled, poor mite. She couldn't make out what was going on. Who was this strange man looking at her? Leslie was almost in tears. He gave Larry a hug and lifted Megan into his arms. Her bottom lip started to tremble. She wasn't too sure until Leslie whispered, 'I'm your daddy!'

Megan's eyes opened wide. She understood the word 'daddy'; the twins had instilled it in her. They had told her stories about their father making it sound magical, but she wasn't too happy. Leslie realised it would take a little while and she would come round when she was ready.

Tea was like a Christmas party; at least, that's how it felt. The excitement was overwhelming, the children all talking at once, asking questions. Leslie seemed to come to life, telling the children stories. It felt almost surreal to be listening to him. His quiet patience was out of character; this wasn't the Leslie I remembered! He had certainly changed. But it didn't matter: I was so happy to be a family again, if only for a little while.

Once tea was over, Jane and Maggie insisted on washing up, hoping to stay up a little later, bless them. After all, this was a special day for everyone, and even little Megan showed no sign of tiredness. I had got her ready for bed, but she was too excited to be able to sleep. Leslie was smitten but he knew it was best to wait for her to come to him. By 10 p.m. everyone was yawning; the day had caught up on us all.

When the children were in bed Leslie had a long soak in the bath – another luxury he had missed. I decided that any more talking could wait until tomorrow. There was so much I wanted to ask, but I realised that he was exhausted. In any case, we could have another air raid through the night and sleep was more important. I left a small bottle of Guinness on the kitchen table for Leslie while I went upstairs to get ready for bed. Fifteen minutes later, I came down to see if Leslie had finished in the bathroom. Lo and behold, he was fast asleep in the chair, the Guinness untouched. No point in disturbing him; the air raids would do that regardless.

Fortunately for us, the sirens didn't go off until early morning. We had managed some sleep. Leslie was oblivious to any noise, and William had to shake him hard.

'Dad, Dad! Wake up – there's an air raid.'

It took a couple of minutes for Leslie to come round. 'What, what's going on?' He jumped to his feet. 'Oh God! Sorry,' he muttered, 'can't remember a thing. An air raid is it? Come on, let's get you inside the shelter.'

I had by this time ferried the children down the stairs. Leslie took Megan from my arms while I made sure they were all tucked in safely. There was no room for us but the twins managed to tuck Megan in between them so that was OK. I suggested that we sheltered under the stairs, but Leslie said unless it became too close for comfort he would stay put. The realisation of what we had to endure while he was away hit him hard, seeing the children tremble when the noise of the anti-aircraft guns hit the skies – it sounded like another dogfight.

'God, Edith! It's unbelievable,' he said. At that moment, the vibration of a bomb exploding further away shook the house. Megan started to cry and she put her arms out for me.

'Mummee,' was one of the few words she had learnt to speak. Leslie was visibly upset but took control. He put his head inside the shelter and reassured them that it would soon be all over, that they were quite safe and that he would make us all a cup of cocoa – that was considered a treat. His voice was calm and gentle and it seemed to do the trick until another bomb was dropped. It sounded a lot closer.

A few minutes later there was a frantic banging on the door. It was Mrs Rogers and the girls from next door. 'May we come in?'

It was obvious that they were in great distress. The girls were almost hysterical. Part of their ceiling in the front bedroom had come down, leaving a choking mist of debris. 'Tom's on duty,' Mrs Rogers cried. 'We just couldn't stay in there on our own. I'm so sorry.'

She suddenly spotted Leslie. 'Oh! Goodness, I didn't know you were here! I hope you don't mind, we—'

'Say no more,' Leslie said, 'you had better shelter under the stairs. This raid isn't over yet.' With everything pitch dark, it was difficult not to stumble, which Mrs Rogers did, landing face down in the hall. It was more panic than anything. Leslie helped her up and guided her into the cupboard where the two girls were crying and shaking. He quickly fetched some water, hoping it would calm them down.

'You will be safe here, it won't last too long. The gunners will chase them off, the worst is over.' His voice sounded reassuring and everyone seemed to calm down. Although the raid only lasted another fifteen minutes, it seemed like eternity.

The following day was warm and sultry. Although the raid finished sometime after 5 a.m, we hadn't bothered to go back to bed. The children, however, were shattered, so after a drink they crawled back upstairs to sleep. Leslie went next door with Mrs Rogers to survey the damage in the bedroom. There were a couple of heavy boxes that had fallen through the ceiling and it was obvious that the attic had been overloaded, with the continual vibrations from bombs being dropped. It was only a matter of time before it happened.

Leslie helped to remove some of the debris before Mr Rogers arrived home, looking the worse for wear. What a night for everyone!

Later that day, Leslie decided to visit the two Miss Hayneses at their corner shop.

'I'll take Megan with me,' he said. 'It will give me a chance to get to know her,' adding, 'I won't be very long.'

He had noticed that Jane, Maggie and Larry were looking wistfully at him. 'Don't worry,' he murmured, 'as soon as I come back we'll all go to the rec.' This was the recreation ground a mile away where there were swings and a play area.

Their faces lit up. 'Yes, please, Daddy!'

It meant a lot to them; after all, they hadn't seen him for so long. They had forgotten how strict he was before. We watched him disappear over the hilltop with Megan perched upon his shoulders. My heart raced for a moment, a sudden fear, but it was only momentary, although Megan was happy to go. I felt uneasy. I wasn't keen on the two Miss Hayneses, maybe because they were besotted with Leslie and he enjoyed the adulation. Suddenly I realised how foolish I was, allowing my imagination to take over. We would only have him home for a few days and then he would be gone. God knows when we would see him again. I told myself that I would make the best of the time we had together, that the children needed this. My problem was that I had been coping on my own for too long and maybe my intuition was wrong.

Leslie kept his word and arrived home an hour later. Megan looked bemused. Her face was covered in chocolate; she'd enjoyed every minute, full of the joys of spring.

Leslie quipped, 'I'm afraid she made a mess of herself… never mind, eh!'

The rest of the day sped by. The children enjoyed the swings, and the novelty of being with their dad was the icing on the cake. Fortunately we had no air raids and the evening was spent playing ludo with the girls and draughts with the boys. Megan had an early bath; her day had tired her out and she fell asleep within minutes when I put her to bed.

Later that evening when everyone was tucked up, Leslie told me that when he gone to visit the Miss Hayneses he had come across a woman who appeared to have suffered a heart attack. It was just outside our local fish and chip shop. Another man who had spotted her from across the road was trying to give aid.

'There wasn't a lot I could do,' Leslie said. 'I had Megan and I couldn't let go of her… I stayed until the ambulance came, but I think it was too late. It made me think of my own mortality. Really strange, especially when I have faced and missed bullets in this war. You forget that people die of natural causes when you are caught up in a bloody battle! Fortunately Megan didn't understand what was going on and when we reached the shop I allowed the Miss Hayneses to give her some chocolate. No child should witness anything like that.'

His voice seem to fade if though a memory of something that he had seen previously was brought back, but whatever it was, he didn't disclose it.

We had four more air raids before Leslie left: three through the night and one through the day. It seemed a way of life for all of us: a matter of survival, no one planned for tomorrow. We were all heavy-hearted to see Leslie go. There was no telling when we would see him again. He had promised to write whenever possible. The house felt empty even though I had the children. I felt alone. How long could I keep this up?

The following Sunday I took the children to Sunday school at the Church of the Good Shepherd, a little church at Rossmore. Eileen and Rita from next door came with us while Tom (Mr Rogers) repaired the ceiling with Mrs Rogers giving a hand. The morning brought a light relief, a change from the daily routine; praying helped to ease the tension. I sometimes wondered what God was doing; seeing all of the horrors of war and suffering, you had to have a strong faith.

On leaving the church we had about a half a mile to walk home. It was a warm sunny day and everything seemed peaceful; not a gun could be heard to remind you of war. However, the remains of homes that had been demolished by bombs could not be missed. I looked away trying hard not to think of what happened to the people who had lived there. Further on I noticed high wire fencing had been erected. Beyond that there were Nissen huts that housed Italians. I wasn't quite sure whether they were prisoners or just kept out of harm's way because of Italy befriending the Germans. Whoever was winning, was their motto, so I was told. It sent a shiver down my spine. There were posters everywhere warning us to be careful to whom we spoke – loose talk costs lives. That was drummed into us so much, we almost became paranoid: anyone that didn't look English, you looked the other way!

School broke up in July for the summer holidays; a heatwave had been forecast for the next few weeks. I was overjoyed because it would mean that the children could play outside and we could have a few picnics. Poole Park was a favourite place. It had a boating lake and a small zoo. I tried to save enough money for the paddle boats; it was the highlight of the day. Everything depended on the air raids, and so you could never tell. You just had to take a chance or you would never go out.

Unfortunately for us we were returning home one day when a raid took place. The sirens were going full blast. The bus we were on had to stop and everyone was ushered into a nearby shelter. Funnily enough, it didn't seem so scary with everyone huddled together. We were all in the same boat, so to speak. There was a dank smell from stagnant water, which had been there since the winter, but no one complained. After all, we were safer inside.

One week after that raid, in the middle of the night, a fierce dogfight took place. It appeared to be right overhead. The anti-aircraft guns could be heard and the noise was deafening. Foolishly I opened the front door to have a look, with William trying to pull me back in. The sky was lit up like a candle, planes darting in and out. I could see red flames of fire spouting through the night sky. Suddenly I heard the choking of an aircraft engine. A plane had been shot down and it was spiralling towards us. I slammed the door quickly and hid inside the cupboard under the stairs. William was sheltering with the children in the front room. There was no room for me. I called out, begging them to stay where they were. I had a really bad feeling about this; it was too close for comfort. And then it happened – the most horrendous explosion. Everything shook; it felt like the roof had been blown off. I could hear things breaking and the children crying out. I thought, Oh my God! Have we been hit? The children!

I vaguely remember banging my head as I tried to reach them. 'Please, please, God,' I cried out. It was pitch-dark and I wasn't able to see. Panic took over. I couldn't hear the children and my heart was pounding so much I could hardly breathe. I fell to the floor and started to crawl, then a little whimper sounded. It was Megan. 'Mummeee!'

My eyes managed to focus in the dark and I could see them all huddled together. It's a miracle, I thought, we are all alive. Who would believe it? There must be a guardian angel. I really thought this was it for us, but not so. I must never lose faith.

The next hours were a blur. The all-clear had been sounded yet we sat together still shaking, unable to move until the early morning light filtered through. A knock on the door brought me to my senses.

'Are you all right in there?' The voice of Tom from next door echoed through the letterbox. Larry leapt to his feet and dashed to open the door. The sound of a man's voice was comforting.

'Hello, Larry, everything OK?' Tom's voice was one of concern. 'Is your mum there?'

By this time we had all gathered in the hall looking like Orphan Annies.

'Thank God,' Tom murmured. 'We were all worried about you. It was a close shave for all of us. Albert Road caught the worst: a row of houses, poor sods! We had a narrow escape.' How true that was.

Most of that week was spent clearing up. Several slates had been blown off the roof. Some of the plaster from the ceiling in the back bedroom had fallen down, leaving a gaping hole. Apart from one or two cracked windows, held together with tape, amazingly we got off lightly. Outside was a war zone. Most of the homes within a five-mile radius where the plane came down suffered damage. The German pilot had released a bomb, which exploded beneath him, causing devastation of the worst kind.

Homes were burnt to a cinder, everywhere was a black mess. William and his friends had cycled round to see the aftermath, even though I had told him not to. When he returned, he looked quite pale and felt physically sick. Although it had all been cordoned off, the sight was unbelievable. He was visibly shocked by what he had seen. The stench alone was enough.

'William,' I cried, 'why did you go? I told you to keep away; people have their work cut out without having children sightseeing. When I tell you not to do a thing, you do not do it!' My anger mixed with anxiety boiled over. 'I have enough to cope with and you are old enough to know better. You're staying in for the rest of the day. Do you hear me?'

Williams face grimaced. He hated being chastised, especially in front of his brother and sisters. Jane, Maggie and Larry were mesmerised; they had never seen me so cross with William before and knew that it was best to keep quiet. However, little Megan, who had a mind of her own, toddled over to William and held her arms out. As young as she was, she sensed that he was upset and wanted to give him a cuddle. William swooped her up and, without giving me a second glance, he stomped out into the garden. I felt breathless with anger and despair. What were things coming to? With all the stress and tension that the war brought, I was becoming paranoid. Every little thing set me off. I expected too much from the children, especially the boys. I adored my sons so intensely that I sometimes forgot that the girls needed my affection just as much. Girls were natural homemakers, I told myself, and were self-sufficient, but secretly I knew it was wrong to think like that. However, I couldn't help how I felt.

July and August became unbearably hot. I kept the curtains closed throughout the day to keep the house cool. The Curtis family had a paddling pool which the children were allowed to use. It was a godsend for me; I managed to do so much around the house. William helped me to paint the kitchen. It had become badly discoloured through dust and smoke. I painted the skirting boards dark brown so marks would not show up. The smell of paint was so strong it made me feel sick. I was thankful that we could keep the doors open.

It was a Thursday morning and we were putting the finishing

touches to the kitchen cupboard when a knock came on the front door. Looking up, I muttered to William, 'If that's Mrs Scott from the corner house wanting to borrow sugar again, say no! We haven't enough for ourselves. Besides she never returns it. Tell her I'm very sorry.'

'Yes, mum,' William answered. His voice sounded tired, he struggled to his feet, and just at that moment the door swung open and there stood Myra!

'Well, you are fine lot,' she said cheerfully. 'Thought you might have opened the door for me!' Her face was all smiles. She winked at William who was looking bemused.

'Well I never!' I said, sounding a little shrill. 'You could have let us know – we would have cleared up. You've caught us on the hop, but that's enough said. I'll put the kettle on.' Turning to William I said, 'Soak the brushes in turps while I make the tea. You've worked hard today, William, I don't know how I would manage without you.'

His face lit up with a quirky grin, just like his father's.

Myra put her arm round him reassuringly. 'You're a credit to everyone,' she murmured. 'I hope my son turns out as well as you!'

I spun round, thinking, What did she say? Suddenly the penny dropped. 'You are not! No, you're not! Myra, are you expecting?'

Her face was a picture; she looked so well. 'Yes, yes I am,' she said, the joy in her voice obvious. 'I can't believe it, Edith, but the doctor confirmed it yesterday. I'm four months. That's why I never let you know I was coming, I wanted to surprise you. I wrote to Albert a couple of weeks ago, telling him that I might be. When he left in the spring, he joked about it. Although we have been trying for over two years, we had almost resigned ourselves to not having a family. I'm so excited; I want to tell the children that they are going to have new cousin. I popped in to see Millie on the way, but only stayed for a short while. She had her friend the barmaid and her children there, and the place was in chaos. I didn't get the chance to tell her about the baby. Besides her friend was smoking like a chimney and you know how I hate cigarettes. I suppose I'm the only one in the family that doesn't smoke.'

Her face puckered up. 'Ooh! Paint smells strong. Shall we go out into the garden? It's this baby. I can't stand certain smells. Haven't had much morning sickness, just the odd day. So far so good.' Myra continued to chat away while I made the tea. William had fetched the children, who were dripping wet from the paddling pool. I laid a tablecloth on the grass under the tree to keep us shaded from the searing sun. It was strange, really: whatever the weather we always drank tea. In winter it warmed you up; in summer it seemed to keep you cool. We were a nation of tea drinkers!

Shortly after 7 p.m. that evening, Myra left to catch the bus. We all stood by the gate waving goodbye until she disappeared over the hilltop. Dear Myra, I thought I was happy for her. This baby would be the making of her, yet why did I feel so niggardly? It had been a peaceful, happy day; I hadn't felt that hungry. Maybe the paint fumes; yes, that's it, I told myself. Once the children are in bed I'll sit outside. The night air will be cool and I can just relax providing there are no air raids. However, just after 11 the sirens went off. I swore under my breath. No rest for the wicked: if I could get my hands on Hitler! The children were in a deep sleep and waking them was hard. I remember Larry leaning against the wall in the hallway. He just slid to the floor, he was so tired. The twins crawled into the shelter with Megan, who was still asleep, which was amazing with all the noise around us. William sheltered under the stairs.

I decided to sit in the chair to be near the children. It seemed an age before the all-clear sounded, but it was only just after midnight. The eerie silence made me jump. I realised there were no sounds coming from the children. Peering inside the shelter, they were all huddled together fast asleep. They must have been exhausted. There was no point in disturbing them. I decided to sleep in the armchair just in case they woke up. My eyes felt heavy and I could feel myself drifting away. The next thing I remember was being woken up by Larry with a cup of tea.

'What time is it?' My voice sounded shrill.

'It's all right, mum,' Larry said. 'We have all washed and dressed. Megan is fine. We didn't want to wake you up because you have been so tired. Anyway it's only 9 a.m. Don't worry, Mum, we are all fine.'

My mind tried to focus as Larry nattered on, but a feeling of nausea swept over me. It didn't take me long to realise that I had felt like this each time I was expecting. Oh no! This couldn't be happening, not again. I really couldn't cope with another baby. I struggled to my feet, feeling so angry with myself. How could I let this happen? My mind was in a whirl. Maybe it was a stomach upset through inhaling the paint. Still, I'd give a little more time before I start to panic. 'Yes,' I told myself, 'it's early days.' A quick wash to freshen myself up and then see to the breakfast. I had a busy day ahead of me.

By midday the heat became almost unbearable. William and Larry had gone to the swimming baths to cool off. Jane and Maggie took Megan to the swings for an hour. They made some jam sandwiches for a picnic, along with a bottle of lemonade to drink. It was a welcome relief to have some free time to myself. It was all go most of the time and with very little sleep, I sometimes became short-tempered.

Today I was going to relax; it was too hot to do much. There was a pile of ironing waiting for me, but that could wait until the evening when it became cooler. I had a feeling we were in for a thunderstorm by the end of the day. I had some dried biscuits and a cold drink and sat out in the garden under the tree, where it was shaded. My mind started to drift. The nagging thought of being pregnant again would not go away. I would give it another couple of weeks and if I still felt the same then I would see the doctor. With all the heat and lack of sleep, it could be that I was just run down. More than likely that was it. I comforted myself with that thought. Yes, I was worrying over nothing, so I would relax and make the best of the time on my own.

Jane and Maggie arrived home just after 3 p.m. looking the worse for wear from the heat. Megan looked rosy-cheeked under her bonnet, but chirpy; she was quite a handful. It appeared that she wanted to walk all the way and wouldn't get in the pushchair, which must have tried the girls' patience. However, once they had a cool drink and a rinse under the cold tap, they were back to normal and went off to meet their friends at the orchard. Megan soon grew tired and fell asleep in my arms and only woke up when the boys came home. They raced round the back with their bikes, making quite a din. Of course, Mrs Ferris (Biddy) came out to complain. Oh dear! This is all I need, I thought, another set-to. I made my apologies to her and promised it wouldn't happen again.

'That's what you always say,' Mrs Ferris screamed. 'We don't have any peace day in, day out!'

Poor woman, she was almost blue in the face and started to splutter. By this time, Mr Ferris came out. Nodding his head at me, he said quietly, 'Sorry about this.' Turning to Mrs Ferris he said, 'Come along, dear, everyone has said they're sorry, you'll make yourself ill, now come in.' Poor man, I felt for him. He was such an inoffensive person and tried to please everyone. To be honest it must be hard for both of them being elderly, what with the war and being surrounded by children, there was no peace for them whatever way you looked at it. Later that evening, I picked a bunch of sweet peas for Biddy, and told William and Larry to take them to her. They didn't look too happy about it, but I thought it was the polite thing to do. We didn't need to fall out with our neighbours.

We had another air raid that night, shortly after 10. It was another dogfight. It didn't last that long, thank goodness, and we managed to have a fairly peaceful night. William, who had been asked to do a paper round throughout the summer holidays, was up at 6 a.m. to make his deliveries. I remember hearing the back door closing as he left. You could hear a pin drop as he pushed his bike around the back. Poor lad, he wasn't going to disturb anyone! By 7.30 I was up and dressed. Feeling nauseous, I decided to make a sweet cup of tea, only to discover the milk had gone off, sod's law! I checked to see if the milkman had been, as there were days when we didn't have fresh milk. Fortunately this day there was. He had left two pints in a bucket of water that I had left there to keep the milk cool. Bless him, I thought.

Once I had my tea I began to feel a little better. I could hear Megan calling out for me. She would be feeling thirsty, I thought. I had better fetch her down before she woke everyone up. However, Larry beat me to it. He appeared in the doorway clasping Megan in his arms.

'Mum! She's soaking wet.' His voice sounded tired. 'It's always me that has to see to her.'

'Sorry, Larry,' I murmured. 'I'll take her, you go back to bed. I'll bring you a cup of tea up later.'

But just at that moment William burst in through the back door. 'Guess what!' he cried, his voice excited. 'A barrage balloon has come down. It's at the end of Sunnyside Road. It's absolutely massive; it's tilted on two roofs. Can we go down and have a look? Please.'

By this time Jane and Maggie had woken and wondered what was going on. There was no stopping them: within minutes they were all dressed and out the door. I was left holding the baby, so to speak! Later that morning I wandered down with Megan to have a look. It was amazing to see. It was gigantic, men on ladders trying to secure it. I had borrowed William's brownie camera to take a picture, but it proved too difficult for me. However, a friend of William's offered. He stood on a wall a short distance away and managed to take a snap. That was a day that we all remembered.

Chapter Twenty-four

By September the doctor confirmed that I was expecting another baby in the spring.

'Are you coping all right?' he asked. 'Things must be difficult for you, with the shortage of food and so many mouths to feed. However, I must stress that you take more care of yourself. You are slightly anaemic so I am going to recommend a tonic to be taken twice a day. In the meantime, I want you rest whenever possible. I know it isn't easy, but you must be sensible about this. Come and see me in another month.'

On the way home I popped in to see Mrs Curtis. I needed to tell someone. I felt inwardly depressed. I didn't want this baby. It was all too much. Once there, I blurted out, 'I don't know how I'm going to manage.' I started to cry convulsively.

'That's it,' Mrs Curtis murmured, 'let it all out. Keeping it all bottled up doesn't do you any good. It'll all work out in the end. Now let's have a nice cup of tea and you can tell me everything, in confidence, of course!'

With the children back at school, time sped by. Myra came to see me when she heard about the baby. 'Well, Edith,' she joked, 'you could have waited.' Looking slightly bemused by my reaction, she murmured, 'Are you all right? I'm only joking, Edith.'

'Forgive me, Myra,' I said, my voice trembling. 'I'm feeling a little bit sorry for myself. I'm not sure that I want this baby. I can't cope with the five children I've got. I'm so tired, Myra.'

'Oh, Edith!' Myra cried. 'This isn't like you, you're the strong one of the family. Whatever happens, you'll get by. Come on, let's have that cup of tea and we'll talk.'

After an hour of confiding in each other, Myra suddenly said, 'Edith, there is something you're not telling me. What's wrong?'

Up to this point, I wasn't going to say anything, but I knew that I had to trust someone and who better than Myra? Hesitating, I said, 'A couple of weeks ago I had to see the doctor for a check-up, and while I was waiting who should walk in but Mrs Stevens from Sunnyside Road. We chatted for a bit, and then she said, "By the way, I went to see my mother in Southampton. It was the beginning of September. I remember I was waiting by the bus stop and I saw your Leslie. I swear it was him. Looked very smart in his uniform. Didn't see me. He strode off and disappeared into a house further on. Mind you, I was quite surprised; thought he was on the front line. My first thoughts were that I had got it wrong, but it could be only a matter of minutes and I saw him again, this time on a bike. He rode past me; definitely was your Leslie!" Mrs Stevens went on and on. Myra, I told her that I knew! But I had no idea what was going on. Since then I have been having all kinds of doubts. Had he come home? What was he doing in Southampton? What am I supposed to think, Myra?'

There was a moment of silence. Myra's face looked slightly angry. 'For goodness' sake, Edith! The woman got it wrong. It must have been someone who looked like Leslie. Honestly, Edith, fancy believing that! The woman is a troublemaker, with nothing better to do. Now listen to me, Edith: Leslie would never come home without you knowing. He would have written to you, right? So stop worrying.'

I nodded in agreement, knowing she talked sense and tried to sound cheerful, but I still felt a niggling doubt. We chatted for ages, then she had to leave to go home.

Myra's baby was born in November, a beautiful little boy. We all went to see them one Sunday afternoon. We stayed for just an hour; there was only one bus back that day and it left at 3.30 so there was very little time, especially with the blackouts. The November evenings were damp and foggy and it was no fun to be out. With the threat of air raids, it was best to be indoors. We had been invited to Millie's for tea, but had decided against it because there would be no buses running and it would be too far to walk home. Our bus stopped at the corner of Churchill Road parallel with Ashley Road. It was quite a hike, even from there.

Once indoors I lit a fire. It was bath night and I had all the school clothes to iron, not my best night by any means. Still, once everything was done I had decided to write to Leslie to tell him about the baby I was expecting. I had put it off for so long, but it had to be done. In my heart I knew he wouldn't be too pleased, but what else could I do?

Trying to eke out the ration coupons was a nightmare. There just wasn't enough to go round, a small portion of butter and cheese didn't last a week. There had been talk of extra rations for larger families, but nothing so far. However, by December 1941, children under two would receive free orange juice and cod liver oil. In my case that would only be for Megan. I had dried milk and dried eggs, which weren't the same as being fresh.

However, I was able to make cakes and tarts and a Welsh cake that didn't require butter or margarine. It tasted bland, but when you're hungry you get used to it. With Christmas round the corner, and with very little money, I decided to make everything. Firstly I knitted three dolls, one each for the girls. I bought the dolls' faces from the haberdashery shop. They only cost a few pence each and when stitched on they looked really sweet. I made the dresses out of an old christening gown and gave each doll a different colour bow. It's surprising what you can do when faced with circumstances such as mine well – most of us.

The boys were a different challenge. William, being the eldest, was passed the toy age and so was Larry, who was into books. So I ended up buying both of them a fountain pen each, which in actual fact came from William's paper round money. He always handed it over to me and only asked for a few coppers back to spend. Any money saved was placed in an old tea caddy for a rainy day. However, in our case it was raining every day!

Christmas sped by and we were into the new year, 1942. By the middle of January, we were knee deep in snow. It was bitterly cold and trying to keep the house warm was difficult. To a certain extent, I relied on handouts. I couldn't afford to be proud and accepted everything that was offered – wood, coal, food and clothes, everything helped. I had previously swapped my clothes coupons for food rations, like sugar, butter and so on… Everyone was doing it in order to survive. Bureaucracy would have frowned upon it, but this was war. There was the black market and the spivs around every corner; opportunists lapped it up.

With the thought of a new baby arriving in the spring, I stored and saved whatever I could. It wasn't going to be easy with another mouth to feed and with the continuing air raids day and night, the deliveries of essential foods and medicines was delayed everywhere. A diet of tinned food kept us going. I remember checking the larder and counting at least twenty tins of peaches! Eight tins of corned beef and Spam. Even so, I would have to eke it out, it wouldn't last long.

My first letter from Leslie arrived at the end of January. It had postmarks all over it. Like everything, it had gone astray and had taken nearly five weeks to reach me. My heart was in my mouth, I wasn't sure of what to expect. Fortunately, it wasn't a telegram. To my surprise it included a crumpled ten-shilling note. I just looked at it in disbelief. It felt like a small fortune. With my hands trembling, I quickly read the letter. It was difficult to distinguish the words because the letter had got wet at some stage, making the words blotchy. From what I could interpret, he was in France with very little contact from the outside world. It was like living in a hellhole. Losing comrades was worse than fighting; the only thing that kept him going was the thought of his family at home. The news about the baby came as a surprise, he wrote.

> I know how difficult it must be for you at this time and having an extra mouth to feed makes it harder so I have enclosed ten shillings to see you through when the baby is born. I miss you all and hope it's not too long before I'm home, please write when you can.
>
> Love, Leslie.

I could feel the tears welling up inside me. All the doubts I had about him disappeared. How foolish I had been, allowing Mrs Stevens to create a barrier of disbelief. Myra was right: it was plain fantasy. Besides, everyone has a double!

By the end of March, I was feeling very tired and worn out. The baby was due in the next couple of weeks and I couldn't wait for it to be over with. Megan was all over the place, walking and talking, into everything. I just didn't have the energy to cope with her. She sensed my tension and rebelled even more.

'The others were never like this. I shall be glad when she is old enough to go to school. God knows how long I can stand it!' Thinking out loud, I muttered. 'Hope it's a boy, even number. Besides boys have better temperaments.'

Realising what I was saying made me stop in my tracks. 'Good Lord! What am I thinking? This is wicked! I must pull myself together! I'm tired and not thinking straight. I need to rest more.'

In the next week, I went to great pains to show Jane and Maggie the things that they would need to do when the new baby arrived. I wanted the girls to be involved, they both needed to feel important at this time. Their faces lit up when I told them they would be in charge especially where Megan was concerned. 'Remember to use the enamel cups,' I said. 'Megan has already broken two china ones pretending to make tea. Better safe than sorry. We need them for when we have visitors.'

With things clearer in my mind, I felt more relaxed. Mrs Rogers had offered to come in during the birth, mainly to keep an eye on Megan and make sure the girls were coping. William and Larry, of course, would do their bit and the Curtises were there if we needed any help. The bombing raids throughout the days seemed to be less frequent, which made it easier for the children at school.

However, it was a new tactic by Hitler to lull us into a false sense of security. For, just a few days before the baby was born, we had three horrendous raids during the day. The schools literally spent the day in the shelters. It was beyond a joke. The following day we had a warning from the Ministry of War that at all times each and every one of us should carry our gas masks; there was a possibility that gas might be used. Vital information had been received. Each child was checked by the teachers at school. I kept mine and Megan's gas masks under the shelf in the larder. Megan's was a Mickey Mouse one. She thought it was something to play with, not knowing the sinister reason why she had to wear it. At first she wasn't too happy about having it over her face until we called it hide and seek with Mickey Mouse. We all put ours on just to let her know there was nothing to be afraid of. I must admit, the adult ones looked a bit alien!

Two days later I woke up in the middle of the night, not through an air raid but through labour pains. Poor William had to dash for the midwife. In his desperation to get dressed, he nearly fell over: he had put two legs in one trouser leg! If it hadn't been so serious it would have been funny! By 7 a.m. it was all over. Another little girl, quite small with fair hair. The children were mesmerised when they saw how small she was. Tiny feet and fingers, just like a doll. I thought I would be disappointed at having another girl, but she was so sweet it didn't matter. The rest of the day was hectic; Mrs Rogers had her hands full. She saw to all the meals, took charge of the washing and ironing. Mrs Curtis took Megan out for the afternoon to give me some peace. Poor Megan wanted to play with the baby and hold her, and was quite upset when she couldn't. I suppose she must have felt a little left out after being the baby of the family for so long, but in time she would get used to it.

We named the new baby Jessica. Jane and Maggie chose it in the end. The boys weren't that bothered, it was all the same to them. Strangely enough, Larry was very attentive and held the baby like she was a china doll. There was no doubt in my mind that he was the gentlest of boys. I knew in my heart that he would always be there for me. He wasn't a mummy's boy, by any means, he often got the better of William when they had a scrap. To be fair, both my boys were princes.

By the summer, the Americans had arrived; some were staying in Bournemouth. It caused a bit of a stir, especially where the ladies were concerned. In fact, it was quite cheering; it was nice to know they were our ally. Of course, there were a few who resented them, but we needed them, even though they had arrived late into the war. The Yanks, as some called them, brought with them nylon stockings, chocolate and chewing gum, rarities to say the least. The young girls were starry-eyed, it was like looking through rose-coloured glasses. They flocked in the square flirtatiously. I suppose we were all curious and a little excited. After all, the only Americans we saw were on film at the picture house!

However they were here to fight against the Germans and it wouldn't be long before they were shipped abroad, and how many would come back? Hundreds of our boys had been killed and it left a void in people's lives everywhere. At times I would imagine all sorts of things. What if anything happened to Leslie? If he never came back?

My whole body would shudder at the thought. Like always, I pulled myself together and pushed it to the back of my mind.

The school holidays soon came round, and with the warm summer weather, life was a little easier. Still, coping with air raids and shortage of food we somehow managed to get by. Jessica was growing fast. She was such a dear little thing, no trouble at all. A far cry from Megan, who was into everything. I didn't have an awful lot of patience with her. She was so stubborn. Typical of girls, I thought. Fortunately, Jane and Maggie took charge of her, which gave me some respite.

William and Larry had turned the top part of the garden into an allotment. They planted carrots, potatoes, cabbages and turnips, a whole variety of vegetables, all from packets of seeds. It would save a lot and put pennies in our pockets. The boys were proud of their achievement, especially when everything started to grow. They spent hours tending to everything. Keeping the bugs off was quite difficult, but it was all worth it.

One Sunday, Myra arrived unexpectedly with baby Thomas in the midst of a thunderstorm. She was drenched, her hair dripping everywhere. She had walked all the way from the bus stop, a good half-mile at least. Thomas was crying, poor little chap, all red in the face.

'Myra,' I cried, grabbing a towel from the airing cupboard, 'what were you thinking of? You should have rung the corner shop and we would have met you off the bus with a brolly. You're soaking wet and look at poor Thomas! What is wrong? Come on, I'll make some tea, Jane and Maggie will take care of the baby, you need to dry off.'

With everyone indoors because of the storm it became a little too crowded in the kitchen and I could see that Myra was agitated. Something was seriously wrong.

'Right! Everyone upstairs,' I cried, 'we need some quiet time here. If you're good we'll have a jam sponge for tea, how about that?'

There was no need to repeat myself – within a few seconds you could hear a pin drop! Looking at Myra I could see tears streaming down her face all the anguish was coming out. She wiped her face with her sleeve and I could see dark circles around her eyes.

'What's happened,' I whispered, 'are you in trouble?'

'No,' she answered, 'it's me. Albert is home, we had a row. I haven't been feeling too well, a few headaches, and he made me see the doctor. I've been feeling sick. The doctor wants me to have some tests. I don't see the need. I'm just run down, that's all. Anyway, Albert started laying the law down and I walked out. Honestly, Edith, it's all too much. I'm so tired; I don't need Albert nagging me.'

'No,' I said quickly 'you don't, but Albert is only concerned. He needs to know that you will be all right. He loves you and Thomas, you're his life and when he's away fighting, that's what keeps him going, what gives him a reason to survive. You must realise this. Don't push him away; he has little time to spare arguing. Does he know that you were coming to me?'

'No! He doesn't,' Myra cried. 'I just left with Thomas when he went to the lavatory, otherwise I wouldn't have been allowed to leave. Sorry, Edith, I needed to get away.'

'No need to apologise,' I whispered, 'you're my sister and I'll always be here for you. Now, first things first: how about that cup of tea? You have a rest. I'll take care of Thomas while you have a nap after. No arguments, mind you!'

While Myra slept, I prepared tea. Jane and Maggie took care of the babies, the storm had cleared up and the sun was shining. We hadn't had an air raid for two nights apart from a false alarm, which gave us a little respite, but like always, it was the lull before the storm, so to speak, so we had to make the best of it. The sponge cake looked quite appetising, with a sprinkle of sugar on top. Larry had gone to the baker's for some bread. Hopefully, there would be some left. I just didn't have time to make any; besides, I didn't have a lot of ingredients left. The house felt peaceful with everyone out, I took the opportunity to have ten minutes on my own before everyone descended on me for tea.

My thoughts for Myra kept nagging at me. It was apparent that she wasn't well. Albert needed to know that she was with me; he would be out of his mind with worry. Yes, the best thing to do was to let William phone the corner shop where Myra lives and they would let Albert know. If the doctor wanted Myra to have tests, then it must be serious. Yes, once tea was over, that would be the sensible thing to do. We had to think of Thomas, too.

Later that evening Albert arrived. He had managed to cadge a lift from a neighbour. He was dressed in his khaki uniform. You could see your face in his shiny boots. His curly hair was greased back. That's what they meant by spit and polish. He almost stood to attention at the door, his face etched with worry.

He said, 'Thanks, Edith, for letting me know. I'm sorry about this.'

'Come in,' I murmured. 'Myra and Thomas are in the front room. You will have peace and quiet in there. We'll be out in the garden, so take as long as you like.'

The evening was muggy, but at least it wasn't raining. It seemed an age before Myra and Albert emerged from the house. By the look on Myra's face I could see that they had reconciled things between them. I felt relieved. Hopefully, she had listened to sense. We all wanted what was best for her. After saying their goodbyes, they left to catch the bus home with little Thomas fast asleep. By September, Myra was diagnosed with a brain tumour. She was operated on, but died. She was only twenty-five.

Coming to terms with Myra's death took its toll on everyone. Albert was a broken man. He was given compassionate leave and moved in with his sister, who took care of Thomas. Most of the family rallied round to help, but it soon became obvious that he wanted to distance himself from us. I understood in one way, but Irene (who lived in Chingford) and Millie took it as a personal affront. After all, she was our sister and Thomas was our nephew. The numbness that we all felt was indescribable, and with the bombardment of war all around, it left us feeling vulnerable and desolate. Gwen and Ivor were unable to come south because of the war; both were working in munitions factories, which made things difficult for them. Like everything, time heals and by 1943 the pain began to ease.

With four of the children in junior school, life was made a little easier by their school hours being the same. And with the constant threat of air raids during the day, I knew William would make sure that they were together when walking home. Several children had been killed by random bombings during home time and when ever there was an air raid, you held your breath until they arrived home safely. It was so nerve-racking that at times I thought of keeping them home from school, but normality was vital and in their best interests. Megan, who was barely three, had grown rapidly. Her constant chatter and her ability to grasp things was amazing. She absolutely doted on Jessica and kept her amused whenever I needed to get on with things. At times she tried my patience, but I bit my lip because I realised that it was just her nature.

On one occasion when she was nearly four, Megan was playing in the back garden when she noticed Mrs Rogers hanging out the washing. Everything was pegged in sizes, very precisely, which was quite amusing. However, Megan, being full of curiosity, had noticed the line of knickers. She called over to Mrs Rogers – wait for it – 'Are the big knickers yours, Mrs Rogers?'

Although I had been indoors at the time, I heard everything clearly. I was mortified. I rushed outside to find Mrs Rogers looking red-faced and most undignified. 'Where are her manners?' she cried. 'She is a naughty little girl!'

'Sorry,' I said, 'it won't happen again. She doesn't understand. I do apologise.'

Grabbing Megan by the hand, I hurried indoors. Of course, there were a few tears when I smacked her bottom. But it didn't make any difference, for the following day Megan was outside chatting away to Mrs Rogers asking her all sorts of things!

Chapter Twenty-five

During the early summer of 1943, there was an outbreak of quinsy, throat disease, mostly among children. It became very serious through the shortage of medicines and some children died. It caused panic throughout. Although the children were being inoculated at school, I still felt vulnerable, with six children to cope with, so every morning I made them gargle with saltwater before they went to school. Not very pleasant but it had to be done. Megan and Jessica, of course, were too young, so I kept them away from groups of children. I became almost paranoid. I disinfected the whole house until it smelt like a hospital. All this and the added complication of headlice nearly drove me to the edge.

Those weeks became a nightmare, especially when Jane complained of a sore throat. She soon lost her appetite and looked sallow. Without hesitation, I sent William for the doctor, who diagnosed quinsy.

'Sorry,' he whispered, 'but I'm afraid she is quite ill. You must keep the other children away from her; it is very contagious. I will give you some medicine, which she must take three times a day. Also she must gargle; salt water will do. In the meantime give her bed baths to keep her cool. I'll call back later this evening.'

Within three days, I was told to prepare for the worst, as the next few hours were critical. I remember sending Larry for the vicar. We needed a miracle and this was the man who would bring it about, so I hoped and prayed. Without the doctor knowing, I had been giving Jane Aspro, a type of aspirin, to keep her temperature down, and also Vicks VapoRub to clear the mucus from her throat. Unfortunately, I forgot to hide them and the doctor discovered them on the mantelpiece. He was not pleased at all and reprimanded me.

'Do you realise how seriously ill Jane is? Please give her what I prescribe; it is vital. The next few hours are crucial.'

The doctor's voice was still ringing in my ears when the vicar arrived. I felt helpless and he was my only hope. Watching him kneel at the side of the bed and pray made me feel humble. I listened as he asked God to make her well. 'She is only a child; take my life and let her live.'

I shall remember those words for the rest of my life. Later that night when Jane was gasping for breath and I didn't know what to do, I prayed, 'Please God, forgive me, but I'm going to use my medicines.'

Placing the Vicks on Jane's tongue, I begged her to swallow. I promised her a sixpence each time she coughed, hoping it would release the mucus that was stopping her from breathing. It seemed like eternity with each cough she made, but it worked and her breathing improved. With the help of an Aspro her temperature came down. She laid there drenched in perspiration looking pallid and still, but she was alive, just!

I washed her gently, hoping and praying that she would pull through. My body ached with tiredness. I could feel myself slipping away, I needed to shut my eyes just for a while. Suddenly there was a knock on the front door. I must have fallen asleep for when I looked at the clock it was gone 6 a.m. I stumbled to the door to find the doctor waiting on the step.

'How is she?' His voice sounding officious, he said, 'If she has made it through the night, then there is hope.'

He sat at the side of the bed and took Jane's temperature and he then took a swab of her throat. There was a few moments silence while he studied the swab.

'Well! This is short of a miracle,' his voice sounded surprised. 'She is going to make it. The worst is over.'

His eyes looked towards the mantelpiece. There was the Vicks and Aspro. I had forgotten to hide them, oh dear! The doctor's face looked mesmerised.

He said slowly, 'Well, I see you never took my advice. Whatever you have faith in, it's worked. You carry on, it's beyond me.' Giving me further instructions, the doctor left promising me he would return later that day. I felt elated, with renewed strength.

The following weeks saw Jane grow stronger. She had great determination and it wasn't long before she was back to normal. It was fortunate that none of the other children had picked anything up; to a certain extent we were quite hardy.

We had our share of air raids throughout the summer and Leslie appeared suddenly one weekend. He had been wounded slightly and was given leave. His time with us was short, forty-eight hours. To say it was chaotic was an understatement. The children were excited, and of course it was the first time that Leslie had seen Jessica. He was thrilled to bits and was reluctant to return, but we were at war. According to Leslie, with the Americans stepping in, the war would soon be over. God save the King!

Of course, like everything, it has to get worse to get better. Hitler was determined to invade Britain and bring it to its knees. However, he hadn't reckoned on the British stalwart breed; he would never crush us no matter what. Mr Churchill's speeches gave the British people confidence.

'We will beat them.' This was his assurance to us all. The raids were continuous throughout. The devastation around us was depressing, shops and houses obliterated. The shortage of food was at its worst and you had to queue for everything. Thank God for ration books or we wouldn't have had much of anything. Even furniture was rationed, apart from those who had been bombed and had lost everything. Those like myself who had very little in the way of furniture as I had chopped chairs up for firewood in one act of desperation, had to make an application for utility furniture. The application was then submitted to the District Assistance Board, who then issued permits to purchase based on points.

Most of Britain's timber came from abroad and with very little reaching us because of the war, there was a shortage. Eventually I received a permit which allowed me sixty points. I managed to buy four chairs at 12/6d each. I had enough points for a bed, but that would have to wait until I could afford it. At that time the girls shared a single bed and the boys shared a double, top to toe. It wasn't ideal, but needs must. Then again, I shared four in a bed when I was a child.

October 1943 will stick in my mind for ever. It was a Friday evening, Jane and Maggie had gone to see Dorothy Chapman, a school friend who lived two doors away. William had gone to the Campaigners, similar to the Scouts, so there was just Larry. Megan and Jessica were in bed. Everything seemed fine so I decided to pop round to see Sophie, a neighbour and friend, who lived around the corner. Larry was playing Draughts with Andy, his friend from down the road, and was pleased for me to go out.

'Don't worry, Mum,' he said, 'I know where you are and if there is an air raid I know what to do.'

I had previously washed my hair, and had put curlers in. My hair was still damp so I wrapped a scarf around my head like the Land Army girls. After all, you had to have a little bit of decorum! It was only a short walk, but it was pitch dark. With all the blackouts there was little or no light to see your way around and it made me feel uneasy even though it was only gone seven. I was glad when I reached the door. My intention was to stay for just an hour, but we got carried away talking and it was past nine when I checked the time.

'Oh!' I cried 'I didn't realise it was that late, sorry, but I had better get back, I don't like to leave the children too long. Thanks for the tea, I'll see you soon.'

Wrapping my coat around me, I hurried along. On turning the corner I became aware of someone standing in the shadows across the road. Instinctively, I quickened my steps, my heart starting to pound. I could hear footsteps behind me. Panic took over and I stumbled. I wanted to scream but nothing came out. The pain in my elbow was excruciating. I had stumbled sideways and my left arm took the blow.

Suddenly I heard a voice of a man. 'Lady! Please, please. I no hurt you, be no afraid. I no hurt you.'

I felt his arms pull me to my feet. I was trembling so much that I almost fainted.

'Please, lady,' the voice cried. 'I am lost. I am Italian, my name Lorenzo. I come from camp. Sorry, lady, I feel sick for home. I want to go home.'

My eyes began to focus in the darkness and I could see the outline of his face. He was crying. Any fear I felt soon disappeared. To say I had lost my senses was an understatement. I suddenly found my voice.

'You had better come with me – wandering around in the dark won't do anyone any good.'

It all sounded surreal, but my instinct told me that this man wasn't dangerous. Once indoors I was able to take stock of things. Standing there in the hallway, this poor young man looked a picture of despair. He was only young, twenty at the most, unshaven and undernourished. His clothes were prison issue. Fear showed in his eyes. The children by this time had gathered in the hallway looking bewildered.

'What's going on, Mum?' William's voice sounded alarmed.

'It's all right,' I said, 'I fell over and this young man helped me. I've grazed my elbow. Go and put the kettle on. How about baked beans on toast for supper? Larry, pull the damper out and let's get the fire going.'

I ushered Lorenzo into the kitchen and sat him down by the fire. Jane and Maggie just stood and stared like he had appeared from outer space.

'For goodness' sake,' I cried, 'you two put the plates in the oven to warm.'

Normally I never cooked late, but it was apparent that this young man hadn't eaten for some time. It was obvious by the way that he stuffed the food into his mouth. It was painful to watch. Once supper was over with, I discreetly asked William to fetch Mr Rogers from next door. Lorenzo had to be returned to the camp. While the girls washed up, I tried to talk to him. I felt so sorry; he was so vulnerable.

From his broken English I learned that he was only eighteen. He had come to England to study, but when the war broke out, things changed. It appeared that his parents had collaborated with the Germans. This was what he was told. He tried to get back to Italy, but ended up being detained and then transferred to the camp. They were all treated well, he said, but he became claustrophobic and very nervous.

'I feel sick for my home,' he cried. 'I find a way out and I run. I get lost. I know I go back to the camp; it is better than lost.' He held my hand. 'Lady, I say thank to you.'

Later that evening, accompanied by Mr Rogers, Lorenzo returned to the camp.

The following day, after a restless night, I went next door to see Mr Rogers. I was very concerned about Lorenzo. It appeared that he had been missing for three days, there had been a search party sent out and the police had been informed, but somehow Lorenzo had managed to avoid capture.

'What will happen to him? He is only a boy, really,' I said, my voice lowering to a whisper. 'Will he be punished?'

Mr Rogers' face grimaced and he said, 'To be honest, Edith, he is incarcerated because he is considered a risk. We are at war and we have lads fighting on the frontline his age and younger. No harm will come to him; he will probably be put on spud peeling for the duration. Remember, this isn't Germany; our prisoners have the life of Riley in comparison. Besides, they are all able to come and go within the camp. I know for a fact that some folk feed them little extras through the wire netting; the guards turn a blind eye now and again. No, Edith, you have no need to worry. Remember, we have to survive. We have to live each day as it comes. There's no handouts for us.' With his words ringing in my ears, I went back indoors, still not convinced.

Several weeks later, William came dashing in. 'Mum!' he said breathlessly. 'I've got a note for you. It's from Lorenzo. We went past the camp after school; he was waiting by the fence and called out. To be honest, Mum, I've seen him several times with the other prisoners inside the camp. A few days ago some of the boys from school were throwing stones at them, calling them traitors. Anyway, they were reported and the headmaster gave them detentions for a month and banned them from going anywhere near the camp again. No one knows about what happened, Mum. Only Andy, and he wouldn't say anything.

'We felt sorry for him, and when the coast was clear we went across to speak to Lorenzo. He wanted me to give this to you. I don't know whether you will be able to read it or not; it's all crumpled and blotchy.'

The writing was poor but we managed to decipher it, bits of Italian and English mixed up. From what we could make out, he was being shipped back home on medical reasons. He wanted to thank me and my family for the kindness we had shown him. He would never forget and we would always be in his prayers.

A wave of sadness swept over me, we were all caught up in a war that took innocence away. It was dog eat dog; we were afraid of each other, throughout Europe no one trusted anyone. God! Would it ever end? Four years of suffering and still no light at the end of the tunnel.

With winter upon us and the continuation of air raids, morale was at its lowest. There was very little fuel or food to be had; it was first in, first served. You could queue for hours and still come away with nothing. It was frustrating and demoralising, but somehow the strength to fight on was always there. Christmas, however, brought some cheer. Mrs Curtis suggested we all got together and pool what we had.

The children were over the moon. It would be one big party for everyone. Where there's a will there's a way! Air raids or not, we were determined to have a good time. Making decorations out of coloured paper kept the children busy. We also went to a carol service the Sunday before Christmas. The church was packed, from babies to grannies. It was held in the afternoon because of the blackouts. Some of the carols were poignant, especially 'Silent Night'. There were tears flowing throughout – sometimes a good cry is a tonic!

Hitler's war continued to rage into 1944. With it came the news that Hitler was planning something more hideous, flying bombs! The news came by radio. Not helping was learning about the Japanese, the horror of the atrocities they were committing in Burma and other countries. It was devastating to learn because Mr Churchill had only just broadcast to the nation that the war was nearing the end and we were winning. It had given us all renewed hope, and then to be dashed like this cast a heavy cloud.

Lord Haw Haw continued spouting propaganda each evening. 'Germany calling, Germany calling' – what an idiot!

The trouble was most people were kept in the dark where information was concerned I suppose what we didn't know was less to worry about. According to news received, these flying bombs would be directed at London and would be unlikely to hit us here in Dorset. Poor London!

In the meantime, life continued, but air raids were constant. Southampton docks took heavy blows, with the odd bomb being dropped close to home. The Germans were becoming more complacent and took more risks. This became apparent when one day in April, a daring raid took place. German bomber planes flew overhead. Their target was Southampton, and the drone of their engines was unbelievably loud. I remember it clearly. It was a Tuesday afternoon and the children were at school, apart from Megan and Jessica. I had just made a pot of tea. Sophie, my friend and neighbour, had called in for a chat. Little Megan had put the cups out. She loved to help. Bless her.

Within a few minutes of sitting down, the sirens had gone off. Grabbing Jessica and Megan we flew to the shelter. It was only a matter of seconds and you could hear the anti-aircraft guns. The vibrations of the planes shook the house; they were flying quite low. Suddenly there was a shattering explosion, then nothing. A few minutes passed, then voices began to filter through from outside. Sophie scrambled out of the shelter. 'Stay where you are, Edith, I'll see what's going on. Something isn't right.'

A few seconds passed and she called out, 'Come and see this!'

With Megan tugging at my arm and little Jessica clinging to me, I emerged into the daylight. The explosion had left a cloud of hazy smoke. Everyone was looking into the sky, and no wonder. Germans! I could see through the haze three men parachuting down. God Almighty! The planes had been shot down. Fire engines could be heard, people were dashing everywhere. Bloody hell! I heard one man call out, 'Let's get the bastards!'

Nothing could prepare me for what happened next. There was a bungalow on the corner of the road where the Corbin family lived. It looked like it had been hit, flames and smoke pouring out. I got caught up in all the panic with everyone racing round with buckets of water. There was very little I could do, having Jessica and Megan to look after. I could only watch helplessly. Jessica was whimpering, poor little mite. She clung to me, her little body shaking. Suddenly I realised that Megan wasn't holding my hand.

'God! Megan where are you?' The realisation that she had wandered off without me knowing gave rise to panic. 'Megan!' I screamed, pushing my way through the crowd. I screamed and screamed. It seemed like no one could hear me until Sophie caught up with me.

'Edith! For goodness' sake, calm down. I saw Megan go into the house about ten minutes ago. I thought you had gone in before her. She is probably inside hiding. Come on, we'll go and look for her.'

Once inside we searched the house from top to bottom, under the beds and in the cupboards, but there was no sign of her. By this time we were joined by Mrs Rogers, who had heard me calling.

'Let me take care of Jessica,' she cried. 'She is frightened with all that's going on. Megan can't be far away. Have you looked in the garden? She might be in the shed.'

'Yes,' I said 'you could be right, the little monkey. There's water on the floor, looks like she has helped herself to a drink. Thank goodness, she can't be far.'

We checked the shed, the coal house and even went next door to ask the Ferrises but found nothing until Sophie noticed what she thought was a sheet caught up in the fruit trees at the end of he garden.

'What's that? It can't be what I'm thinking, Edith.' Her face looked pallid. My heart missed a beat.

'Oh God, Sophie! It can't be—'

Without thinking clearly, I raced up the garden, trampling all over the vegetable patch as I did so. Slowing down I could hear a voice.

'*Danke, klein Mädchen*.'

Pulling the branches away, I gasped at what I saw. There in the midst lying on the ground was a German pilot. He was covered in blood, his leg looked broken, his clothes torn to shreds. And there was Megan kneeling beside him with a mug of water, giving him sips of it. I was speechless. Megan's little face, covered in smut, smiled up at me.

My first instinct was to grab her, but something stopped me. The look on the German's face was one of pain and fear. He looked like he was dying. This wasn't happening, it was too surreal. Gathering my senses, I whispered to Megan, 'Come with me, sweetheart, put the cup down. We'll go and fetch the doctor for the poor man.'

Megan's face changed. 'No, Mummy! I don't want to, he is thirsty!'

Before I could say anything more, Sophie and two Home Guards appeared. The looks on their faces was one of disbelief.

'Bloody hell! We got a live one here! He's come a cropper!'

They edged towards him and knelt down. It was obvious that the German's injuries were severe. One of the guards muttered, 'I think he's had it; better get him to hospital. He's a prisoner of war, whatever way you look at it. You ladies should go. This no place for a child to be. We'll take care of everything.'

I picked Megan up and hurried away. Sophie followed behind. Her face was ashen and she was trembling.

The next couple of hours we were confined to the house. An ambulance arrived along with a military vehicle. The top of the garden was cordoned off. People were gathered outside the house, hoping to get a glimpse. As the German was brought out on the stretcher, one or two people shouted obscenities. Others just stared, mostly out of curiosity. Watching from the window I felt only pity, not just for the German but for all those stood there. War brought out the worst in some of us. Were we justified because of what we had suffered? Only God knew the answer.

Chapter Twenty-six

On 6 June 1944, D-Day, an invasion took place on the beaches of Normandy by British and American forces. Thousands of men took part, including Canadians. This was the greatest day of the war which had been planned for months. It was bloody and there was great loss of life.

The Luftwaffe set their path for the flying bombs, the dreaded Doodle Bug (V1). London was targeted, the bombs wreaked chaos and carnage killing thousands. Many British and American airmen sacrificed their lives attacking the bombs and rocket sites. Because of this they saved London from worse levels of destruction and also saved tens of thousands of lives. We in the far south had our first experience some weeks later. With the Doodle Bug, you heard the dreadful drone first. It was hideous. You waited and once the noise stopped you knew that the bomb was about to drop. The suspense was awful. You didn't know where it would hit. You closed your eyes and held your breath and prayed to God that it would miss you! Hundreds of these bombs were fired in so many hours, it was constant.

I remember one night. I was putting the milk bottles out when the sirens went off. It could only have been a matter of seconds when I heard the drone of a Doodle Bug. I stood transfixed, looking into the night sky. To me what I saw in the pitch darkness looked like a basket of fire. It was the flames spouting from the bomb. It was horrifying. It seemed so close. I slammed the door and called out to the children. They almost fell down the stairs in their haste. Poor Maggie held Jessica, and within minutes they were in the shelter. I hid under the stairs with William and Larry as there wasn't room in the shelter for all of us. Suddenly the noise of the bomb stopped. The silence felt evil. We put our hands over our ears. The anticipation of waiting was sickening, then we heard an almighty blast. It dropped a few miles away, although it felt very near. We learned later that it was in Poole.

There were many more near misses with fire baskets (Doodle Bugs) but we were very fortunate not to be hit. However, there was worse to come with Hitler's V2 rockets. We listened to the news on the wireless. It wasn't good, but Mr Churchill responded in such a way. His speeches to the nation were always positive; he was Britain's anchor. Lord Haw Haw still managed to spout his propaganda. As soon as he came on we use to switch it over and listened to Vera Lynn singing. She was the forces sweetheart and loved by everyone. My favourite song that she sang was 'The White Cliffs of Dover'. Her songs instilled cheer in all of us. Some evenings in the winter we would sit around the fire and join in, singing at the top of our voices. It made us feel good inside. Of course, we weren't sure what the neighbours thought!

During August of 1944, Leslie's regiment returned home from France, but not for long, though. They were based at Bovington camp and managed to come home for a weekend. Walking down the road in full uniform and his backpack, he was cheered by the neighbours. What a welcome. This was given to any soldier who returned no matter what. We made the best of the weekend and the children were in their element. With the weather at its best, we managed a couple of picnics free of air raids. Although Leslie appeared relaxed with the children, it was obvious that he had changed. He seemed distant, almost a stranger to me. I put it down to the stress of the war. It had certainly taken its toll. Little was said and I didn't ask any questions. He would tell me in his own time, so I thought. It was sad to wave him goodbye when he left, not knowing when we would see him again. I watched him disappear over the top of the hill, he never looked back once. This bloody war! The feeling of despair was hard to shake off.

Aftermath

The following week Mrs Curtis offered to take the children for a day out. She had friends in Shaftesbury, who lived out in the wilds, a cottage surrounded by fields and horses. Freedom for the children to run around in, the girls were very excited. William and Larry made their own arrangements, which left me with time to myself. What a luxury. I decided to make the best of it. A trip to

Bournemouth for window-shopping and a walk through the gardens. The seaside was off-limits. Barricaded with barbed wire. I suppose it was the same all along the coastline. Some had concrete bunkers, all to keep the enemy out. But today I was going to fantasise and try to enjoy the time on my own.

Once the children had set off, I made the beds and tidied up, had a quick wash and ironed my best dress. It was old but pretty, patterned with tiny flowers. I always felt smart when I wore it. I had tanned stockings and buckled shoes, which I kept in mothballs and only wore on special occasions. Today was special. I stood and looked in the mirror. 'Yes, you'll do,' I said to myself. I dabbed some Poppy scent behind my ears before setting out.

Bournemouth was hustle and bustle. Looking around the square, I noticed the gypsies with their baskets of flowers and heather. 'Lucky heather, lady?' they called out. It was supposed to be unlucky to refuse, but it was only superstition. However, I wasn't going to tempt providence! I handed a rather wizened old gypsy a couple of coppers. 'You've had a long, hard struggle, my dear,' she clasped my hand and murmured. 'Your life is going to change dramatically. Your path is mapped out for you. It's in the stars!'

Feeling quite unnerved, I pulled my hand away. I thanked her and hurried off thinking, I have six children, what could possibly change?

After looking through the shops – some were boarded up, awaiting repairs – I made my way to the gardens. It was cool among the trees. A welcome relief from the searing sun. I found a bench and sat down; it felt so peaceful. Looking around me I noticed one or two people having a picnic lunch. Others just strolled away from the hustle and bustle. On the far side of me were the tennis courts and a small café alongside, which I mentally noted.

The place was alive with squirrels and small birds hopping all around. Most of them were fairly tame and came right up to you. One squirrel brazenly jumped on to the bench hoping for some small morsel of food, chance would be a fine thing! There was never any stale bread in my household to feed any creature. How sad was that, but that was war.

My thoughts started to drift until a voice said, 'A penny for them.' It was Joyce, my good neighbour from Cheltenham Road. 'Fancy seeing you here! Where are the children?'

Her voice was excited as she bombarded me with questions. We sat there for almost an hour, catching up on all that had happened. Joyce and Ted had moved in with her mother as soon as the war started because she lived alone and wasn't prepared to budge. She lived on the outskirts of Corfe Castle in a two-bedroom cottage. It had been fairly shielded from the air raids compared to other parts of the country. Unfortunately, her mother became ill and passed away and after a few months they decided to move back to Parkstone. Ted was now working in an ammunition factory. After we made arrangements to meet up again, Joyce left to catch the early bus.

Feeling thirsty, I made my way to the café and as I did so I noticed a group of American servicemen on the far side of the tennis courts. It was quite common these days. Wherever you went you saw a Yank. Many of them had charmed the local girls, which had caused resentment among tight-knit families. The saying was, 'While the cat's away, the mice do play'. It caused heartache for some, but this was war and you took every day as it came, not knowing what tomorrow would bring. Who were we to judge?

There were just a few people in the café. I ordered a cup of tea and a rock cake and sat down in the corner by the window, where I could see across the gardens. It all looked so peaceful. I felt good and really relaxed. It had been a long time since I had time on my own. I was going to relish this.

The lady serving brought my tea and cake across. She smiled and placed a half a sugar knob in the saucer; needless to say this was a little extra, one I didn't expect, especially with all the rationing. Sipping my tea, my mind started to wander. It was hard to imagine peacetime again, waking up each day with the knowledge that there were no more air raids, no sirens, no bombs, no blackouts and plenty of food for everyone.

Suddenly my thoughts were interrupted by the loud voices of the American servicemen entering the café. There were six in all. They appeared to be oblivious to anyone else around them. My attention was drawn to them by the fact that they all appeared to have received injuries, arms in slings, one with crutches, another with a patch across his face. Of course, the penny dropped, these men had been shipped back here to recover. Realising I was staring; I turned my face towards the window, not wanting to draw attention to myself by my bad manners. Finishing my tea off, I made my way to the counter to pay. As I did so one of the Americans said, 'Good day to you, ma'am.'

Feeling slightly embarrassed, I turned to acknowledge and noticed the one with the patch on his face and a stubbly beard giving me a hard look. Almost like he had seen a ghost. Feeling uncomfortable, I smiled and left making my way through the gardens. It was time for me to go home. I had just reached the path leading to the square when I heard a voice call 'Hey, wait a minute.'

I turned to see who it could be. My heart missed a beat. Hurrying towards me was an American serviceman. As he got closer, I realised it was one from the café, the one with the patch on his face. What on earth could he want?

He was quite breathless when he reached me. 'Sorry, didn't mean to scare you. My apologies. Please, I know you. Forgive me for the intrusion.'

To say I was shocked was an understatement. I was lost for words, looking into his face it seemed familiar. It was the eyes, piercing blue eyes. Eyes that I seemed to remember. Oh! My God, it couldn't be…

My legs went weak beneath me. 'Please, who are you?' My voice seemed almost a whisper. 'It can't be you.'

'Yes, it's me, Peter.' His voice trembled as he spoke. 'And you are Edith. I thought I was seeing things. I can't believe it. Forgive me. This must be a shock to you. It certainly is for me. Please come and sit down.'

We sat down on a bench nearby. There was a few moments' silence as we gained our composure; my whole body was trembling with emotion. This man sat next to me, was he my Peter? How many years ago – he disappeared. I thought he was dead. My head was swimming. I felt unable to speak.

'It's OK, Edith, you're not seeing a ghost. I'm real, this is me,

Peter.' His voice had changed from the polished accent that I remembered. It had an American drawl which was alien to me, but there was no doubt that this was Peter. His appearance had changed and of course he was older. He looked thinner and it was obvious that he was badly scarred. The patch across his face covered most of the injury. I learned later that he was hit by shrapnel, not just his face, but his arm and leg, which were covered by his uniform.

The next half-hour sped by. Peter explained very briefly how he came to be here in Bournemouth, mainly to convalesce. Half of his platoon had been killed or injured. Those that had survived had been shipped back.

'I know you deserve an explanation of what happened years ago,' he said his voice lowered to almost a whisper. 'Believe me, Edith, I cannot imagine what you must have gone through. I need to tell you what happened, but not now. Please can we meet again? There is so much that needs to be said.'

'Yes,' I replied, 'you're right. There is and I have a family to get back to.'

His face looked shocked, almost as if time had stood still for me and nothing had changed. It all felt surreal, like I would wake up and it was all a dream, but no, this was real. I suddenly wanted to run away. It was all too much. However, I knew that I had to meet again if only to find out what had happened, I owed it to myself. We made arrangements to meet a couple of days later.

Chapter Twenty-seven

The bus was full on the way home and I had to stand part of the way. I felt confused and angry inside, so much that I went past my stop which made it a long walk home. Fortunately, the children had only just arrived back. They were full of excitement and couldn't wait to tell me about their day. Poor Mrs Curtis looked absolutely shattered.

'You've got your work cut out, Edith,' she said laughing. 'We've had a smashing time. No problems getting them to sleep tonight. The girls have made me a cup of tea. Very welcome too.'

After having a natter about the events of the day, Mrs Curtis left. Megan and Jessica were ready for bed; it had been a long day for them. A quick wash and they were in bed and asleep in minutes. William and Larry came home just after 7 p.m. 'We're starving, Mum,' they cried, 'can we have fish and chips?'

Of course, Jane and Maggie wanted some as well, and to be honest I was feeling pretty peckish after the long walk. 'Let's see,' I said, 'have we enough money? Better check the tea caddy. You had better make it quick; they close in another half-hour. Blackout, don't forget.'

William said he would go while we laid the table. Later that evening the sirens went off, but it was only short-lived. A false alarm. Wish they would make their minds up. Back and forward with Jessica and Megan wasn't funny, so I decided to let them sleep in the shelter just in case we had another alarm. I was past being tired and settled in the armchair for the rest of the night. I wasn't going to sleep – I had too much to think about. Coming to terms with seeing Peter was haunting me. I would never have thought in a million years that this could happen – the Peter I knew and loved was a stranger to me now.

With piles of washing to be done, I was up at the crack of dawn. The sun was filtering through. It was going to be another scorching day. I put the boiler on and got the scrub board out; the mangle was in the yard. By 9 a.m. I had done two lines of washing and the smell of washing powder wafted through the house. The children hated it. I think it was because it made me hot and short-tempered, which meant they would have to tiptoe round me!

By midday I had finished all the chores. The children had gone out with their friends, just Jessica, Megan and I were left. Later that afternoon we went to the park as they both loved the swings. The sound of their laughter was a tonic. Looking around me, watching other mums with their children running round excitedly, made me forget it was wartime. It was hilarious to watch them on the slide. Of course, I had to watch little Jessica. She was becoming a tomboy like Megan, fearless and intrepid. It was a good thing really. If anything happened to me they would have the strength to cope, please God…

Friday was the day that I was going to meet Peter. I made the pretence of having to have my eyes tested. Jane and Maggie were left to look after Jessica and Megan.

'I'll only be an hour or two,' I told them, trying to be matter of fact, 'you know where everything is. Any problems, go next door.'

Feeling slightly guilty, I waved goodbye and set off. I had arranged to meet Peter at the café in the gardens. To say that I was nervous was an understatement. It was like going back in time, but the past was the past. It would never be the same. We had the war to prove that.

Peter was waiting by the tennis court when I arrived. It was hard to recognise him with the familiar picture I had stored in my head all that time ago. A feeling of apprehension swept over me. It was just like meeting a stranger until he smiled and held his hand out.

'Hello, Edith. Glad you were able to make it. To be truthful I wasn't really sure you'd come, after all this time and the shock. Who could blame you? Anyway, you're here and I need to explain, if is the last thing I do.' His voice sounded sad even though he was smiling. 'How about a cup of tea?'

The café was quiet and we were able to sit near the window. It took a few minutes before Peter was able to speak. 'Where to begin, that's the question.' His voice was almost a whisper. 'I've dreamed of this moment, of being able to tell you, to see you once again. I never really thought that it would happen. Believe me, I searched.'

Looking at his face, I could see how difficult it was, there was no doubt he had suffered.

'It's all right, Peter,' I murmured, 'just tell me. I need to know. We both owe it to each other, so come on.'

Once he started to talk, the old Peter came to the surface. His mannerisms were the same as I remembered. As the tale unfolded, I could not contain my amazement. What started out as an ordinary day all those years ago turned into a nightmare for all. Peter had finished his course at the bank in Chicago and was due to catch the train to New York at 8 that morning. He was accompanied by another colleague named Byron Fritz, who had been on the same course. They arrived early at the station, when Byron complained of feeling unwell.

'Keep an eye on my luggage, Peter,' he said, 'I need to use the men's room. Must be something I ate.'

After twenty minutes of waiting, Peter became concerned. He put all the luggage together by the station master's office and dashed to see what had happened. On entering the men's room, he found Byron unconscious and bleeding from the head. His first reaction was to go for help, but before he could do so, he was attacked from behind. He felt a crushing blow and then nothing. When he came to he was on a train bound for Canada.

'I could not remember anything; I didn't know who I was and what I was doing on the train. There was one other person in the compartment, who asked if I was OK. I said I didn't feel well and that I couldn't remember anything or where I had come from. The next thing I was being escorted off the train. I ended up in a Canadian hospital with total amnesia. The doctors had said that the blow to the head had caused the memory loss and it would be impossible to say when it would return, if ever.'

According to the police, the luggage that Peter had with him belonged to a Byron Fritz with a Canadian address and they naturally assumed that he was Byron. While Peter convalesced, the police made enquiries. It appeared that he had a wife and a little boy that were living in Toronto. Peter accepted their word and arrangements were made to bring his wife and child to see him. 'You cannot imagine how I felt.' Peter's voice sounded strained. 'There standing by my bed was this woman and child who I had no recollection of. The best part of it was she pretended to know me.

' "Darling Byron," she cried, "what has happened to you? We have been frantic with worry." She threw her arms around me. I felt no emotion. It was so surreal. The little boy just stood there, unable to say anything. I learned later that he couldn't remember me because I had apparently left when he was only two. Of course, this was part of a big plan that I found out about three years later.'

Peter explained that he eventually left hospital and went to live in Toronto with his said wife Olga and son Nicholas. The first few months were a nightmare, trying to adjust and adapt to a new life came very hard. In time he found a job in a bank in the centre of Toronto. After a while, he came to accept that this was his life. Olga had told him that they had met seven years previously at a conference and were married within a year. Nicolas was born nine months later. Life was blissful, according to Olga, until he was sent on a sabbatical for a year to Chicago, which meant promotion and a higher salary. During that time he had very little contact with Olga and Nicholas and only managed to return home a couple of times, which put a strain on their marriage.

He was offered a permanent post in Chicago, including a large house.

However, Olga was reluctant to move to another country; it was too much upheaval, as she was settled in Canada, she said. After many discussions, it was decided that he would return to his old job and stay in Canada. Shortly before he was due home, there was a terrible storm which hit Chicago leaving devastation everywhere. It appeared that Byron went missing, presumed dead up until the time he was found on the train, and that's when Peter came in.

'Life would have continued the same and my identity covered up,' Peter said, 'except that providence stepped in. I was leaving the bank one day when I was hit by a car that mounted the sidewalk. I woke up in hospital with severe concussion, within a couple of days I was having flashbacks. My memory was coming back. The doctors put it down to side effects caused by the medication and shrugged it off, but I knew different. Olga came to see me, and immediately I saw her, I started to recall other things. None of it added up. Fortunately I never let on to Olga; my sixth sense told me not to. I needed things to come together, a clear picture.

'While I was convalescing and alone in the house, I made a search through Olga's papers. I found an envelope hidden inside one of her briefcases. It told me all I needed to know. Byron had been a Russian agent, and so was Olga. Nothing could prepare me for it. To say I felt afraid was an understatement. I knew my life would be in danger if Olga discovered my secret. So I played dumb until I could figure out what to do.

'My main concern was for Nicholas. I had come to love him as if he was my own; how could I leave him? He was innocent in all this. Although Olga was his natural mother, she had no maternal feelings and treated Nicholas like her ward. I had to get away somehow. I could go to the police and explain but I knew it would be difficult to prove. My papers showed me as a natural Canadian. It was so well planned and Olga had made it quite clear to the doctors that I had suffered a mental breakdown in the past. Even if the police in Canada investigated, my life would be in danger by the very fact that Olga would know. God knows what these people were capable of!'

Peter told me that the safest thing for him to do was to leave the country. Fortunately for him, Olga had to go away to a conference for three days, which gave him the opportunity to prepare. He had a Canadian passport in the name of Byron Fritz and while searching through Olga's papers, he found Nicholas's passport. It would be a risk, but he would take Nicholas with him. Firstly, he would have to talk to him and explain his plans without alarming him. As far as Nicholas was concerned, Peter was his real father and he absolutely worshipped him. There was no love from Olga, who sometimes treated him with contempt and distanced herself from him, so naturally Nicholas turned to Peter.

'I loathed the way she treated him,' Peter said. 'She was unattractive to me and our so-called marriage was a sham.'

After assuring Nicholas that he would take care of him, he

booked two tickets to New York. On arrival, he reported straight away to the police. At first they viewed him with suspicion, but after delving into the archives of unsolved cases, they found Peter's files. Once it was established it was authentic, Peter was interviewed by several detectives. With Peter's account of what had happened, they were able to piece things together. The seriousness of what they had discovered made it essential for them to place Peter and Nicholas in a safe house.

After several weeks, Peter learned what had happened that fatal day. It appeared that Byron was part of a ring of Russian infiltrators who had planned sabotage against America and Canada. Byron had been placed in New York to initiate plans. He worked alongside Peter at the bank and both were sent to Chicago on a course. During that time, Byron had accepted bribes and had become a liability. The day of his return to New York, he was contacted by one of his Russian patriarchs. A meeting was arranged at the station. After making excuses of feeling ill, Byron left to go to the men's room, leaving Peter on the platform looking after the luggage.

What happened next wasn't planned. If Peter had stayed and not gone in search of Byron, things would have been different, but when Peter found Byron, he sealed his own fate. According to the police, Byron had been murdered because he had revealed information. Unfortunately Peter walked in on it. They knocked him unconscious and his identity was swapped. They needed to get rid of Byron's body before the police discovered what was going on. The fact that Peter was found with amnesia was a bonus for them and that was when Olga came on the scene. Poor Peter became the scapegoat for a Russian spy ring.

'Living in a world that had been fogbound with amnesia had kept me alive,' Peter continued with emotion in his voice. 'It would have proved fatal if I had started to remember my past earlier on. I must have had a guardian angel: the years went by and I was none the wiser, but the day I was knocked down I had my life back. It must have been a year later after I reported to the police that I was able to leave the safe house. In that time, Olga had been arrested, along with her patriarchs. The whole ring was blown apart and several arrests were made throughout America and Canada. I was free to go wherever I wished. Eventually we moved to New England and settled down. Nicholas adapted quickly and made friends at his new school.

'After six months I decided to come back to England to search for you and my family. The police had made enquiries earlier on, but no luck. Leaving Nicholas with friends, I flew back to London, only to find that you had moved on and the house now belonged to a French family. I eventually traced Fanny, who had never married and returned to England after Mother died. We were both in shock at the revelations and we cried uncontrollably; it was all too much to bear.

'Once we had come to terms with everything, Fanny and I decided to try and find you. After trying numerous addresses, including Somerset House, we traced Rose and Charlie. To be honest, I didn't recognise them; they had both aged so much and were living in very poor conditions with five children. To say they were shocked was an understatement. Eventually Rose confessed that the last time she had heard from you was when you were living in Swanage. You had met somebody else and didn't want to return to London again; you were very happy with your new life.

'Although I knew in my heart after all this time, you had moved on. I felt devastated. Everyone thought I was dead – how could I possibly imagine that you would be there waiting? To look for you further would be pointless and selfish. After much soul-searching, we returned to New England. With no family left in London, Fanny decided to come with me, the prospect of not seeing each other again for some time was unthinkable. Nicholas was over the moon; to have an aunty was more than he could wish for.

'Life took on a new meaning until war broke out in Europe. I had American citizenship; eventually I was called up when we entered the war. We had a few weeks' training and we were then flown to England. Later we were shipped to France. To say I was prepared would be a lie; it was a shock to the system. God knows, Edith, it's a hideous war. I'm one of the lucky ones; I can live with my injuries. It's my buddies that I left behind who won't be coming home. That's the worst part of it. I'll never forget.

'We arrived here in Bournemouth after spending six weeks in

hospital. Once we have convalesced here, we will be shipped back to the States. Edith, I can't believe that I'm here talking to you. I never for one moment thought that I would ever see you again.'

Listening to Peter made me feel humble. In all the years that had passed, my thoughts of Peter had faded. It was part of my life that I had put away in a box and stored, never to be opened again. At first I wished I had never met him; there would have been no pain. Not knowing was the worst: was he alive, was he dead? Horrible images had haunted me and I almost gave up, but here I was, sitting next to Peter after all this time. It took a war to bring us together – what irony, or was it just fate?

A few moments passed before I was able to speak. When I did, my voice was almost a whisper.

'I'm so sorry. It feels so unreal. I can't begin to understand what you have been through; it's like something out of a book. But it isn't – you're here, it's real. It's hard to take it all in. There is so much that I need to tell you as well. You know I'm married. I have six children; my husband is in the army. Where? I don't know.'

My voice seemed to echo as I continued to tell my story. Peter listened intently not once interrupting me. When I had finished, he held my hand. We sat silently for a while. There was nothing more to tell. Even so we both knew that the bond we once had was still there. God in heaven, where do we go from here?

Having agreed that we would continue to see each other, arrangements were made that we would meet whenever it was possible. Time was short; Peter could be shipped back to America at any time. Although my head told me it was futile, my heart ruled. All I knew was that I had never stopped loving him. I wanted to spend as much time with him before he left my life again. Juggling everything was difficult, but somehow I managed.

School term started and the children went back, giving me more time to myself. In between air raids and coping with the shortage of food, I still managed my rendezvous. The happiness I felt blotted out any feelings of guilt. The fact that Peter had changed physically made no difference; his scars were quite shocking, but that was all they were: scars. He was the same man and I loved him for his strength of character.

October came with the news that Peter was returning to the States. He needed skin grafts. The military hospital there had the specialists. Although it was expected, we both felt unprepared. The thought of not seeing each other again was too much to bear. I told myself that I had a family, a husband away fighting a relentless war. How selfish of me! But it made no difference to how I felt. The last afternoon we spent together, we vowed that that we would never lose touch.

'I shall be back once the war is over,' Peter said. 'I've missed England. I'm a Brit at heart, my roots are here.'

It was heartbreaking to say goodbye. For days I felt numb inside. The knowledge that he had gone from my life again was hard to accept. If it hadn't been for the children depending on me, I would have gone to pieces. Six weeks later I received a postcard saying, 'All is well', signed 'P'. It made my Christmas.

By the end of January 1945, it was confirmed that I was expecting again. I had ignored all of the signs, pretending that I had just put weight on. The thought of having another mouth to feed was depressing. How would I cope? We barely had enough food to live on as it was; it just wasn't fair. Rumours that the war would soon be over made no difference; the truth was I didn't want another baby. With six children already, it wouldn't be fair on them; a life of hand-me-downs was a dismal prospect. With Leslie away at war, there was no way that I could let him know; maybe it was for the best. I had no options but to accept the situation. I was too far gone.

Doodlebugs continued to bombard London. Most of the coastlines were battered, too. News filtered through that the war was coming to an end. As much as we wanted to believe it, we could not imagine Hitler giving up; he was a madman who wanted to rule the world. There had been attempts to assassinate him by his own henchmen but they had sadly failed. Anyone that showed the slightest disloyalty was executed.

In the meantime the news that thousands of Jews had been systematically tortured and executed in concentration camps was printed in the national newspapers. It was horrific to read, and there was more to come. It was beyond anyone's imagination that these terrible atrocities could have happened, but they did.

Americans and our boys witnessed the aftermath. The shocking memory of what they saw would stay with them for ever.

Chapter Twenty-eight

Life in the south continued the same. Bread was so scarce that you were only allowed one loaf per family whenever you could buy it. Making your own bread wasn't easy. There were very few ingredients to be had. Consequently everything tasted bland, but when you are hungry you will eat anything. The children were thin, although healthy considering the circumstances. Malt and cod liver oil were given out in spoonfuls at school. The children loathed it, but it was compulsory. Our ration of sweets I put aside for them. It was something to look forward to when they returned from school.

By March the Allied forces overran the Nazi regime and crossed the Rhine; they took Germany. It was confirmed that Adolph Hitler had committed suicide. The news of this lifted our spirits. It felt like a light at the end of the tunnel. The war was coming to an end, so we hoped. Dared we celebrate? Mrs Curtis was the first to suggest a celebration, although the Rogers next door thought it would be complacent to do so.

'The war isn't over yet! We don't know for sure.' Mr Rogers was adamant. 'Is Hitler dead? Then I'll believe it!' He stood there in his tin helmet; it was almost like he enjoyed being in the Home Guard, God bless him!

I suppose he was right but it didn't make any difference – we went ahead and celebrated. We laid the kitchen table and filled it with whatever we could; there was lemonade for the children, a couple of bottles of Guinness for the grown-ups, sandwiches and home-made cake. It wasn't much, but it was a feast to us. Mrs Rogers with her girls joined in, regardless of what had been said. After all, this was the first sign of peace after nearly six years of war. We had to be positive. Later we sat round the fire and we sang all the songs of hope. 'Keep the Home Fires burning, while your heart is yearning', 'Bless them all, bless them all, the long and the short and the tall', 'It's a Long Way to Tipperary, it's a long way to go'. Our voices were hoarse by the end of the evening, but did we feel good!

The next few weeks brought news, good and bad. Our casualties had been enormous. The King and Queen had been out and about, viewing the bomb sites around London, as they had done several times throughout the war, which boosted morale. However, the signs were that the war was coming to an end and the newspapers were full of it. Maybe my baby would be born in peacetime. I could feel the baby kick. Not long now, just a few more weeks and everything would be over.

In the meantime Easter was upon us. It was spring – it brought with it the warmth of the sun. The schools had closed for the holidays. There was excitement in the air, a feeling of optimism, hope, peace. Then news filtered through that Germany was about to surrender, and in May an unconditional surrender was signed. The war was over!

We celebrated with street parties; trestle tables filled with food lined the streets. Union Jacks hung from every window. It was a sight to behold. No more blackouts, no more sirens, no more bombs. It was in everyone's mind, peace at last.

I stood by the window, looking out. I could swear that I could hear marching and whistling from afar, 'Keep the Home Fires burning'. God bless.

Epilogue

After the war, Peter stayed in America. Edith decided that her family was more important and when Leslie returned they stayed together. Edith's children grew up to start their own families and are all alive and well. Edith lost touch with some of her friends because of the war and this is why some of their stories are incomplete.

Printed in Great Britain
by Amazon